my **LITTLE** PONY

Friendship is Magic

WRITTEN BY
Christina Rice, Ted Anderson, & Katie Cook

ART BY
Agnes Garbowska, Brenda Hickey, & Andy Price

COLORS BY
Agnes Garbowska WITH COLOR ASSIST BY Lauren Perry,
Brenda Hickey, Andy Price, & Heather Breckel

LETTERS BY
Neil Uyetake

SERIES EDITS BY
Bobby Curnow

COVER BY
Andy Price

COLLECTION EDITS BY
Justin Eisinger
& Alonzo Simon

COLLECTION DESIGN BY
Neil Uyetake

PUBLISHER
Ted Adams

Special thanks to Meghan McCarthy, Eliza Hart, Ed Lane, Beth Artale, and Michael Kelly.

For international rights, contact licensing@idwpublishing.com

ISBN: 978-1-63140-688-1

20 19 18 17   3 4 5 6

® Licensed By: [Hasbro logo]

www.IDWPUBLISHING.com

Ted Adams, CEO & Publisher
Greg Goldstein, President & COO
Robbie Robbins, EVP/Sr. Graphic Artist
Chris Ryall, Chief Creative Officer/Editor-in-Chief
Matthew Ruzicka, CPA, Chief Financial Officer
Dirk Wood, VP of Marketing
Lorelei Bunjes, VP of Digital Services
Jeff Webber, VP of Licensing, Digital and Subsidiary Rights
Jerry Bennington, VP of New Product Development

Facebook: facebook.com/idwpublishing
Twitter: @idwpublishing
YouTube: youtube.com/idwpublishing
Tumblr: tumblr.idwpublishing.com
Instagram: instagram.com/idwpublishing

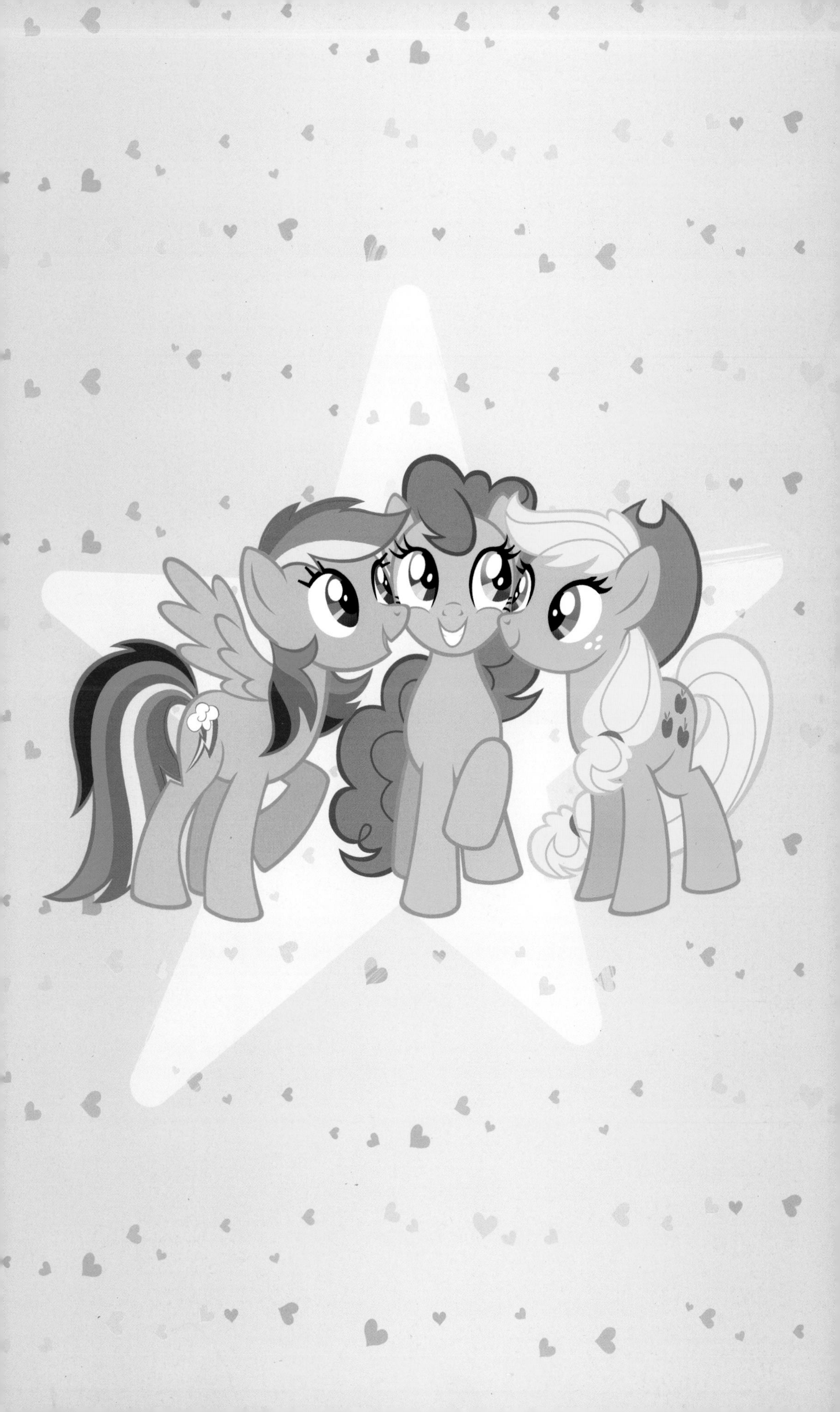

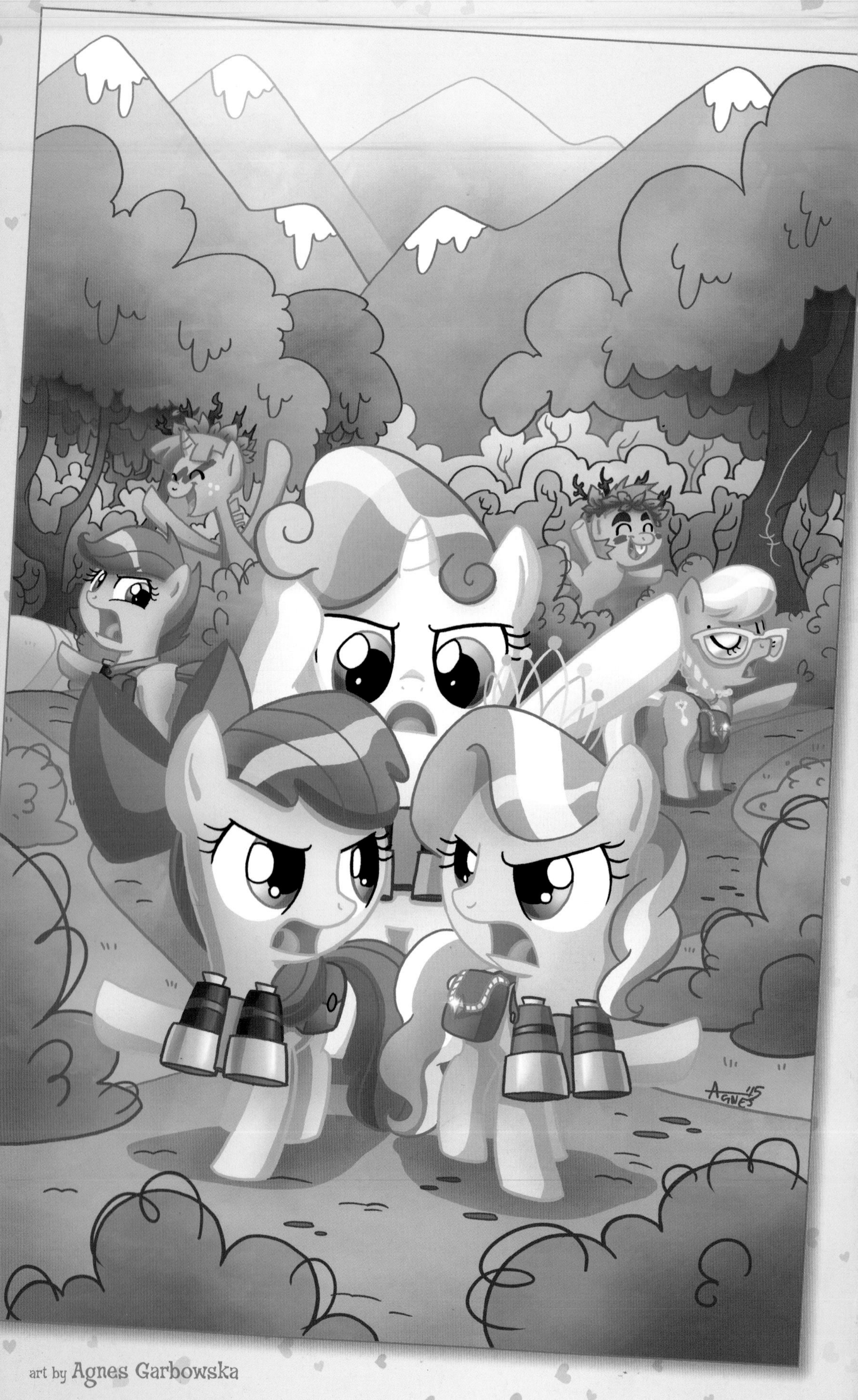

art by Agnes Garbowska

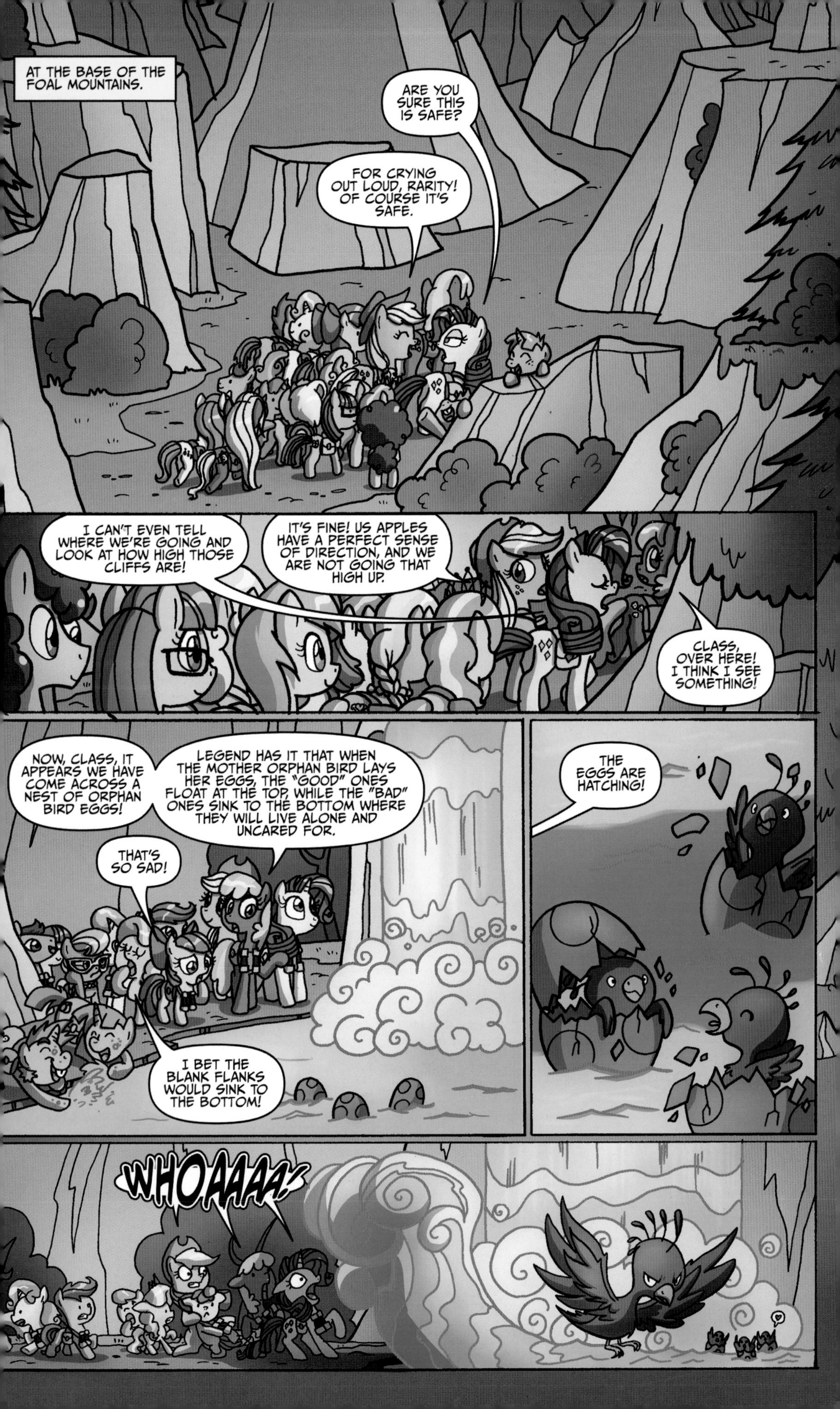
AT THE BASE OF THE FOAL MOUNTAINS.
ARE YOU SURE THIS IS SAFE?
FOR CRYING OUT LOUD, RARITY! OF COURSE IT'S SAFE.
I CAN'T EVEN TELL WHERE WE'RE GOING AND LOOK AT HOW HIGH THOSE CLIFFS ARE!
IT'S FINE! US APPLES HAVE A PERFECT SENSE OF DIRECTION, AND WE ARE NOT GOING THAT HIGH UP.
CLASS, OVER HERE! I THINK I SEE SOMETHING!
NOW, CLASS, IT APPEARS WE HAVE COME ACROSS A NEST OF ORPHAN BIRD EGGS!
LEGEND HAS IT THAT WHEN THE MOTHER ORPHAN BIRD LAYS HER EGGS, THE "GOOD" ONES FLOAT AT THE TOP, WHILE THE "BAD" ONES SINK TO THE BOTTOM WHERE THEY WILL LIVE ALONE AND UNCARED FOR.
THAT'S SO SAD!
I BET THE BLANK FLANKS WOULD SINK TO THE BOTTOM!
THE EGGS ARE HATCHING!
WHOAAAA!

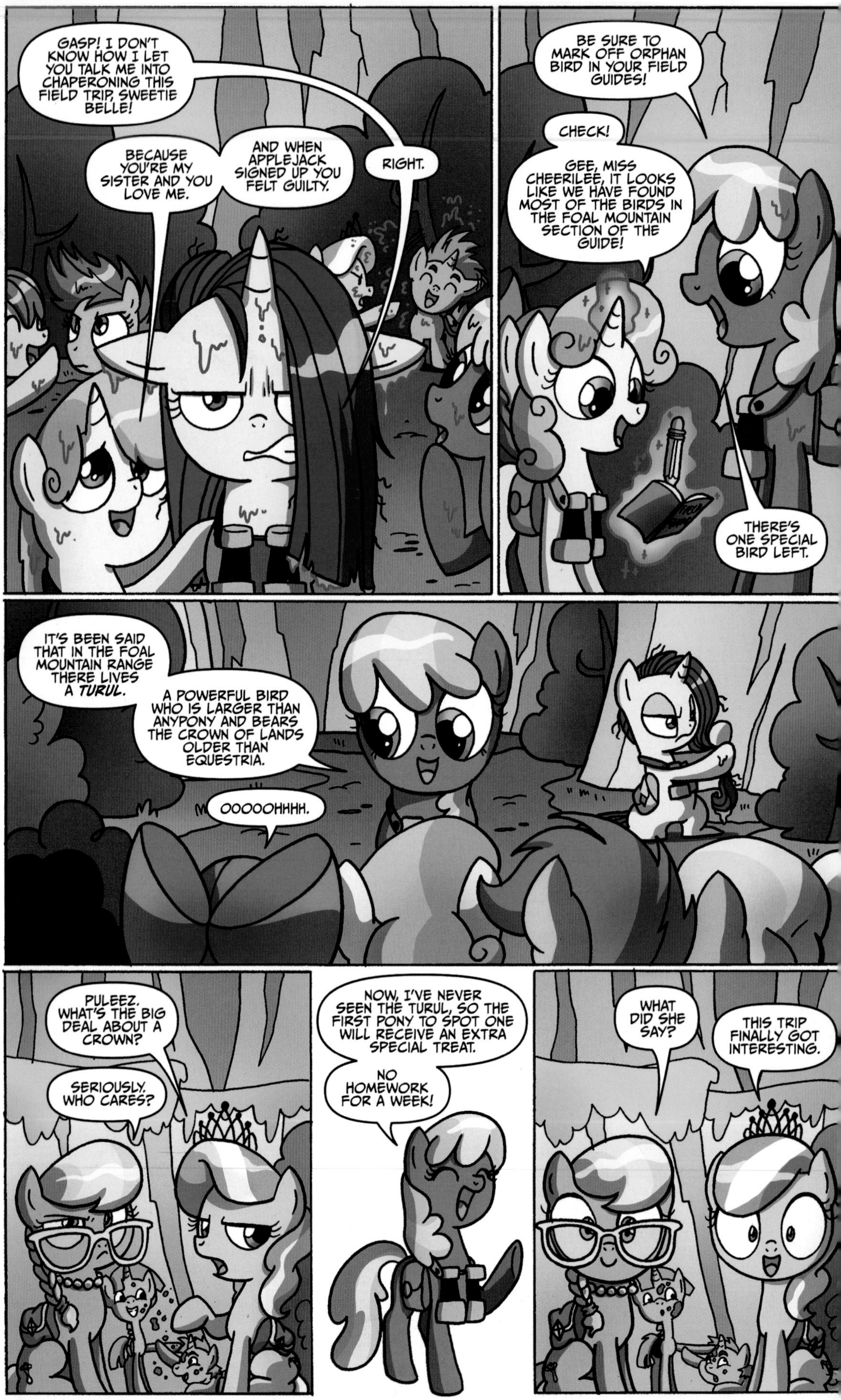
GASP! I DON'T KNOW HOW I LET YOU TALK ME INTO CHAPERONING THIS FIELD TRIP, SWEETIE BELLE!
BECAUSE YOU'RE MY SISTER AND YOU LOVE ME.
AND WHEN APPLEJACK SIGNED UP YOU FELT GUILTY.
RIGHT.
BE SURE TO MARK OFF ORPHAN BIRD IN YOUR FIELD GUIDES!
CHECK!
GEE, MISS CHEERILEE, IT LOOKS LIKE WE HAVE FOUND MOST OF THE BIRDS IN THE FOAL MOUNTAIN SECTION OF THE GUIDE!
THERE'S ONE SPECIAL BIRD LEFT.
IT'S BEEN SAID THAT IN THE FOAL MOUNTAIN RANGE THERE LIVES A *TURUL*.
A POWERFUL BIRD WHO IS LARGER THAN ANYPONY AND BEARS THE CROWN OF LANDS OLDER THAN EQUESTRIA.
OOOOOHHHH.
PULEEZ. WHAT'S THE BIG DEAL ABOUT A CROWN?
SERIOUSLY. WHO CARES?
NOW, I'VE NEVER SEEN THE TURUL, SO THE FIRST PONY TO SPOT ONE WILL RECEIVE AN EXTRA SPECIAL TREAT.
NO HOMEWORK FOR A WEEK!
WHAT DID SHE SAY?
THIS TRIP FINALLY GOT INTERESTING.

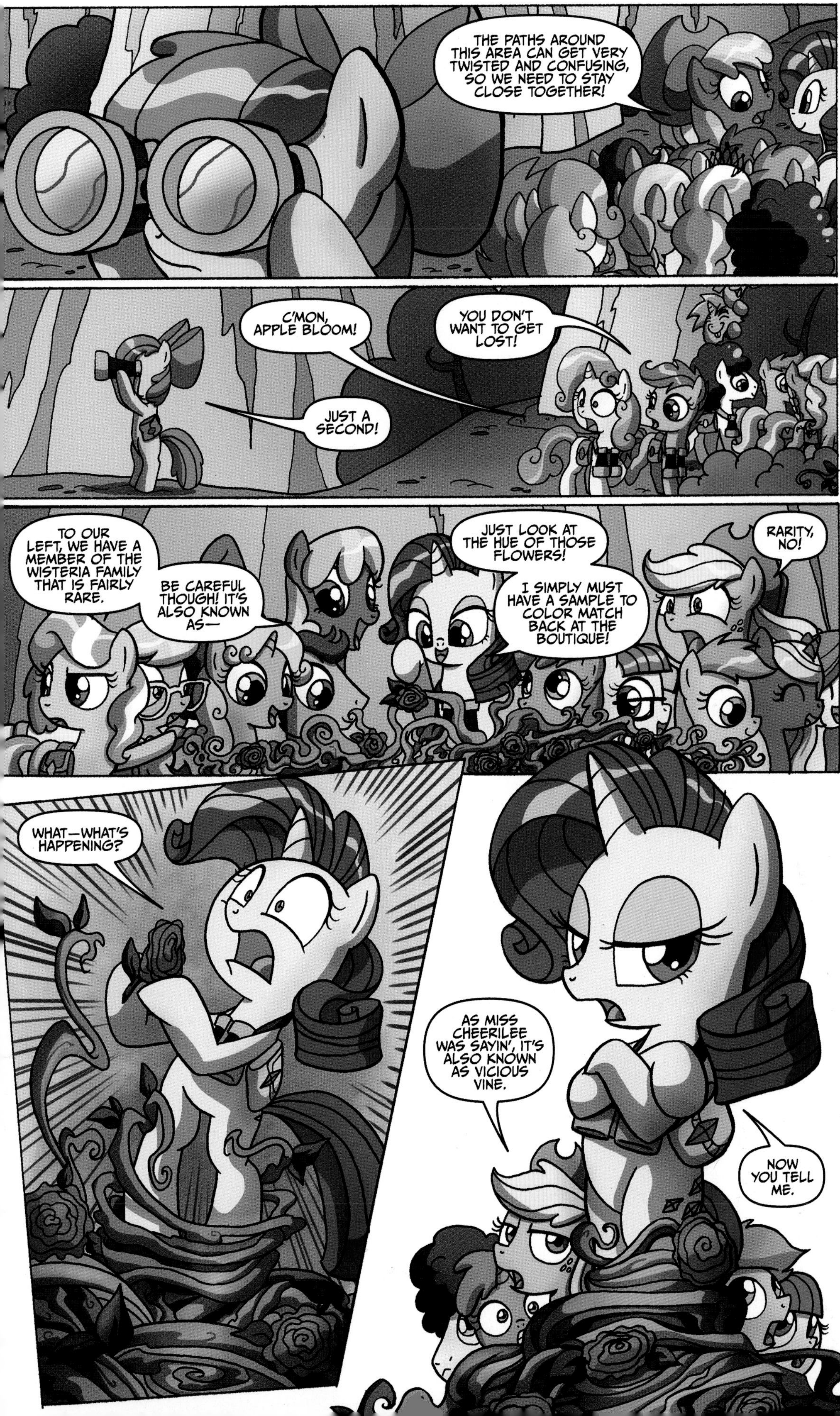
THE PATHS AROUND THIS AREA CAN GET VERY TWISTED AND CONFUSING, SO WE NEED TO STAY CLOSE TOGETHER!
C'MON, APPLE BLOOM!
YOU DON'T WANT TO GET LOST!
JUST A SECOND!
TO OUR LEFT, WE HAVE A MEMBER OF THE WISTERIA FAMILY THAT IS FAIRLY RARE.
BE CAREFUL THOUGH! IT'S ALSO KNOWN AS—
JUST LOOK AT THE HUE OF THOSE FLOWERS!
I SIMPLY MUST HAVE A SAMPLE TO COLOR MATCH BACK AT THE BOUTIQUE!
RARITY, NO!
WHAT—WHAT'S HAPPENING?
AS MISS CHEERILEE WAS SAYIN', IT'S ALSO KNOWN AS VICIOUS VINE.
NOW YOU TELL ME.

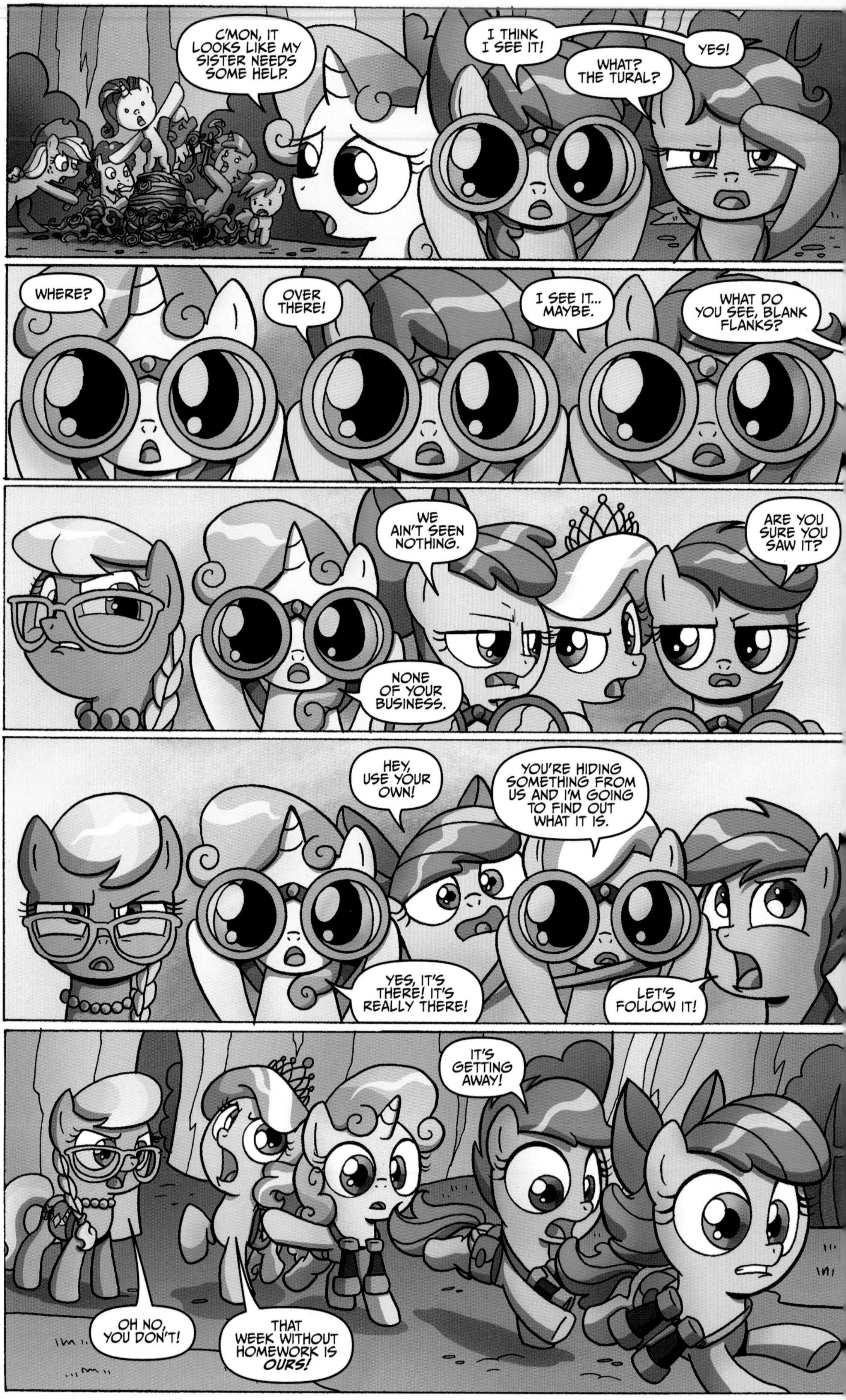
C'MON, IT LOOKS LIKE MY SISTER NEEDS SOME HELP.
I THINK I SEE IT!
WHAT? THE TURAL?
YES!
WHERE?
OVER THERE!
I SEE IT... MAYBE.
WHAT DO YOU SEE, BLANK FLANKS?
WE AIN'T SEEN NOTHING.
ARE YOU SURE YOU SAW IT?
NONE OF YOUR BUSINESS.
HEY, USE YOUR OWN!
YOU'RE HIDING SOMETHING FROM US AND I'M GOING TO FIND OUT WHAT IT IS.
YES, IT'S THERE! IT'S REALLY THERE!
LET'S FOLLOW IT!
IT'S GETTING AWAY!
OH NO, YOU DON'T!
THAT WEEK WITHOUT HOMEWORK IS OURS!

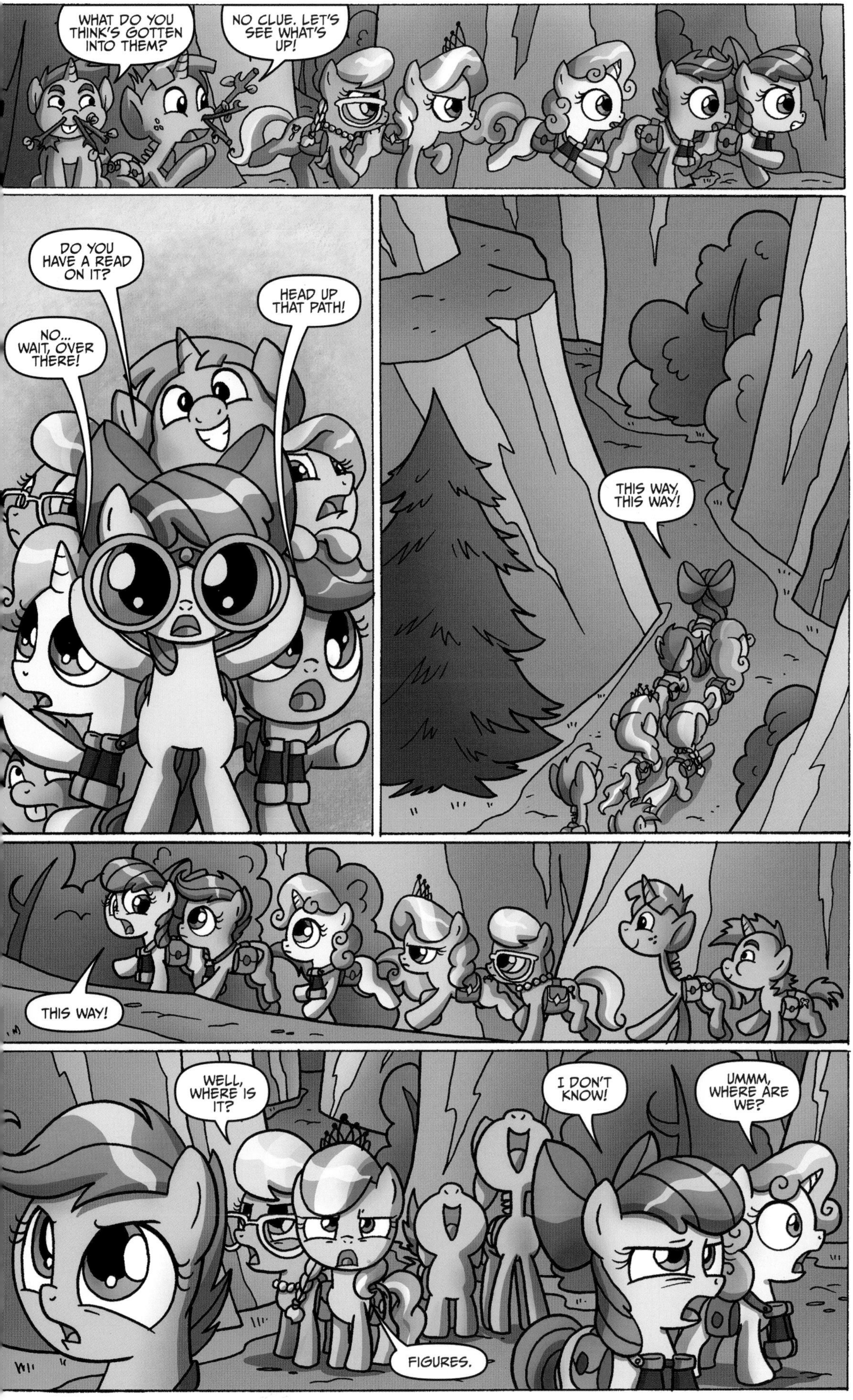
WHAT DO YOU THINK'S GOTTEN INTO THEM?
NO CLUE. LET'S SEE WHAT'S UP!
DO YOU HAVE A READ ON IT?
NO... WAIT, OVER THERE!
HEAD UP THAT PATH!
THIS WAY, THIS WAY!
THIS WAY!
WELL, WHERE IS IT?
I DON'T KNOW!
UMMM, WHERE ARE WE?
FIGURES.

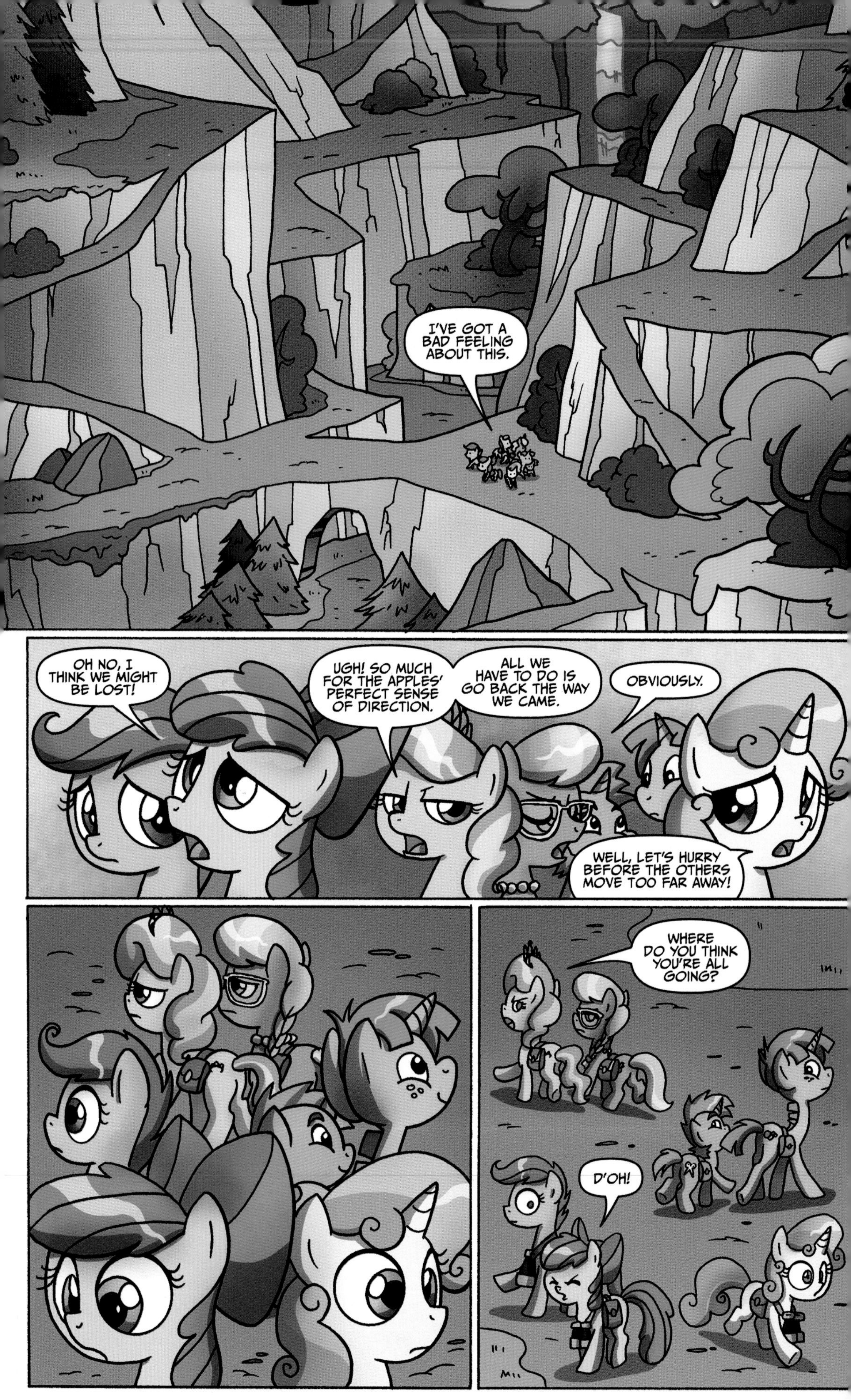
I'VE GOT A BAD FEELING ABOUT THIS.
OH NO, I THINK WE MIGHT BE LOST!
UGH! SO MUCH FOR THE APPLES' PERFECT SENSE OF DIRECTION.
ALL WE HAVE TO DO IS GO BACK THE WAY WE CAME.
OBVIOUSLY.
WELL, LET'S HURRY BEFORE THE OTHERS MOVE TOO FAR AWAY!
WHERE DO YOU THINK YOU'RE ALL GOING?
D'OH!

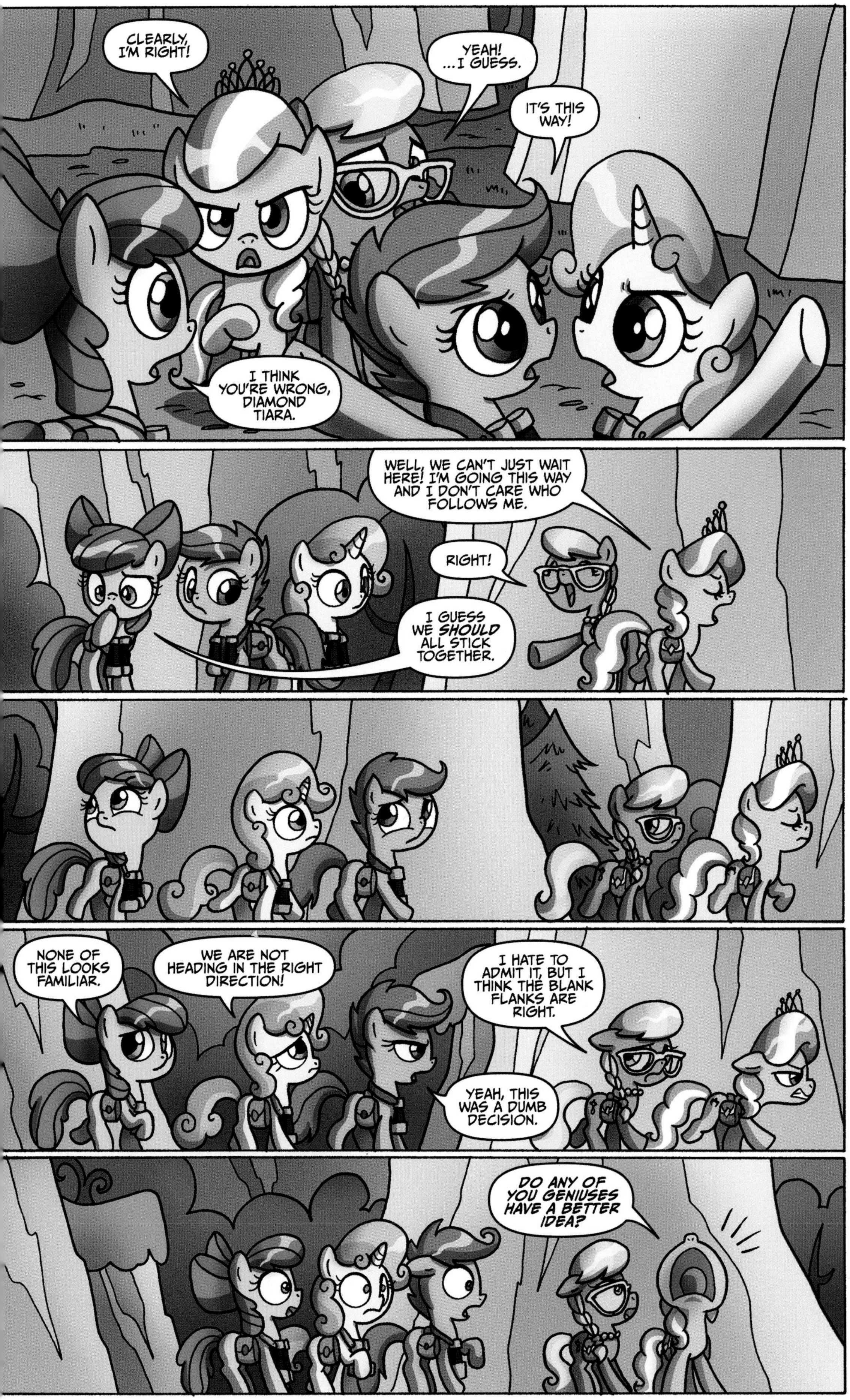

CLEARLY, I'M RIGHT!
YEAH! ...I GUESS.
IT'S THIS WAY!
I THINK YOU'RE WRONG, DIAMOND TIARA.
WELL, WE CAN'T JUST WAIT HERE! I'M GOING THIS WAY AND I DON'T CARE WHO FOLLOWS ME.
RIGHT!
I GUESS WE SHOULD ALL STICK TOGETHER.
NONE OF THIS LOOKS FAMILIAR.
WE ARE NOT HEADING IN THE RIGHT DIRECTION!
I HATE TO ADMIT IT, BUT I THINK THE BLANK FLANKS ARE RIGHT.
YEAH, THIS WAS A DUMB DECISION.
DO ANY OF YOU GENIUSES HAVE A BETTER IDEA?

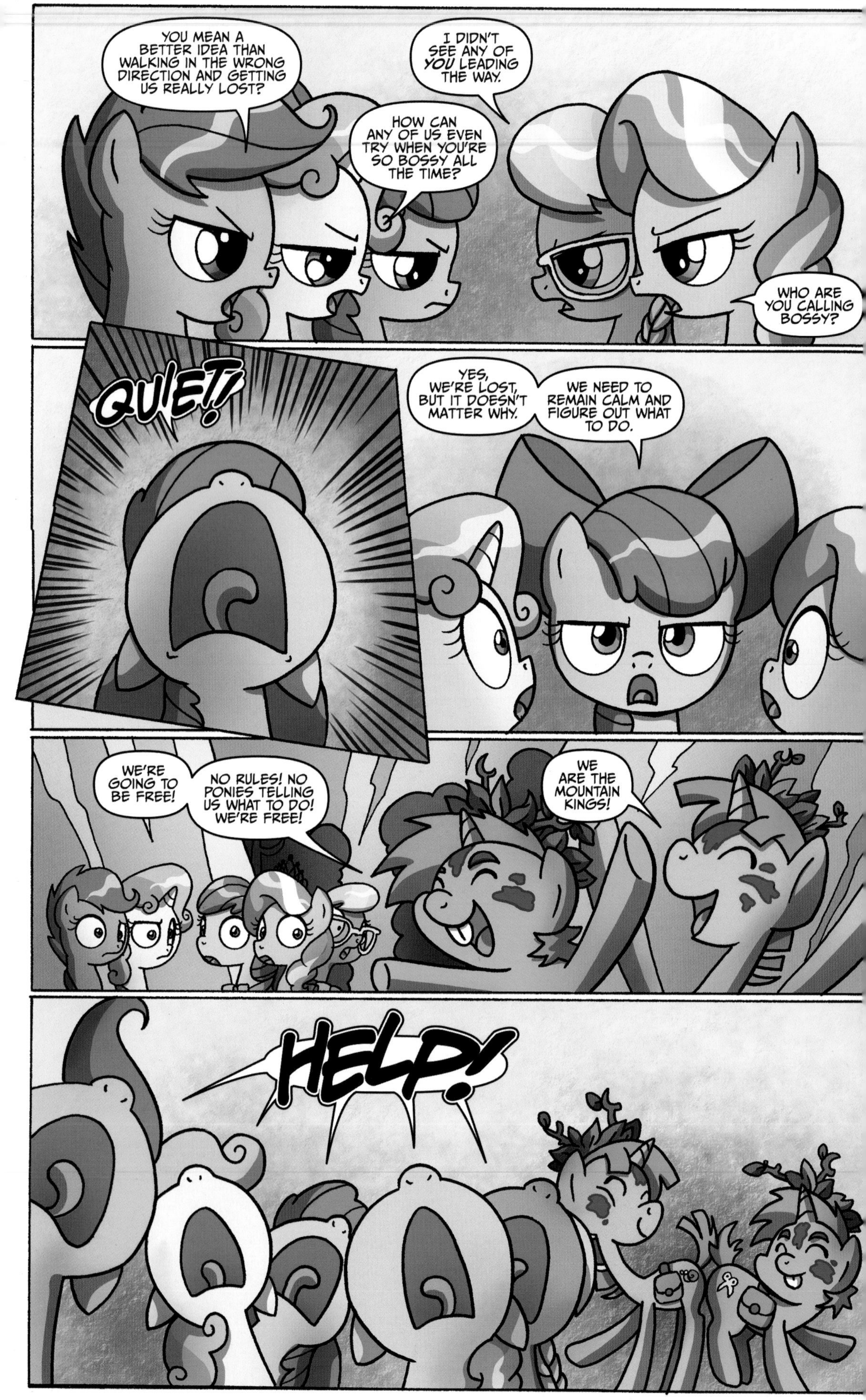

YOU MEAN A BETTER IDEA THAN WALKING IN THE WRONG DIRECTION AND GETTING US REALLY LOST?
I DIDN'T SEE ANY OF YOU LEADING THE WAY.
HOW CAN ANY OF US EVEN TRY WHEN YOU'RE SO BOSSY ALL THE TIME?
WHO ARE YOU CALLING BOSSY?
QUIET!
YES, WE'RE LOST, BUT IT DOESN'T MATTER WHY.
WE NEED TO REMAIN CALM AND FIGURE OUT WHAT TO DO.
WE'RE GOING TO BE FREE!
NO RULES! NO PONIES TELLING US WHAT TO DO! WE'RE FREE!
WE ARE THE MOUNTAIN KINGS!
HELP!

MAYBE WE SHOULD JUST STAY PUT AND LET THE OTHERS FIND US.

YOU'RE RIGHT, MAYBE THEY HEARD US YELLING!

AND THEY'LL COME LOOKING!

WE ARE GOING TO STAY PUT AND LET THE OTHERS FIND US!

GREAT IDEA!

I JUST SAID THAT...

DID YOU HEAR THAT?

HEAR WHAT? IS IT SIS AND APPLEJACK?

ROOOOOAAAAARRRRRRRRRRRR

ON SECOND THOUGHT, MAYBE WE SHOULD GET OUT OF HERE.

THE MOUNTAIN KINGS ARE INCLINED TO AGREE.

ROOOOOAAAARRRRR

RUN!

WHAAAAA!

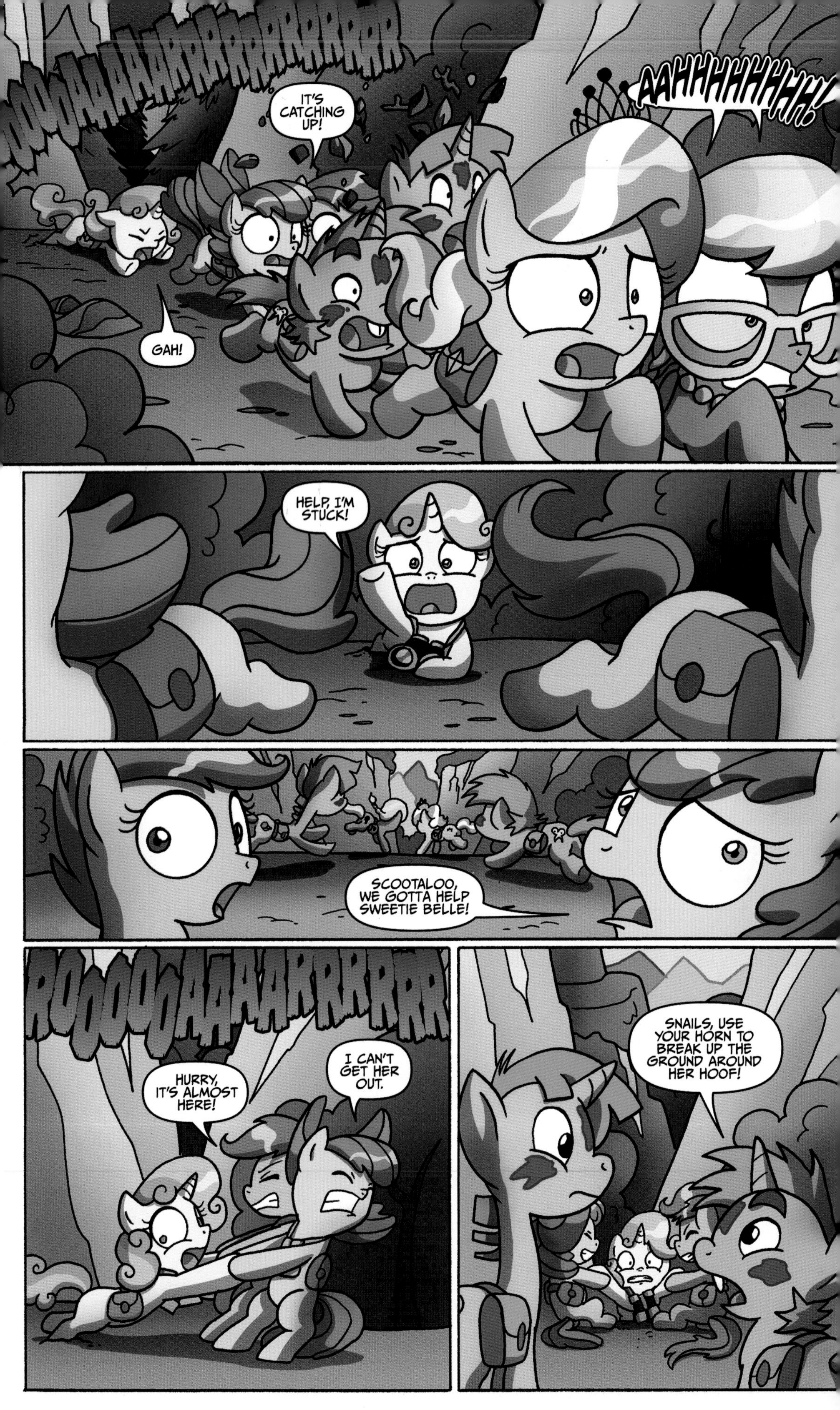
ROOOOAAAAARRRRRRRRRRRR
IT'S CATCHING UP!
AAHHHHHHHH!
GAH!
HELP, I'M STUCK!
SCOOTALOO, WE GOTTA HELP SWEETIE BELLE!
ROOOOOAAAAARRRRRR
HURRY, IT'S ALMOST HERE!
I CAN'T GET HER OUT.
SNAILS, USE YOUR HORN TO BREAK UP THE GROUND AROUND HER HOOF!

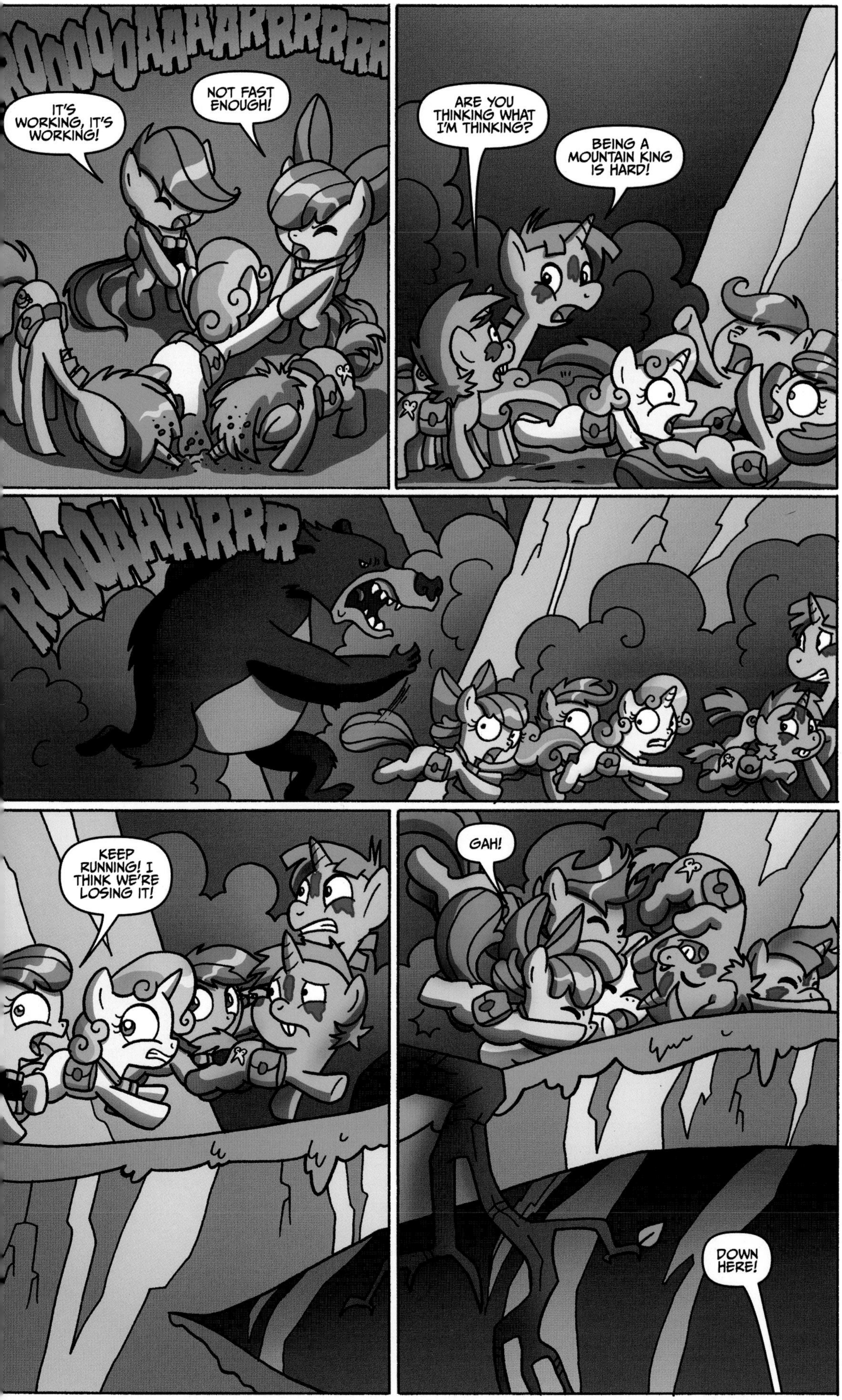
ROOOOOAAAARRRRRR
IT'S WORKING, IT'S WORKING!
NOT FAST ENOUGH!
ARE YOU THINKING WHAT I'M THINKING?
BEING A MOUNTAIN KING IS HARD!
ROOOAAARRR
KEEP RUNNING! I THINK WE'RE LOSING IT!
GAH!
DOWN HERE!

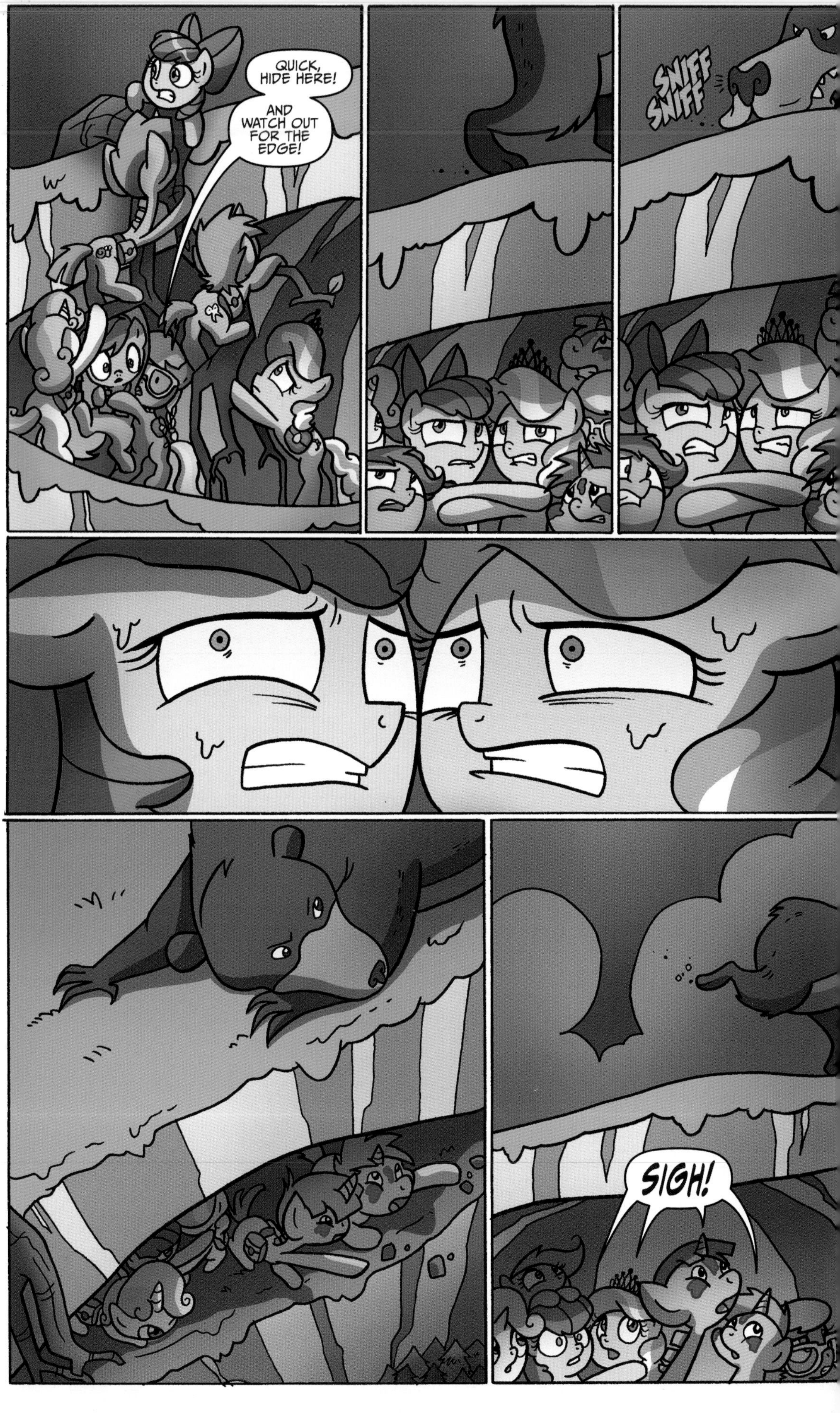
QUICK, HIDE HERE!
AND WATCH OUT FOR THE EDGE!
SNIFF SNIFF
SIGH!

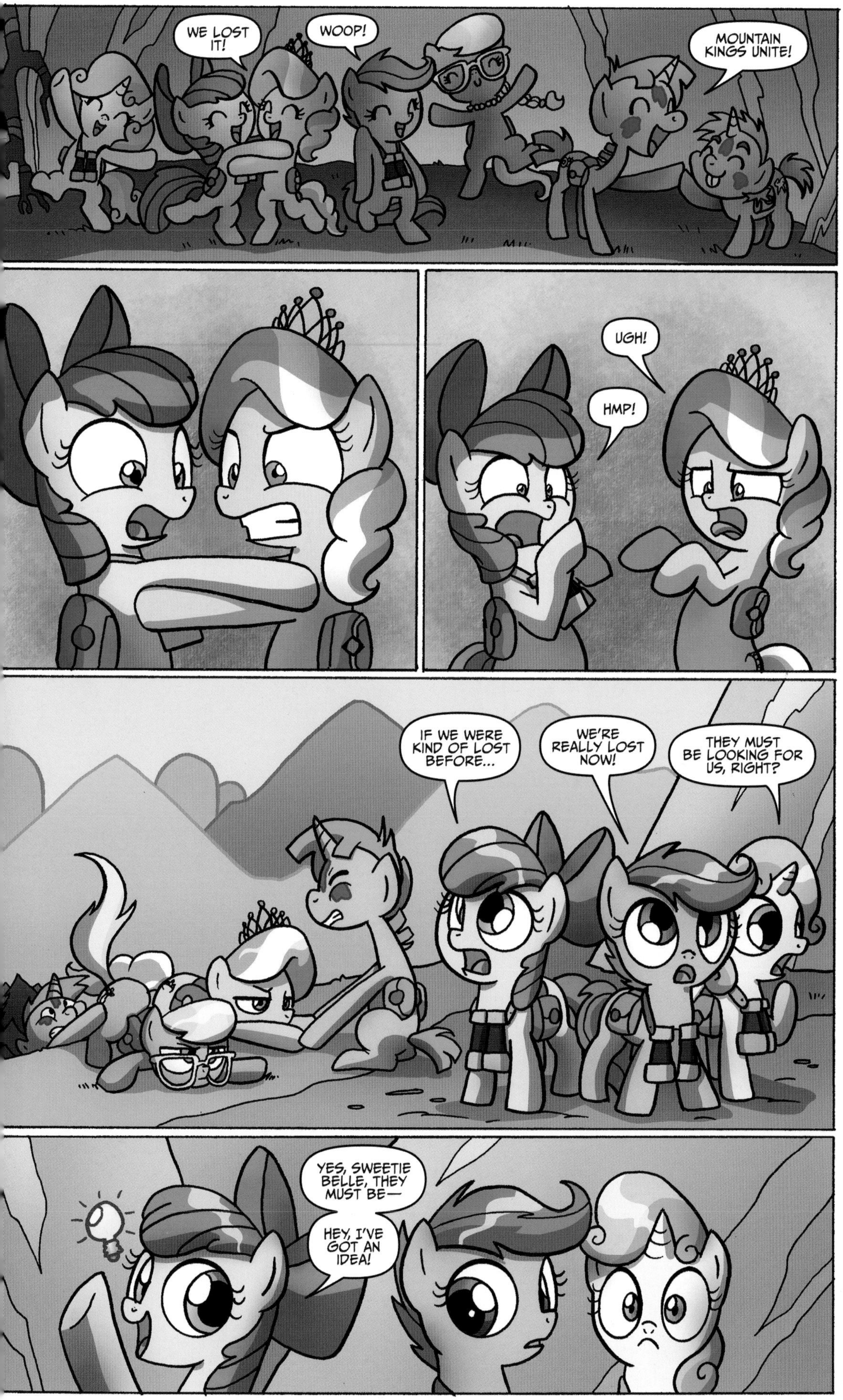
WE LOST IT!
WOOP!
MOUNTAIN KINGS UNITE!
UGH!
HMP!
IF WE WERE KIND OF LOST BEFORE...
WE'RE REALLY LOST NOW!
THEY MUST BE LOOKING FOR US, RIGHT?
YES, SWEETIE BELLE, THEY MUST BE—
HEY, I'VE GOT AN IDEA!

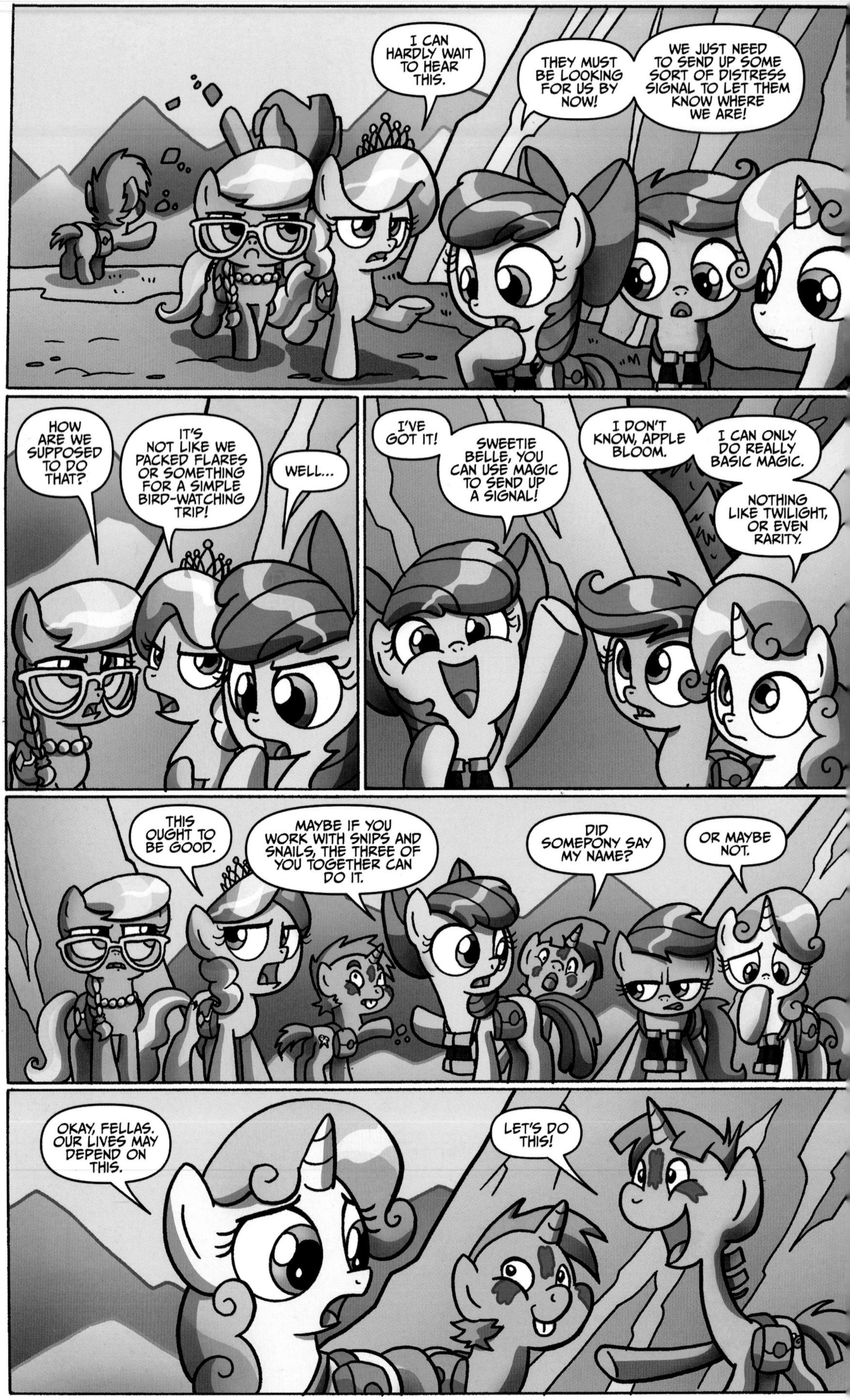
I CAN HARDLY WAIT TO HEAR THIS.
THEY MUST BE LOOKING FOR US BY NOW!
WE JUST NEED TO SEND UP SOME SORT OF DISTRESS SIGNAL TO LET THEM KNOW WHERE WE ARE!
HOW ARE WE SUPPOSED TO DO THAT?
IT'S NOT LIKE WE PACKED FLARES OR SOMETHING FOR A SIMPLE BIRD-WATCHING TRIP!
WELL...
I'VE GOT IT!
SWEETIE BELLE, YOU CAN USE MAGIC TO SEND UP A SIGNAL!
I DON'T KNOW, APPLE BLOOM.
I CAN ONLY DO REALLY BASIC MAGIC.
NOTHING LIKE TWILIGHT, OR EVEN RARITY.
THIS OUGHT TO BE GOOD.
MAYBE IF YOU WORK WITH SNIPS AND SNAILS, THE THREE OF YOU TOGETHER CAN DO IT.
DID SOMEPONY SAY MY NAME?
OR MAYBE NOT.
OKAY, FELLAS. OUR LIVES MAY DEPEND ON THIS.
LET'S DO THIS!

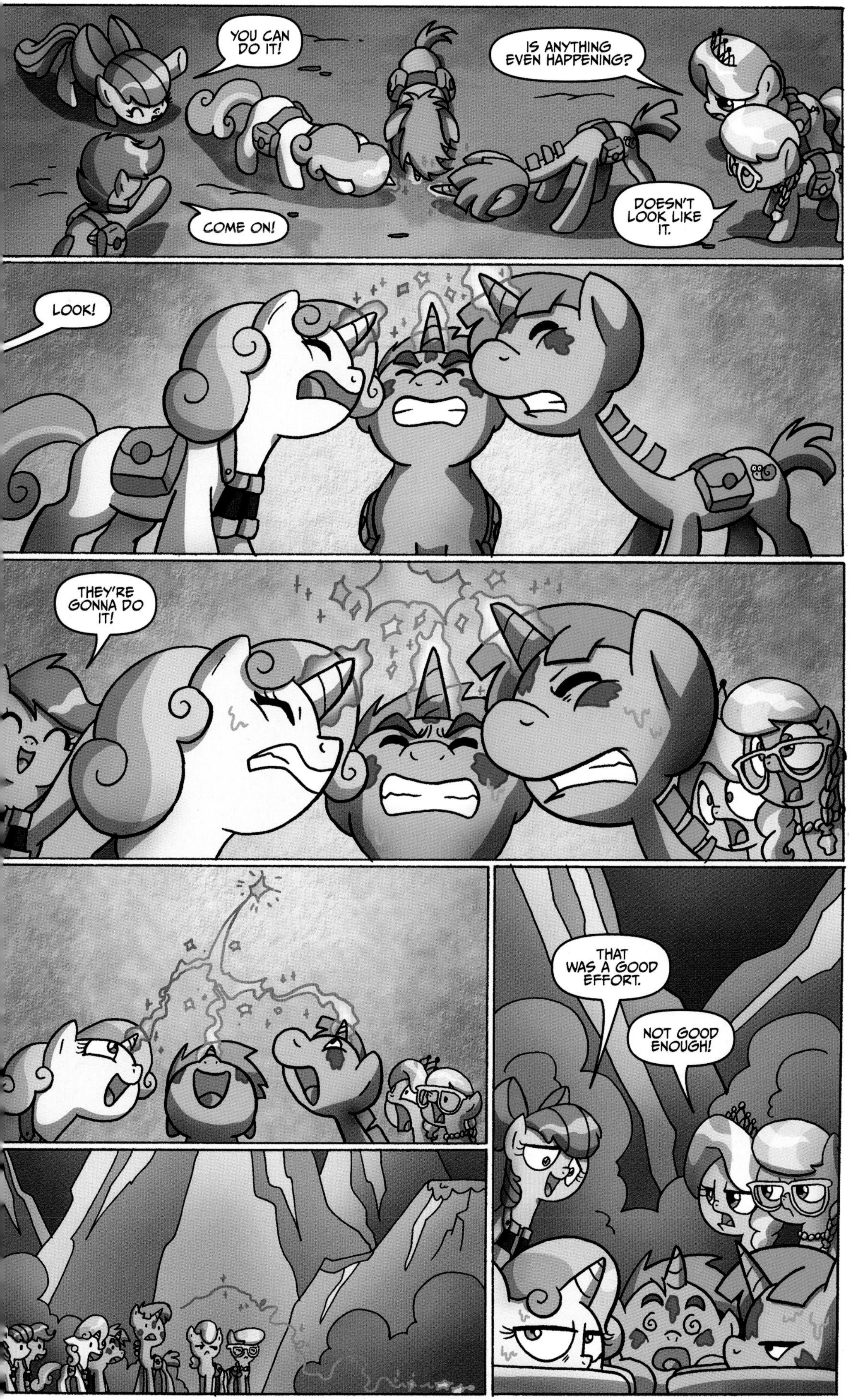
YOU CAN DO IT!
COME ON!
IS ANYTHING EVEN HAPPENING?
DOESN'T LOOK LIKE IT.
LOOK!
THEY'RE GONNA DO IT!
THAT WAS A GOOD EFFORT.
NOT GOOD ENOUGH!

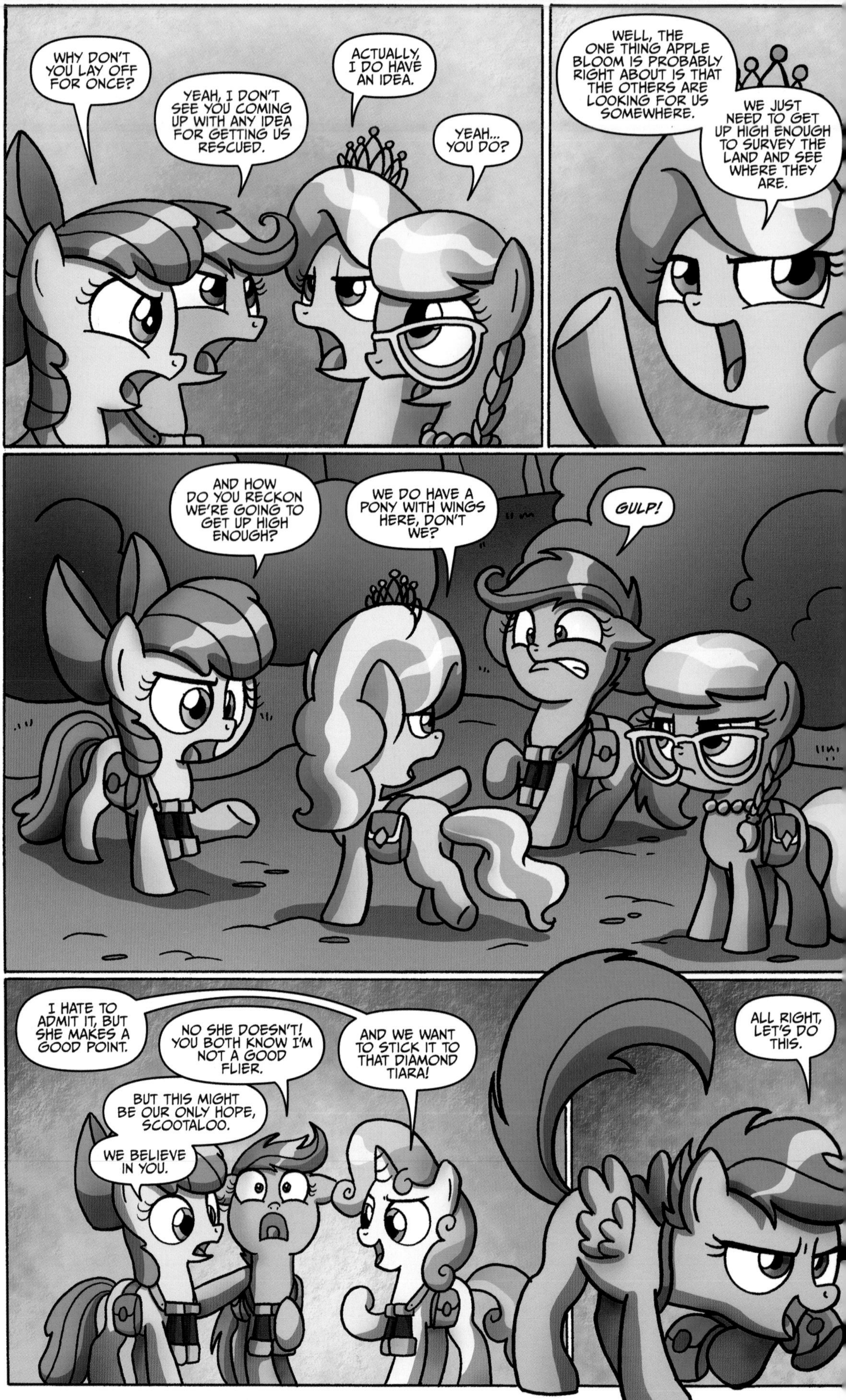
WHY DON'T YOU LAY OFF FOR ONCE?
YEAH, I DON'T SEE YOU COMING UP WITH ANY IDEA FOR GETTING US RESCUED.
ACTUALLY, I DO HAVE AN IDEA.
YEAH... YOU DO?
WELL, THE ONE THING APPLE BLOOM IS PROBABLY RIGHT ABOUT IS THAT THE OTHERS ARE LOOKING FOR US SOMEWHERE.
WE JUST NEED TO GET UP HIGH ENOUGH TO SURVEY THE LAND AND SEE WHERE THEY ARE.
AND HOW DO YOU RECKON WE'RE GOING TO GET UP HIGH ENOUGH?
WE DO HAVE A PONY WITH WINGS HERE, DON'T WE?
GULP!
I HATE TO ADMIT IT, BUT SHE MAKES A GOOD POINT.
NO SHE DOESN'T! YOU BOTH KNOW I'M NOT A GOOD FLIER.
AND WE WANT TO STICK IT TO THAT DIAMOND TIARA!
BUT THIS MIGHT BE OUR ONLY HOPE, SCOOTALOO.
WE BELIEVE IN YOU.
ALL RIGHT, LET'S DO THIS.

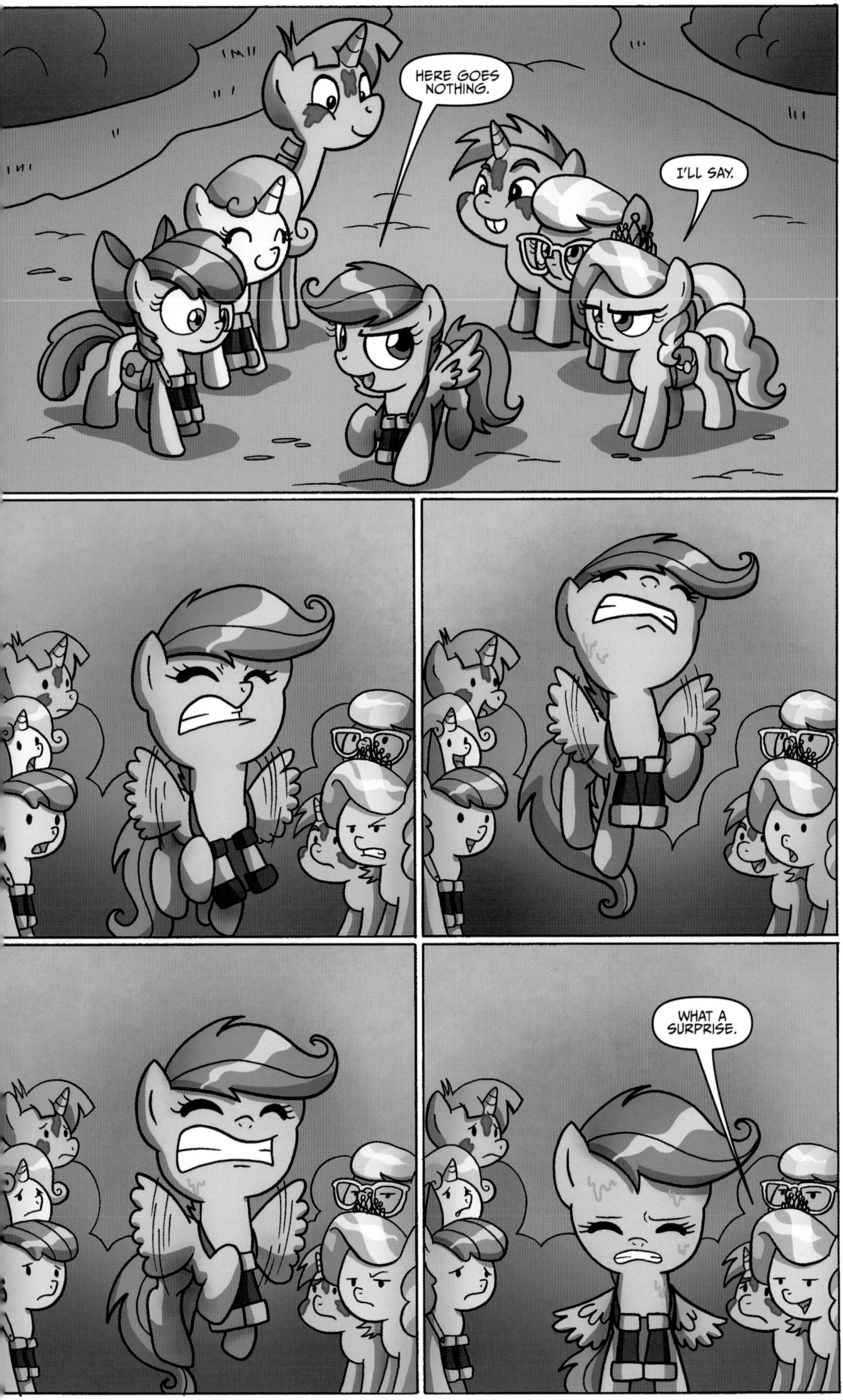
HERE GOES NOTHING.
I'LL SAY.
WHAT A SURPRISE.

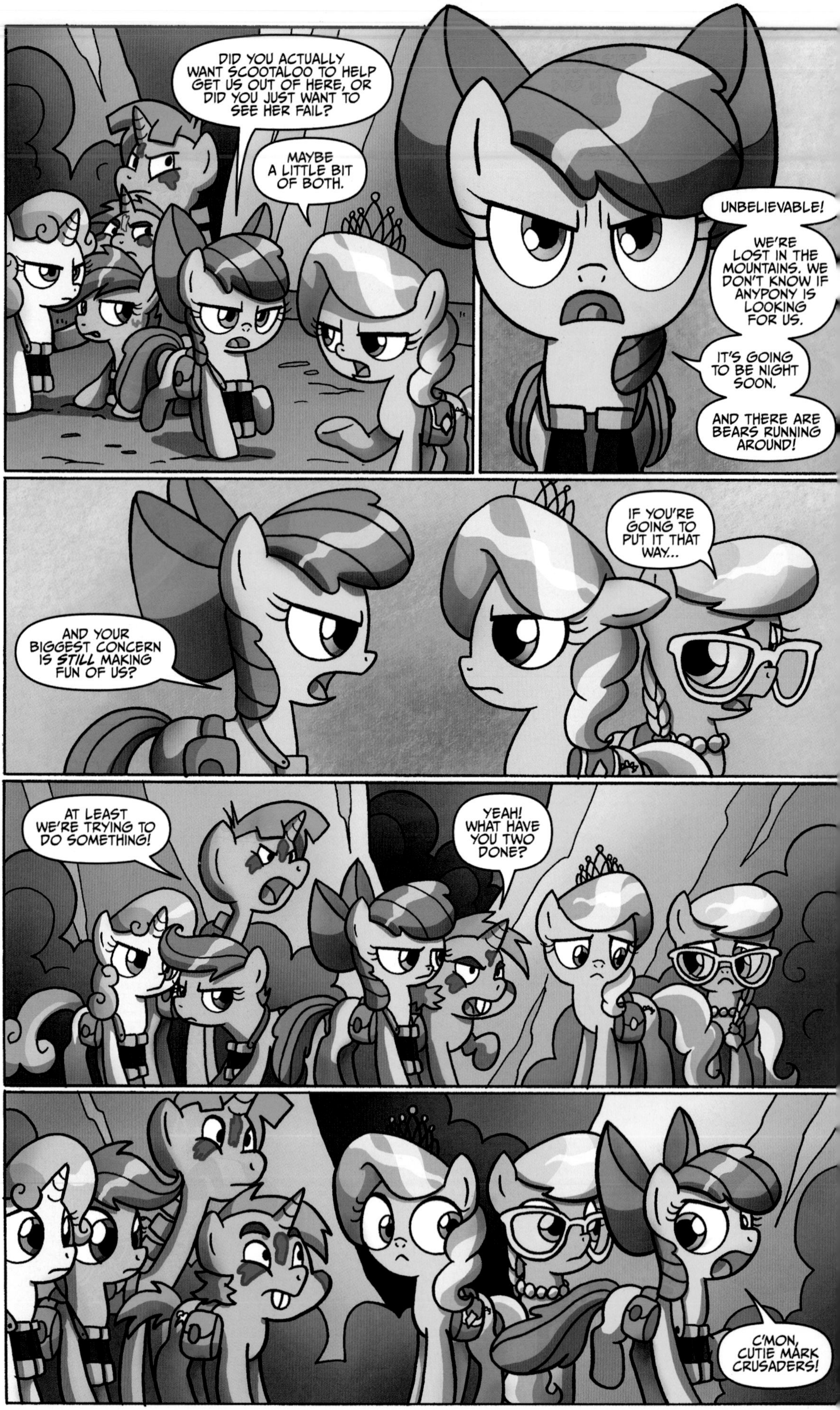
DID YOU ACTUALLY WANT SCOOTALOO TO HELP GET US OUT OF HERE, OR DID YOU JUST WANT TO SEE HER FAIL?
MAYBE A LITTLE BIT OF BOTH.
UNBELIEVABLE!
WE'RE LOST IN THE MOUNTAINS. WE DON'T KNOW IF ANYPONY IS LOOKING FOR US.
IT'S GOING TO BE NIGHT SOON.
AND THERE ARE BEARS RUNNING AROUND!
AND YOUR BIGGEST CONCERN IS *STILL* MAKING FUN OF US?
IF YOU'RE GOING TO PUT IT THAT WAY...
AT LEAST WE'RE TRYING TO DO SOMETHING!
YEAH! WHAT HAVE YOU TWO DONE?
C'MON, CUTIE MARK CRUSADERS!

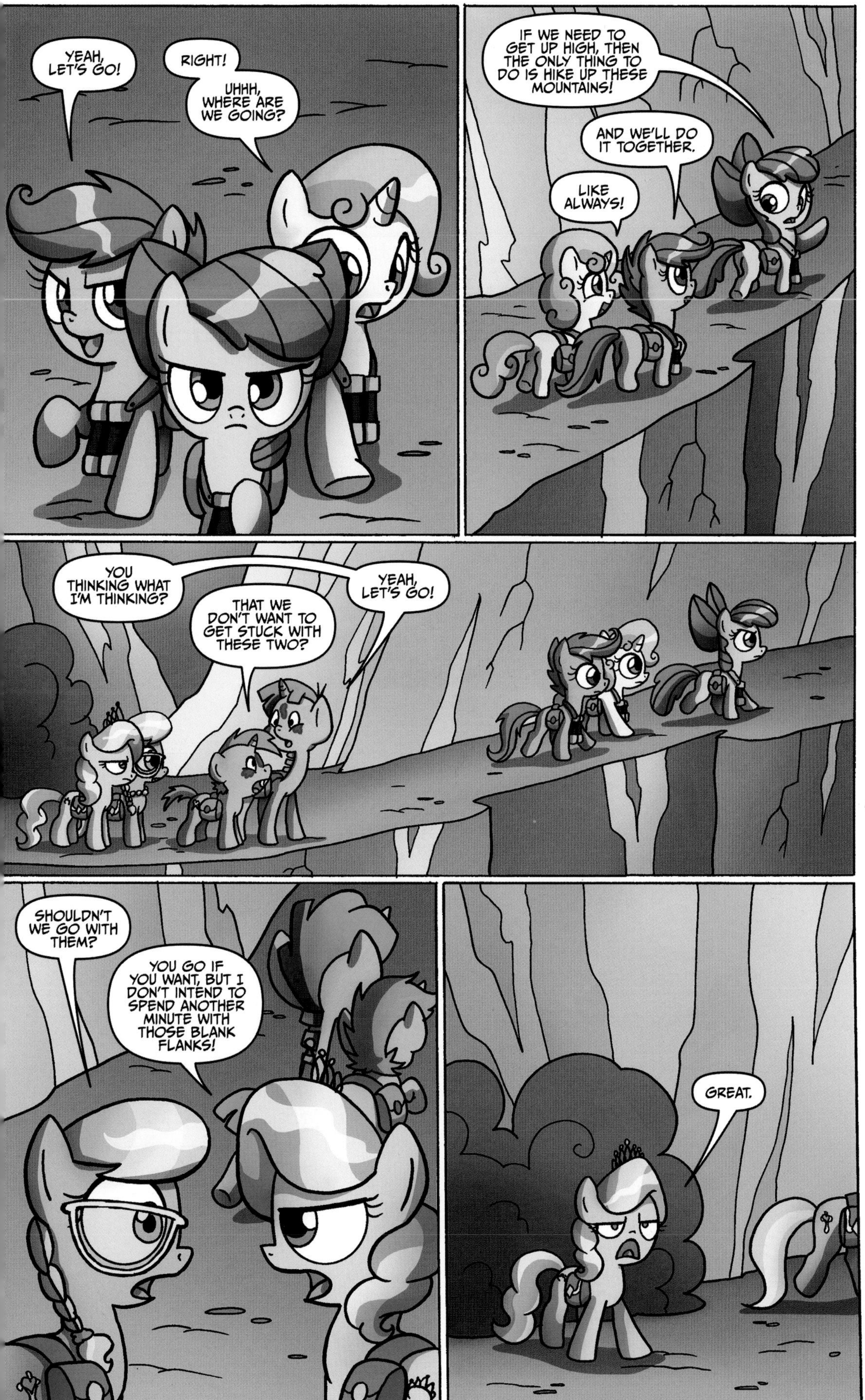
YEAH, LET'S GO!
RIGHT!
UHHH, WHERE ARE WE GOING?
IF WE NEED TO GET UP HIGH, THEN THE ONLY THING TO DO IS HIKE UP THESE MOUNTAINS!
AND WE'LL DO IT TOGETHER.
LIKE ALWAYS!
YOU THINKING WHAT I'M THINKING?
THAT WE DON'T WANT TO GET STUCK WITH THESE TWO?
YEAH, LET'S GO!
SHOULDN'T WE GO WITH THEM?
YOU GO IF YOU WANT, BUT I DON'T INTEND TO SPEND ANOTHER MINUTE WITH THOSE BLANK FLANKS!
GREAT.

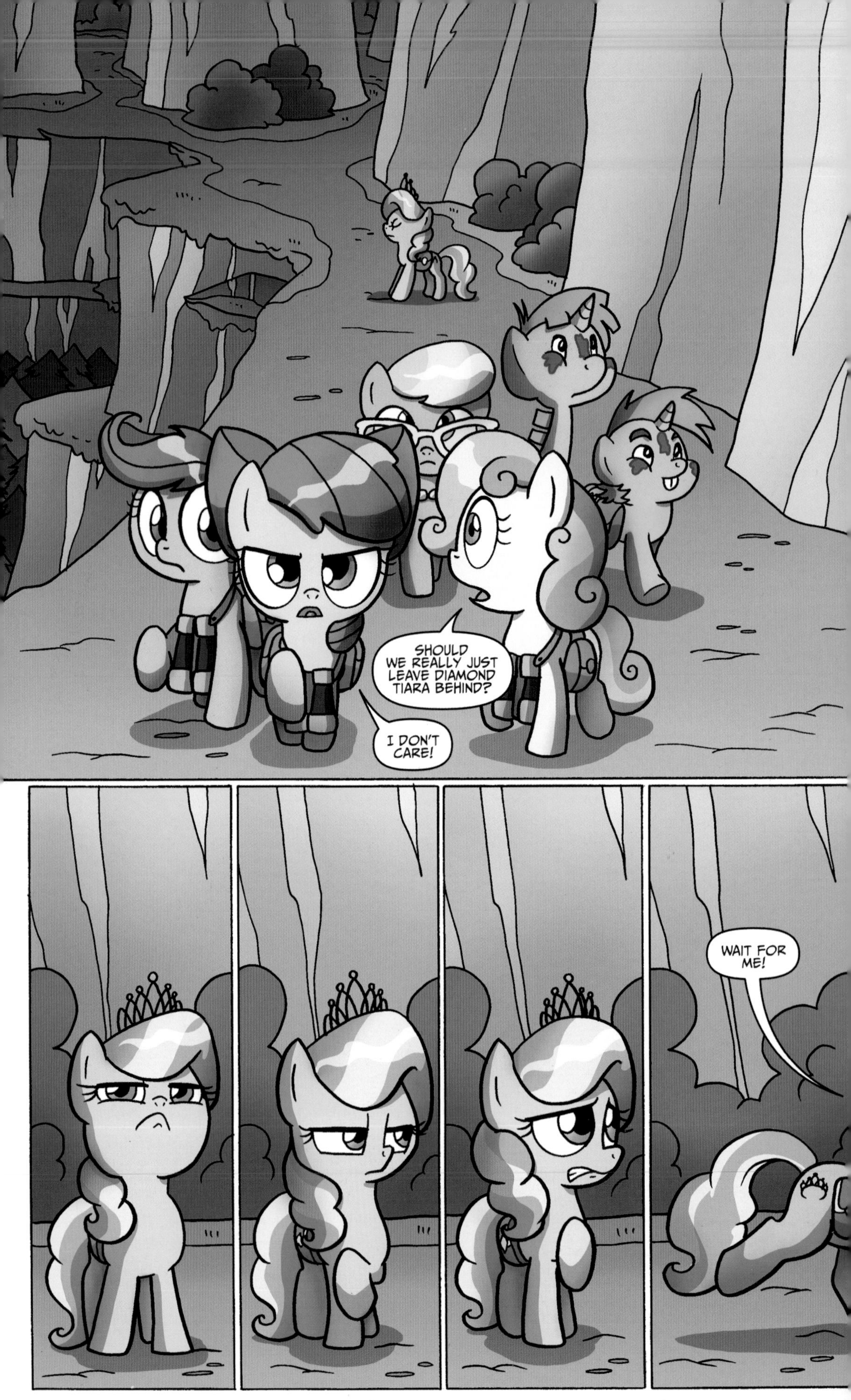
SHOULD WE REALLY JUST LEAVE DIAMOND TIARA BEHIND?
I DON'T CARE!
WAIT FOR ME!

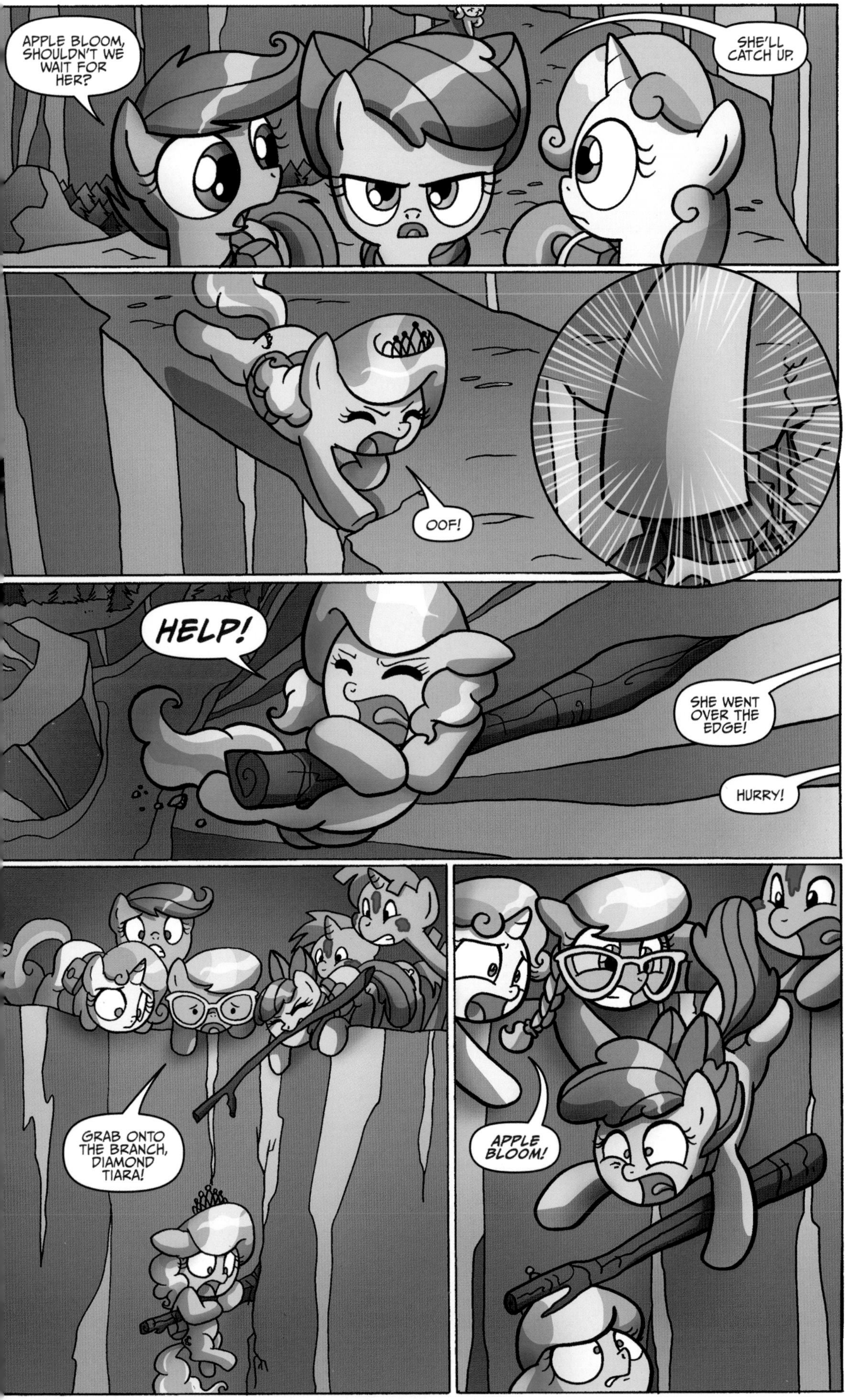
APPLE BLOOM, SHOULDN'T WE WAIT FOR HER?
SHE'LL CATCH UP.
OOF!
HELP!
SHE WENT OVER THE EDGE!
HURRY!
GRAB ONTO THE BRANCH, DIAMOND TIARA!
APPLE BLOOM!

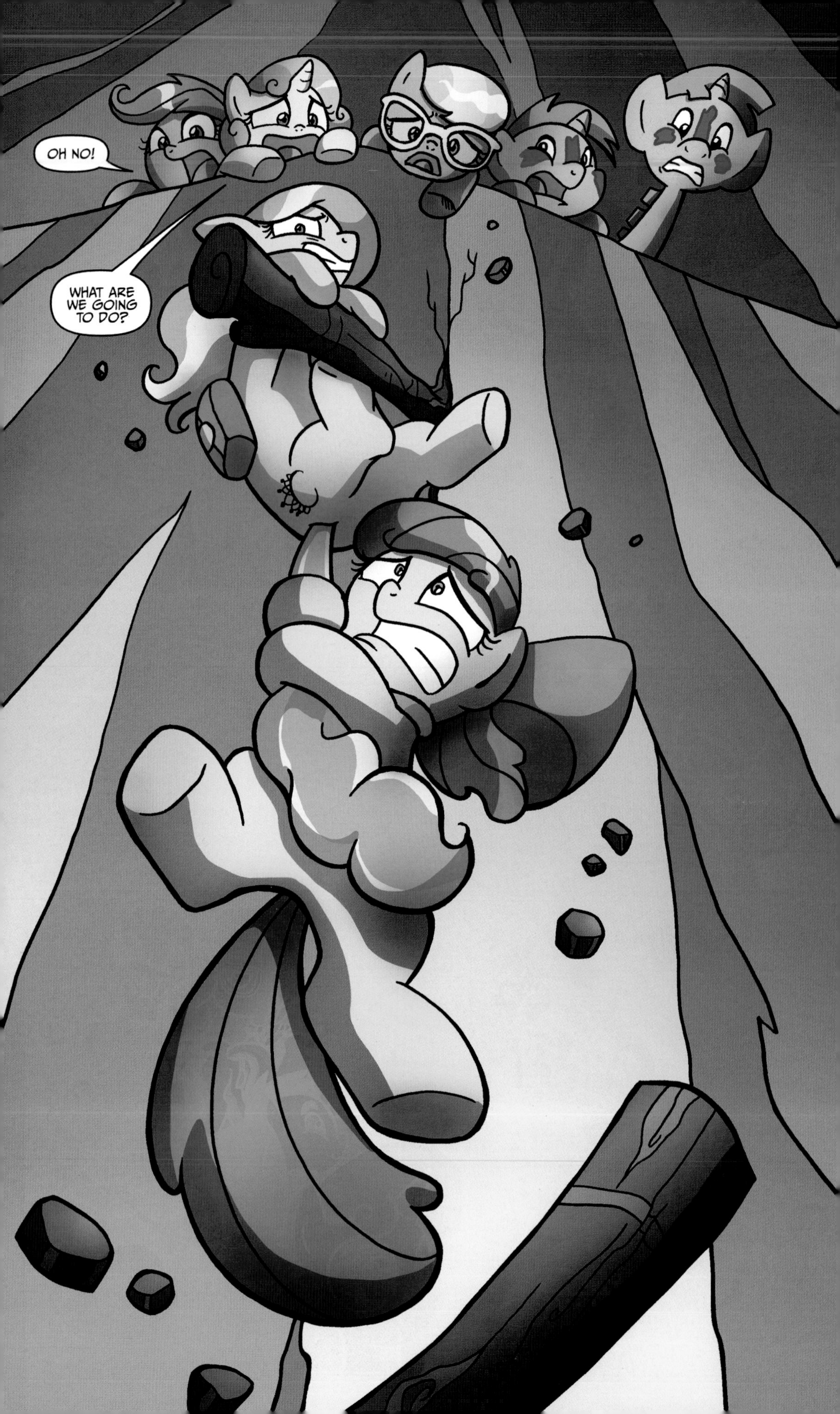
OH NO!
WHAT ARE WE GOING TO DO?

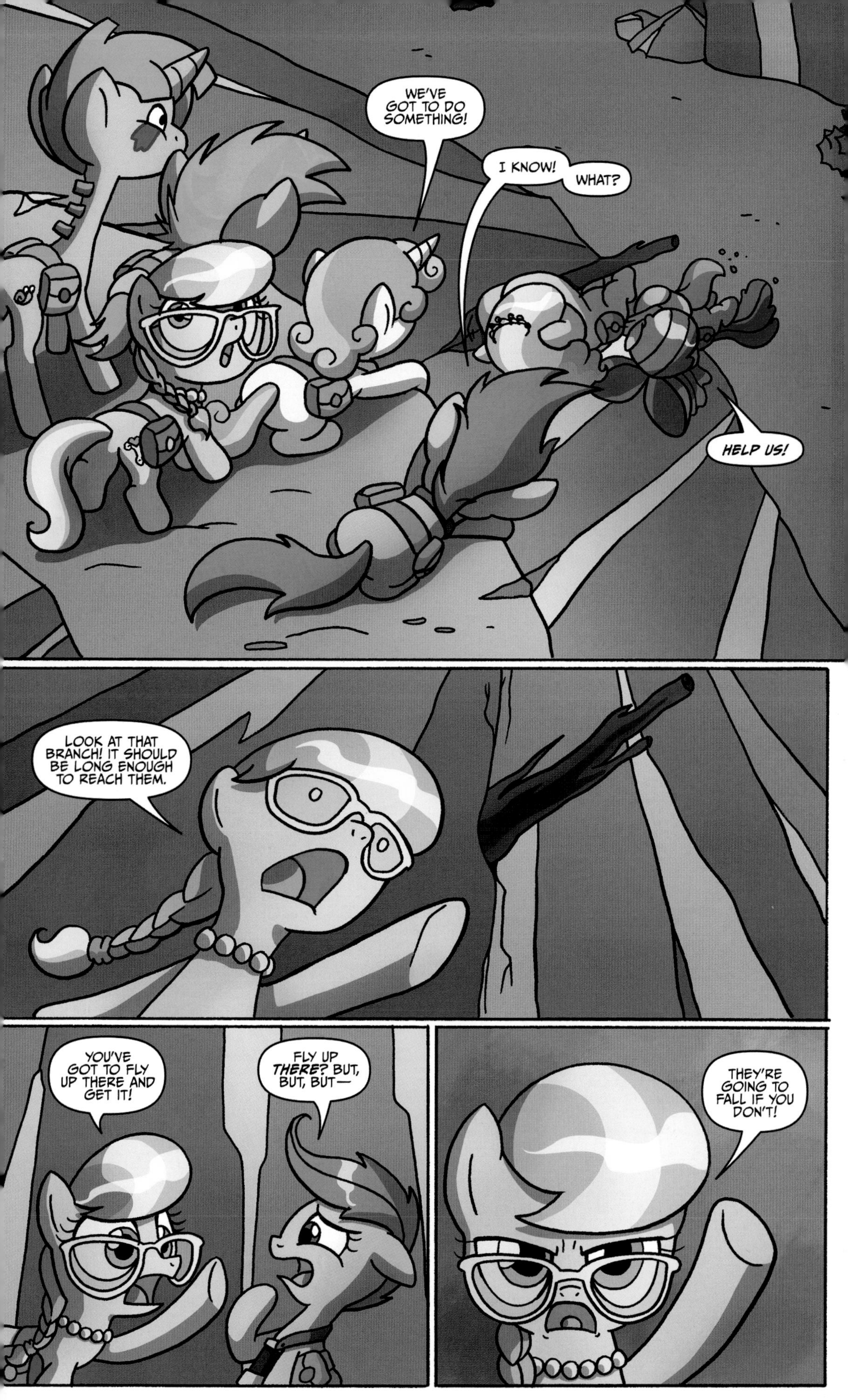
WE'VE GOT TO DO SOMETHING!
I KNOW!
WHAT?
HELP US!
LOOK AT THAT BRANCH! IT SHOULD BE LONG ENOUGH TO REACH THEM.
YOU'VE GOT TO FLY UP THERE AND GET IT!
FLY UP *THERE*? BUT, BUT, BUT—
THEY'RE GOING TO FALL IF YOU DON'T!

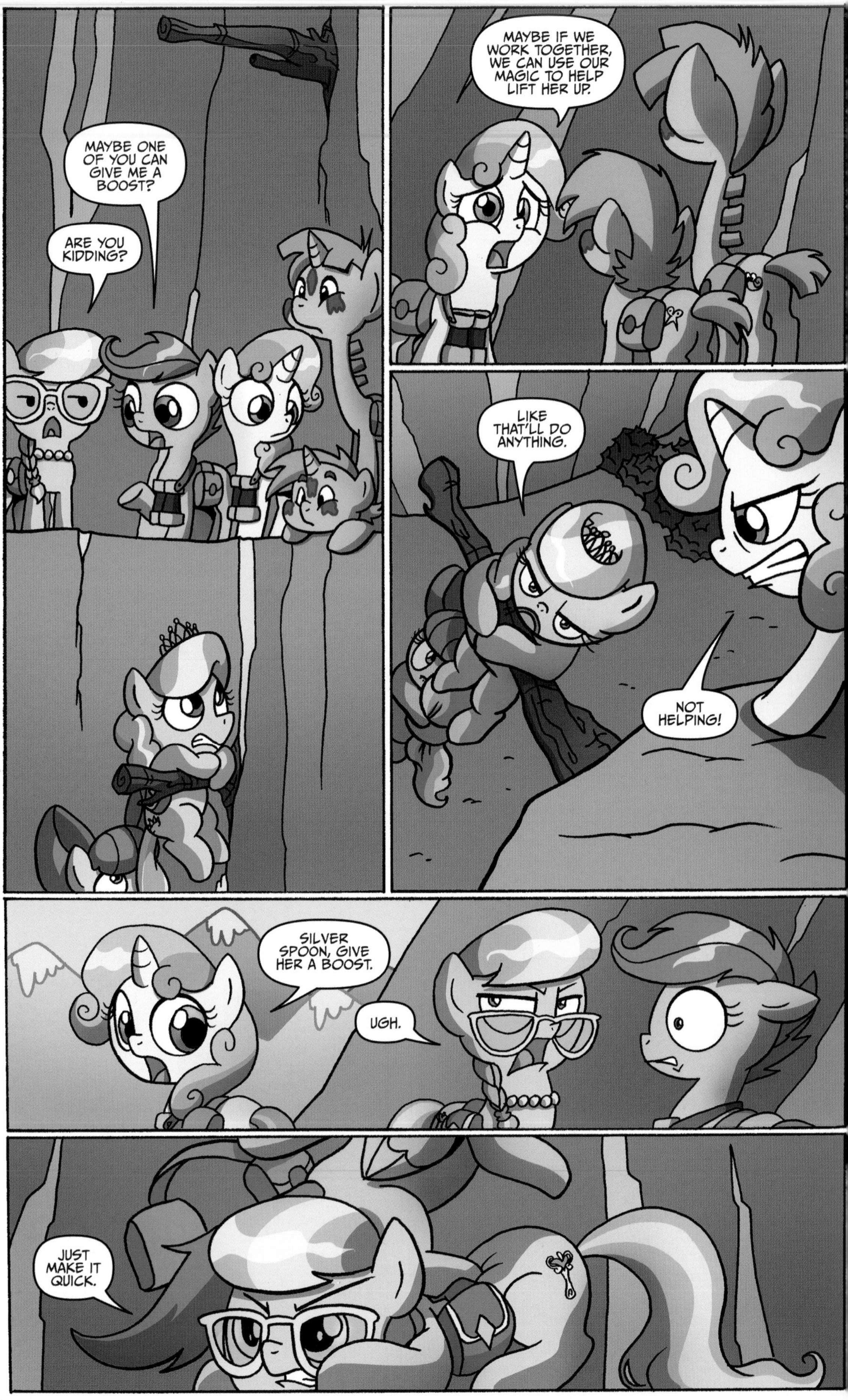
MAYBE ONE OF YOU CAN GIVE ME A BOOST?
ARE YOU KIDDING?
MAYBE IF WE WORK TOGETHER, WE CAN USE OUR MAGIC TO HELP LIFT HER UP.
LIKE THAT'LL DO ANYTHING.
NOT HELPING!
SILVER SPOON, GIVE HER A BOOST.
UGH.
JUST MAKE IT QUICK.

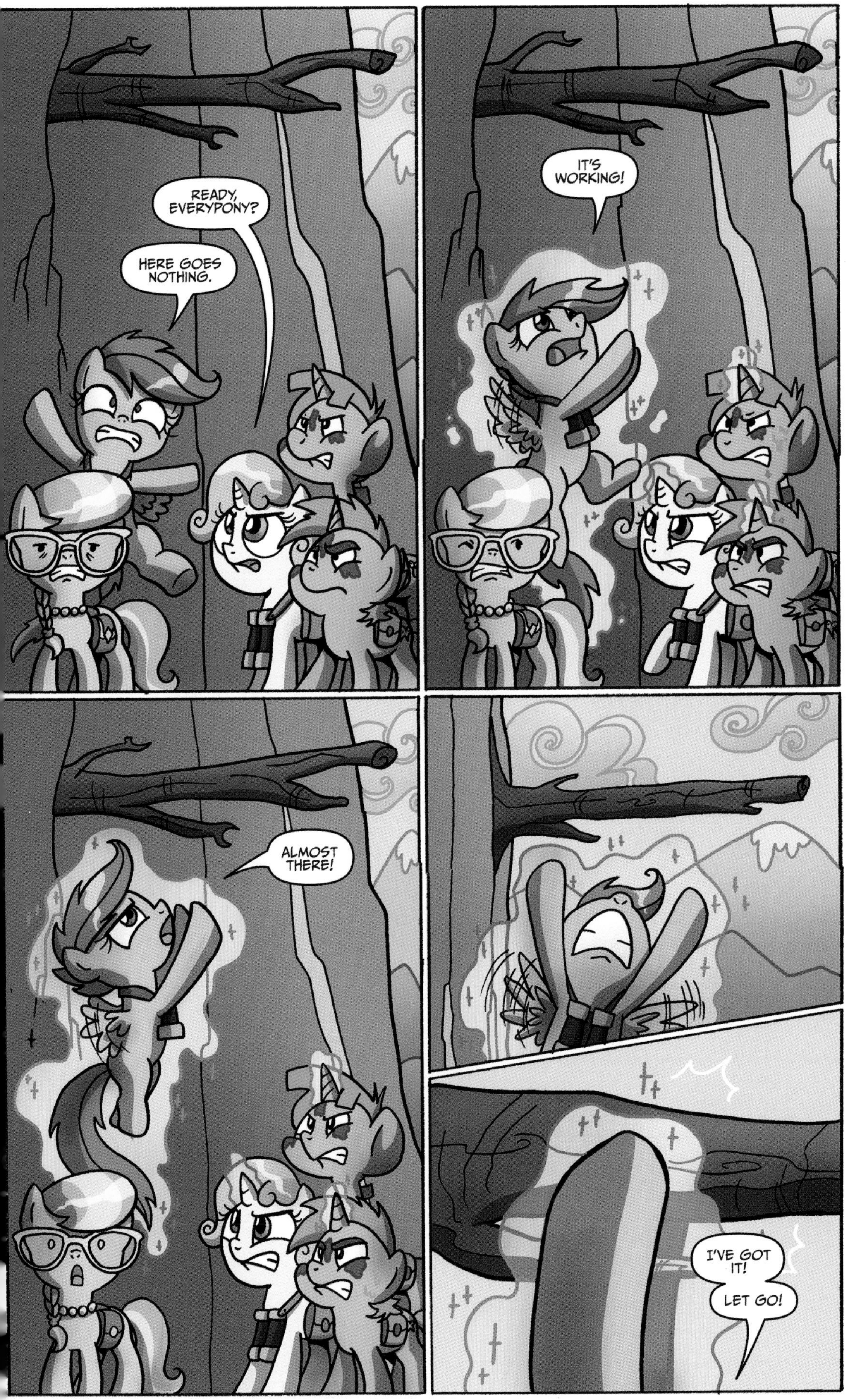
READY, EVERYPONY?
HERE GOES NOTHING.
IT'S WORKING!
ALMOST THERE!
I'VE GOT IT!
LET GO!

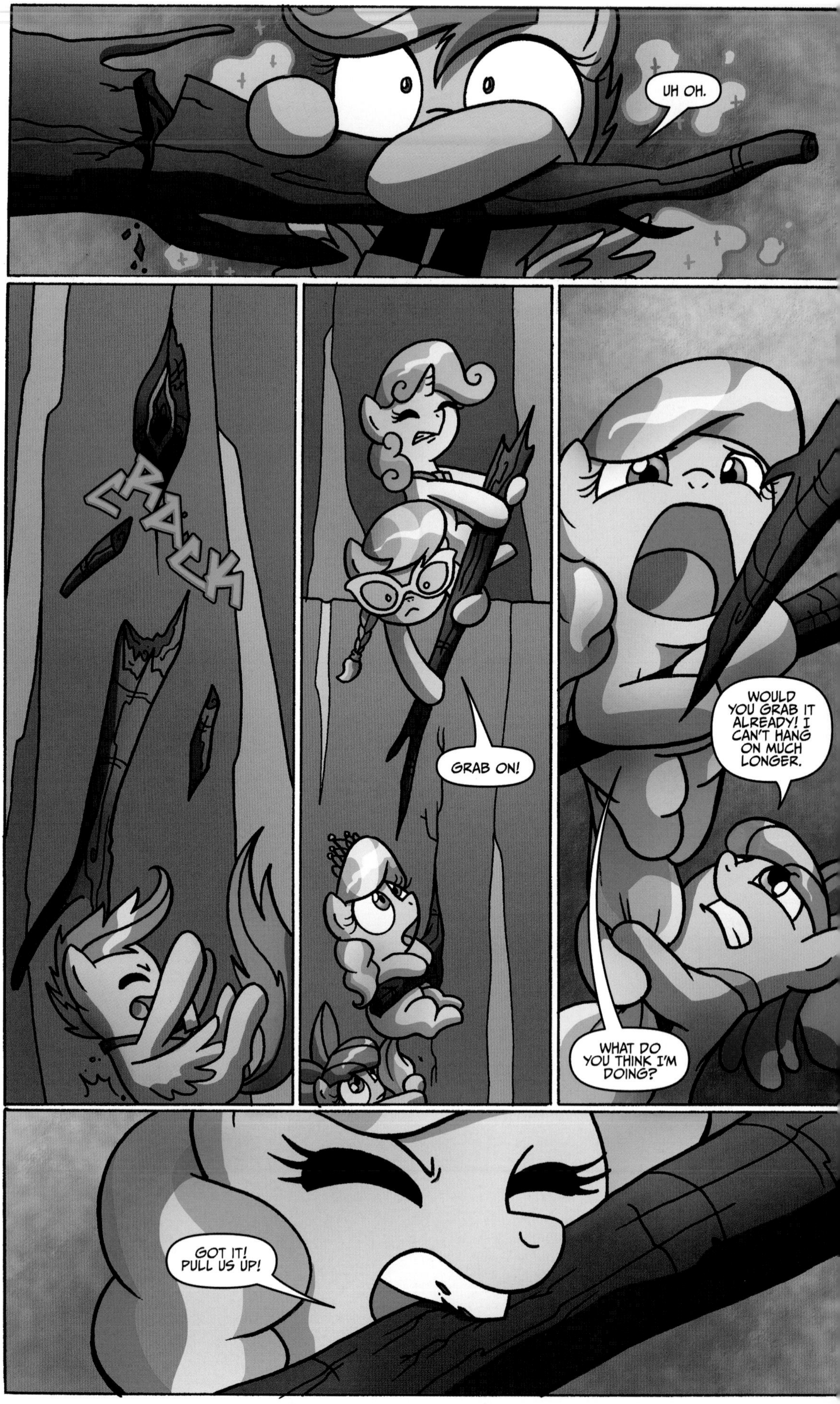
UH OH.
CRACK
GRAB ON!
WOULD YOU GRAB IT ALREADY! I CAN'T HANG ON MUCH LONGER.
WHAT DO YOU THINK I'M DOING?
GOT IT! PULL US UP!

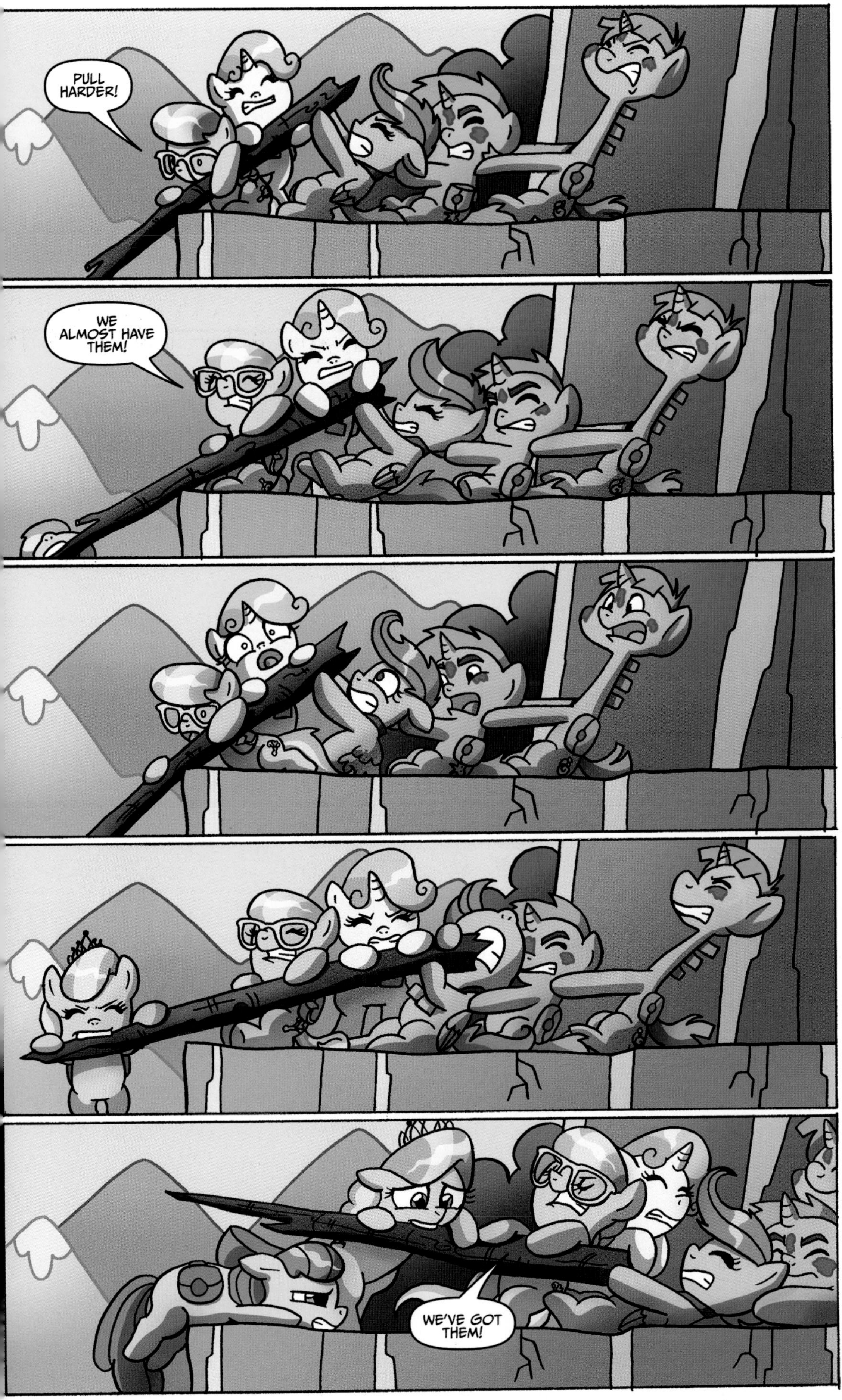
PULL HARDER!
WE ALMOST HAVE THEM!
WE'VE GOT THEM!

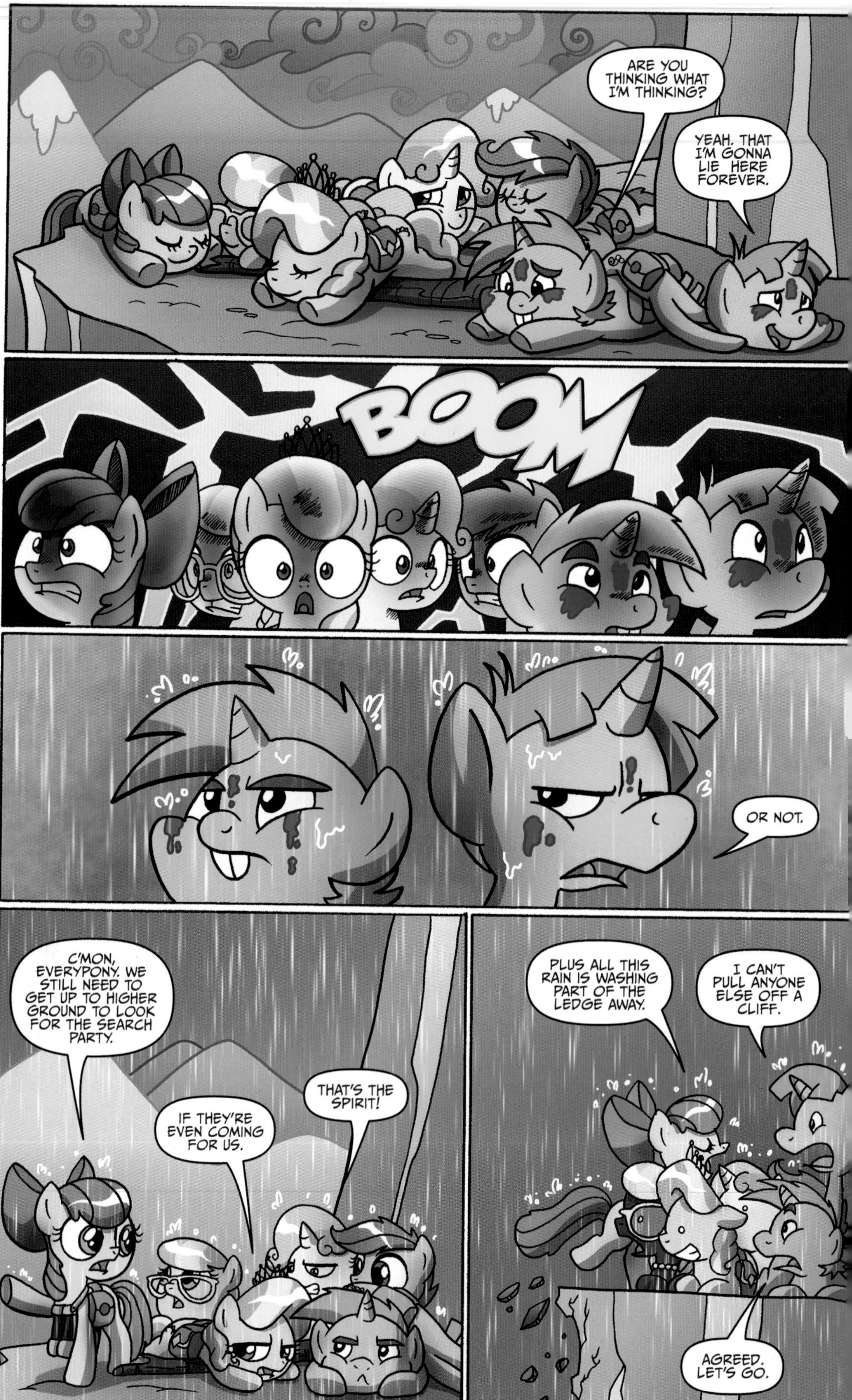
ARE YOU THINKING WHAT I'M THINKING?
YEAH. THAT I'M GONNA LIE HERE FOREVER.
BOOM
OR NOT.
C'MON, EVERYPONY. WE STILL NEED TO GET UP TO HIGHER GROUND TO LOOK FOR THE SEARCH PARTY.
IF THEY'RE EVEN COMING FOR US.
THAT'S THE SPIRIT!
PLUS ALL THIS RAIN IS WASHING PART OF THE LEDGE AWAY.
I CAN'T PULL ANYONE ELSE OFF A CLIFF.
AGREED. LET'S GO.

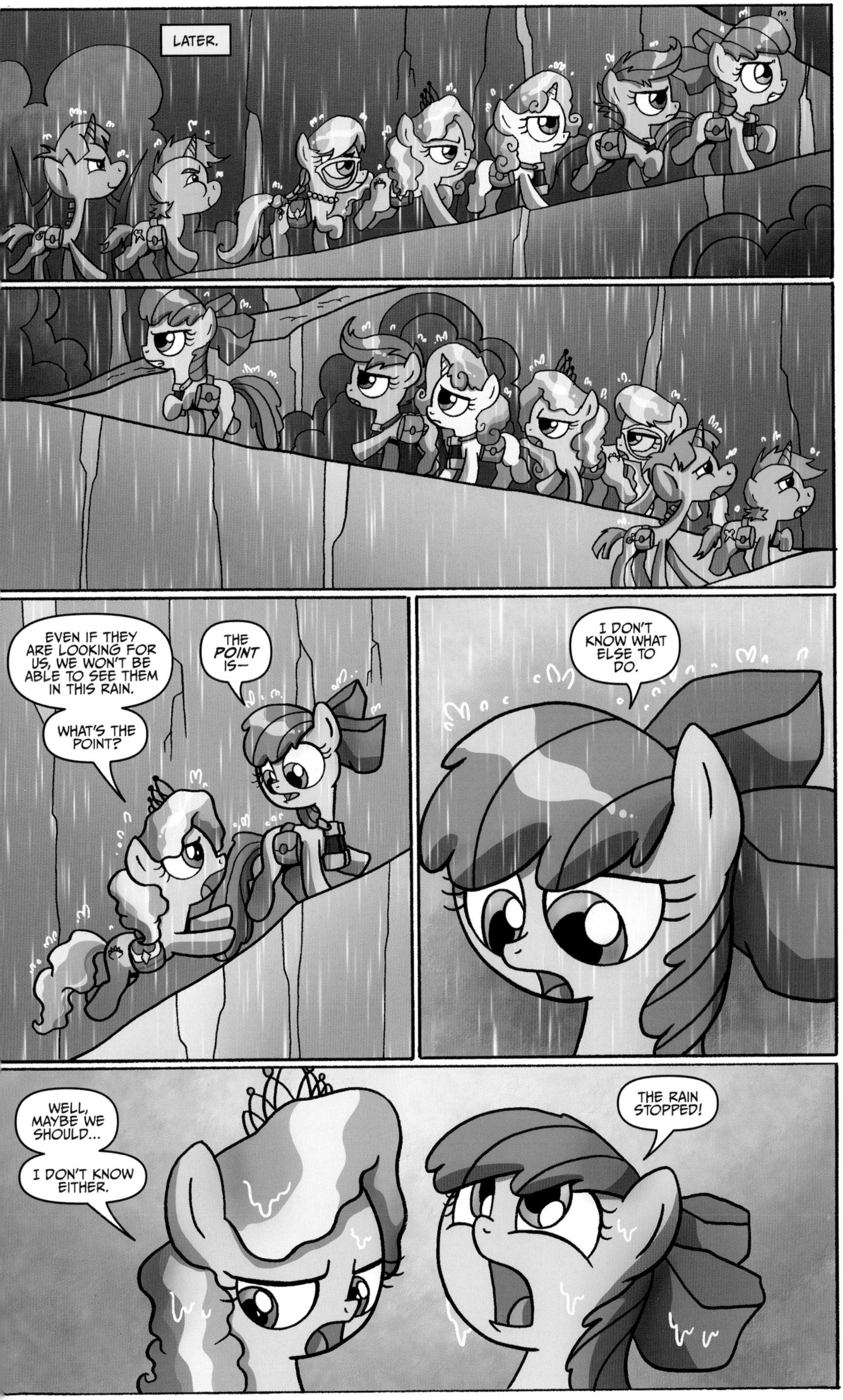
LATER.
EVEN IF THEY ARE LOOKING FOR US, WE WON'T BE ABLE TO SEE THEM IN THIS RAIN.
WHAT'S THE POINT?
THE *POINT* IS—
I DON'T KNOW WHAT ELSE TO DO.
WELL, MAYBE WE SHOULD...
I DON'T KNOW EITHER.
THE RAIN STOPPED!

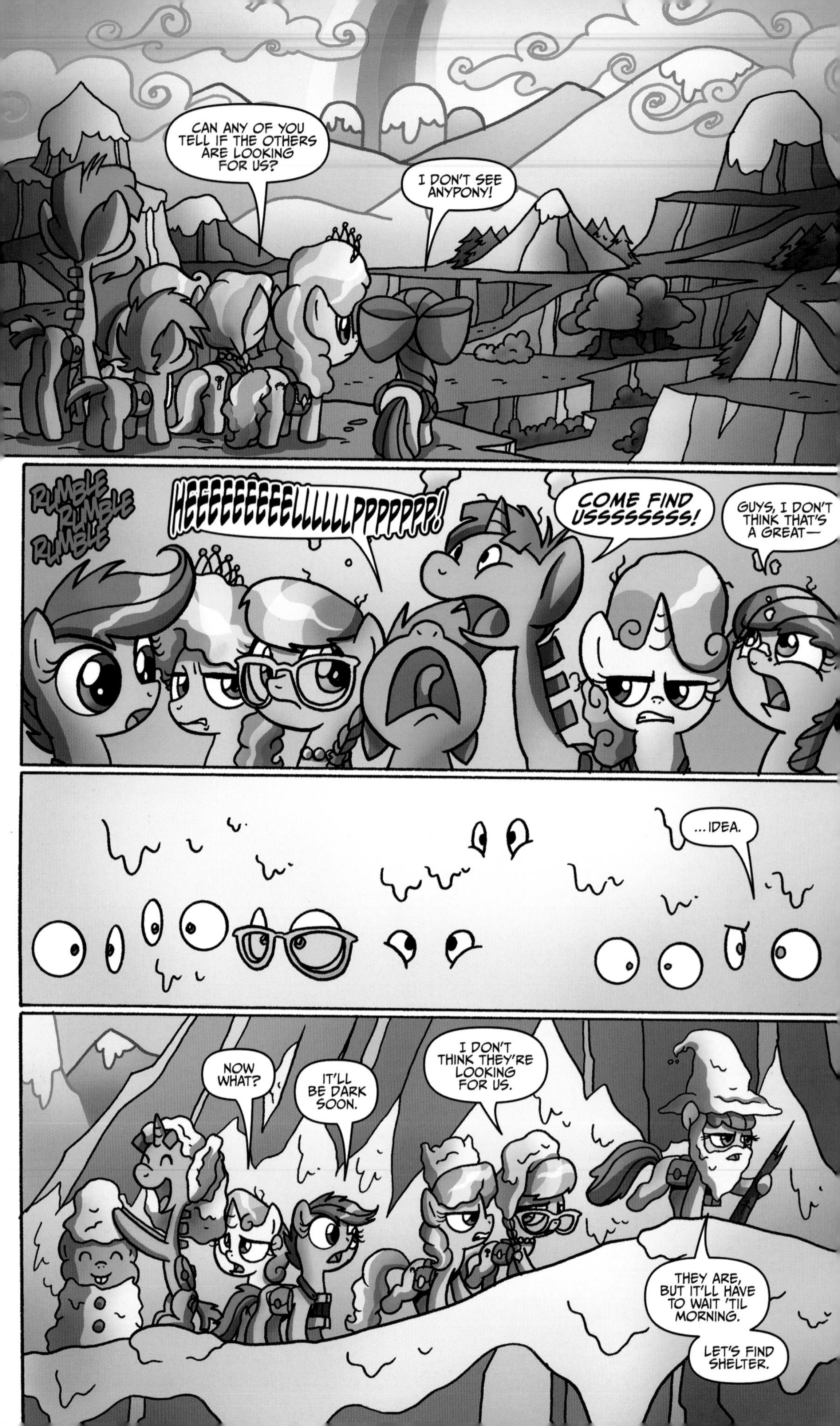
CAN ANY OF YOU TELL IF THE OTHERS ARE LOOKING FOR US?
I DON'T SEE ANYPONY!
RUMBLE RUMBLE RUMBLE
HEEEEEEEEEELLLLLLPPPPPPP!
COME FIND USSSSSSSS!
GUYS, I DON'T THINK THAT'S A GREAT—
...IDEA.
NOW WHAT?
IT'LL BE DARK SOON.
I DON'T THINK THEY'RE LOOKING FOR US.
THEY ARE, BUT IT'LL HAVE TO WAIT 'TIL MORNING.
LET'S FIND SHELTER.

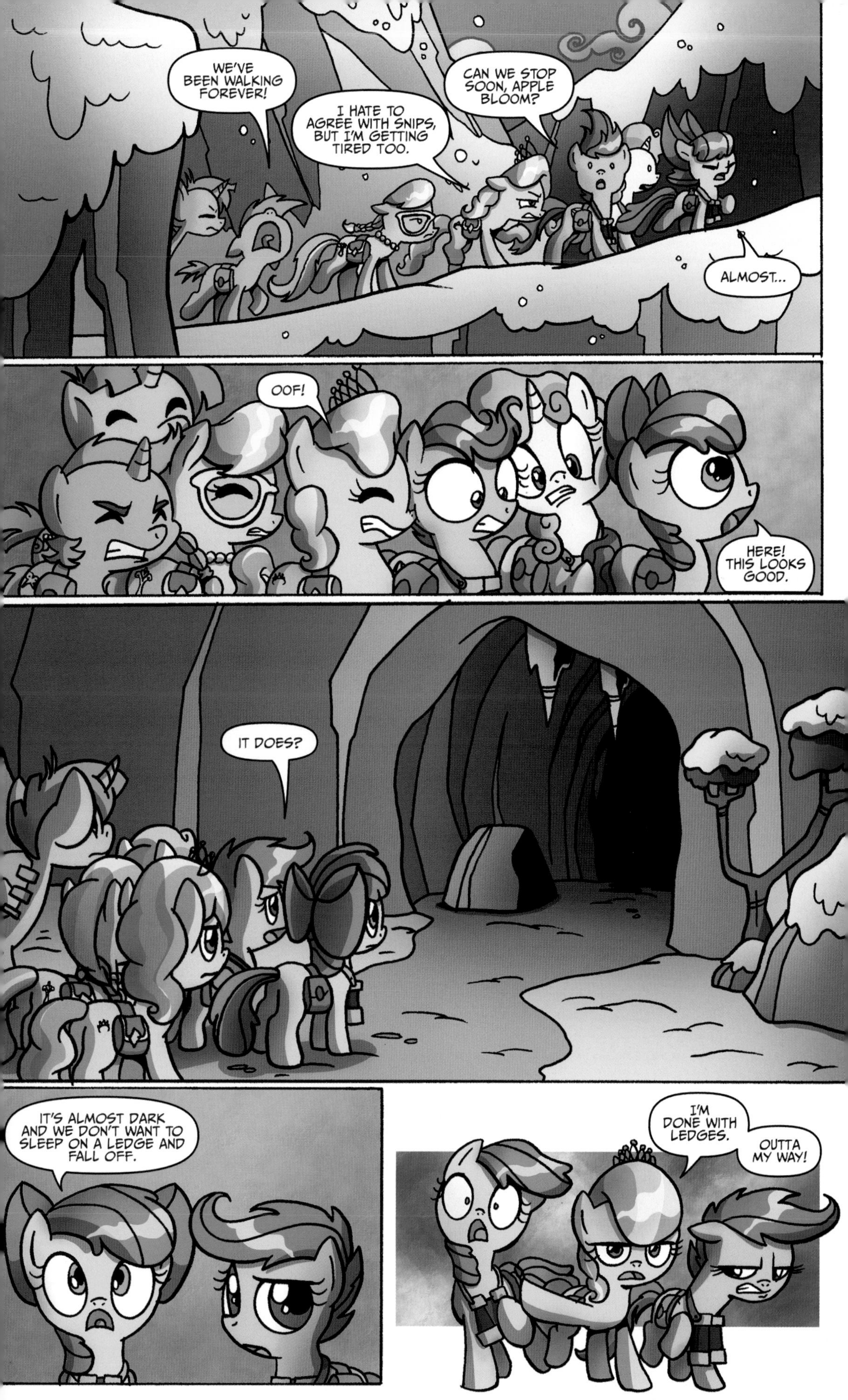
WE'VE BEEN WALKING FOREVER!
I HATE TO AGREE WITH SNIPS, BUT I'M GETTING TIRED TOO.
CAN WE STOP SOON, APPLE BLOOM?
ALMOST...
OOF!
HERE! THIS LOOKS GOOD.
IT DOES?
IT'S ALMOST DARK AND WE DON'T WANT TO SLEEP ON A LEDGE AND FALL OFF.
I'M DONE WITH LEDGES.
OUTTA MY WAY!

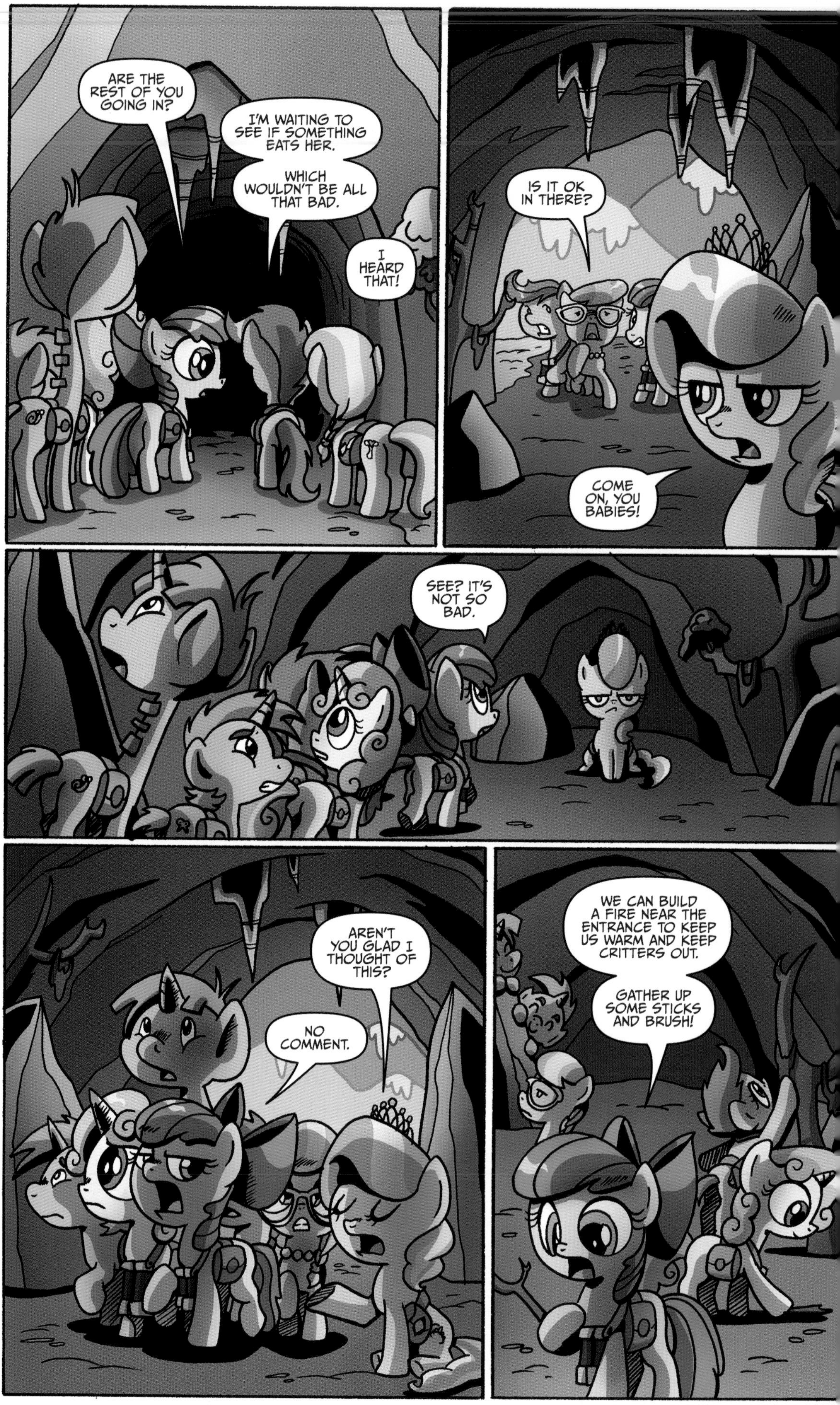
ARE THE REST OF YOU GOING IN?
I'M WAITING TO SEE IF SOMETHING EATS HER.
WHICH WOULDN'T BE ALL THAT BAD.
I HEARD THAT!
IS IT OK IN THERE?
COME ON, YOU BABIES!
SEE? IT'S NOT SO BAD.
AREN'T YOU GLAD I THOUGHT OF THIS?
NO COMMENT.
WE CAN BUILD A FIRE NEAR THE ENTRANCE TO KEEP US WARM AND KEEP CRITTERS OUT.
GATHER UP SOME STICKS AND BRUSH!

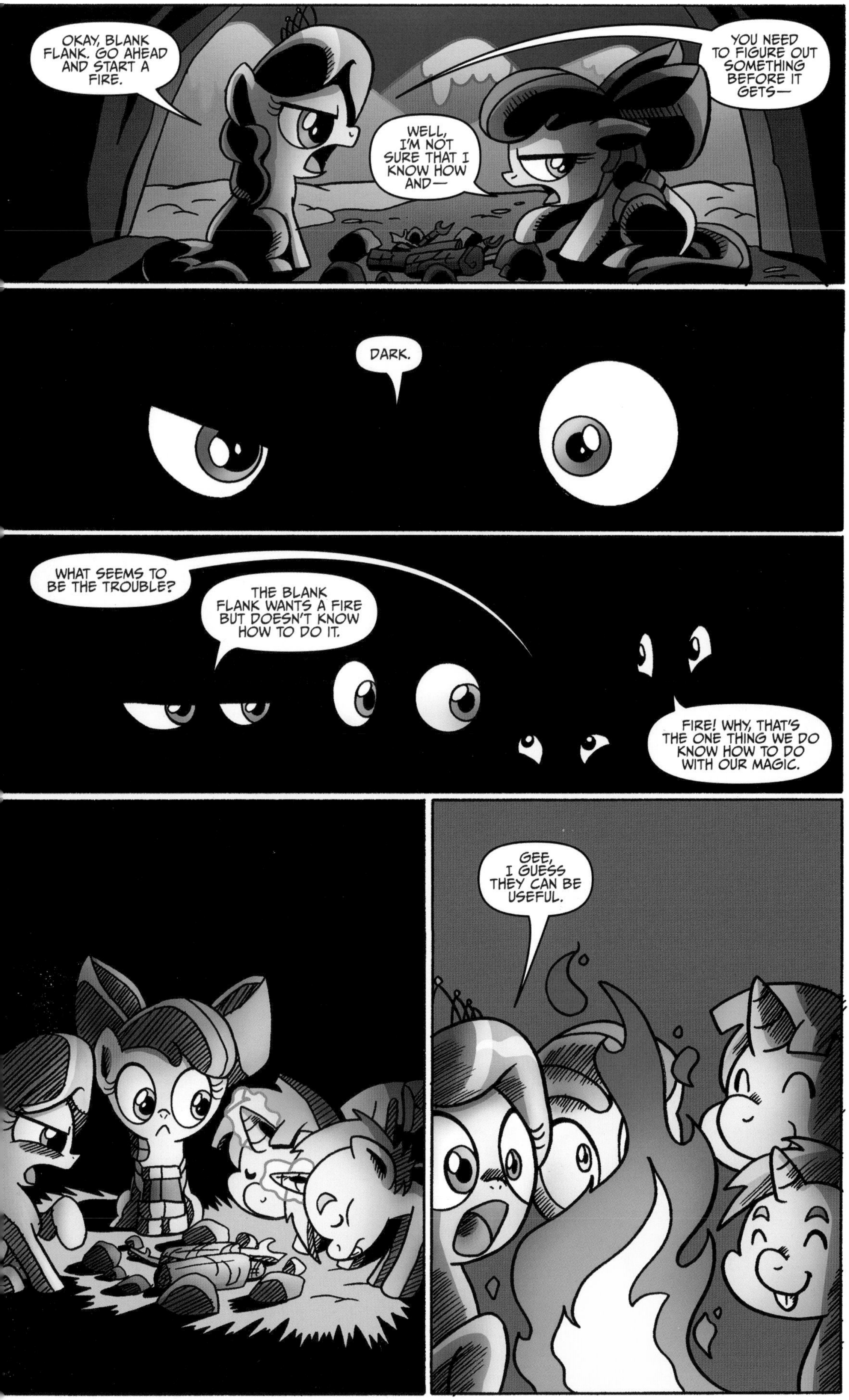
OKAY, BLANK FLANK. GO AHEAD AND START A FIRE.
WELL, I'M NOT SURE THAT I KNOW HOW AND—
YOU NEED TO FIGURE OUT SOMETHING BEFORE IT GETS—
DARK.
WHAT SEEMS TO BE THE TROUBLE?
THE BLANK FLANK WANTS A FIRE BUT DOESN'T KNOW HOW TO DO IT.
FIRE! WHY, THAT'S THE ONE THING WE DO KNOW HOW TO DO WITH OUR MAGIC.
GEE, I GUESS THEY CAN BE USEFUL.

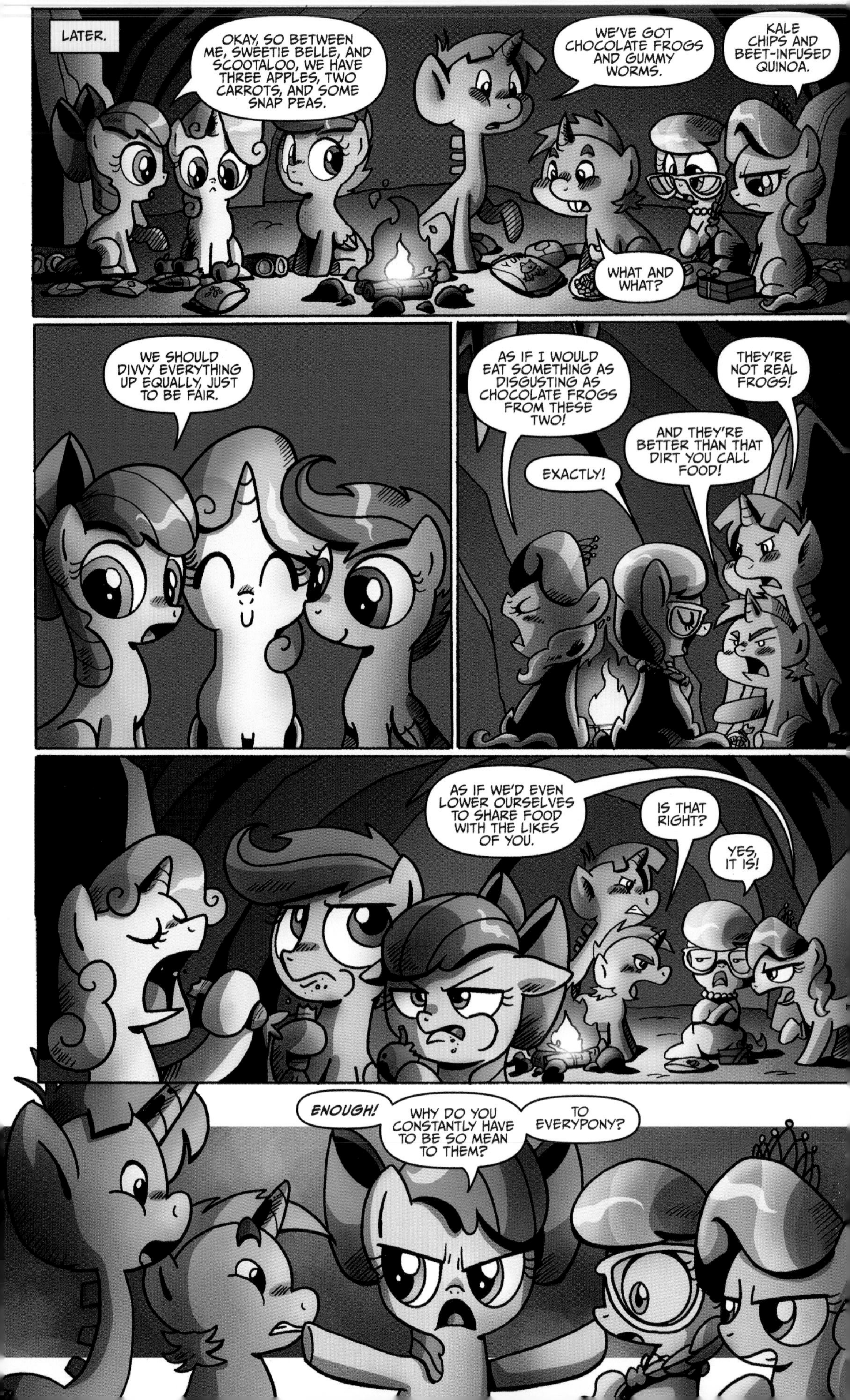
LATER.
OKAY, SO BETWEEN ME, SWEETIE BELLE, AND SCOOTALOO, WE HAVE THREE APPLES, TWO CARROTS, AND SOME SNAP PEAS.
WE'VE GOT CHOCOLATE FROGS AND GUMMY WORMS.
KALE CHIPS AND BEET-INFUSED QUINOA.
WHAT AND WHAT?
WE SHOULD DIVVY EVERYTHING UP EQUALLY, JUST TO BE FAIR.
AS IF I WOULD EAT SOMETHING AS DISGUSTING AS CHOCOLATE FROGS FROM THESE TWO!
THEY'RE NOT REAL FROGS!
EXACTLY!
AND THEY'RE BETTER THAN THAT DIRT YOU CALL FOOD!
AS IF WE'D EVEN LOWER OURSELVES TO SHARE FOOD WITH THE LIKES OF YOU.
IS THAT RIGHT?
YES, IT IS!
ENOUGH!
WHY DO YOU CONSTANTLY HAVE TO BE SO MEAN TO THEM?
TO EVERYPONY?

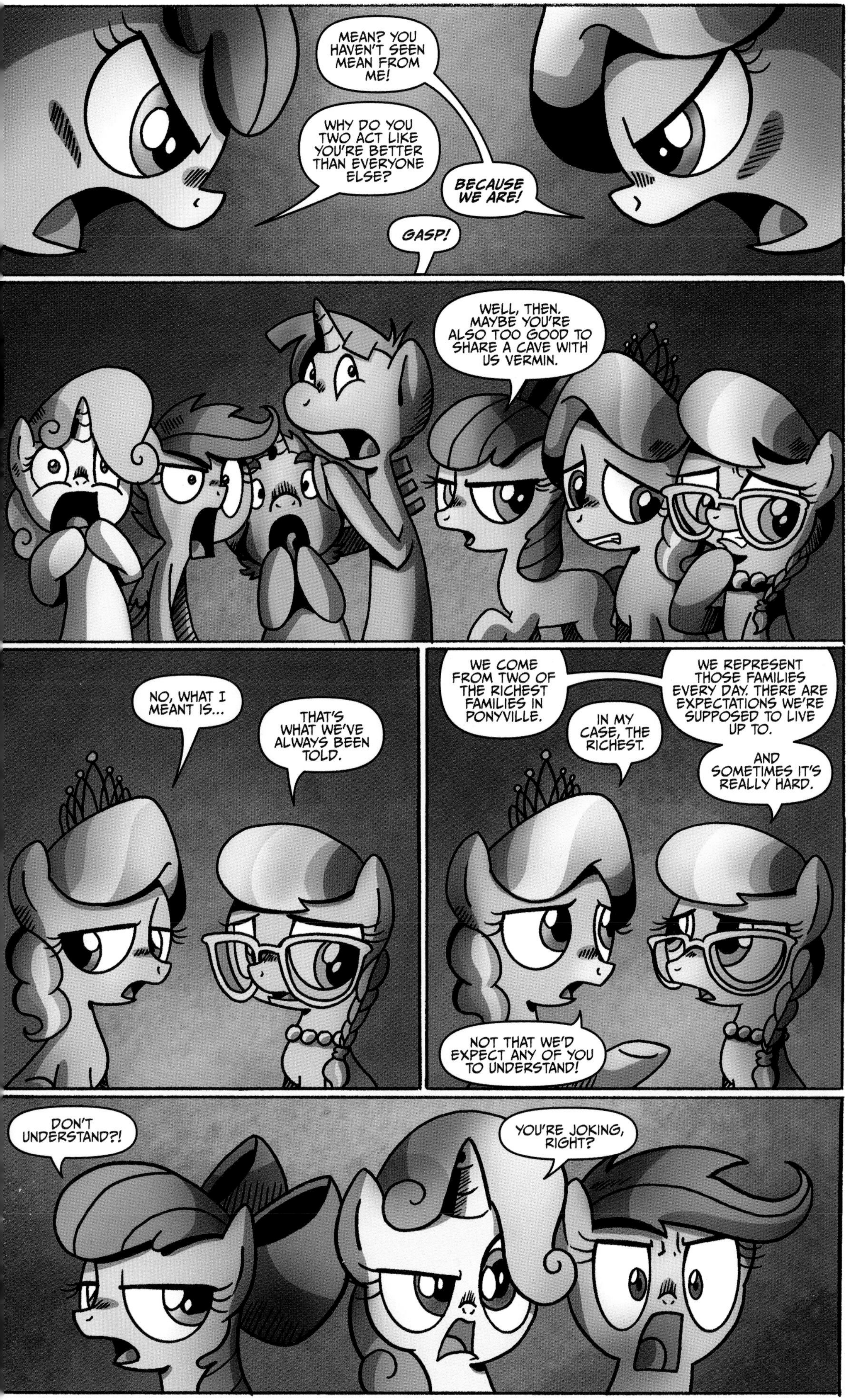
MEAN? YOU HAVEN'T SEEN MEAN FROM ME!
WHY DO YOU TWO ACT LIKE YOU'RE BETTER THAN EVERYONE ELSE?
BECAUSE WE ARE!
GASP!
WELL, THEN. MAYBE YOU'RE ALSO TOO GOOD TO SHARE A CAVE WITH US VERMIN.
NO, WHAT I MEANT IS...
THAT'S WHAT WE'VE ALWAYS BEEN TOLD.
WE COME FROM TWO OF THE RICHEST FAMILIES IN PONYVILLE.
IN MY CASE, THE RICHEST.
WE REPRESENT THOSE FAMILIES EVERY DAY. THERE ARE EXPECTATIONS WE'RE SUPPOSED TO LIVE UP TO.
AND SOMETIMES IT'S REALLY HARD.
NOT THAT WE'D EXPECT ANY OF YOU TO UNDERSTAND!
DON'T UNDERSTAND?!
YOU'RE JOKING, RIGHT?

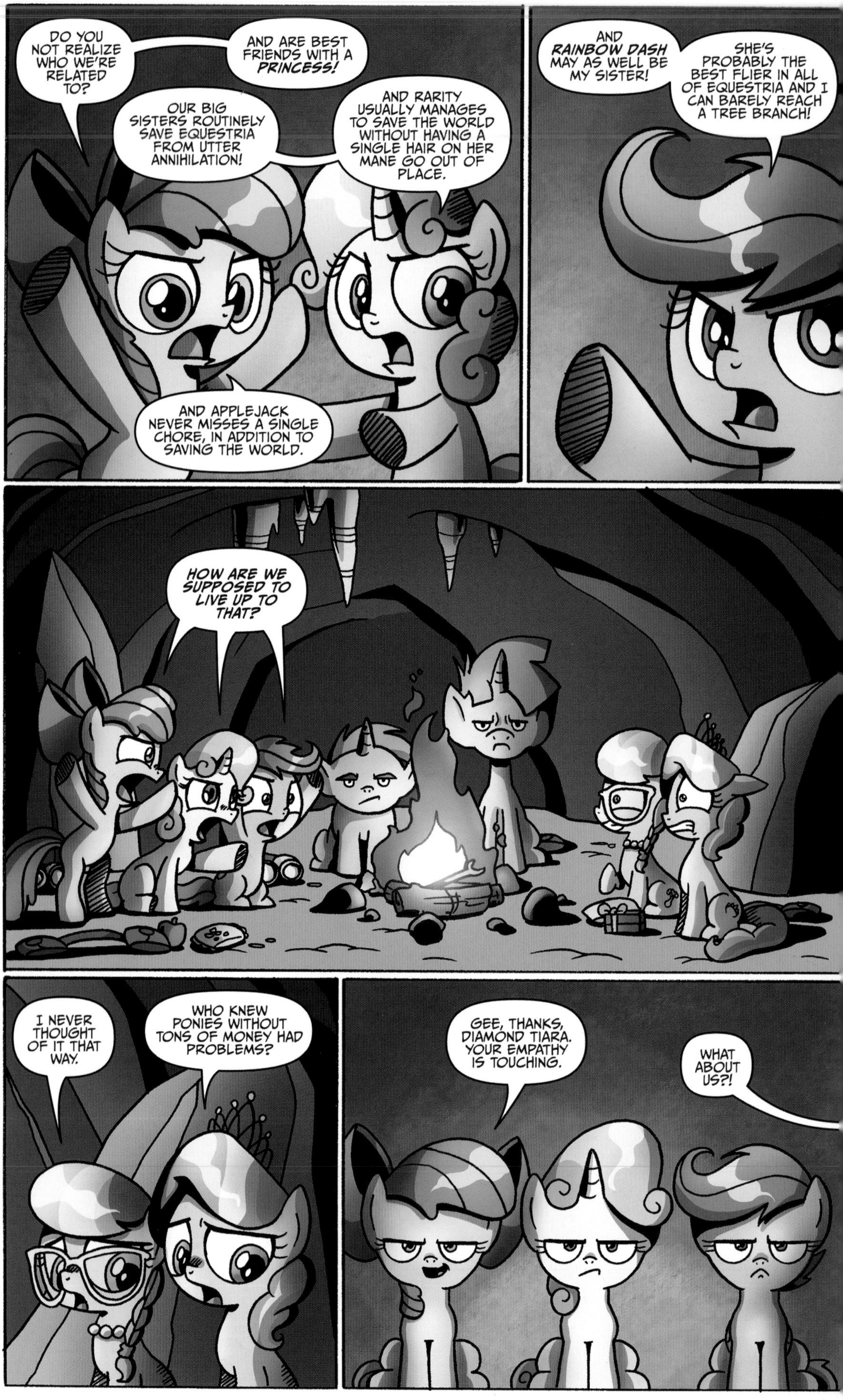
DO YOU NOT REALIZE WHO WE'RE RELATED TO?
AND ARE BEST FRIENDS WITH A *PRINCESS!*
OUR BIG SISTERS ROUTINELY SAVE EQUESTRIA FROM UTTER ANNIHILATION!
AND RARITY USUALLY MANAGES TO SAVE THE WORLD WITHOUT HAVING A SINGLE HAIR ON HER MANE GO OUT OF PLACE.
AND APPLEJACK NEVER MISSES A SINGLE CHORE, IN ADDITION TO SAVING THE WORLD.
AND *RAINBOW DASH* MAY AS WELL BE MY SISTER!
SHE'S PROBABLY THE BEST FLIER IN ALL OF EQUESTRIA AND I CAN BARELY REACH A TREE BRANCH!
HOW ARE WE SUPPOSED TO LIVE UP TO THAT?
I NEVER THOUGHT OF IT THAT WAY.
WHO KNEW PONIES WITHOUT TONS OF MONEY HAD PROBLEMS?
GEE, THANKS, DIAMOND TIARA. YOUR EMPATHY IS TOUCHING.
WHAT ABOUT US?!

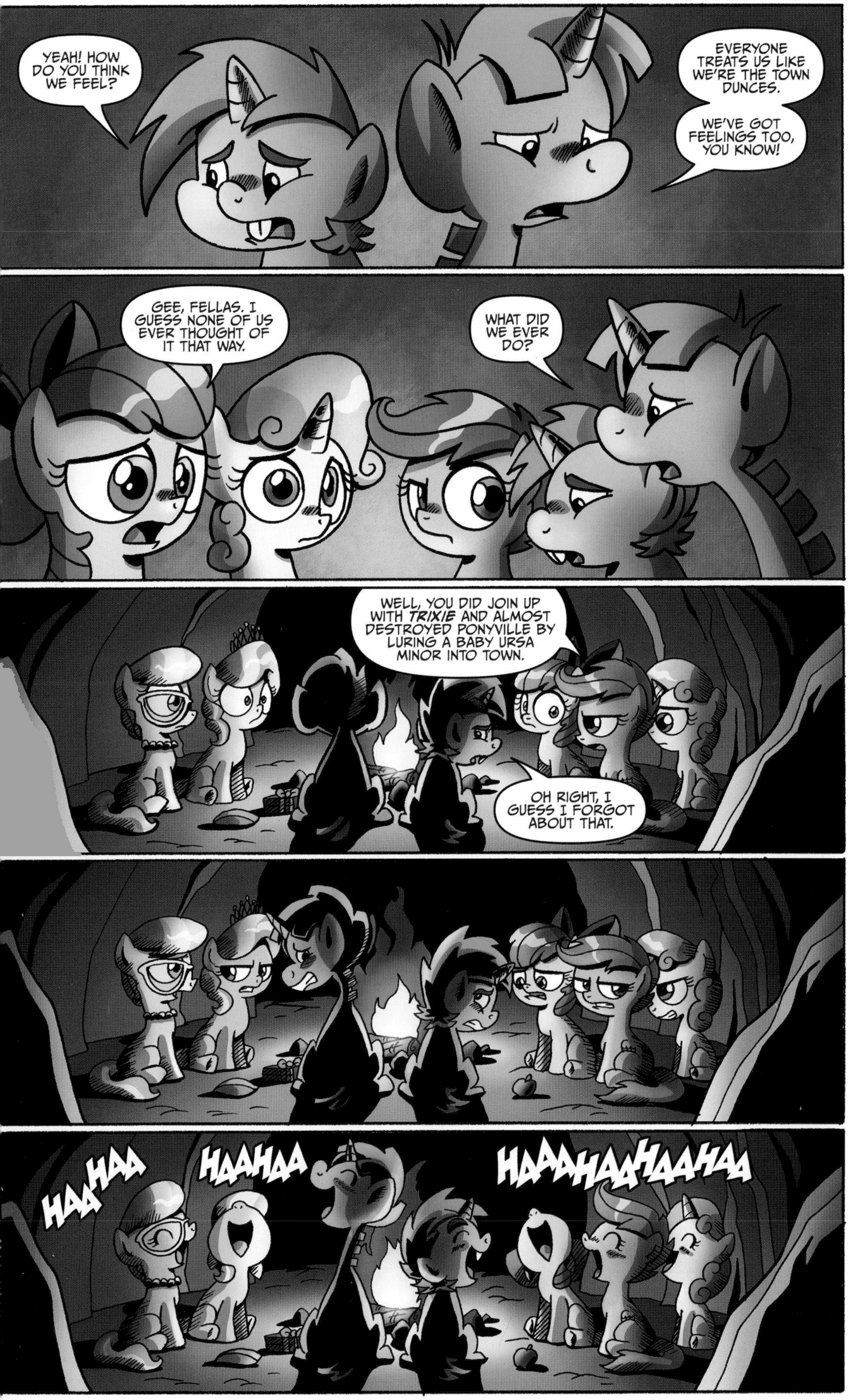

YEAH! HOW DO YOU THINK WE FEEL?
EVERYONE TREATS US LIKE WE'RE THE TOWN DUNCES.
WE'VE GOT FEELINGS TOO, YOU KNOW!
GEE, FELLAS. I GUESS NONE OF US EVER THOUGHT OF IT THAT WAY.
WHAT DID WE EVER DO?
WELL, YOU DID JOIN UP WITH *TRIXIE* AND ALMOST DESTROYED PONYVILLE BY LURING A BABY URSA MINOR INTO TOWN.
OH RIGHT, I GUESS I FORGOT ABOUT THAT.
HAAHAA
HAAHAA
HAAHAAHAAHAA

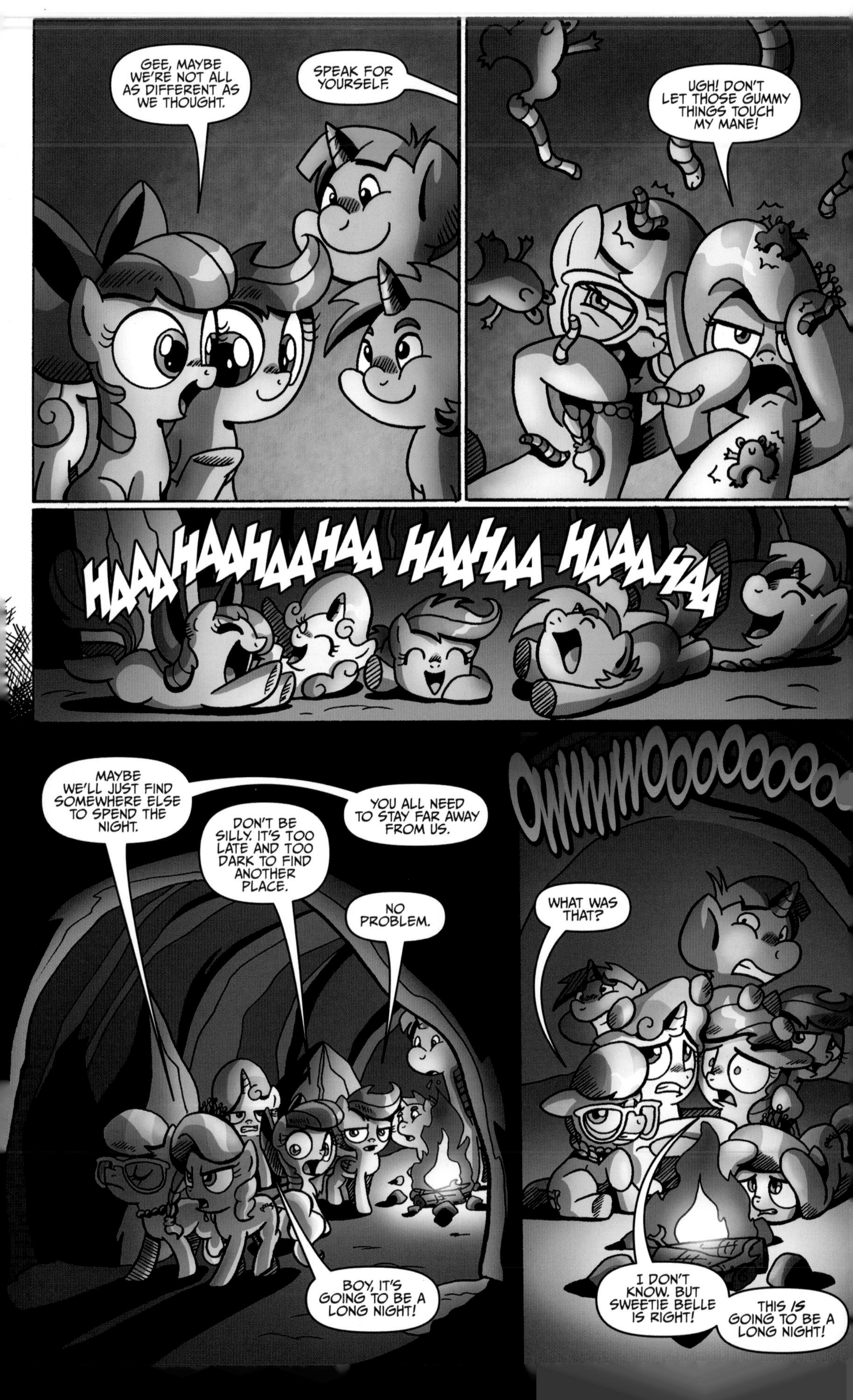
GEE, MAYBE WE'RE NOT ALL AS DIFFERENT AS WE THOUGHT.
SPEAK FOR YOURSELF.
UGH! DON'T LET THOSE GUMMY THINGS TOUCH MY MANE!
HAAAHAAHAAHAA HAAHAA HAAAHAA
MAYBE WE'LL JUST FIND SOMEWHERE ELSE TO SPEND THE NIGHT.
YOU ALL NEED TO STAY FAR AWAY FROM US.
DON'T BE SILLY. IT'S TOO LATE AND TOO DARK TO FIND ANOTHER PLACE.
NO PROBLEM.
BOY, IT'S GOING TO BE A LONG NIGHT!
OWWWWOOOOOOOOO
WHAT WAS THAT?
I DON'T KNOW. BUT SWEETIE BELLE IS RIGHT!
THIS *IS* GOING TO BE A LONG NIGHT!

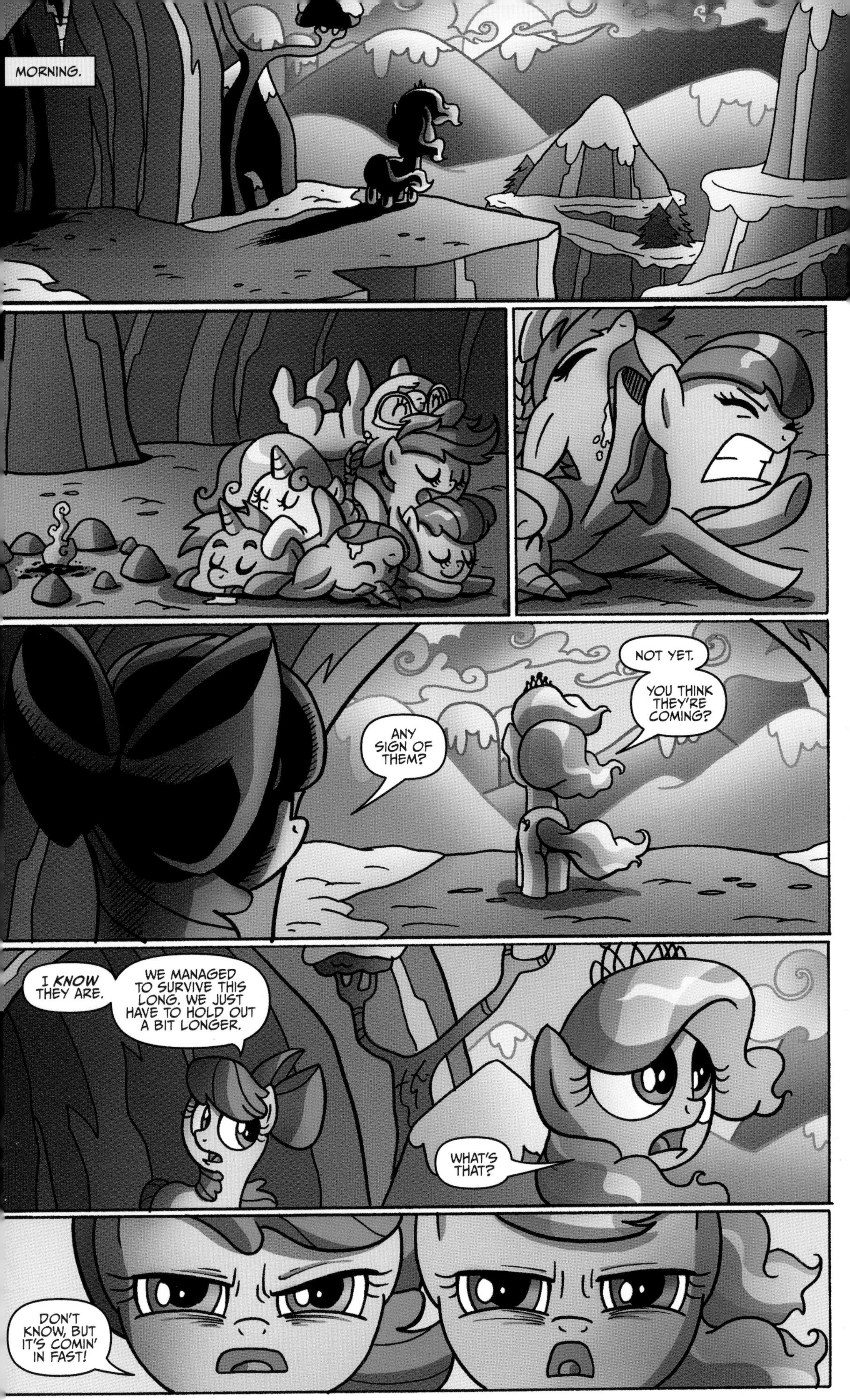
MORNING.
ANY SIGN OF THEM?
NOT YET.
YOU THINK THEY'RE COMING?
I KNOW THEY ARE.
WE MANAGED TO SURVIVE THIS LONG. WE JUST HAVE TO HOLD OUT A BIT LONGER.
WHAT'S THAT?
DON'T KNOW, BUT IT'S COMIN' IN FAST!

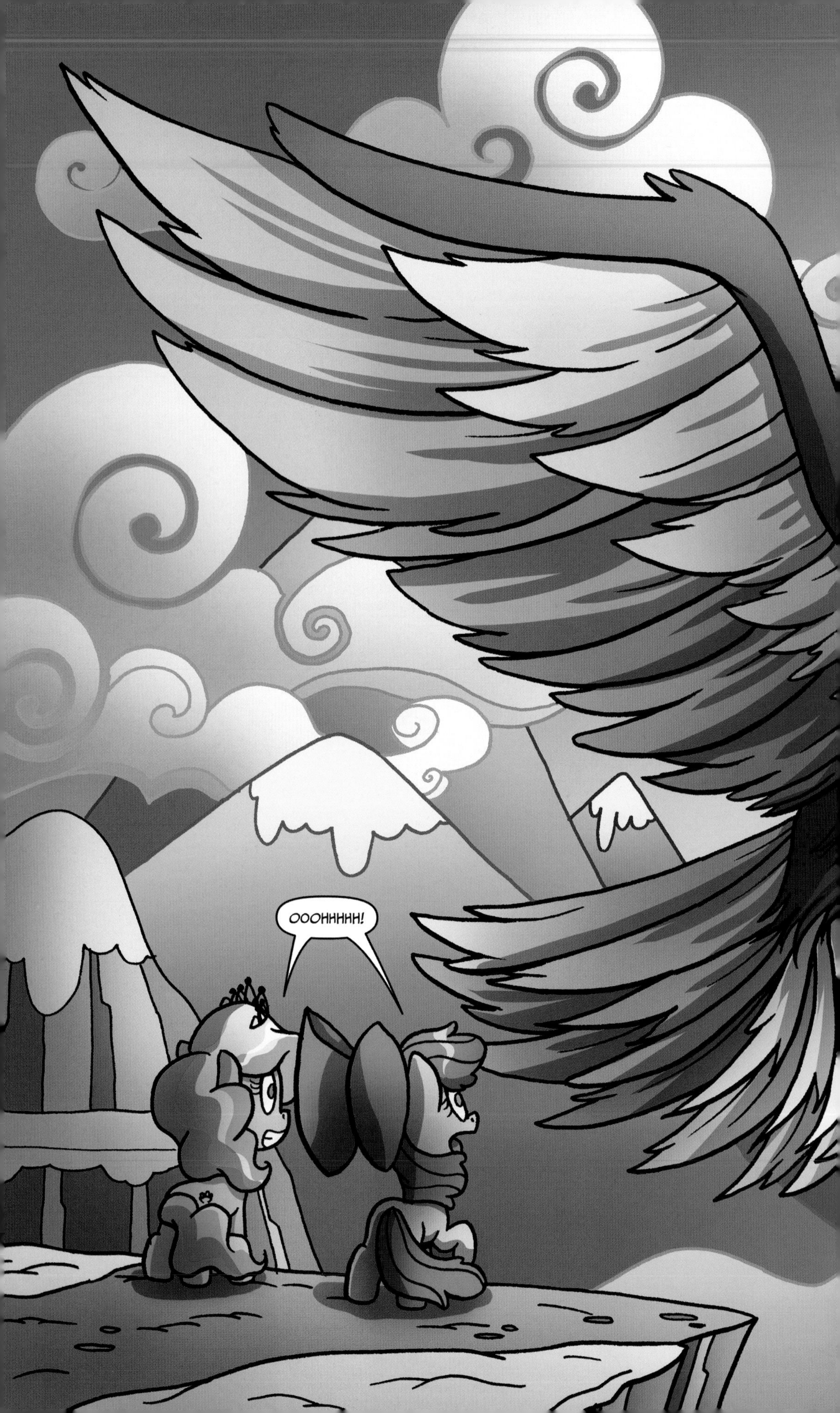
OOOHHHHH!

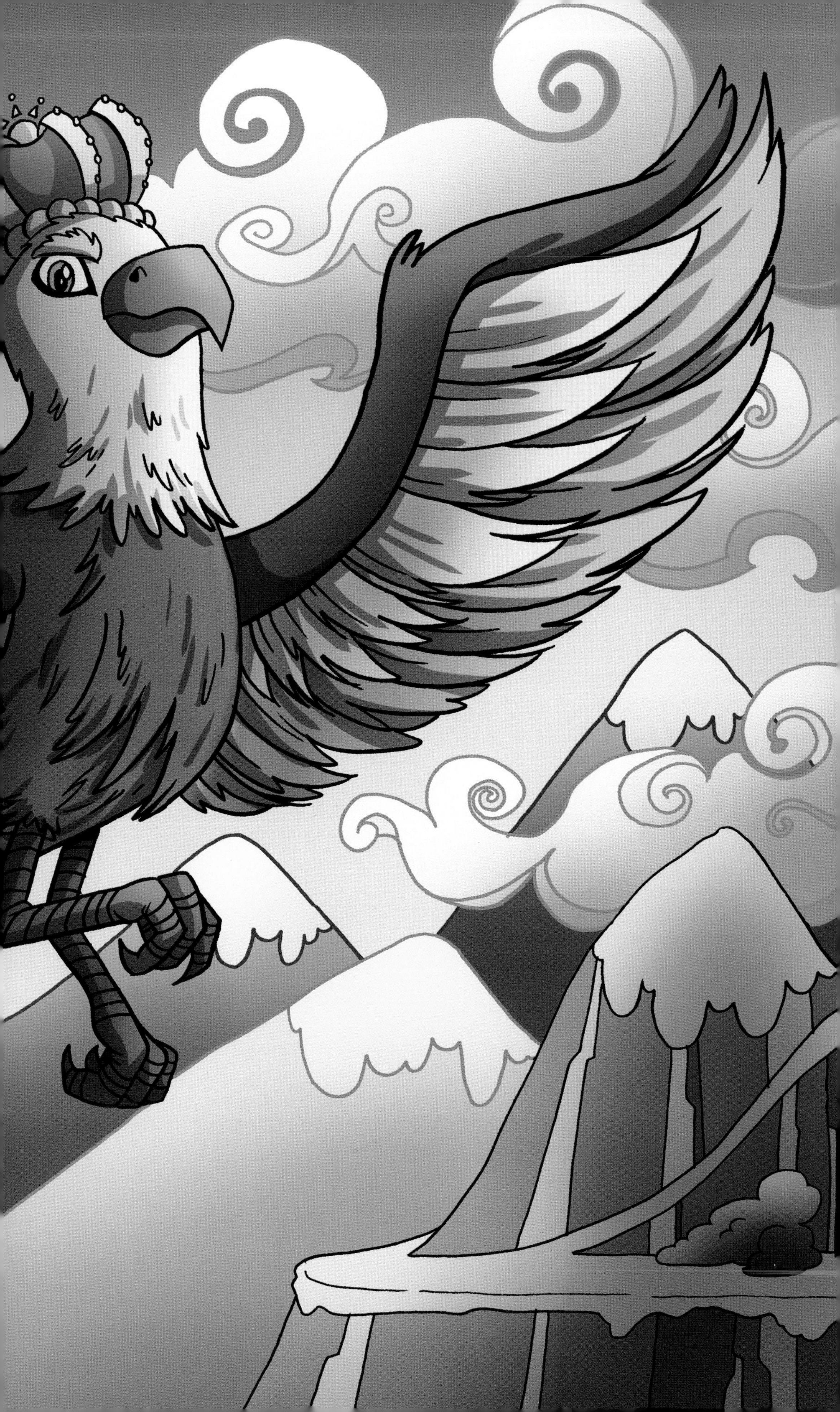

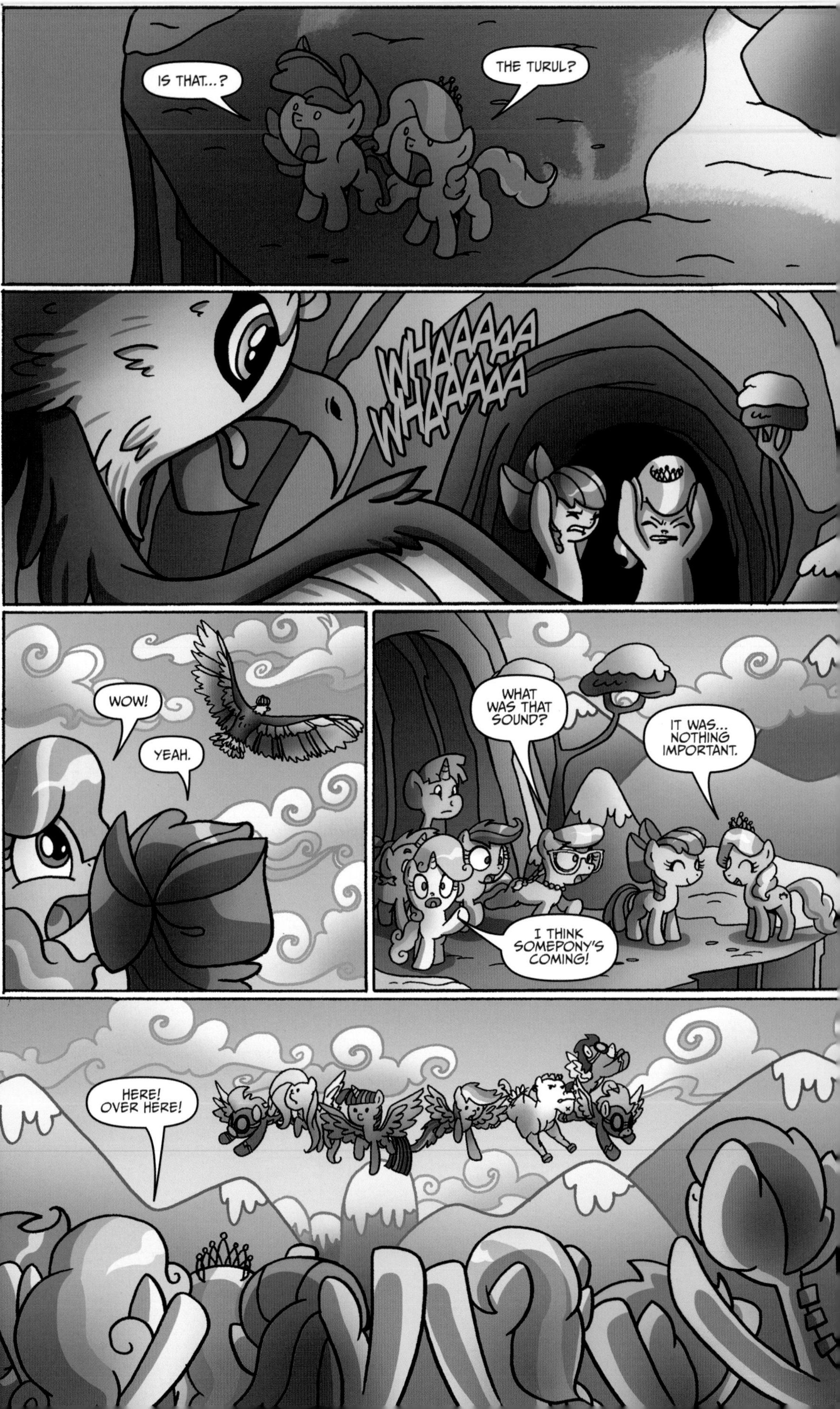
IS THAT...?
THE TURUL?
WHAAAAA WHAAAAA WHAAAAA
WOW!
YEAH.
WHAT WAS THAT SOUND?
IT WAS... NOTHING IMPORTANT.
I THINK SOMEPONY'S COMING!
HERE! OVER HERE!

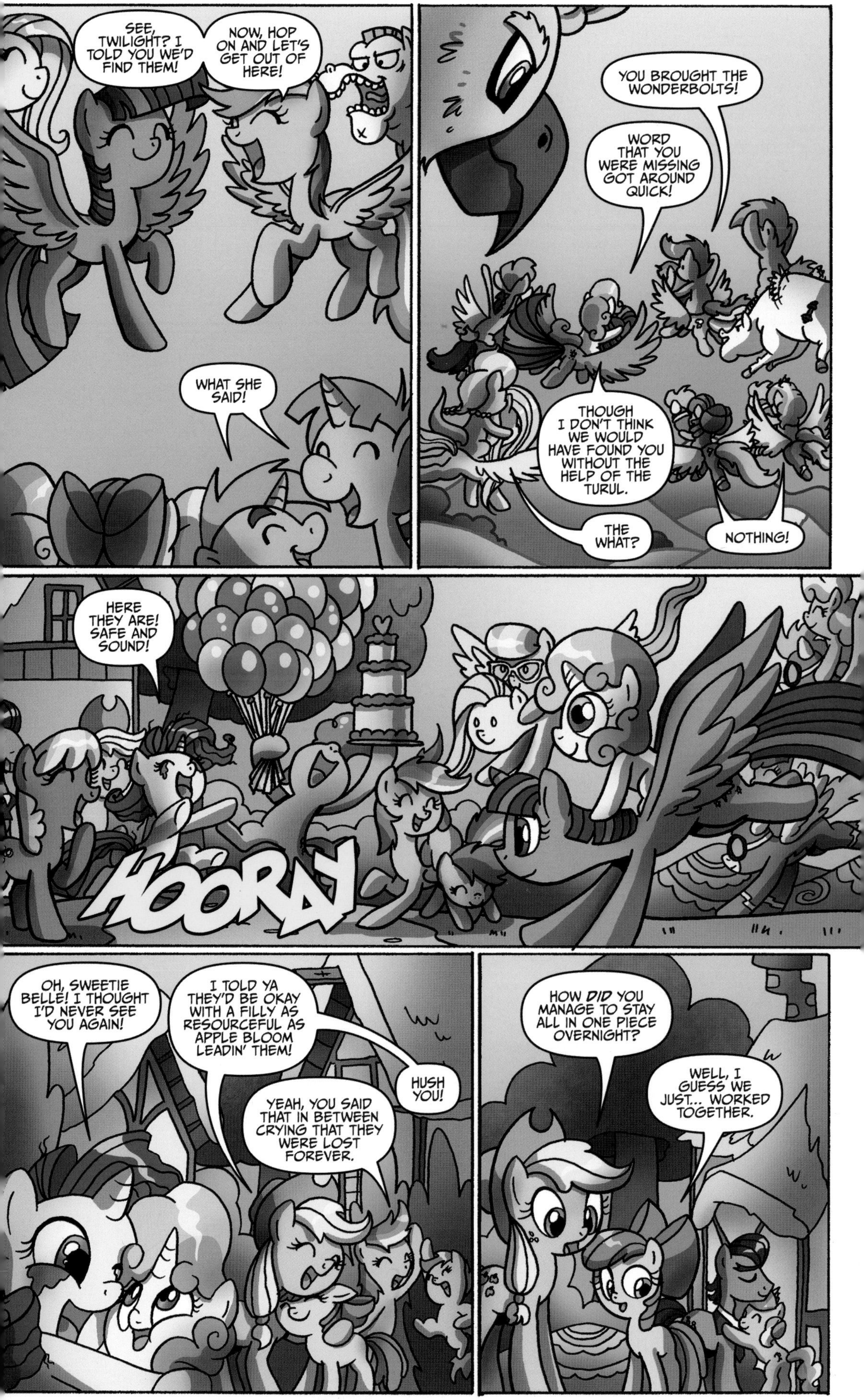
SEE, TWILIGHT? I TOLD YOU WE'D FIND THEM!
NOW, HOP ON AND LET'S GET OUT OF HERE!
WHAT SHE SAID!
YOU BROUGHT THE WONDERBOLTS!
WORD THAT YOU WERE MISSING GOT AROUND QUICK!
THOUGH I DON'T THINK WE WOULD HAVE FOUND YOU WITHOUT THE HELP OF THE TURUL.
THE WHAT?
NOTHING!
HERE THEY ARE! SAFE AND SOUND!
HOORAY
OH, SWEETIE BELLE! I THOUGHT I'D NEVER SEE YOU AGAIN!
I TOLD YA THEY'D BE OKAY WITH A FILLY AS RESOURCEFUL AS APPLE BLOOM LEADIN' THEM!
HUSH YOU!
YEAH, YOU SAID THAT IN BETWEEN CRYING THAT THEY WERE LOST FOREVER.
HOW *DID* YOU MANAGE TO STAY ALL IN ONE PIECE OVERNIGHT?
WELL, I GUESS WE JUST... WORKED TOGETHER.

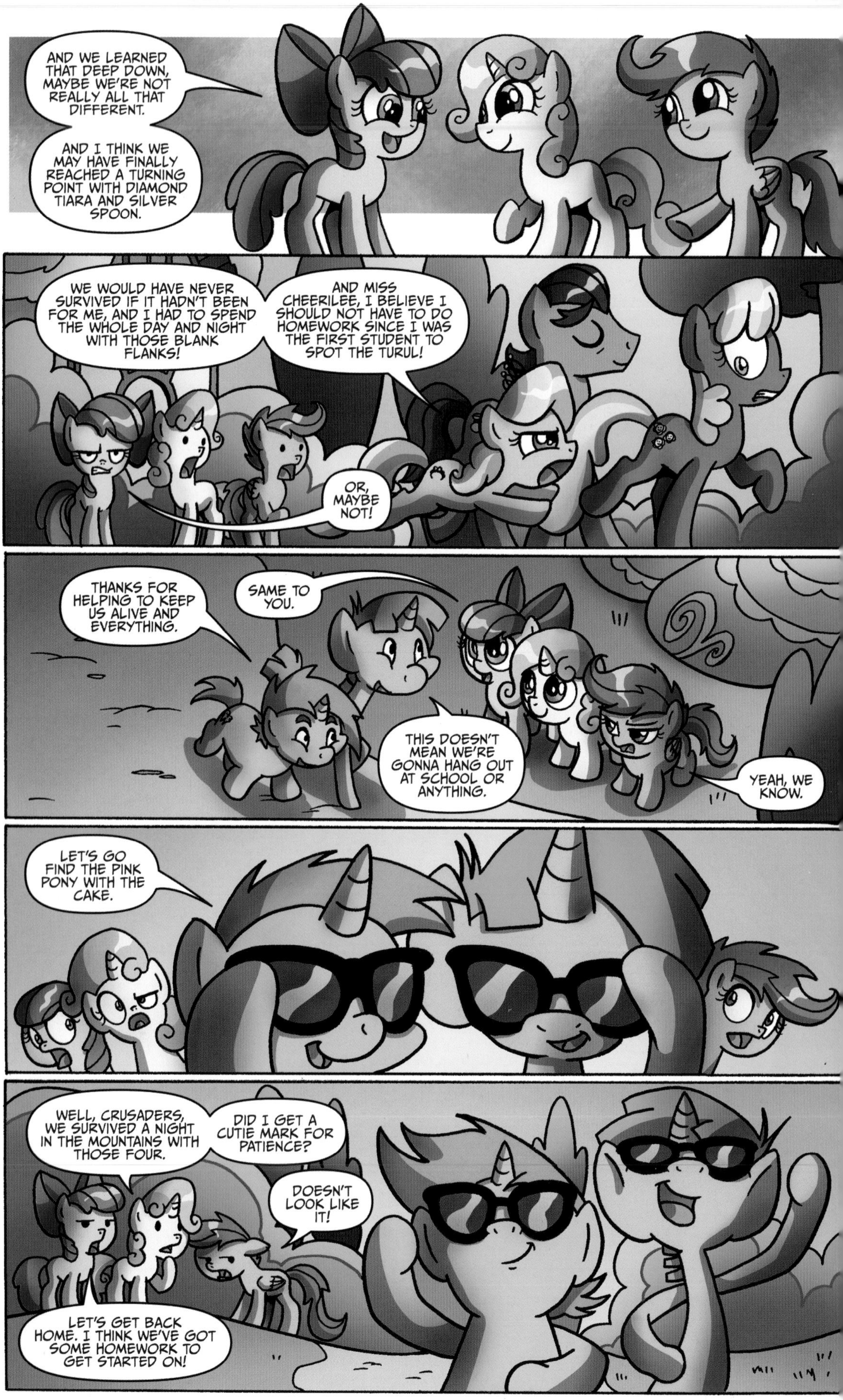
AND WE LEARNED THAT DEEP DOWN, MAYBE WE'RE NOT REALLY ALL THAT DIFFERENT.
AND I THINK WE MAY HAVE FINALLY REACHED A TURNING POINT WITH DIAMOND TIARA AND SILVER SPOON.
WE WOULD HAVE NEVER SURVIVED IF IT HADN'T BEEN FOR ME, AND I HAD TO SPEND THE WHOLE DAY AND NIGHT WITH THOSE BLANK FLANKS!
AND MISS CHEERILEE, I BELIEVE I SHOULD NOT HAVE TO DO HOMEWORK SINCE I WAS THE FIRST STUDENT TO SPOT THE TURUL!
OR, MAYBE NOT!
THANKS FOR HELPING TO KEEP US ALIVE AND EVERYTHING.
SAME TO YOU.
THIS DOESN'T MEAN WE'RE GONNA HANG OUT AT SCHOOL OR ANYTHING.
YEAH, WE KNOW.
LET'S GO FIND THE PINK PONY WITH THE CAKE.
WELL, CRUSADERS, WE SURVIVED A NIGHT IN THE MOUNTAINS WITH THOSE FOUR.
DID I GET A CUTIE MARK FOR PATIENCE?
DOESN'T LOOK LIKE IT!
LET'S GET BACK HOME. I THINK WE'VE GOT SOME HOMEWORK TO GET STARTED ON!

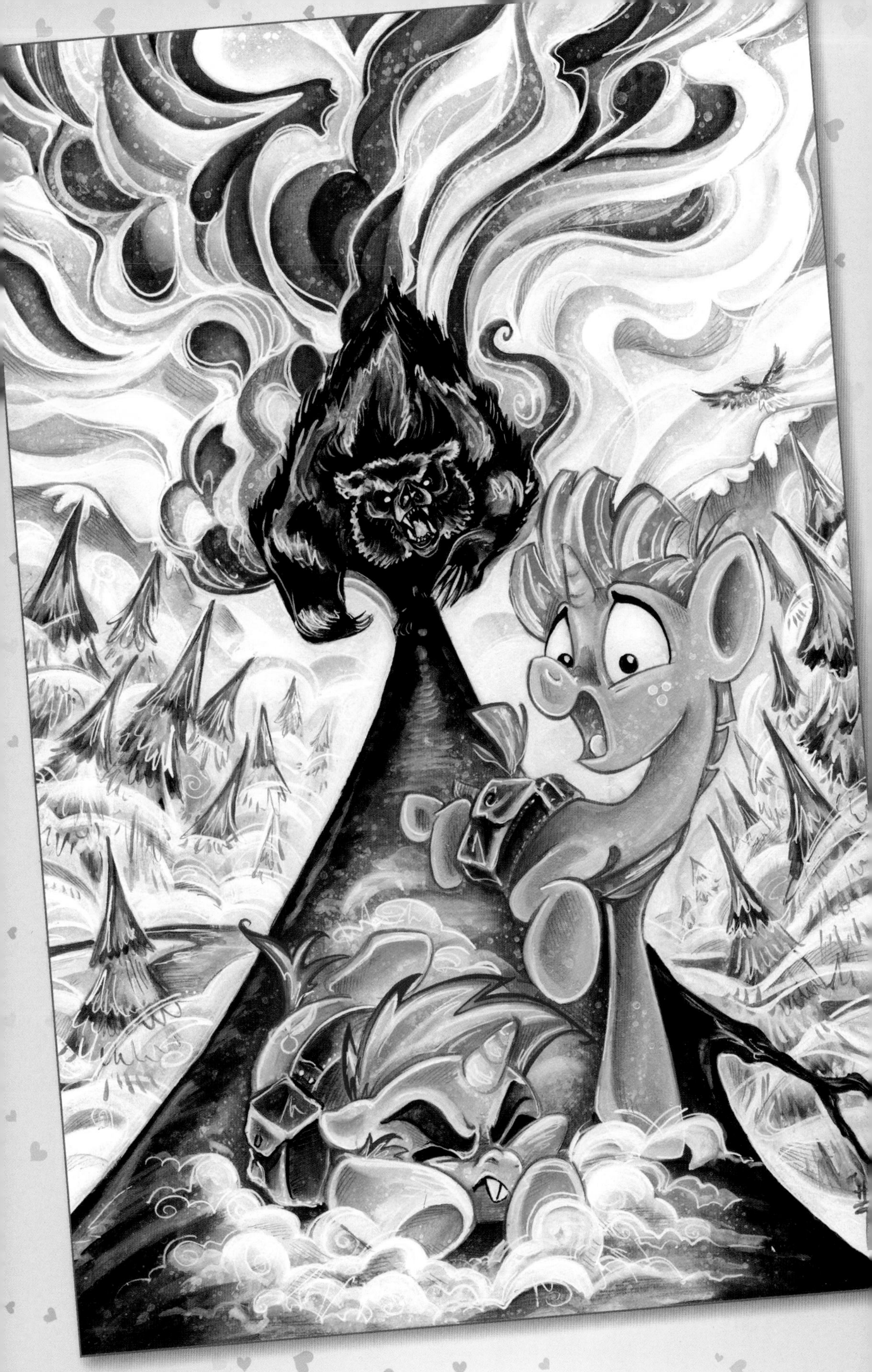

art by Sara Richard

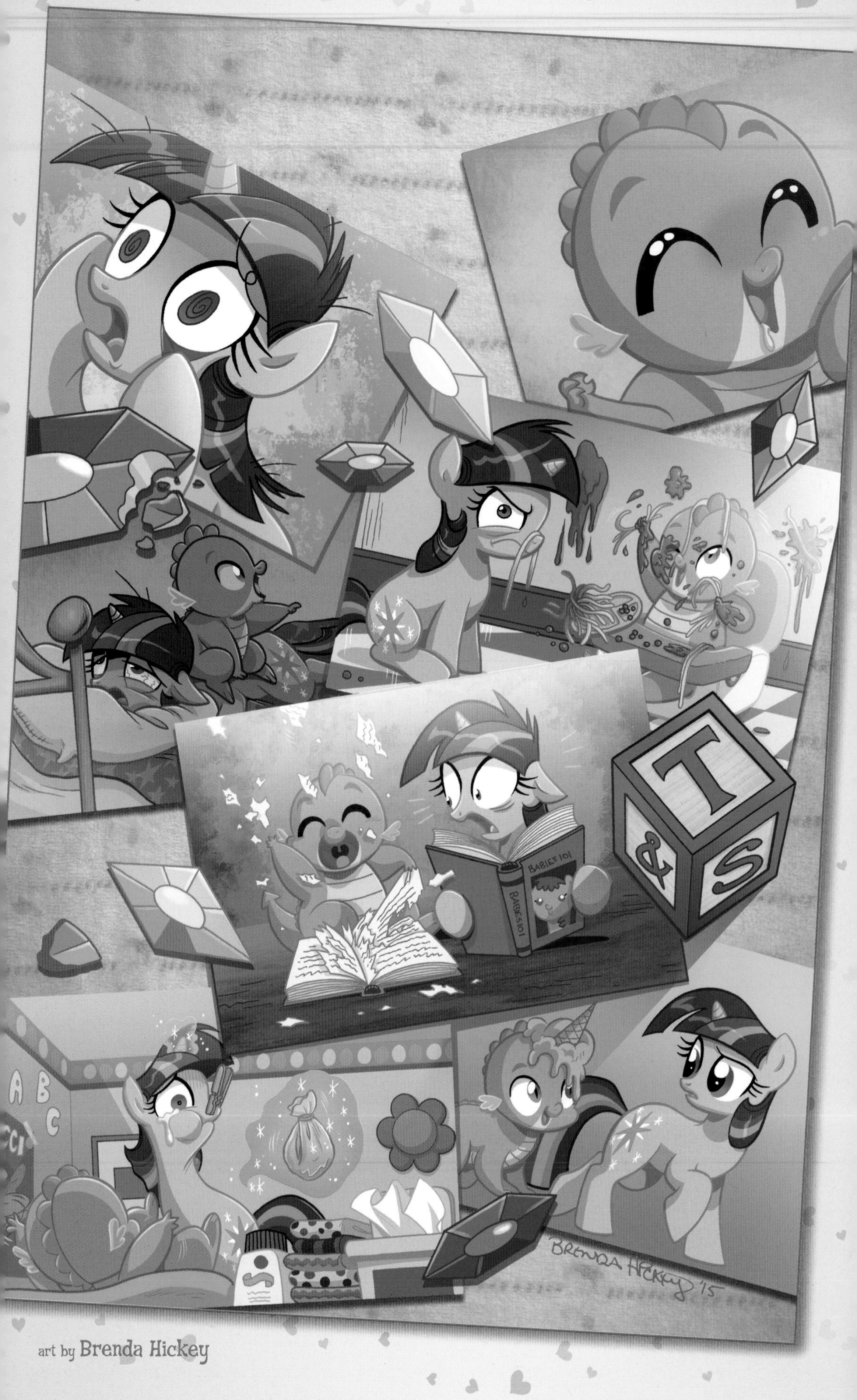
BABIES 101
BABIES 101
T
&
S
A
B
C
BRENDA HICKEY '15

art by Brenda Hickey

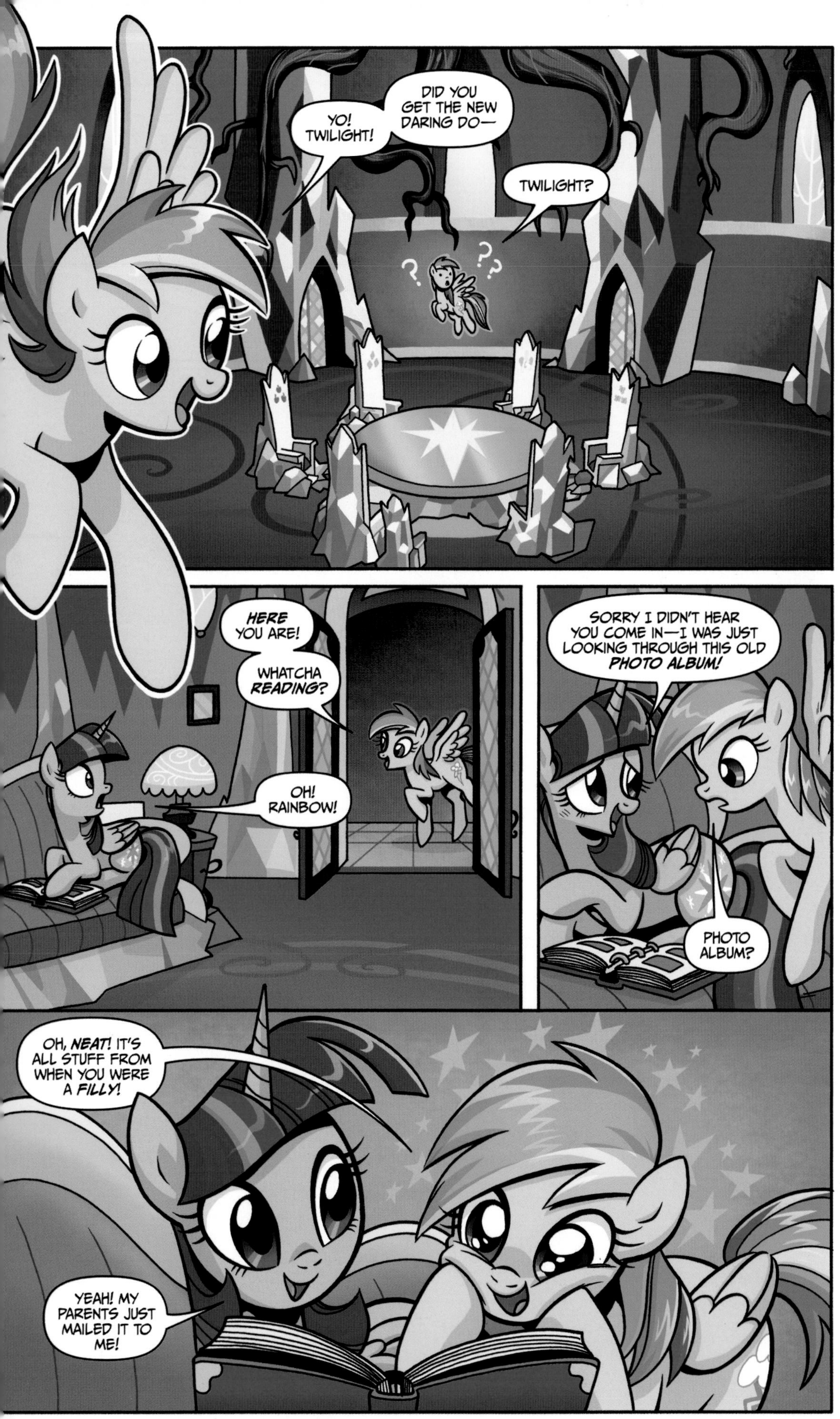
YO! TWILIGHT!
DID YOU GET THE NEW DARING DO—
TWILIGHT?
?
??
HERE YOU ARE!
WHATCHA READING?
OH! RAINBOW!
SORRY I DIDN'T HEAR YOU COME IN—I WAS JUST LOOKING THROUGH THIS OLD PHOTO ALBUM!
PHOTO ALBUM?
OH, NEAT! IT'S ALL STUFF FROM WHEN YOU WERE A FILLY!
YEAH! MY PARENTS JUST MAILED IT TO ME!

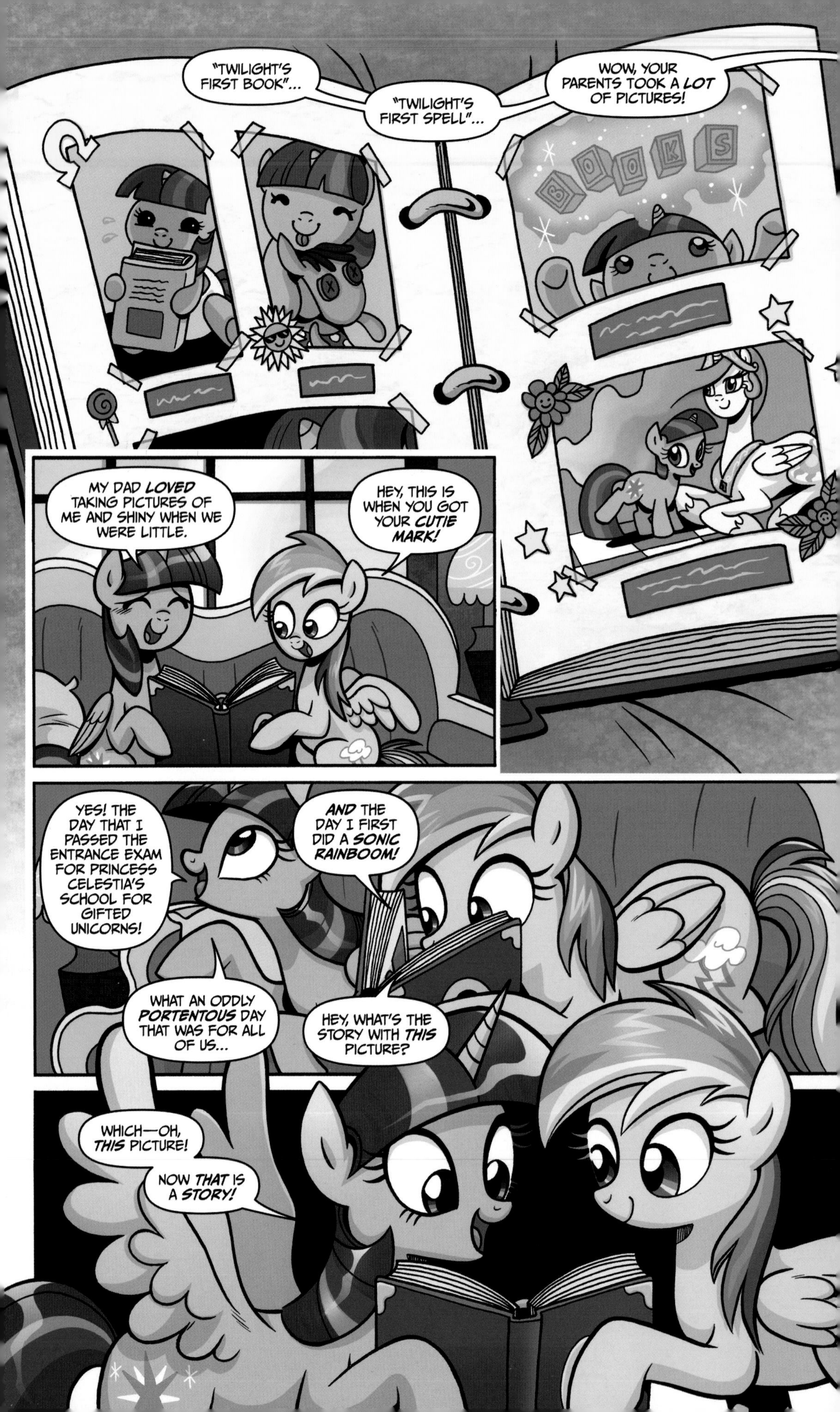
"TWILIGHT'S FIRST BOOK"...
"TWILIGHT'S FIRST SPELL"...
WOW, YOUR PARENTS TOOK A LOT OF PICTURES!
BOOKS
MY DAD LOVED TAKING PICTURES OF ME AND SHINY WHEN WE WERE LITTLE.
HEY, THIS IS WHEN YOU GOT YOUR CUTIE MARK!
YES! THE DAY THAT I PASSED THE ENTRANCE EXAM FOR PRINCESS CELESTIA'S SCHOOL FOR GIFTED UNICORNS!
AND THE DAY I FIRST DID A SONIC RAINBOOM!
WHAT AN ODDLY PORTENTOUS DAY THAT WAS FOR ALL OF US...
HEY, WHAT'S THE STORY WITH THIS PICTURE?
WHICH—OH, THIS PICTURE!
NOW THAT IS A STORY!

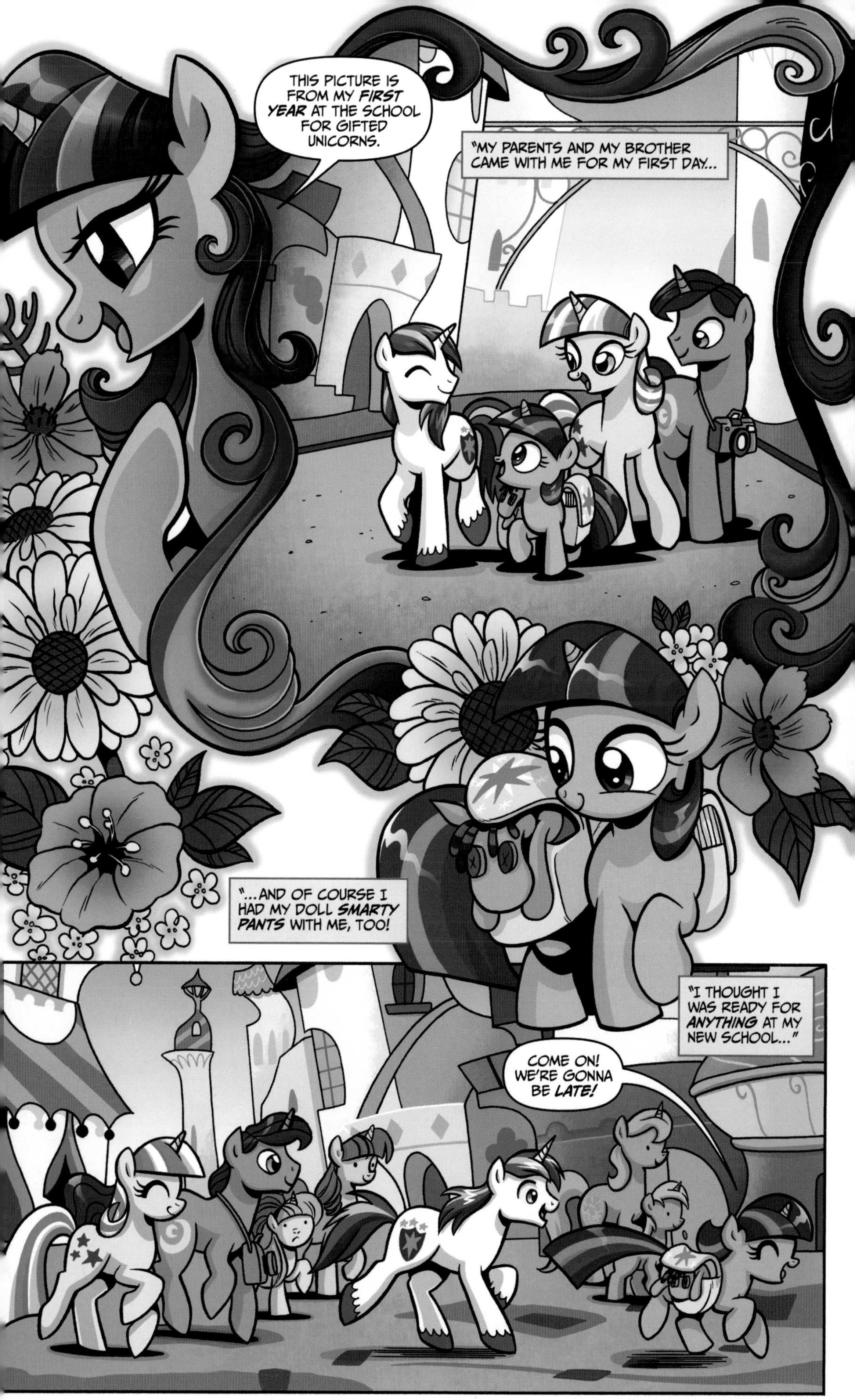
THIS PICTURE IS FROM MY *FIRST YEAR* AT THE SCHOOL FOR GIFTED UNICORNS.
"MY PARENTS AND MY BROTHER CAME WITH ME FOR MY FIRST DAY...
"...AND OF COURSE I HAD MY DOLL *SMARTY PANTS* WITH ME, TOO!
"I THOUGHT I WAS READY FOR *ANYTHING* AT MY NEW SCHOOL..."
COME ON! WE'RE GONNA BE *LATE!*

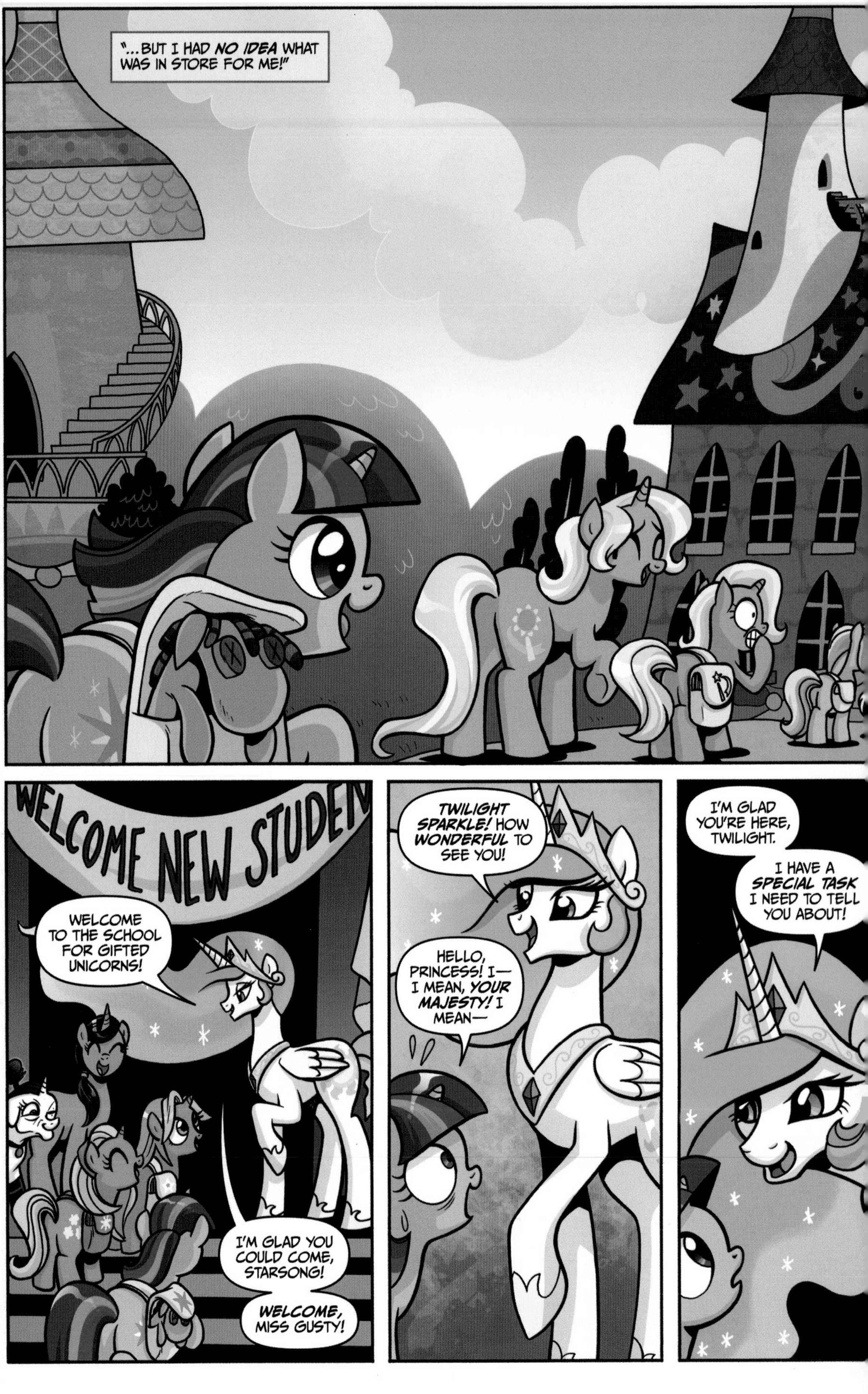
"...BUT I HAD NO IDEA WHAT WAS IN STORE FOR ME!"
WELCOME NEW STUDEN
WELCOME TO THE SCHOOL FOR GIFTED UNICORNS!
I'M GLAD YOU COULD COME, STARSONG!
WELCOME, MISS GUSTY!
TWILIGHT SPARKLE! HOW WONDERFUL TO SEE YOU!
HELLO, PRINCESS! I— I MEAN, YOUR MAJESTY! I MEAN—
I'M GLAD YOU'RE HERE, TWILIGHT.
I HAVE A SPECIAL TASK I NEED TO TELL YOU ABOUT!

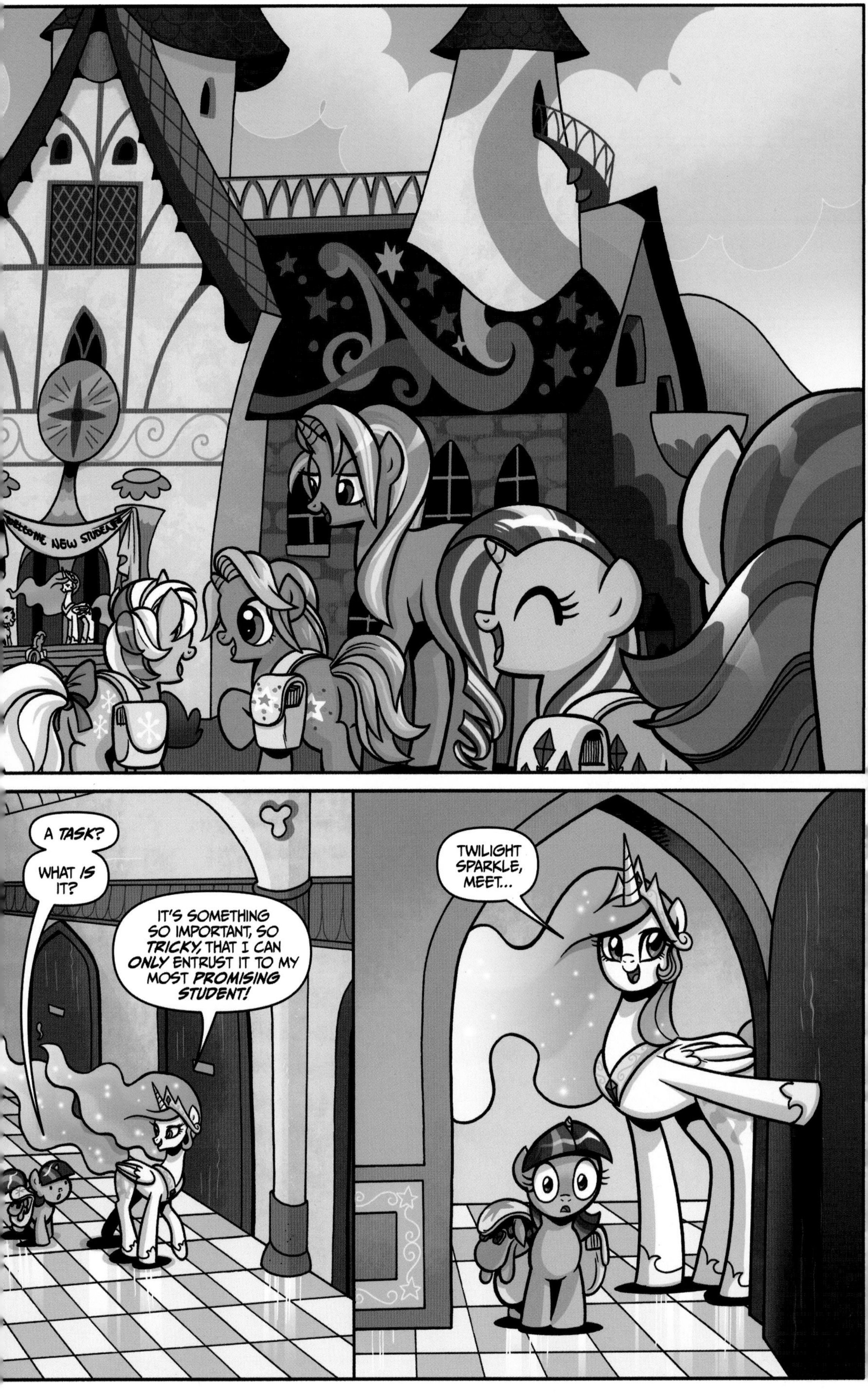
A *TASK*?
WHAT *IS* IT?
IT'S SOMETHING SO IMPORTANT, SO *TRICKY*, THAT I CAN *ONLY* ENTRUST IT TO MY MOST ***PROMISING STUDENT!***
TWILIGHT SPARKLE, MEET...

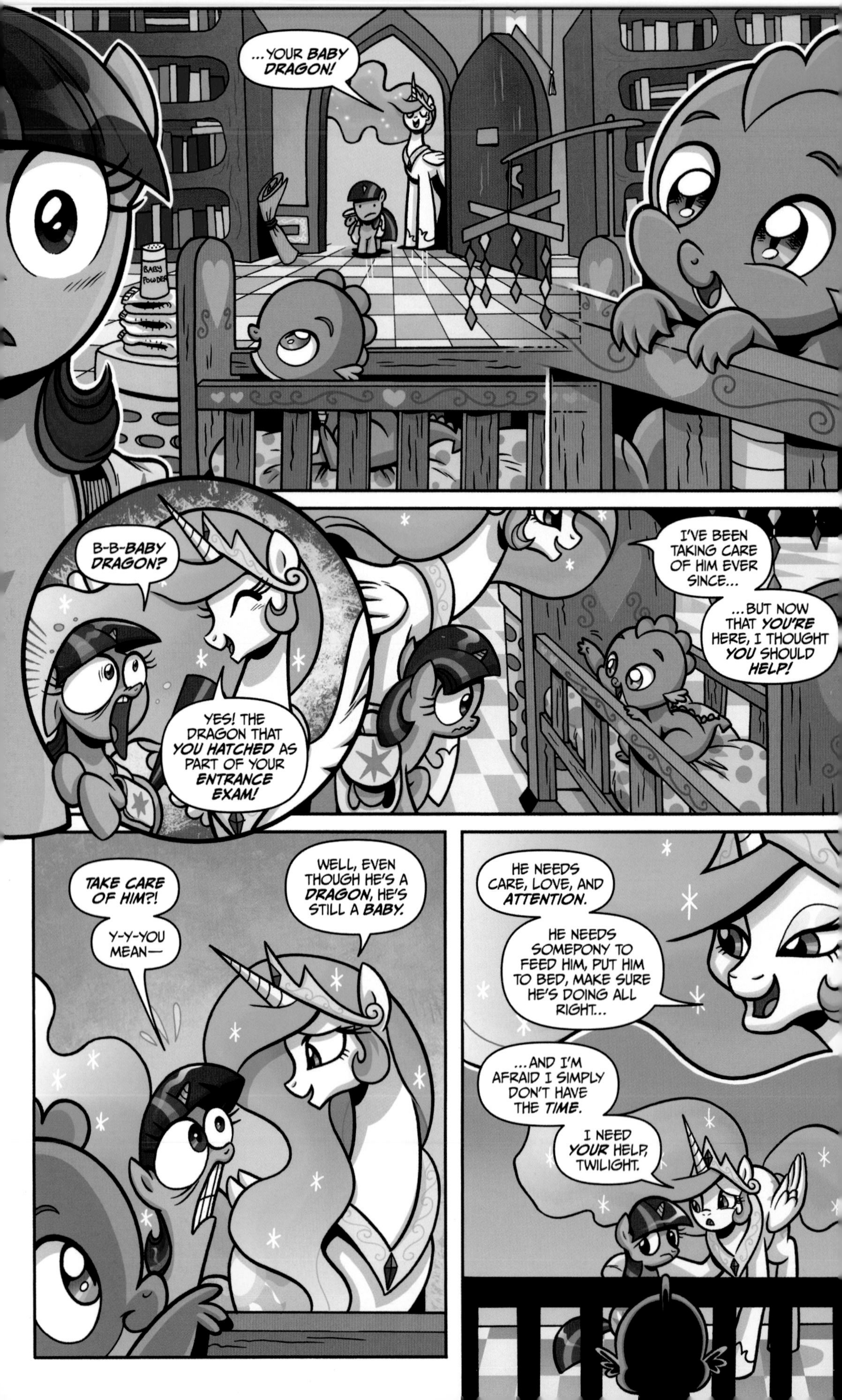
...YOUR BABY DRAGON!
BABY POWDER
B-B-BABY DRAGON?
YES! THE DRAGON THAT YOU HATCHED AS PART OF YOUR ENTRANCE EXAM!
I'VE BEEN TAKING CARE OF HIM EVER SINCE...
...BUT NOW THAT YOU'RE HERE, I THOUGHT YOU SHOULD HELP!
TAKE CARE OF HIM?!
Y-Y-YOU MEAN—
WELL, EVEN THOUGH HE'S A DRAGON, HE'S STILL A BABY.
HE NEEDS CARE, LOVE, AND ATTENTION.
HE NEEDS SOMEPONY TO FEED HIM, PUT HIM TO BED, MAKE SURE HE'S DOING ALL RIGHT...
...AND I'M AFRAID I SIMPLY DON'T HAVE THE TIME.
I NEED YOUR HELP, TWILIGHT.

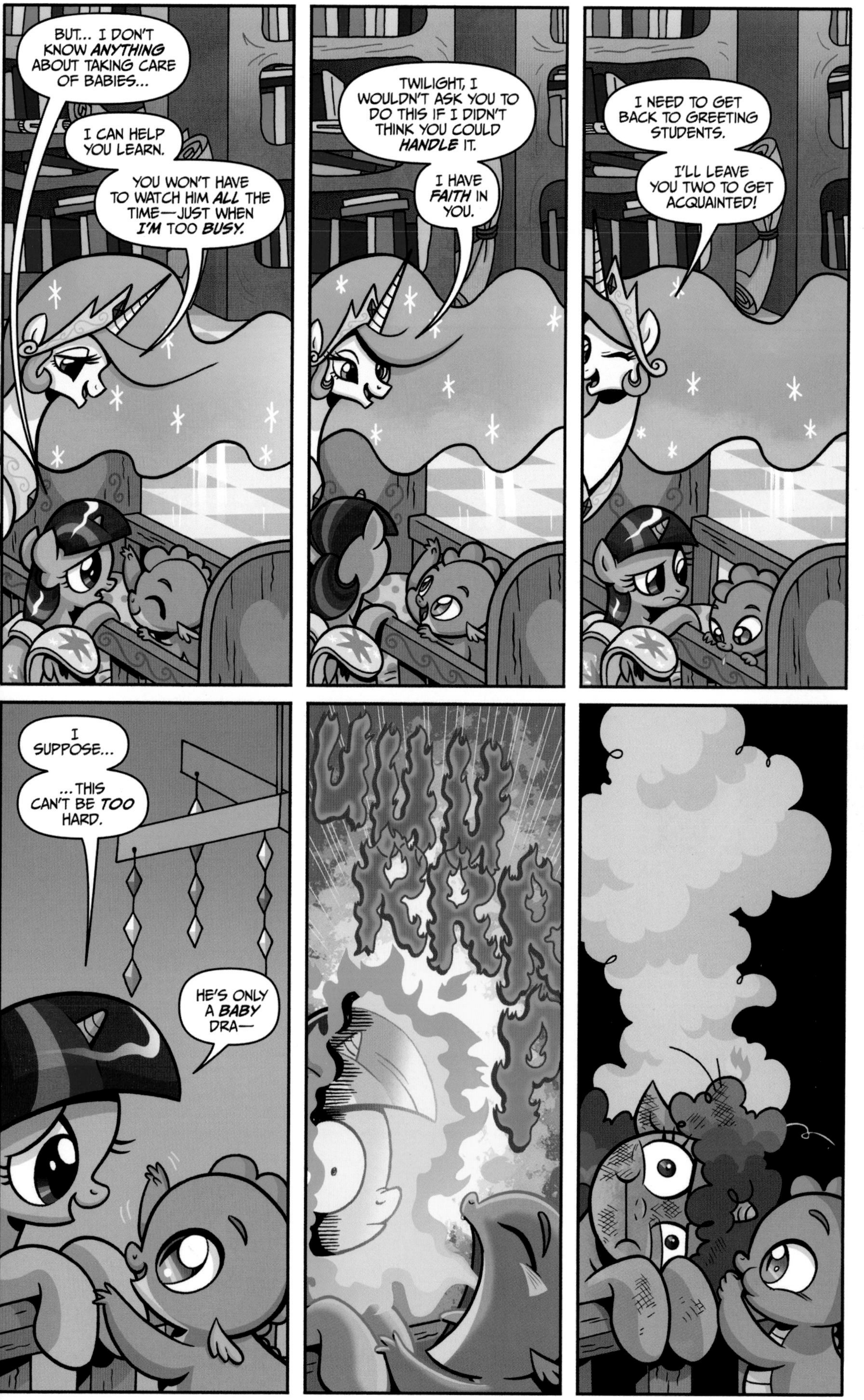

BUT... I DON'T KNOW ANYTHING ABOUT TAKING CARE OF BABIES...
I CAN HELP YOU LEARN.
YOU WON'T HAVE TO WATCH HIM ALL THE TIME—JUST WHEN I'M TOO BUSY.
TWILIGHT, I WOULDN'T ASK YOU TO DO THIS IF I DIDN'T THINK YOU COULD HANDLE IT.
I HAVE FAITH IN YOU.
I NEED TO GET BACK TO GREETING STUDENTS.
I'LL LEAVE YOU TWO TO GET ACQUAINTED!
I SUPPOSE...
...THIS CAN'T BE TOO HARD.
HE'S ONLY A BABY DRA—

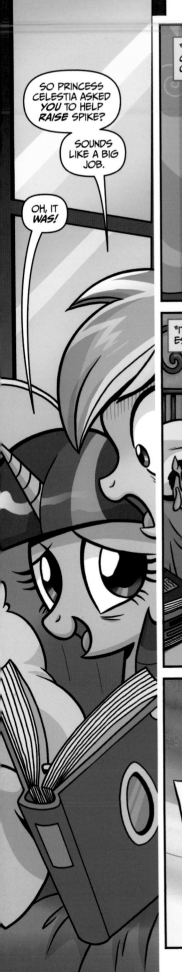

SO PRINCESS CELESTIA ASKED *YOU* TO HELP *RAISE* SPIKE?

SOUNDS LIKE A BIG JOB.

OH, IT *WAS!*

"I LEARNED AS MUCH AS I COULD ABOUT TAKING CARE OF *BABIES,* BUT..."

YOU DON'T HAVE *ANY* BOOKS ON RAISING *DRAGONS?*

I'M SORRY! NOPONY'S EVER *WRITTEN* ONE!

"IT WAS DIFFICULT, ESPECIALLY AT FIRST..."

OKAY, YOUR *CRIB* IS SET UP, I'VE GOT YOUR *TOYS,* YOUR *BOOKS,* YOUR *BLANKETS...*

YOU'VE BEEN *FED,* YOU'VE HAD YOUR *NAP...*

—OH *NO!*

AND I'VE GOT CLASS!

I CAN'T BE *LATE* FOR MY *FIRST DAY!*

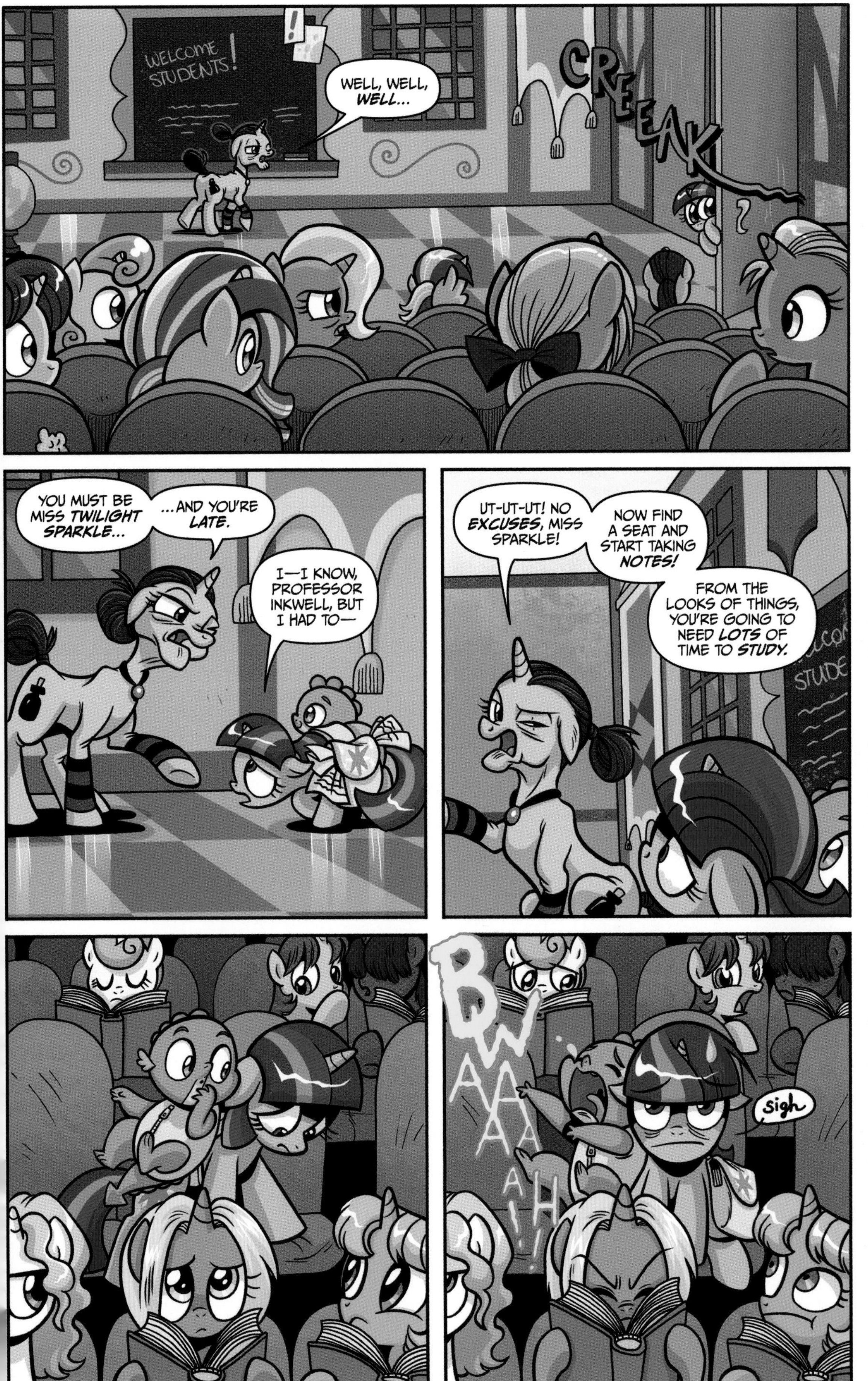
WELCOME STUDENTS!
!
WELL, WELL, WELL...
CREEEAK
?
YOU MUST BE MISS TWILIGHT SPARKLE...
...AND YOU'RE LATE.
I—I KNOW, PROFESSOR INKWELL, BUT I HAD TO—
UT-UT-UT! NO EXCUSES, MISS SPARKLE!
NOW FIND A SEAT AND START TAKING NOTES!
FROM THE LOOKS OF THINGS, YOU'RE GOING TO NEED LOTS OF TIME TO STUDY.
BWAAAAAH!!!
sigh

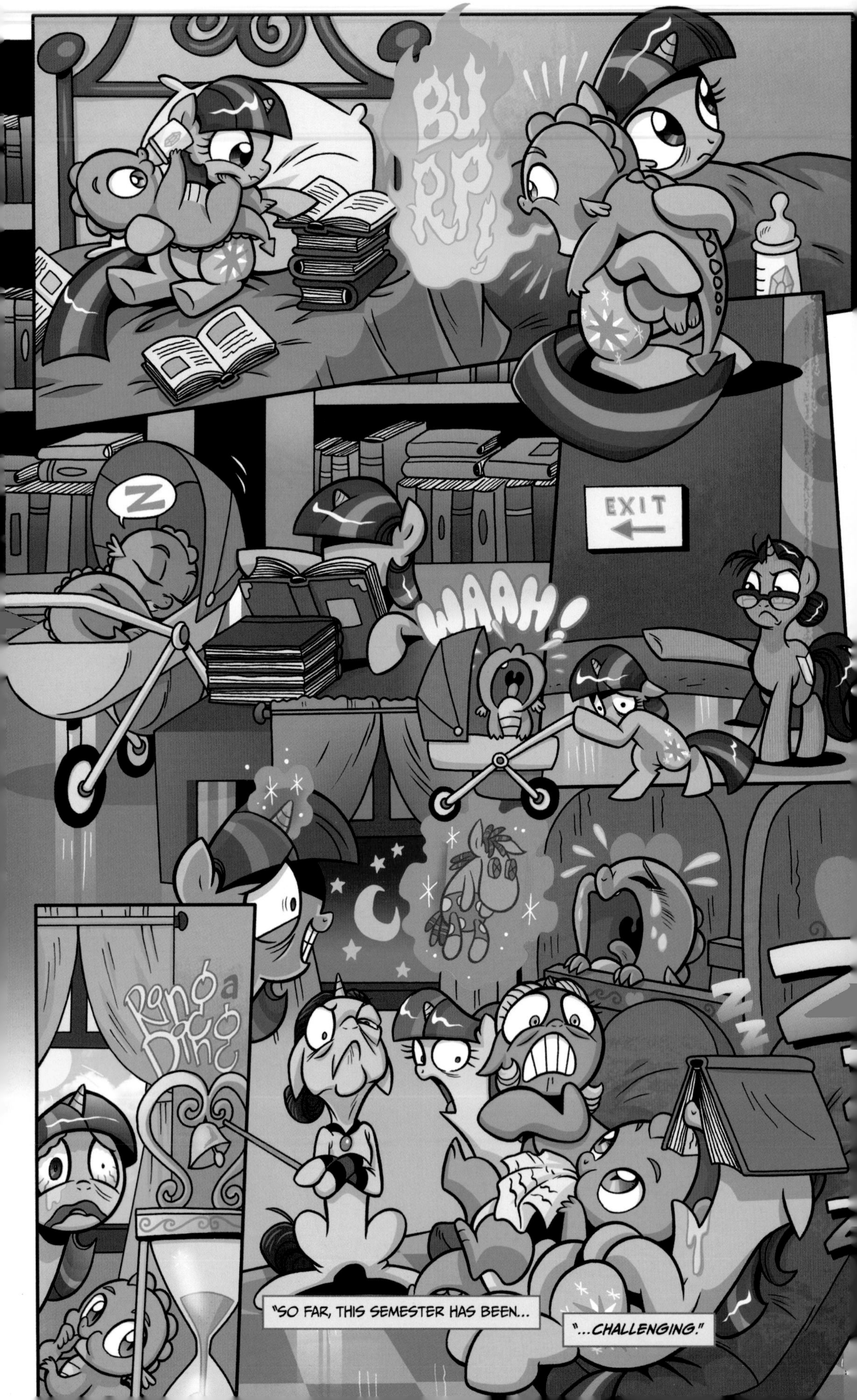
BURP!
Z
EXIT
WAAH!
Ring a Ding Ding
"SO FAR, THIS SEMESTER HAS BEEN...
"...CHALLENGING."

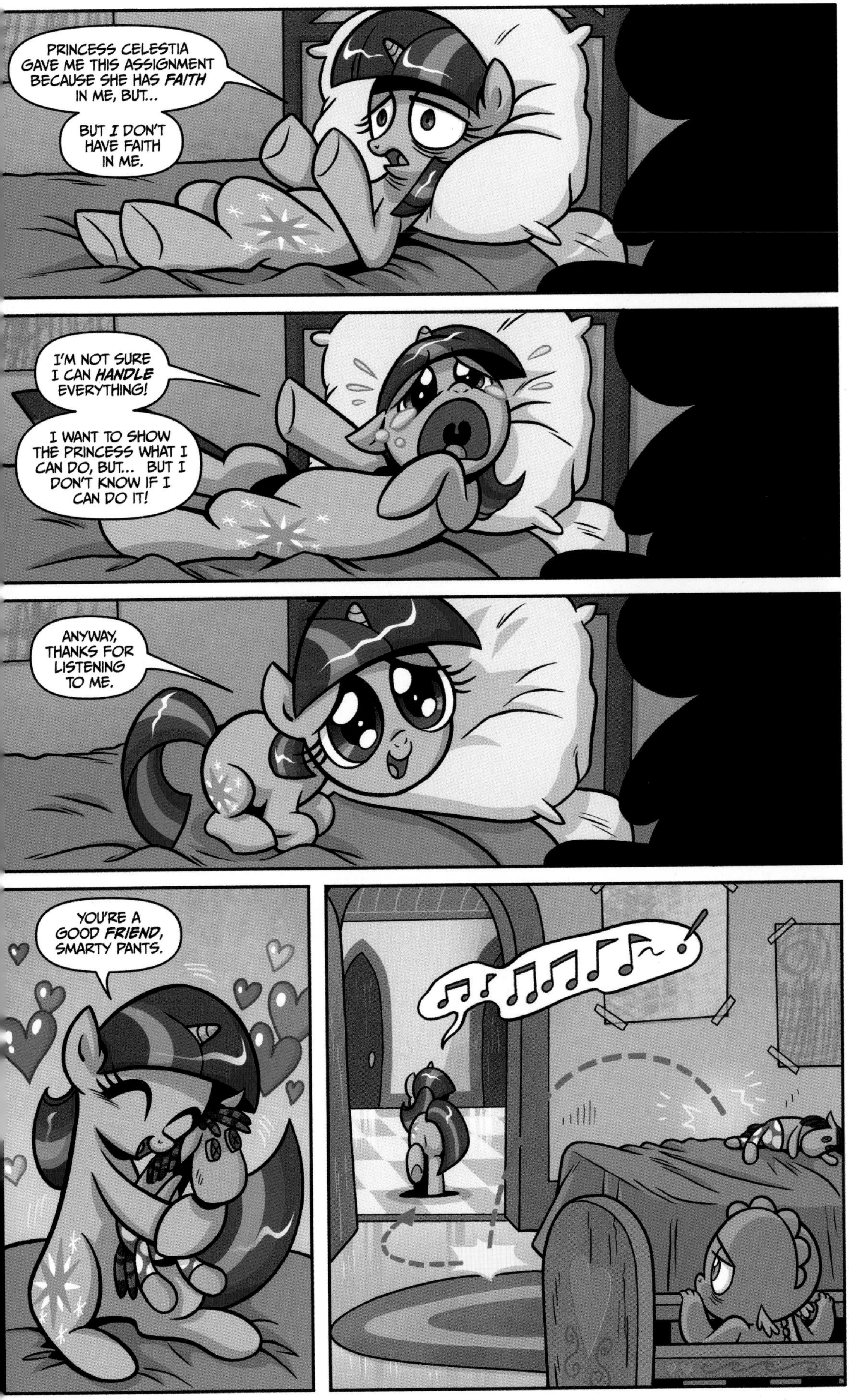
PRINCESS CELESTIA GAVE ME THIS ASSIGNMENT BECAUSE SHE HAS *FAITH* IN ME, BUT...
BUT *I* DON'T HAVE FAITH IN ME.
I'M NOT SURE I CAN *HANDLE* EVERYTHING!
I WANT TO SHOW THE PRINCESS WHAT I CAN DO, BUT... BUT I DON'T KNOW IF I CAN DO IT!
ANYWAY, THANKS FOR LISTENING TO ME.
YOU'RE A GOOD *FRIEND*, SMARTY PANTS.

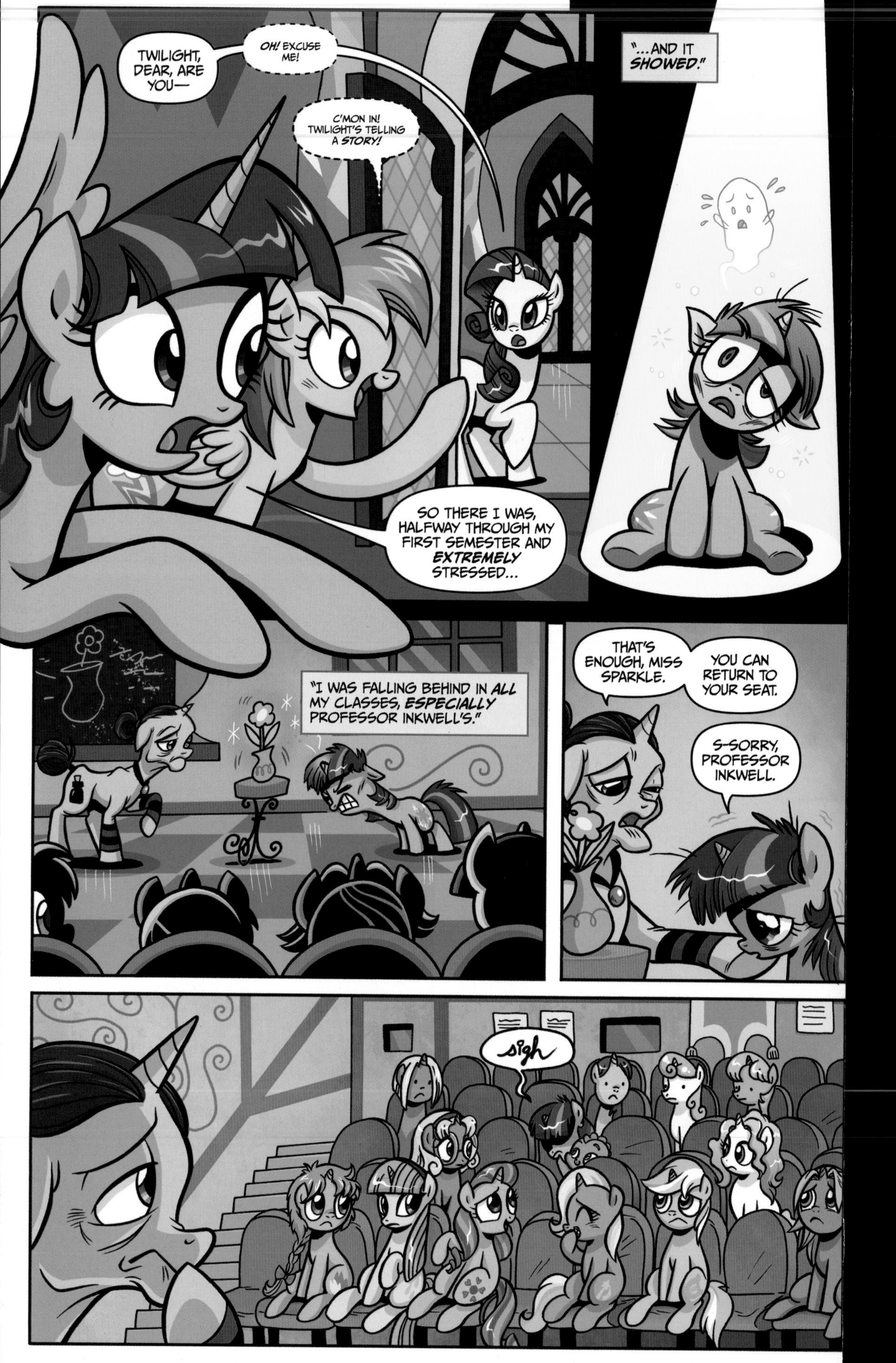
TWILIGHT, DEAR, ARE YOU—
OH! EXCUSE ME!
C'MON IN! TWILIGHT'S TELLING A STORY!
SO THERE I WAS, HALFWAY THROUGH MY FIRST SEMESTER AND EXTREMELY STRESSED...
"...AND IT SHOWED."
"I WAS FALLING BEHIND IN ALL MY CLASSES, ESPECIALLY PROFESSOR INKWELL'S."
THAT'S ENOUGH, MISS SPARKLE.
YOU CAN RETURN TO YOUR SEAT.
S-SORRY, PROFESSOR INKWELL.
sigh

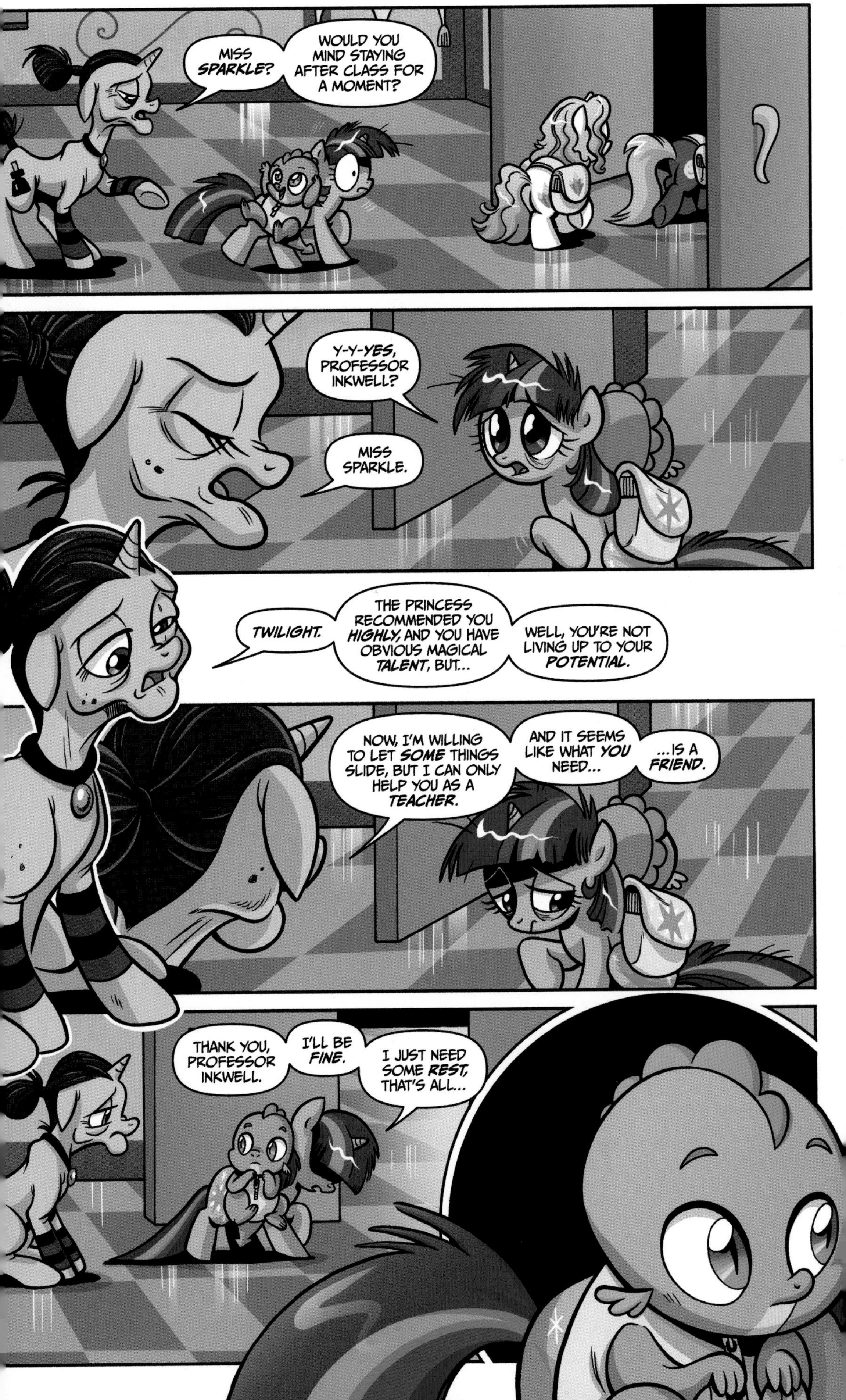

MISS SPARKLE?
WOULD YOU MIND STAYING AFTER CLASS FOR A MOMENT?
Y-Y-YES, PROFESSOR INKWELL?
MISS SPARKLE.
TWILIGHT.
THE PRINCESS RECOMMENDED YOU HIGHLY, AND YOU HAVE OBVIOUS MAGICAL TALENT, BUT...
WELL, YOU'RE NOT LIVING UP TO YOUR POTENTIAL.
NOW, I'M WILLING TO LET SOME THINGS SLIDE, BUT I CAN ONLY HELP YOU AS A TEACHER.
AND IT SEEMS LIKE WHAT YOU NEED...
...IS A FRIEND.
THANK YOU, PROFESSOR INKWELL.
I'LL BE FINE.
I JUST NEED SOME REST, THAT'S ALL...

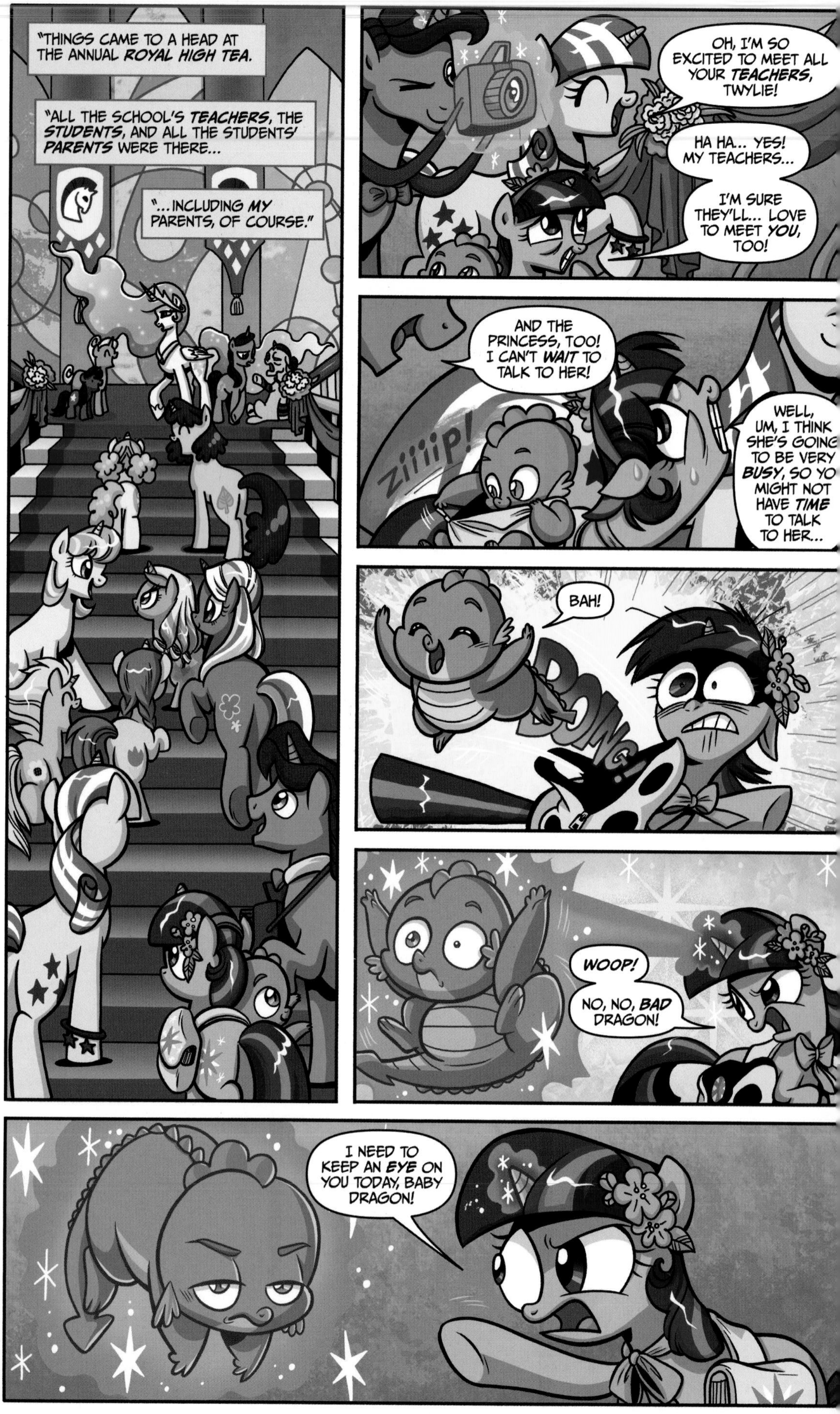
"THINGS CAME TO A HEAD AT THE ANNUAL *ROYAL HIGH TEA*.
"ALL THE SCHOOL'S *TEACHERS*, THE *STUDENTS*, AND ALL THE STUDENTS' *PARENTS* WERE THERE...
"...INCLUDING *MY* PARENTS, OF COURSE."
OH, I'M SO EXCITED TO MEET ALL YOUR *TEACHERS*, TWYLIE!
HA HA... YES! MY TEACHERS...
I'M SURE THEY'LL... LOVE TO MEET *YOU*, TOO!
AND THE PRINCESS, TOO! I CAN'T *WAIT* TO TALK TO HER!
ZIIIIP!
WELL, UM, I THINK SHE'S GOING TO BE VERY *BUSY*, SO YO MIGHT NOT HAVE *TIME* TO TALK TO HER...
BAH!
BOING
WOOP!
NO, NO, *BAD* DRAGON!
I NEED TO KEEP AN *EYE* ON YOU TODAY, BABY DRAGON!

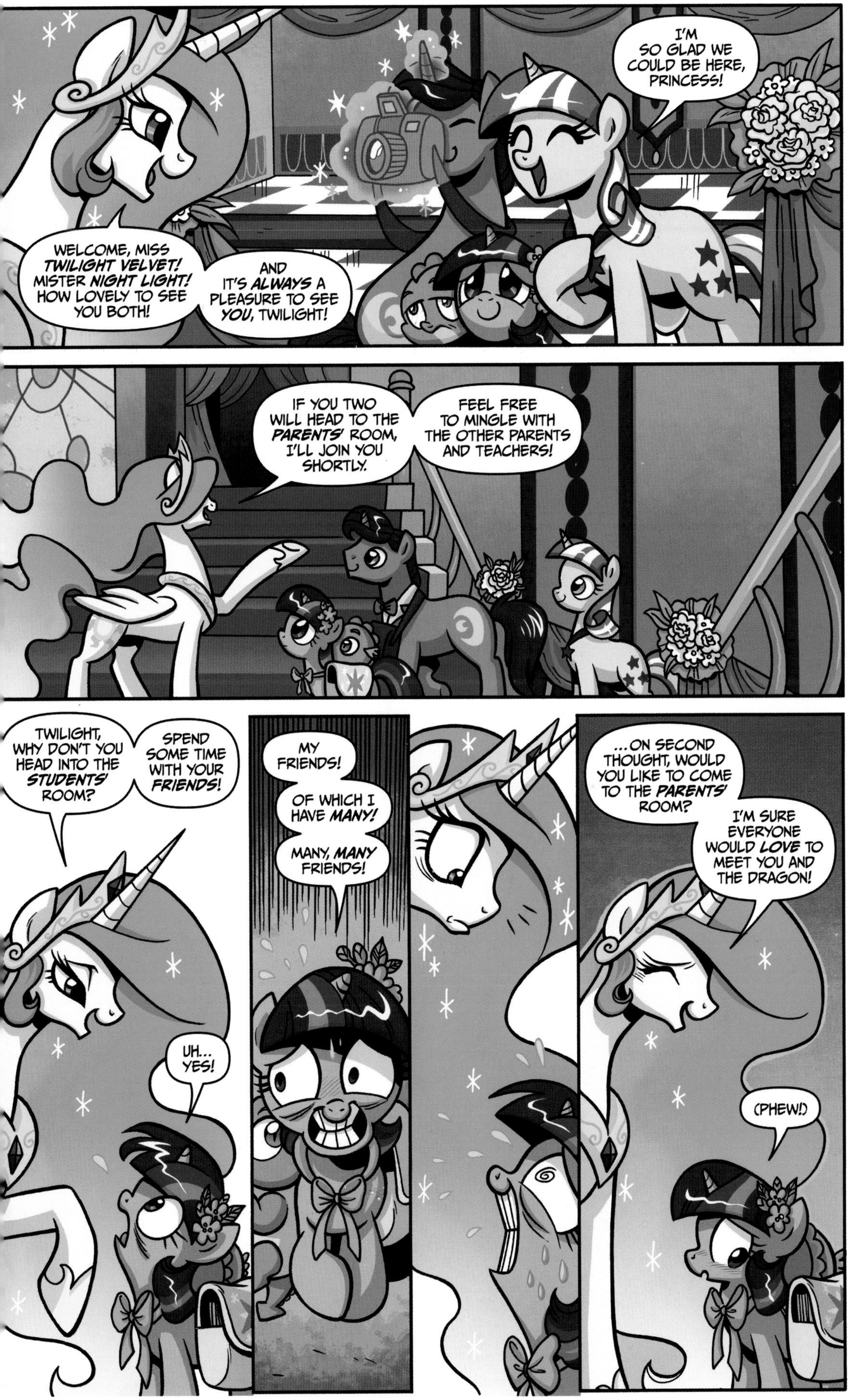
I'M SO GLAD WE COULD BE HERE, PRINCESS!
WELCOME, MISS TWILIGHT VELVET! MISTER NIGHT LIGHT! HOW LOVELY TO SEE YOU BOTH!
AND IT'S ALWAYS A PLEASURE TO SEE YOU, TWILIGHT!
IF YOU TWO WILL HEAD TO THE PARENTS' ROOM, I'LL JOIN YOU SHORTLY.
FEEL FREE TO MINGLE WITH THE OTHER PARENTS AND TEACHERS!
TWILIGHT, WHY DON'T YOU HEAD INTO THE STUDENTS' ROOM?
SPEND SOME TIME WITH YOUR FRIENDS!
UH... YES!
MY FRIENDS!
OF WHICH I HAVE MANY!
MANY, MANY FRIENDS!
...ON SECOND THOUGHT, WOULD YOU LIKE TO COME TO THE PARENTS' ROOM?
I'M SURE EVERYONE WOULD LOVE TO MEET YOU AND THE DRAGON!
(PHEW!)

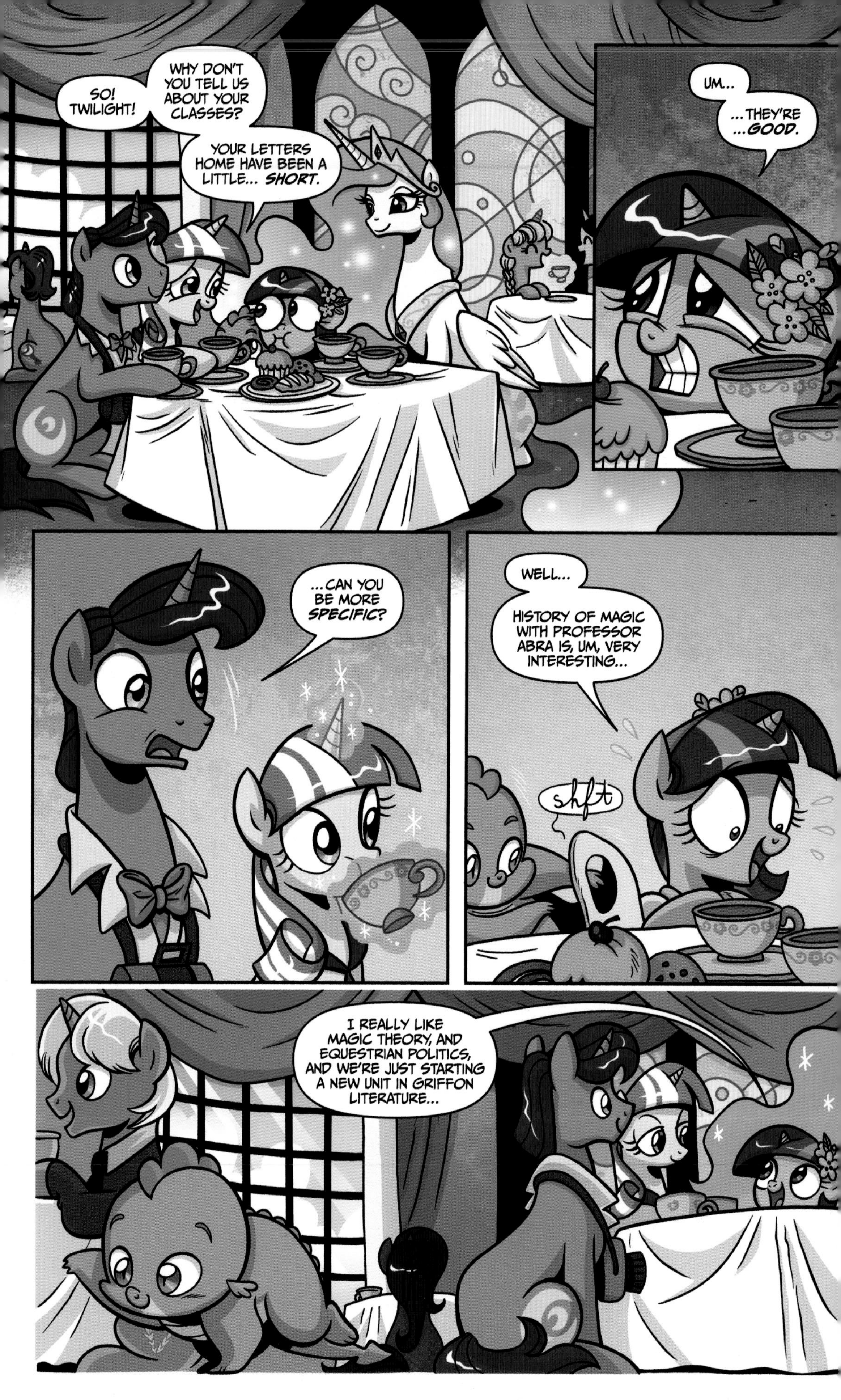
SO! TWILIGHT!
WHY DON'T YOU TELL US ABOUT YOUR CLASSES?
YOUR LETTERS HOME HAVE BEEN A LITTLE... SHORT.
UM...
...THEY'RE ...GOOD.
...CAN YOU BE MORE SPECIFIC?
WELL...
HISTORY OF MAGIC WITH PROFESSOR ABRA IS, UM, VERY INTERESTING...
shft
I REALLY LIKE MAGIC THEORY, AND EQUESTRIAN POLITICS, AND WE'RE JUST STARTING A NEW UNIT IN GRIFFON LITERATURE...

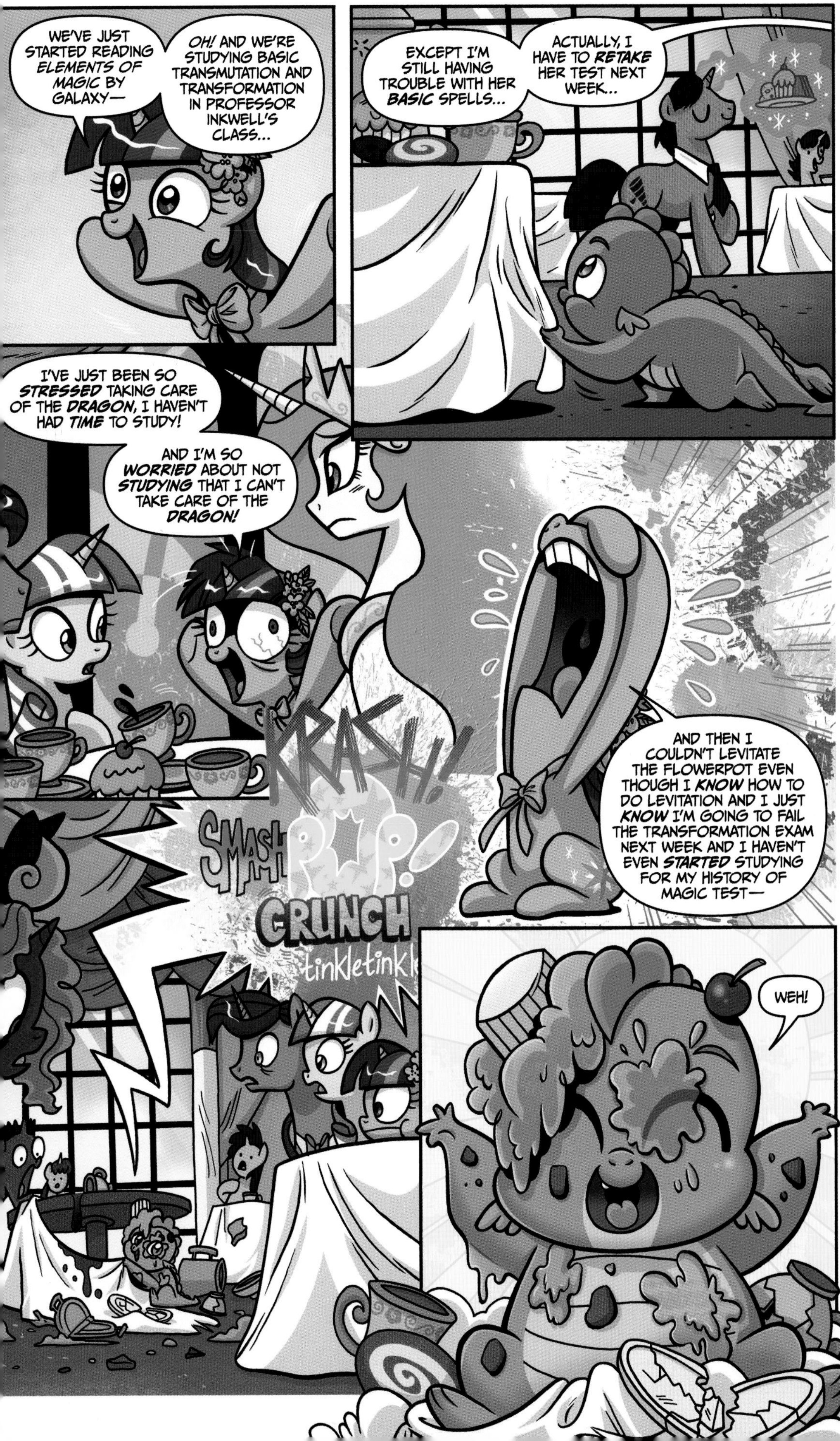
WE'VE JUST STARTED READING ELEMENTS OF MAGIC BY GALAXY—
OH! AND WE'RE STUDYING BASIC TRANSMUTATION AND TRANSFORMATION IN PROFESSOR INKWELL'S CLASS...
EXCEPT I'M STILL HAVING TROUBLE WITH HER BASIC SPELLS...
ACTUALLY, I HAVE TO RETAKE HER TEST NEXT WEEK...
I'VE JUST BEEN SO STRESSED TAKING CARE OF THE DRAGON, I HAVEN'T HAD TIME TO STUDY!
AND I'M SO WORRIED ABOUT NOT STUDYING THAT I CAN'T TAKE CARE OF THE DRAGON!
AND THEN I COULDN'T LEVITATE THE FLOWERPOT EVEN THOUGH I KNOW HOW TO DO LEVITATION AND I JUST KNOW I'M GOING TO FAIL THE TRANSFORMATION EXAM NEXT WEEK AND I HAVEN'T EVEN STARTED STUDYING FOR MY HISTORY OF MAGIC TEST—
KRASH!
SMASH
POP!
CRUNCH
tinkletinkle
WEH!

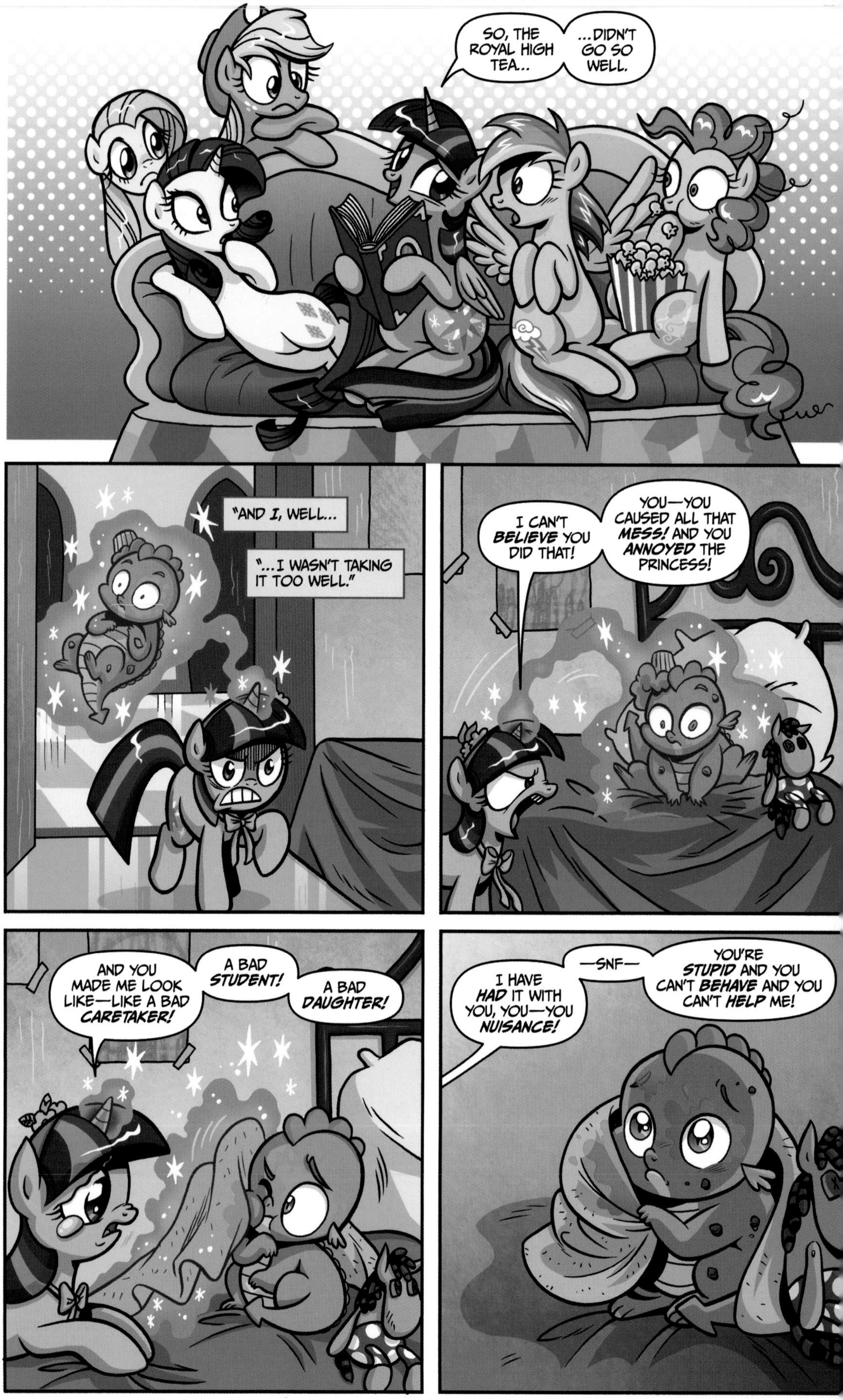
SO, THE ROYAL HIGH TEA...
...DIDN'T GO SO WELL.
"AND I, WELL...
"...I WASN'T TAKING IT TOO WELL."
I CAN'T BELIEVE YOU DID THAT!
YOU—YOU CAUSED ALL THAT MESS! AND YOU ANNOYED THE PRINCESS!
AND YOU MADE ME LOOK LIKE—LIKE A BAD CARETAKER!
A BAD STUDENT!
A BAD DAUGHTER!
I HAVE HAD IT WITH YOU, YOU—YOU NUISANCE!
—SNF—
YOU'RE STUPID AND YOU CAN'T BEHAVE AND YOU CAN'T HELP ME!

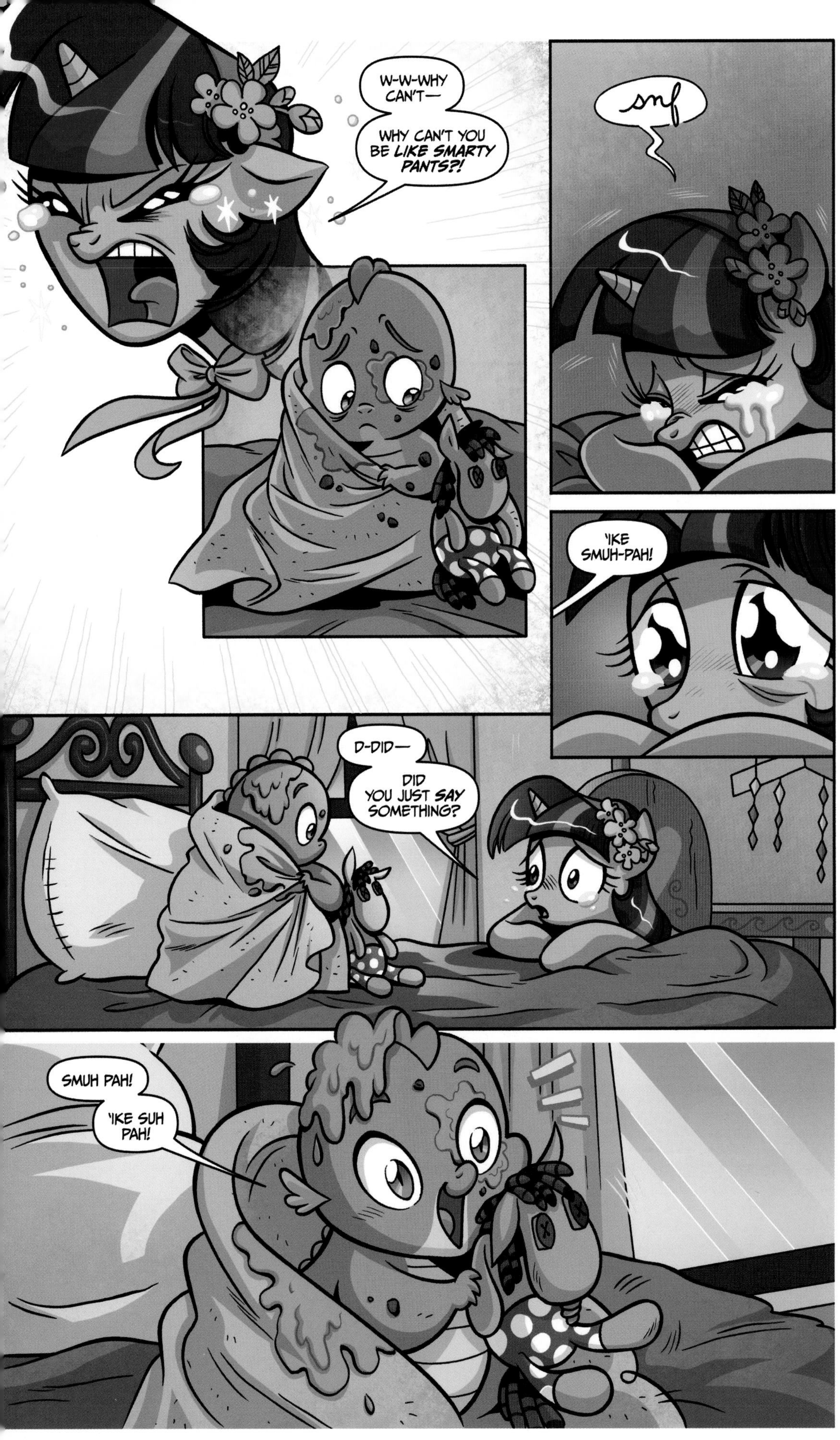
W-W-WHY CAN'T—
WHY CAN'T YOU BE LIKE SMARTY PANTS?!
snf
'IKE SMUH-PAH!
D-DID—
DID YOU JUST SAY SOMETHING?
SMUH PAH!
'IKE SUH PAH!

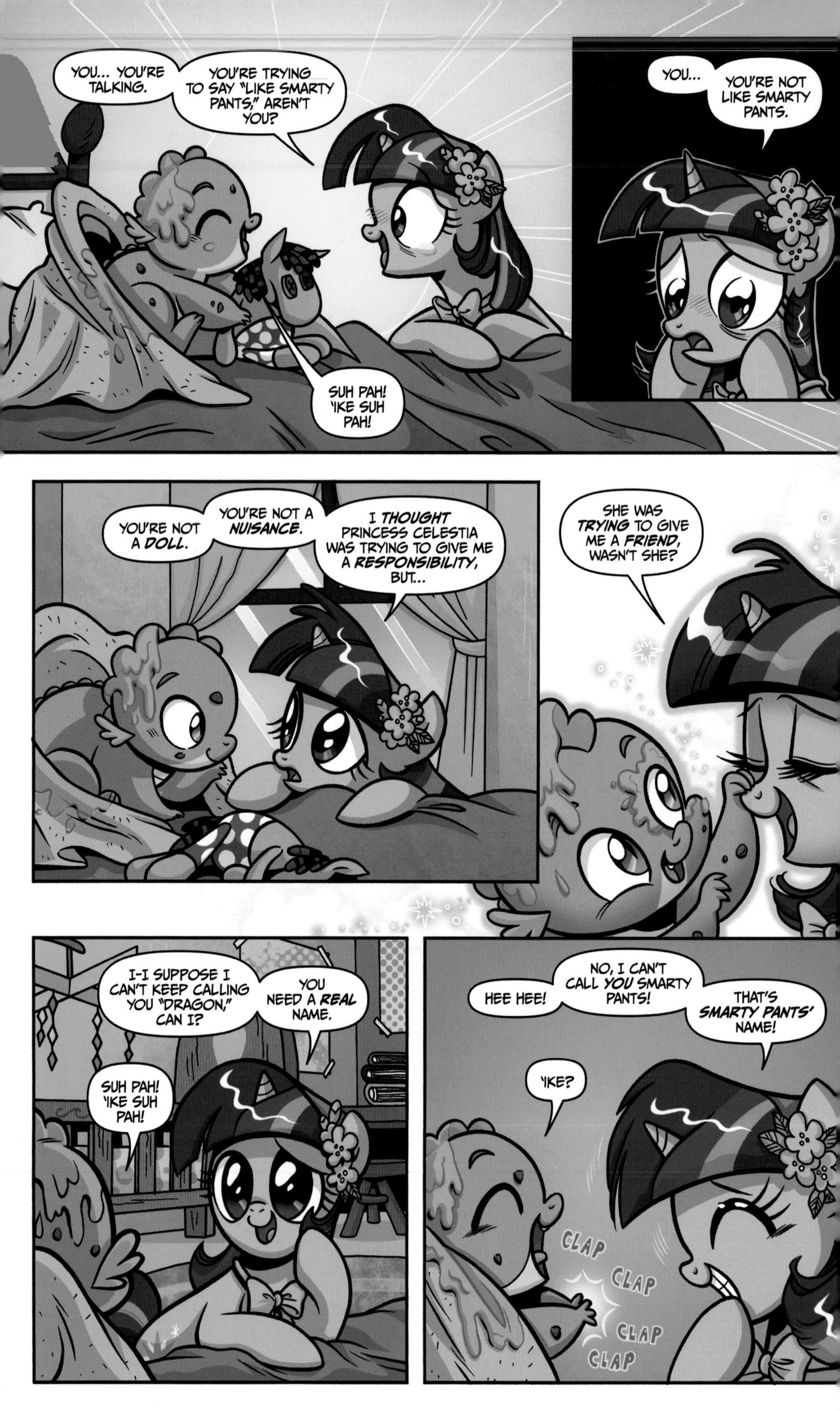

YOU... YOU'RE TALKING.
YOU'RE TRYING TO SAY "LIKE SMARTY PANTS," AREN'T YOU?
SUH PAH! 'IKE SUH PAH!
YOU...
YOU'RE NOT LIKE SMARTY PANTS.
YOU'RE NOT A DOLL.
YOU'RE NOT A NUISANCE.
I THOUGHT PRINCESS CELESTIA WAS TRYING TO GIVE ME A RESPONSIBILITY, BUT...
SHE WAS TRYING TO GIVE ME A FRIEND, WASN'T SHE?
I-I SUPPOSE I CAN'T KEEP CALLING YOU "DRAGON," CAN I?
YOU NEED A REAL NAME.
SUH PAH! 'IKE SUH PAH!
HEE HEE!
NO, I CAN'T CALL YOU SMARTY PANTS!
THAT'S SMARTY PANTS' NAME!
'IKE?
CLAP
CLAP
CLAP
CLAP

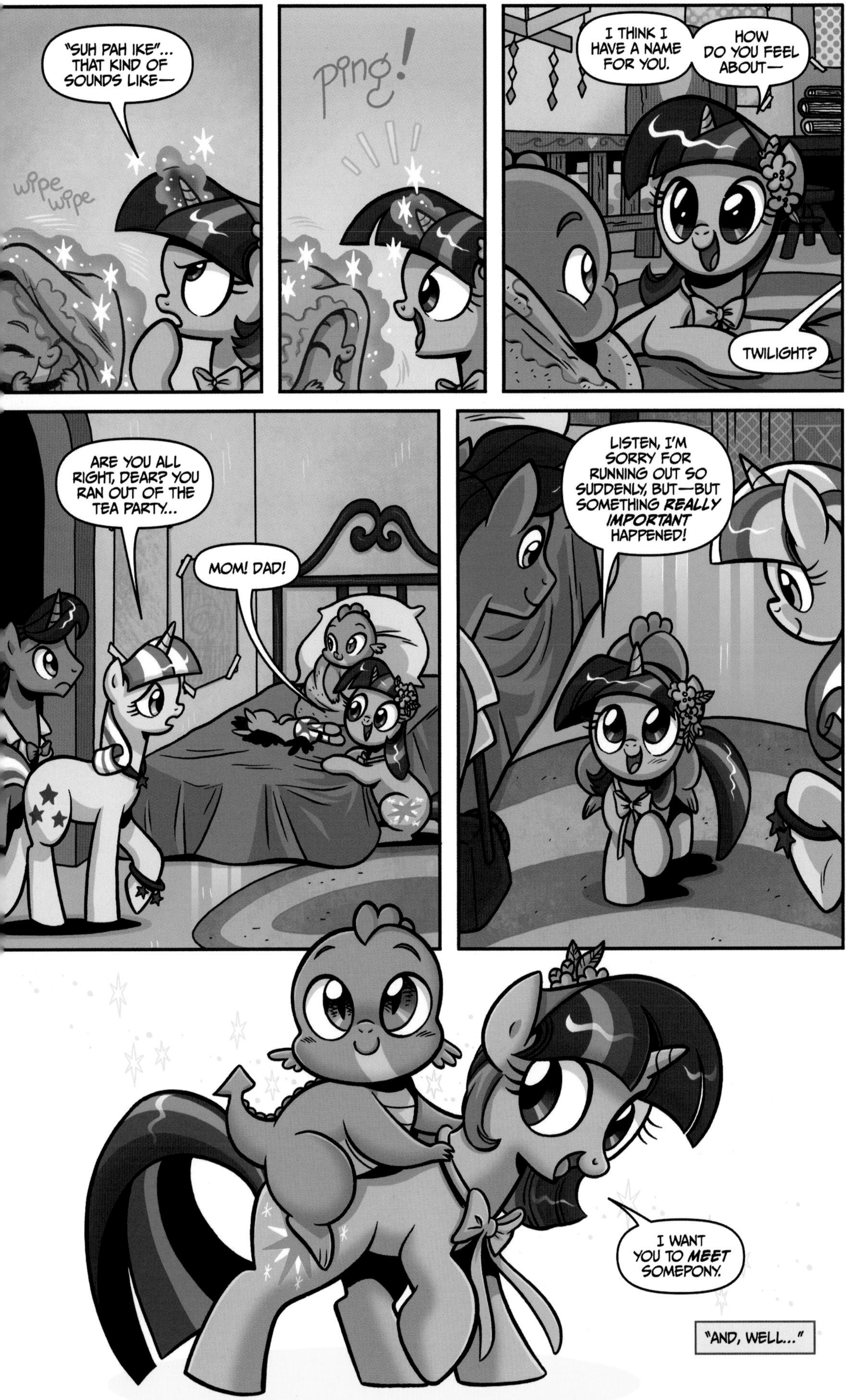
"SUH PAH IKE"... THAT KIND OF SOUNDS LIKE—
wipe wipe
ping!
I THINK I HAVE A NAME FOR YOU.
HOW DO YOU FEEL ABOUT—
TWILIGHT?
ARE YOU ALL RIGHT, DEAR? YOU RAN OUT OF THE TEA PARTY...
MOM! DAD!
LISTEN, I'M SORRY FOR RUNNING OUT SO SUDDENLY, BUT—BUT SOMETHING *REALLY IMPORTANT* HAPPENED!
I WANT YOU TO *MEET* SOMEPONY.
"AND, WELL..."

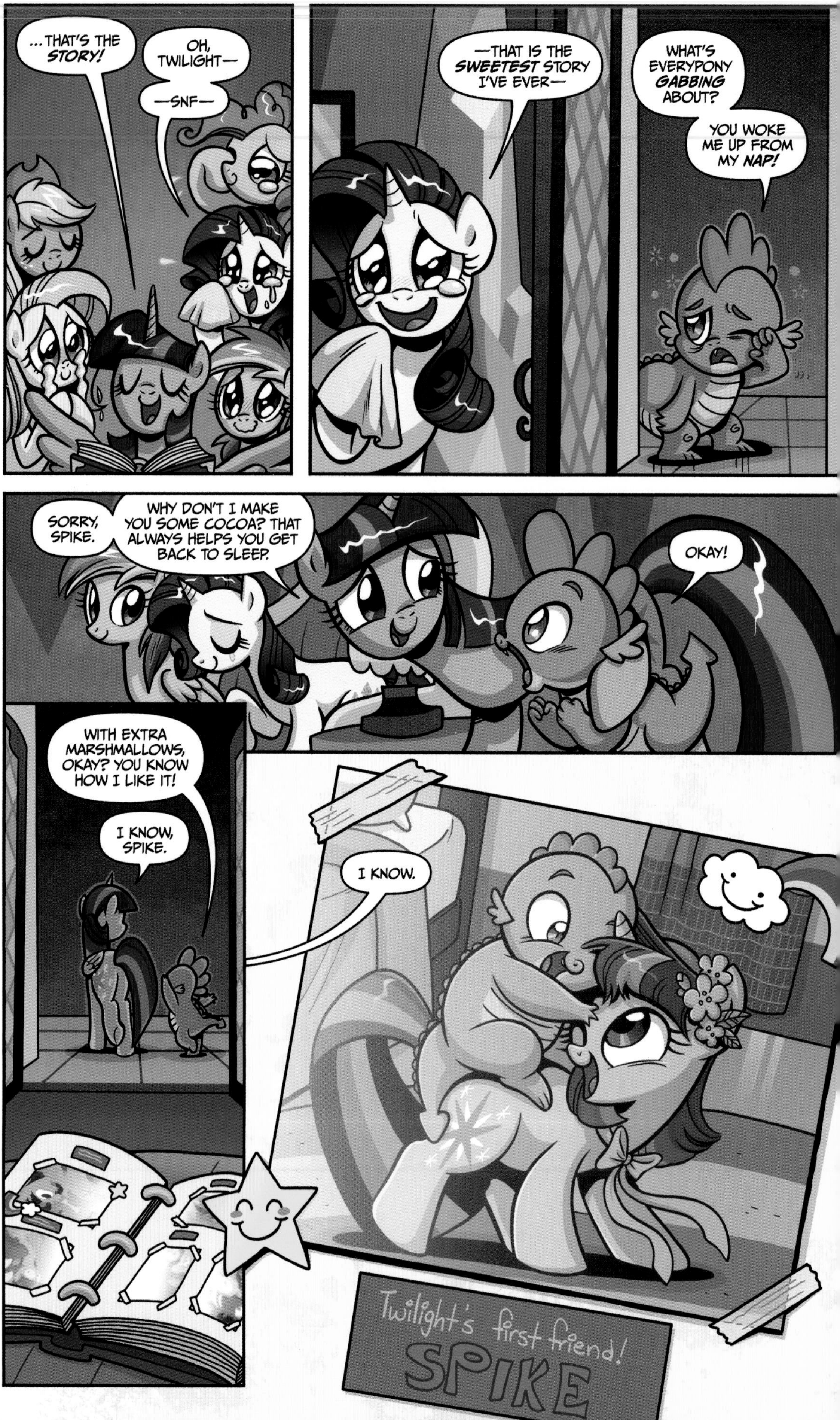
...THAT'S THE STORY!
OH, TWILIGHT—
—SNF—
—THAT IS THE SWEETEST STORY I'VE EVER—
WHAT'S EVERYPONY GABBING ABOUT?
YOU WOKE ME UP FROM MY NAP!
SORRY, SPIKE.
WHY DON'T I MAKE YOU SOME COCOA? THAT ALWAYS HELPS YOU GET BACK TO SLEEP.
OKAY!
WITH EXTRA MARSHMALLOWS, OKAY? YOU KNOW HOW I LIKE IT!
I KNOW, SPIKE.
I KNOW.
Twilight's first friend!
SPIKE

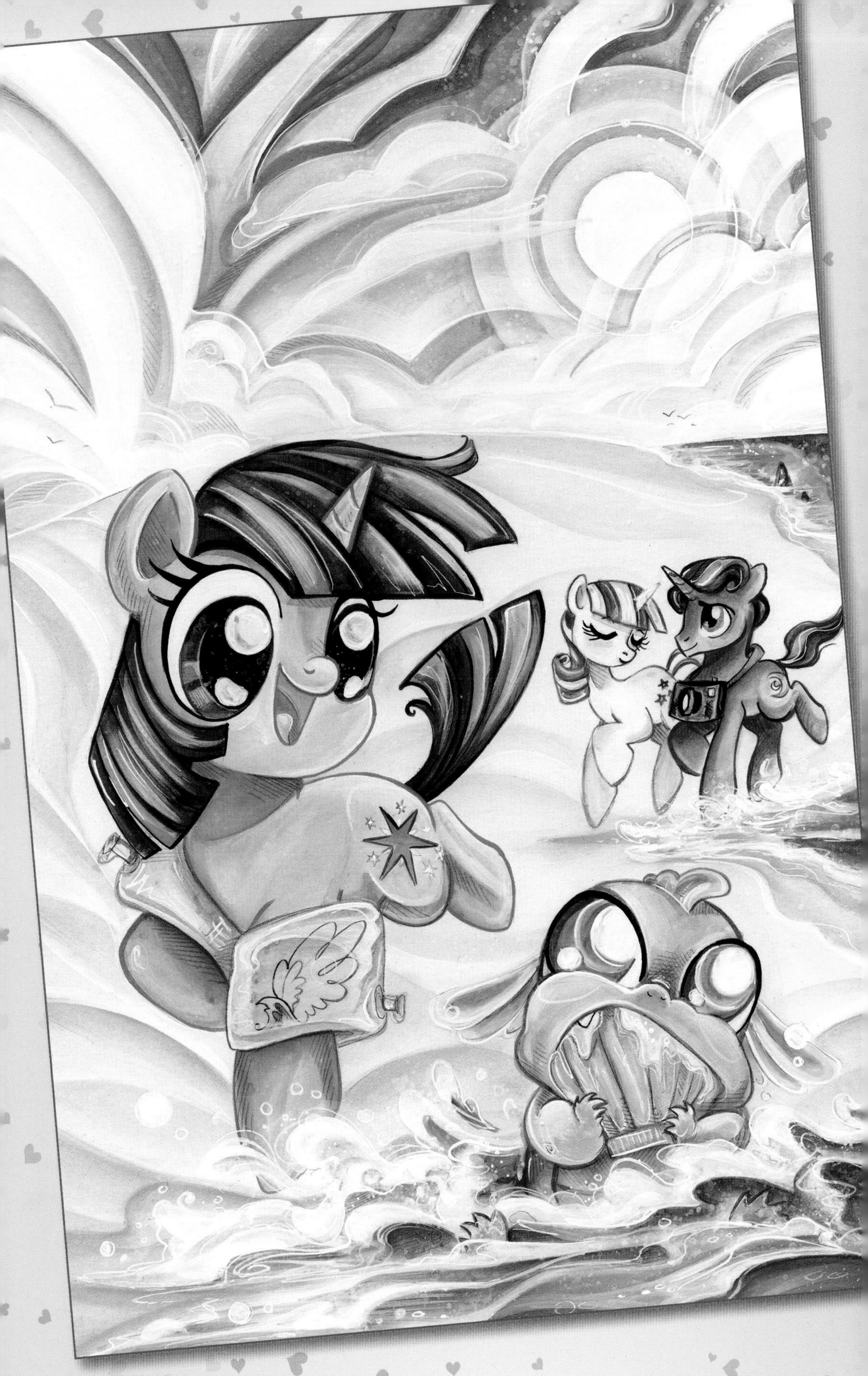

art by Sara Richard

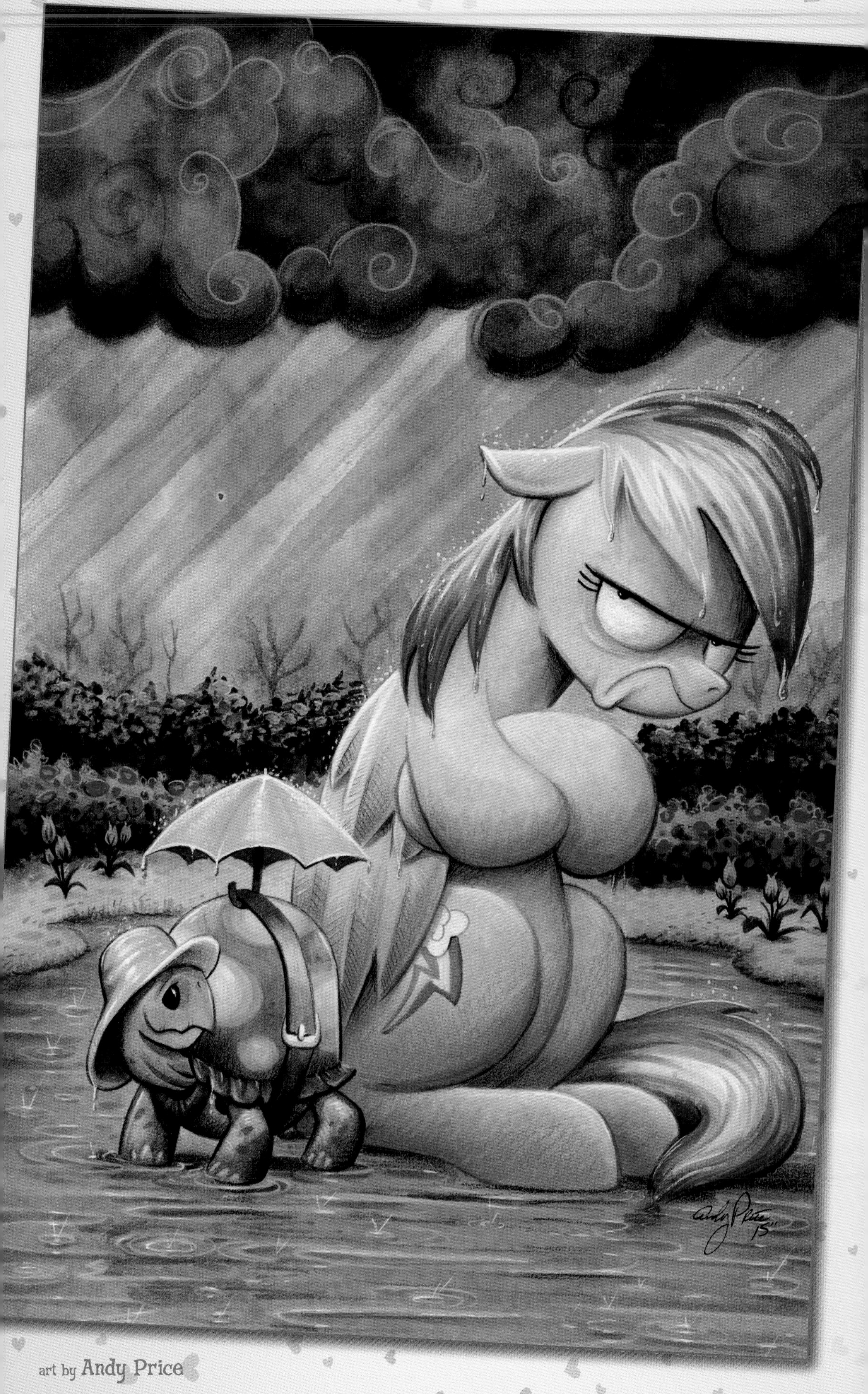

art by Andy Price

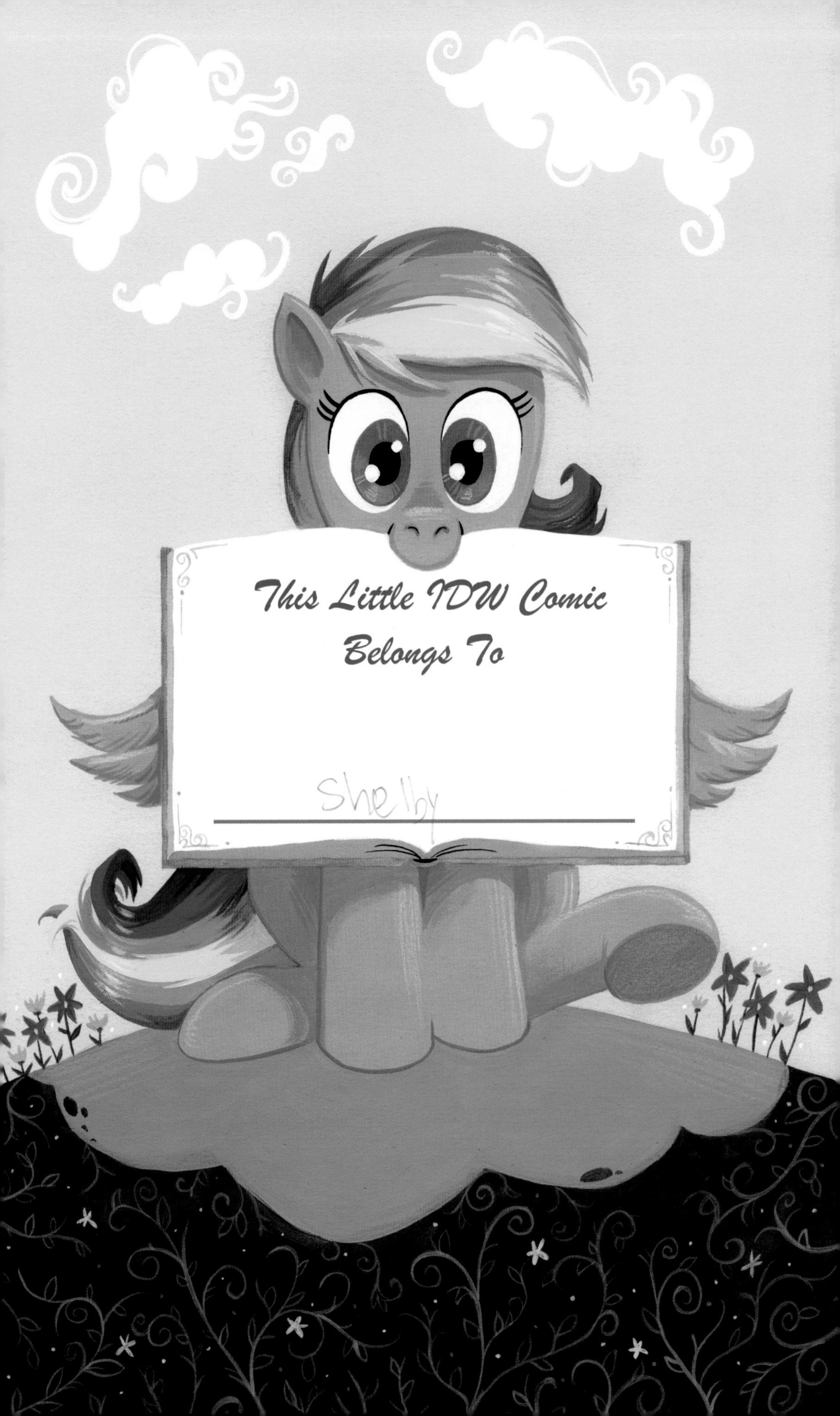
This Little IDW Comic
Belongs To
Shelby

Here in Ponyville the days are bright.
There's always a joy alight.
Ponies are smiling in the day-to-day cheer,
their faces you'll rarely see sneer.

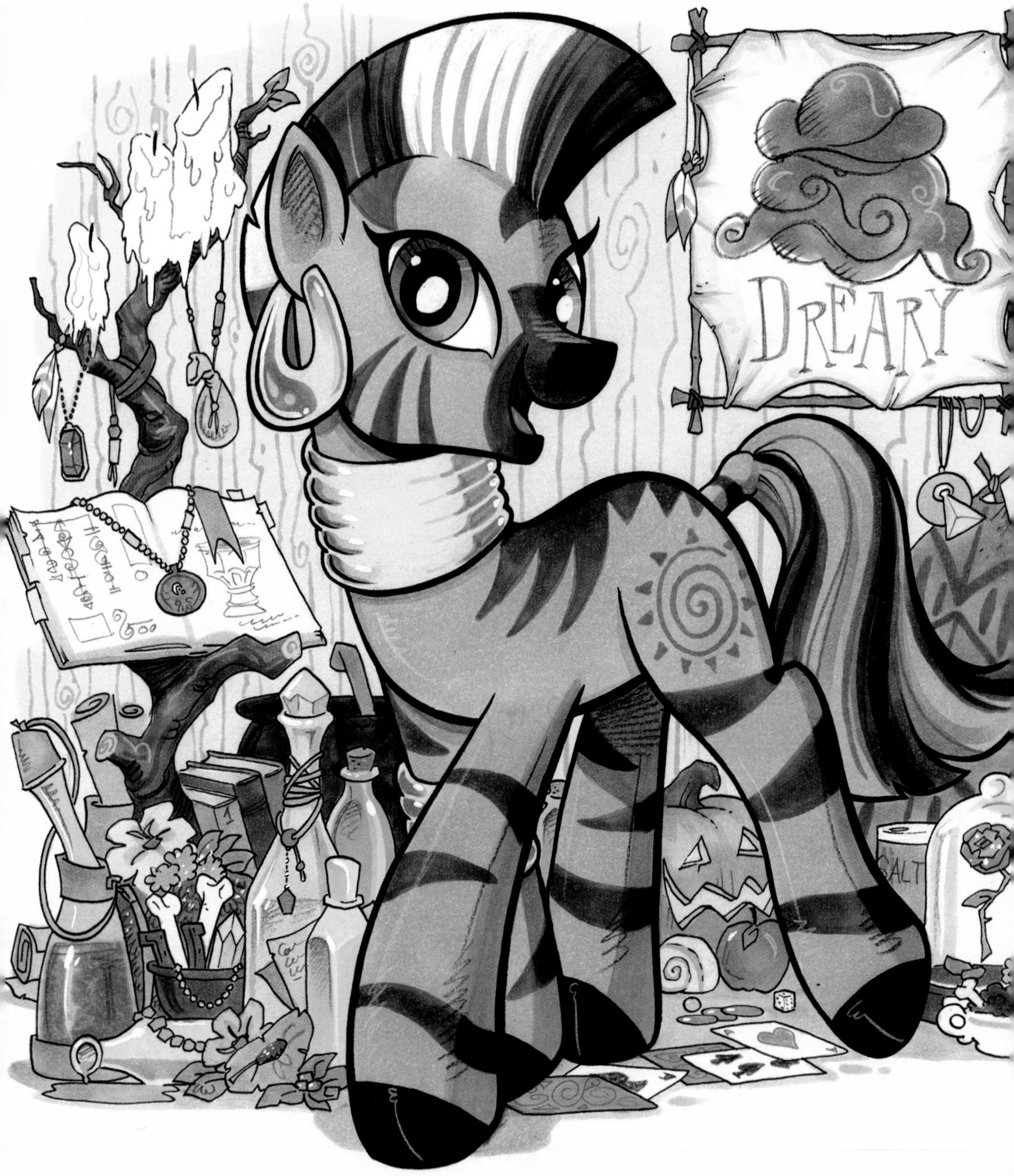
DREARY
SALT

However, my friends, things are not always right,
and when those days come, we must try not to fright.
For those days when the Drearies appear,
we must do our best to stay a good peer.

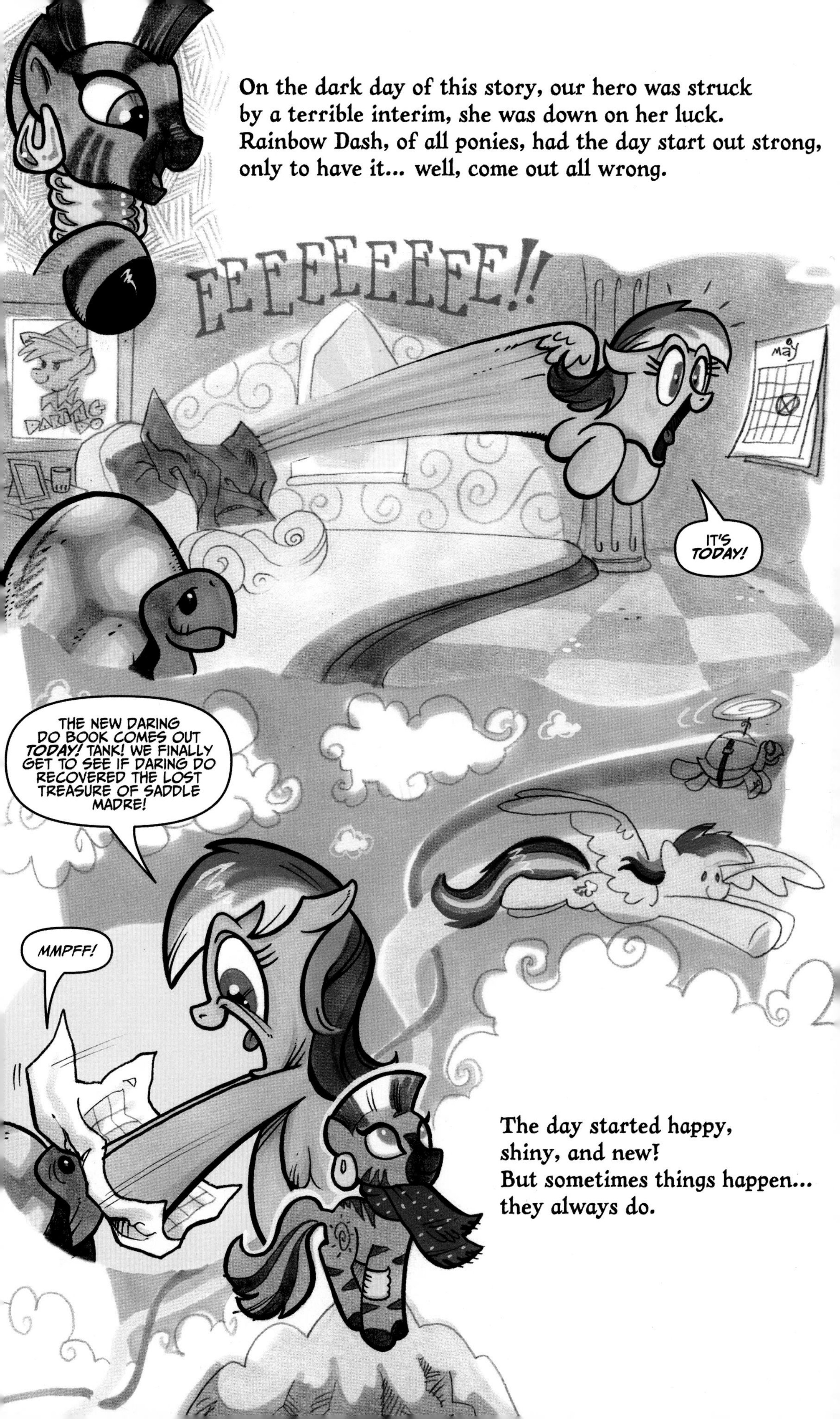
On the dark day of this story, our hero was struck
by a terrible interim, she was down on her luck.
Rainbow Dash, of all ponies, had the day start out strong,
only to have it... well, come out all wrong.
EEEEEEEEE!!
IT'S *TODAY!*
THE NEW DARING DO BOOK COMES OUT *TODAY!* TANK! WE FINALLY GET TO SEE IF DARING DO RECOVERED THE LOST TREASURE OF SADDLE MADRE!
MMPFF!
The day started happy,
shiny, and new!
But sometimes things happen...
they always do.

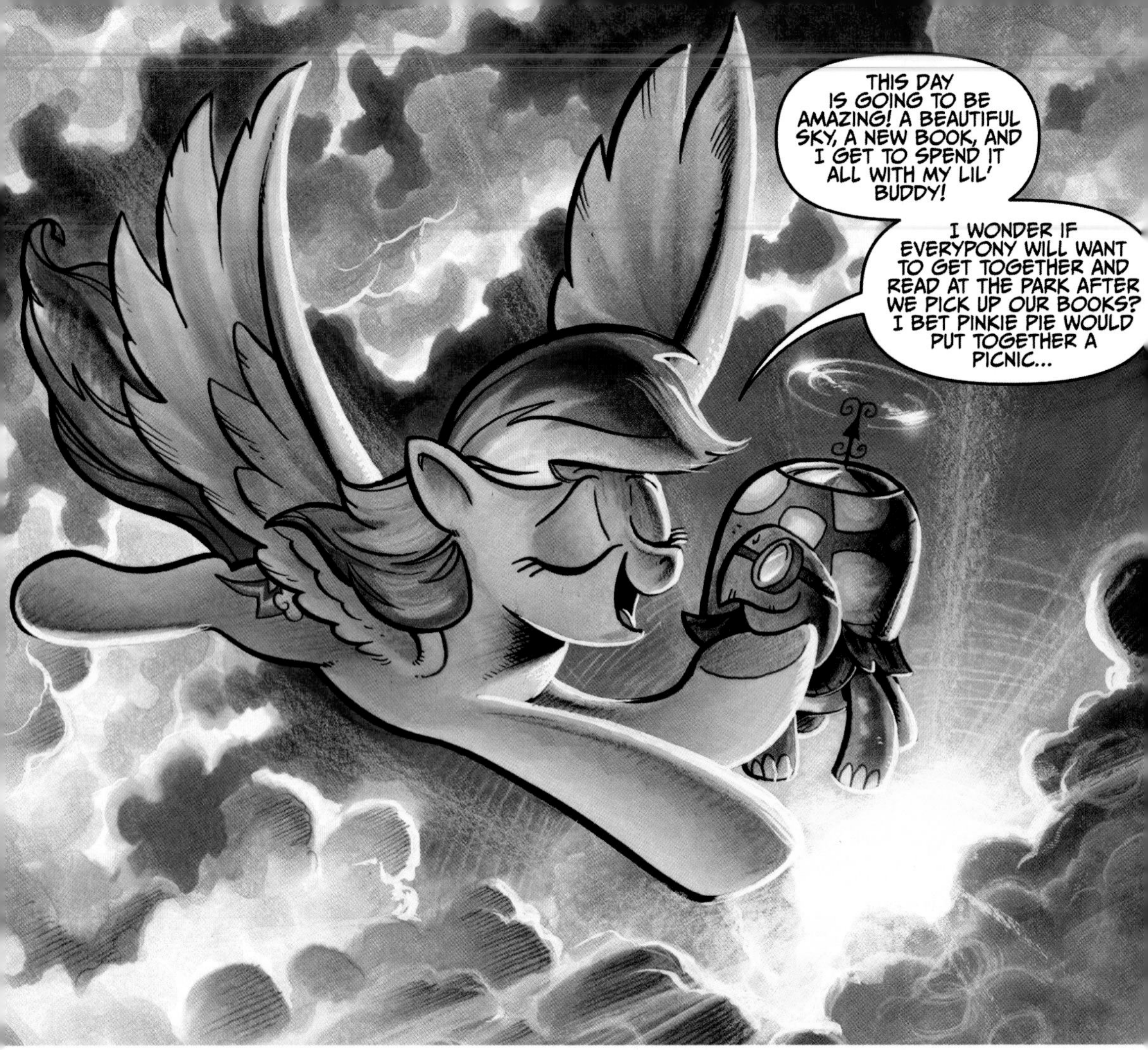
THIS DAY IS GOING TO BE AMAZING! A BEAUTIFUL SKY, A NEW BOOK, AND I GET TO SPEND IT ALL WITH MY LIL' BUDDY!
I WONDER IF EVERYPONY WILL WANT TO GET TOGETHER AND READ AT THE PARK AFTER WE PICK UP OUR BOOKS? I BET PINKIE PIE WOULD PUT TOGETHER A PICNIC...

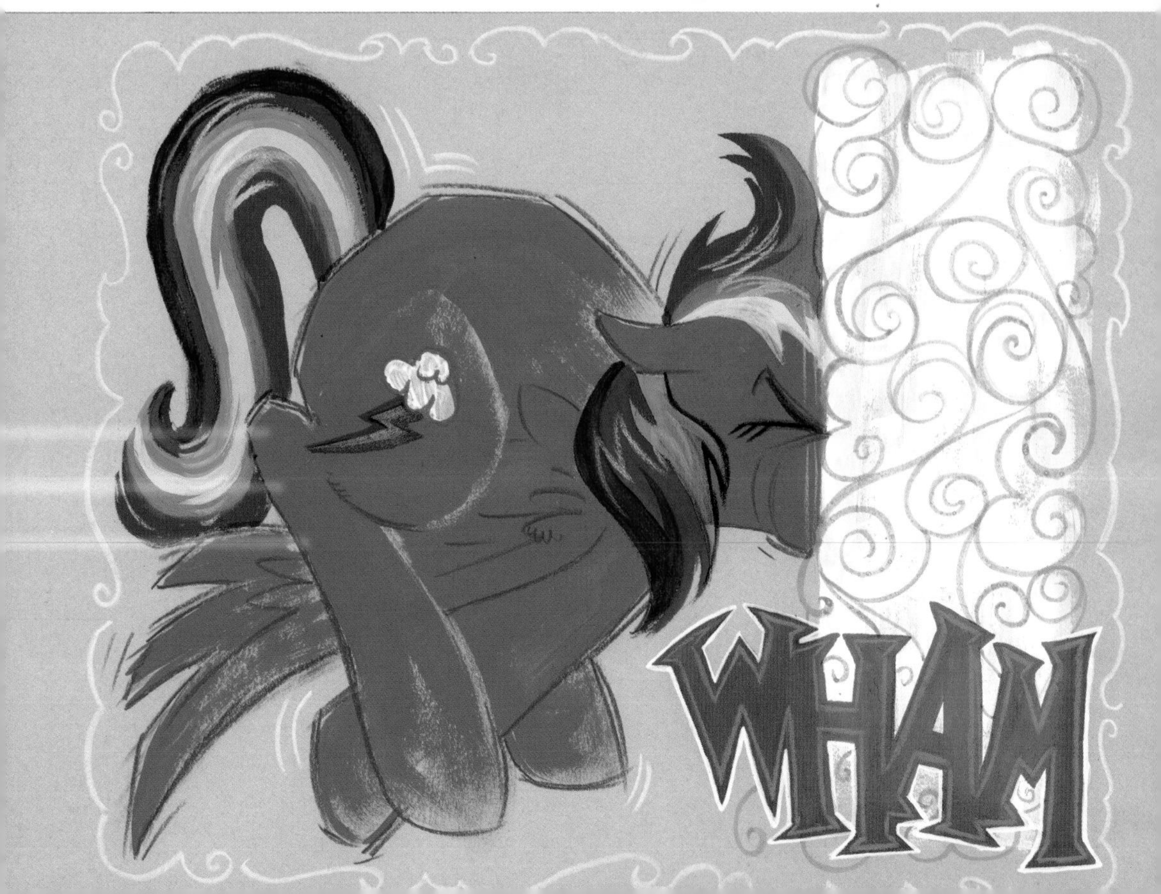
WHAM

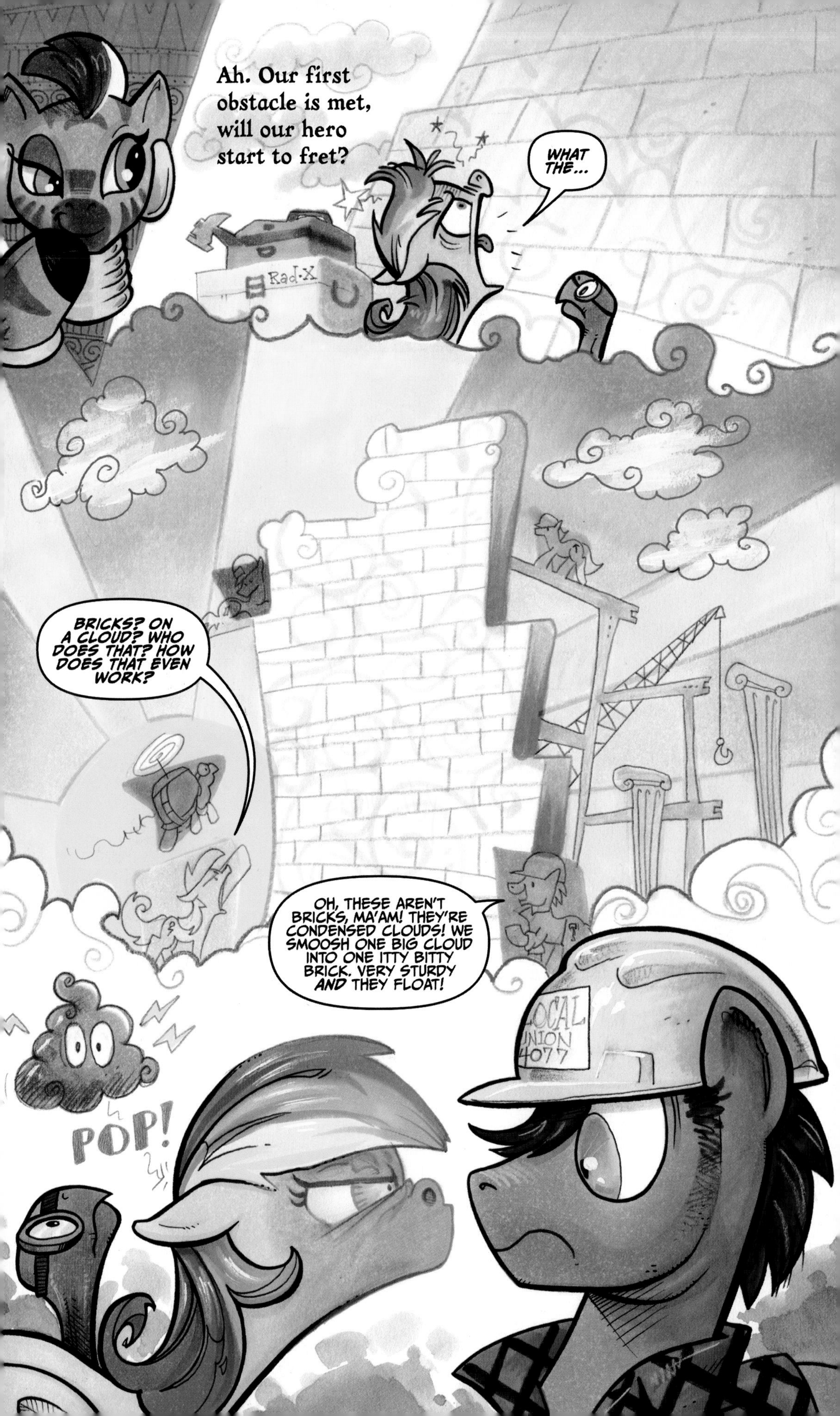
Ah. Our first obstacle is met, will our hero start to fret?
Rad-X
WHAT THE...
BRICKS? ON A CLOUD? WHO DOES THAT? HOW DOES THAT EVEN WORK?
OH, THESE AREN'T BRICKS, MA'AM! THEY'RE CONDENSED CLOUDS! WE SMOOSH ONE BIG CLOUD INTO ONE ITTY BITTY BRICK. VERY STURDY AND THEY FLOAT!
LOCAL UNION 4077
POP!

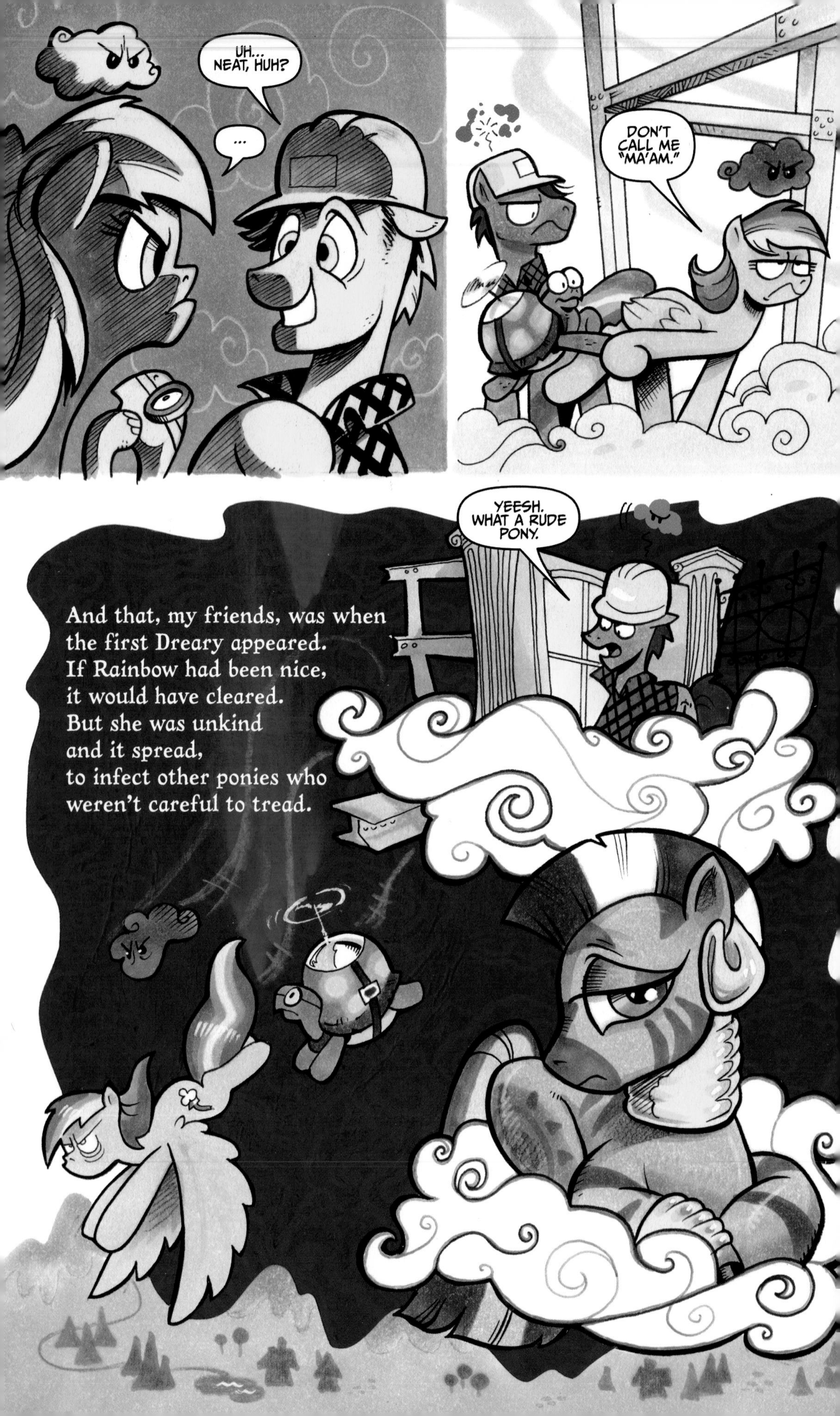
UH... NEAT, HUH?
...
DON'T CALL ME "MA'AM."
YEESH. WHAT A RUDE PONY.
And that, my friends, was when
the first Dreary appeared.
If Rainbow had been nice,
it would have cleared.
But she was unkind
and it spread,
to infect other ponies who
weren't careful to tread.

The Drearies will roll upon us all in a wave,
unless certain ponies begin to behave.
If we all remain kindhearted, friendly, and true...
then heads will clear up and moods not stay blue.

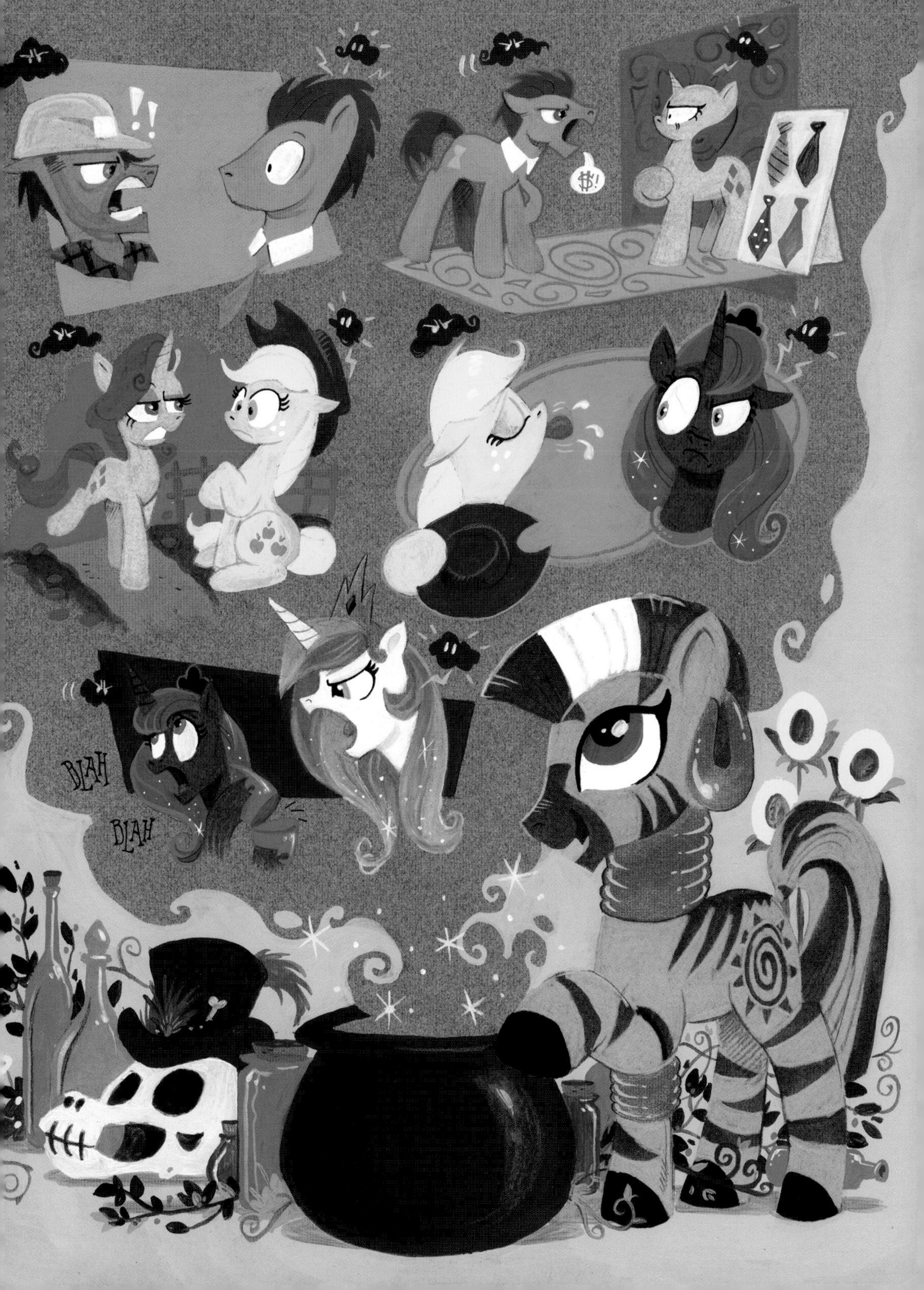
$!
BLAH
BLAH

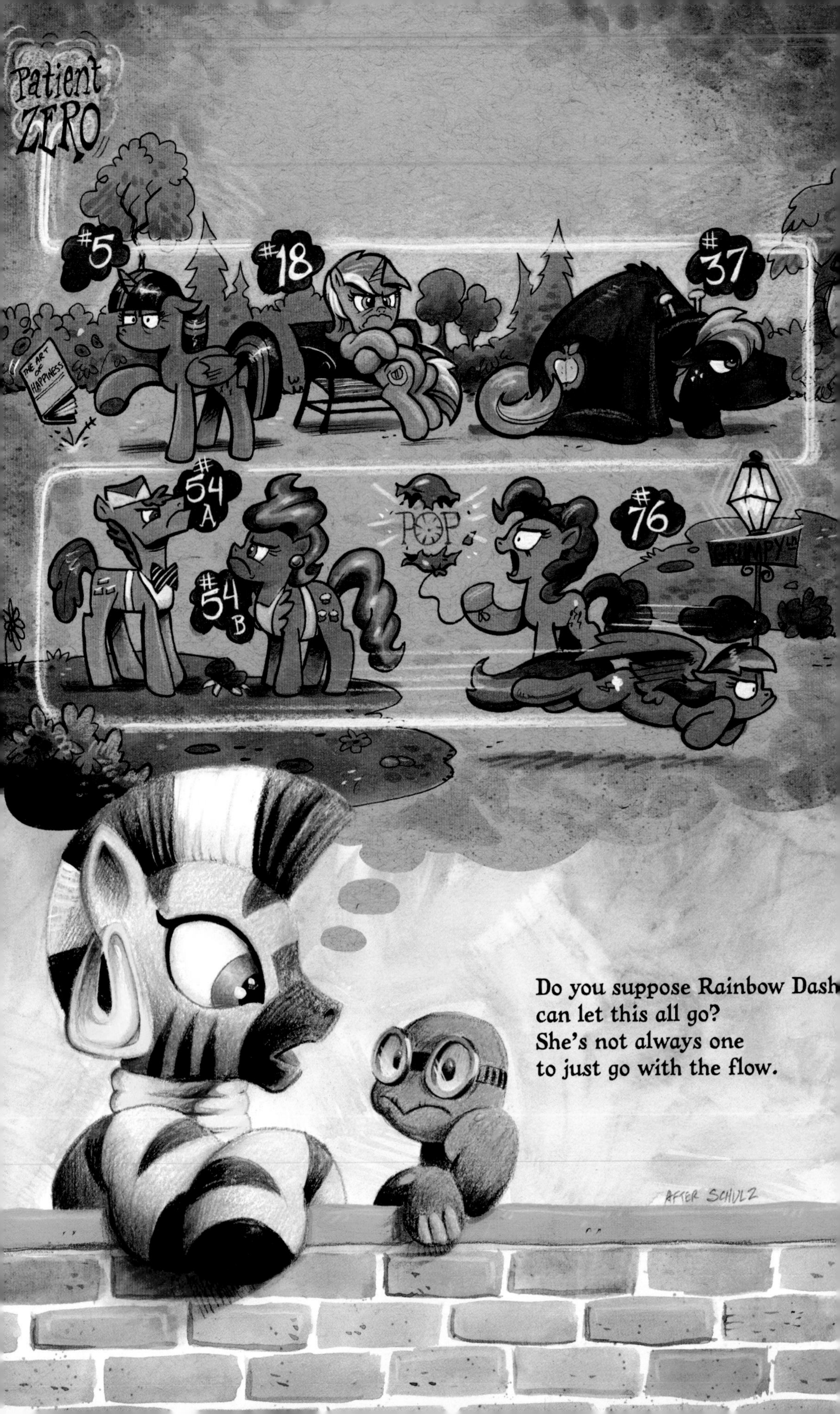
Patient ZERO
#5
THE ART OF HAPPINESS
#18
#37
#54 A
#54 B
POP
#76
GRUMPY LN
AFTER SCHULZ

Do you suppose Rainbow Dash
can let this all go?
She's not always one
to just go with the flow.

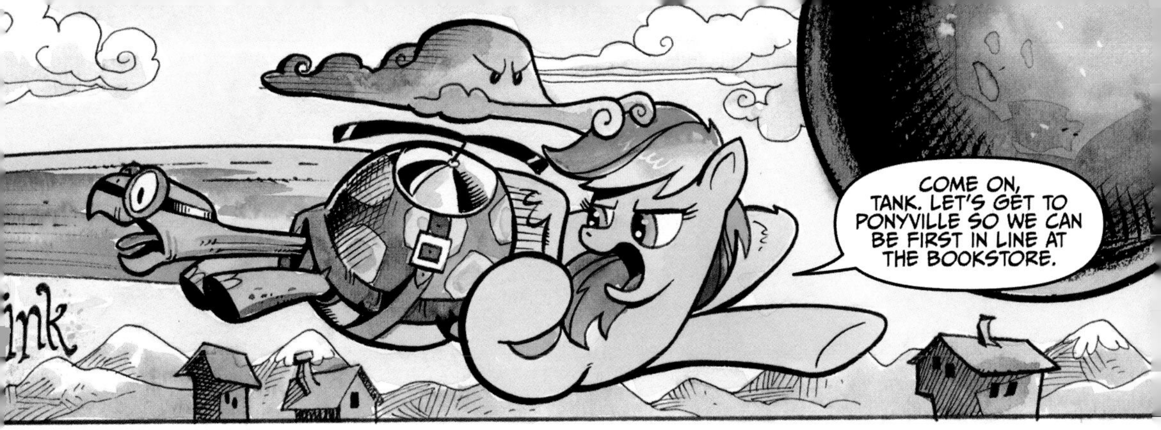
ink
COME ON, TANK. LET'S GET TO PONYVILLE SO WE CAN BE FIRST IN LINE AT THE BOOKSTORE.

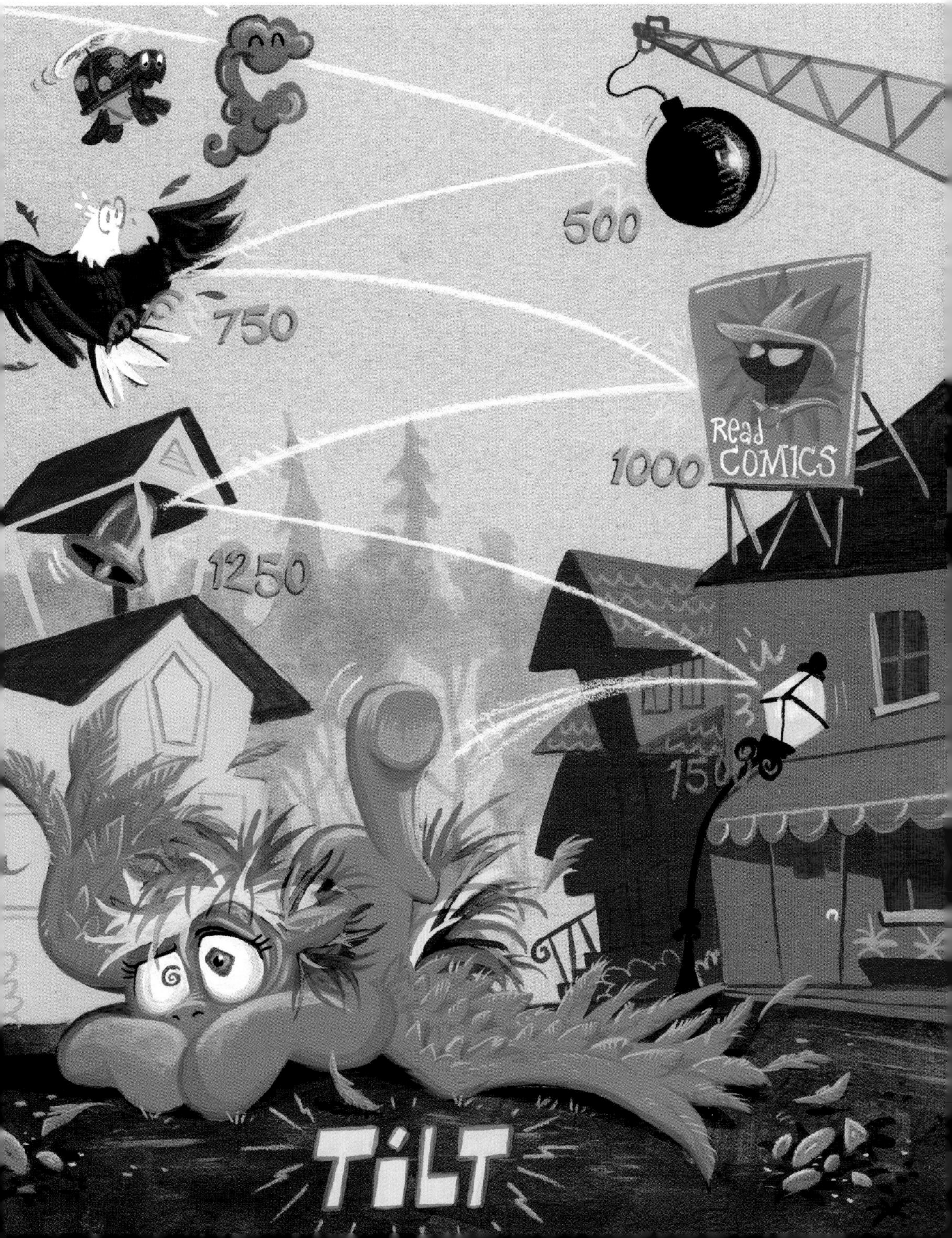
500
750
Read COMICS
1000
1250
TiLT

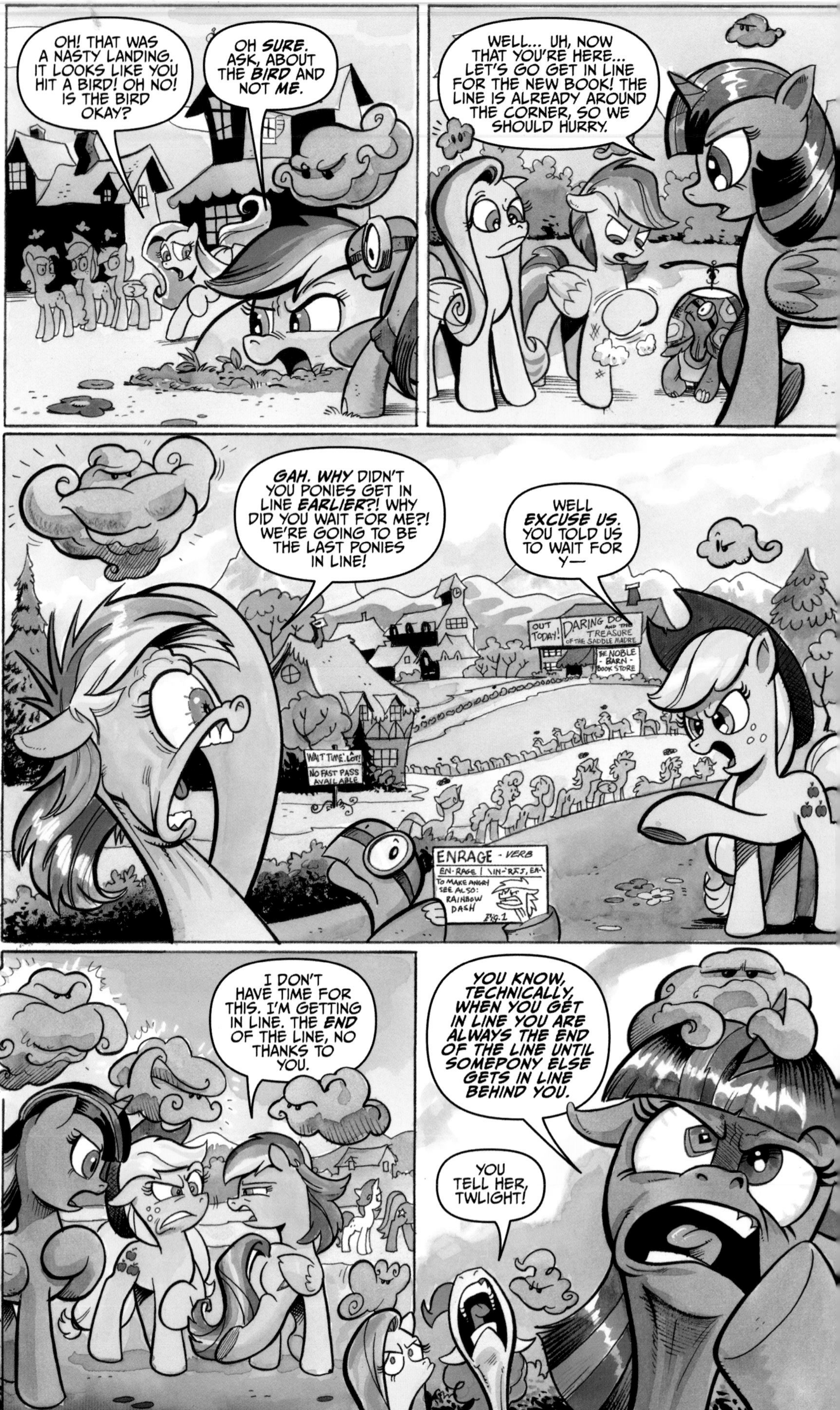

OH! THAT WAS A NASTY LANDING. IT LOOKS LIKE YOU HIT A BIRD! OH NO! IS THE BIRD OKAY?
OH SURE. ASK, ABOUT THE BIRD AND NOT ME.
WELL... UH, NOW THAT YOU'RE HERE... LET'S GO GET IN LINE FOR THE NEW BOOK! THE LINE IS ALREADY AROUND THE CORNER, SO WE SHOULD HURRY.
GAH. WHY DIDN'T YOU PONIES GET IN LINE EARLIER?! WHY DID YOU WAIT FOR ME?! WE'RE GOING TO BE THE LAST PONIES IN LINE!
WELL EXCUSE US. YOU TOLD US TO WAIT FOR Y—
OUT TODAY!
DARING DO AND THE TREASURE OF THE SADDLE MADRE
THE NOBLE BARN BOOK STORE
WAIT TIME: A LOT!
NO FAST PASS AVAILABLE
ENRAGE - VERB
TO MAKE ANGRY
SEE ALSO: RAINBOW DASH
I DON'T HAVE TIME FOR THIS. I'M GETTING IN LINE. THE END OF THE LINE, NO THANKS TO YOU.
YOU KNOW, TECHNICALLY, WHEN YOU GET IN LINE YOU ARE ALWAYS THE END OF THE LINE UNTIL SOMEPONY ELSE GETS IN LINE BEHIND YOU.
YOU TELL HER, TWLIGHT!

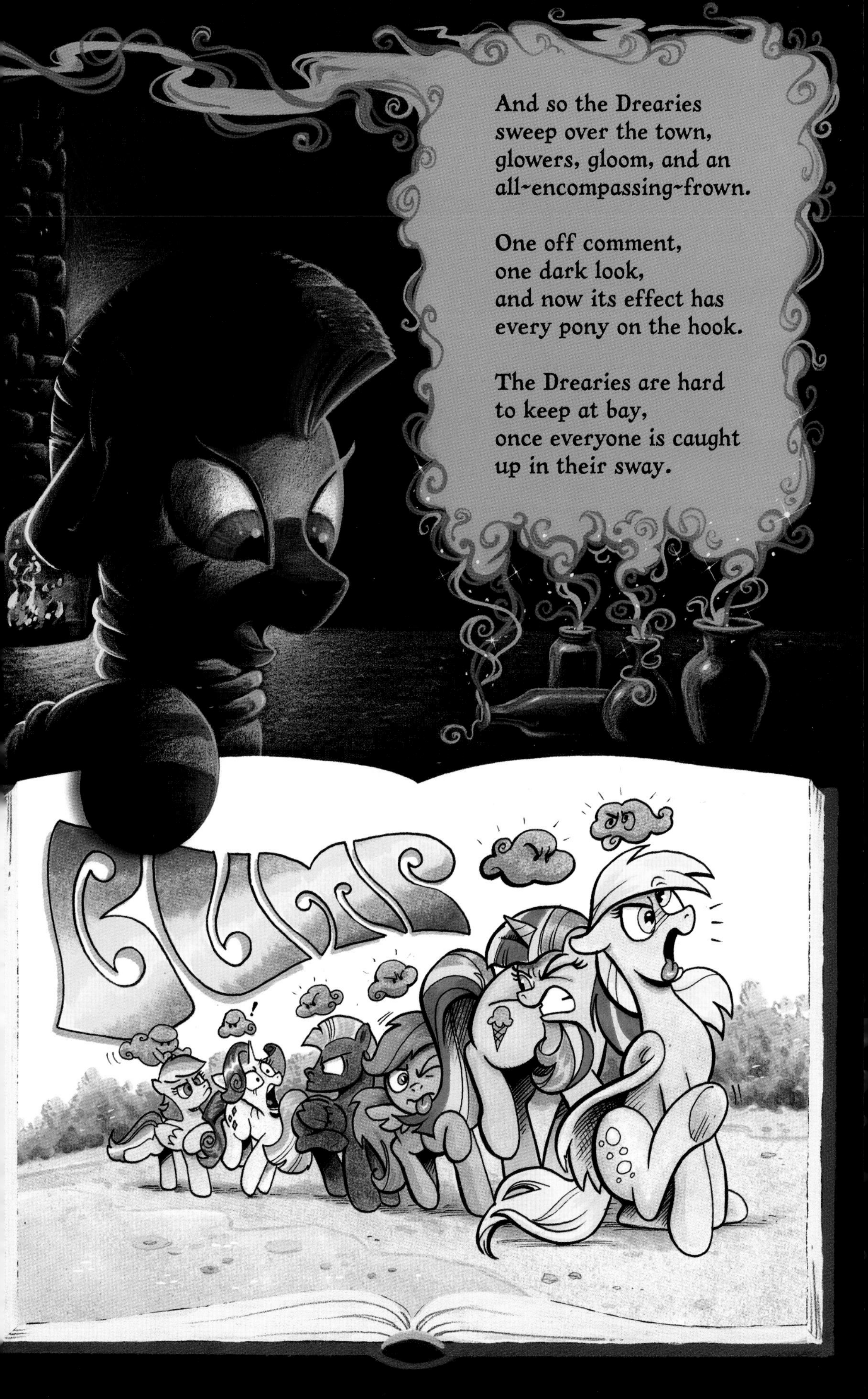
And so the Drearies
sweep over the town,
glowers, gloom, and an
all~encompassing~frown.

One off comment,
one dark look,
and now its effect has
every pony on the hook.

The Drearies are hard
to keep at bay,
once everyone is caught
up in their sway.

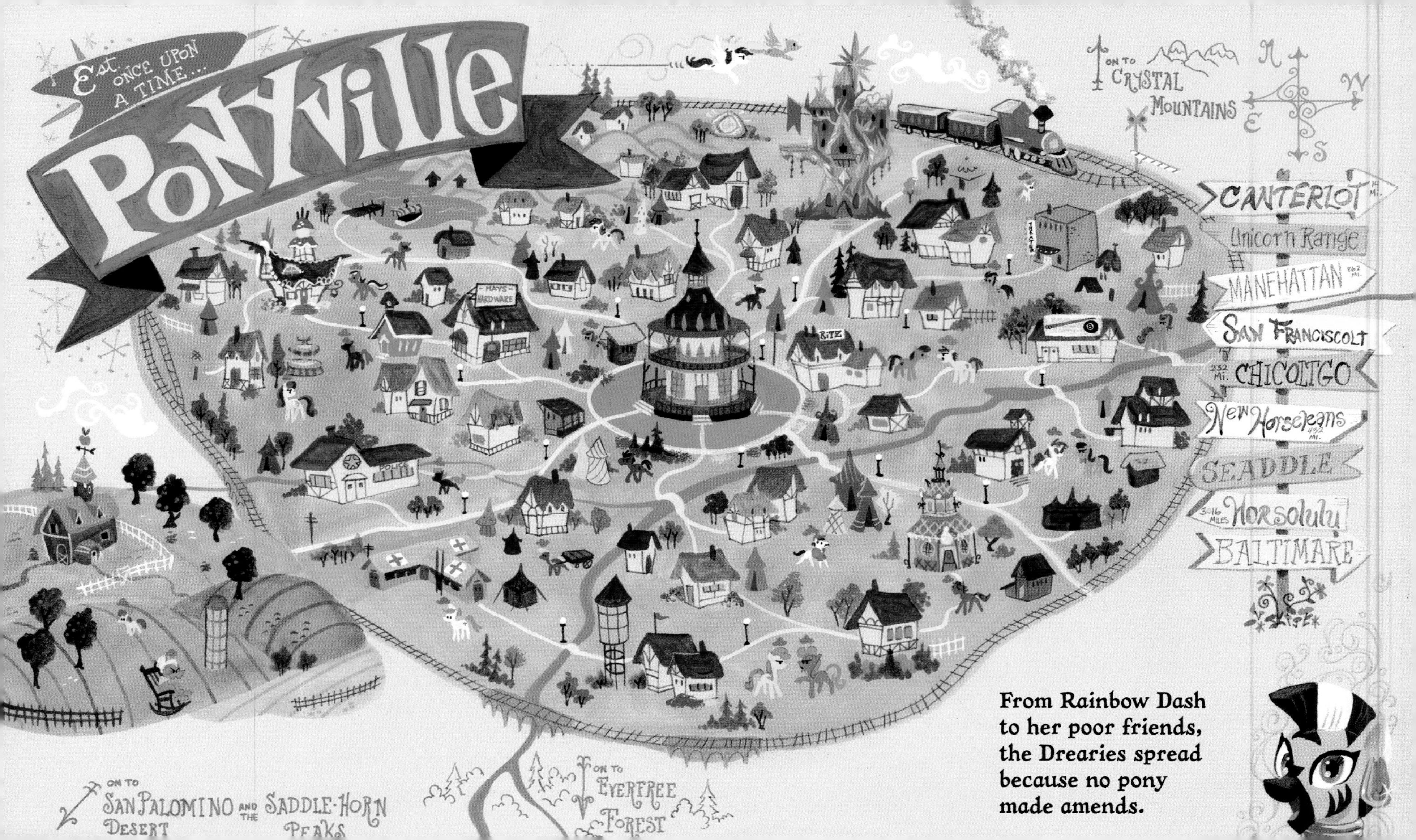
Est. ONCE UPON A TIME...
PONYVILLE
ON TO CRYSTAL MOUNTAINS
N
W
E
S
CANTERLOT 14 MI.
Unicorn Range
MANEHATTAN 862 MI.
SAN FRANCISCOLT
232 MI. CHICOLTGO
New Horseleans 432 MI.
SEADDLE
3016 MILES Horsolulu
BALTIMARE
THEATER
MAYS HARDWARE
RITZ
POLICE
ON TO SAN PALOMINO DESERT AND THE SADDLE-HORN PEAKS
ON TO EVERFREE FOREST

From Rainbow Dash
to her poor friends,
the Drearies spread
because no pony
made amends.

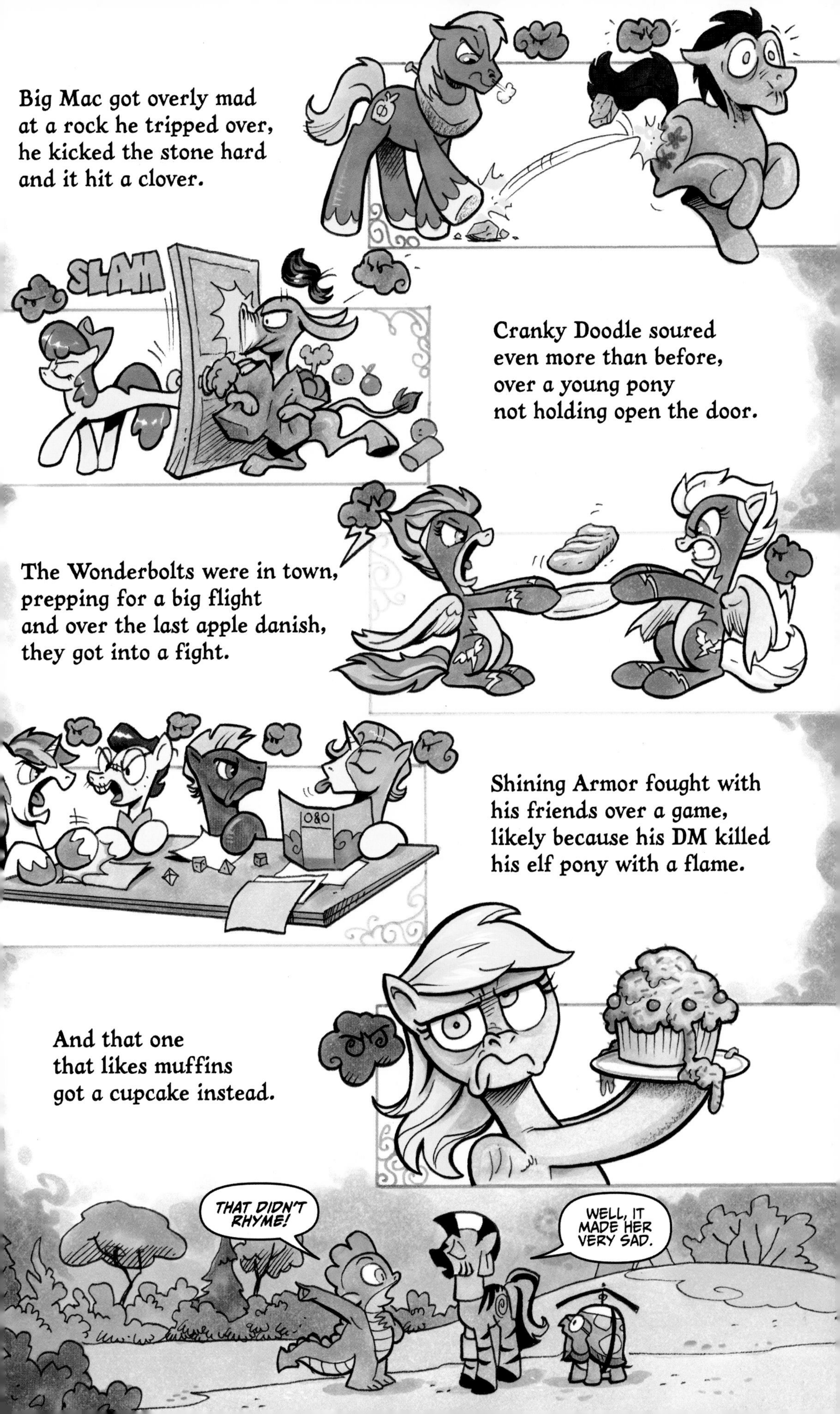
Big Mac got overly mad
at a rock he tripped over,
he kicked the stone hard
and it hit a clover.
SLAM
Cranky Doodle soured
even more than before,
over a young pony
not holding open the door.
The Wonderbolts were in town,
prepping for a big flight
and over the last apple danish,
they got into a fight.
Shining Armor fought with
his friends over a game,
likely because his DM killed
his elf pony with a flame.
And that one
that likes muffins
got a cupcake instead.
THAT DIDN'T RHYME!
WELL, IT MADE HER VERY SAD.

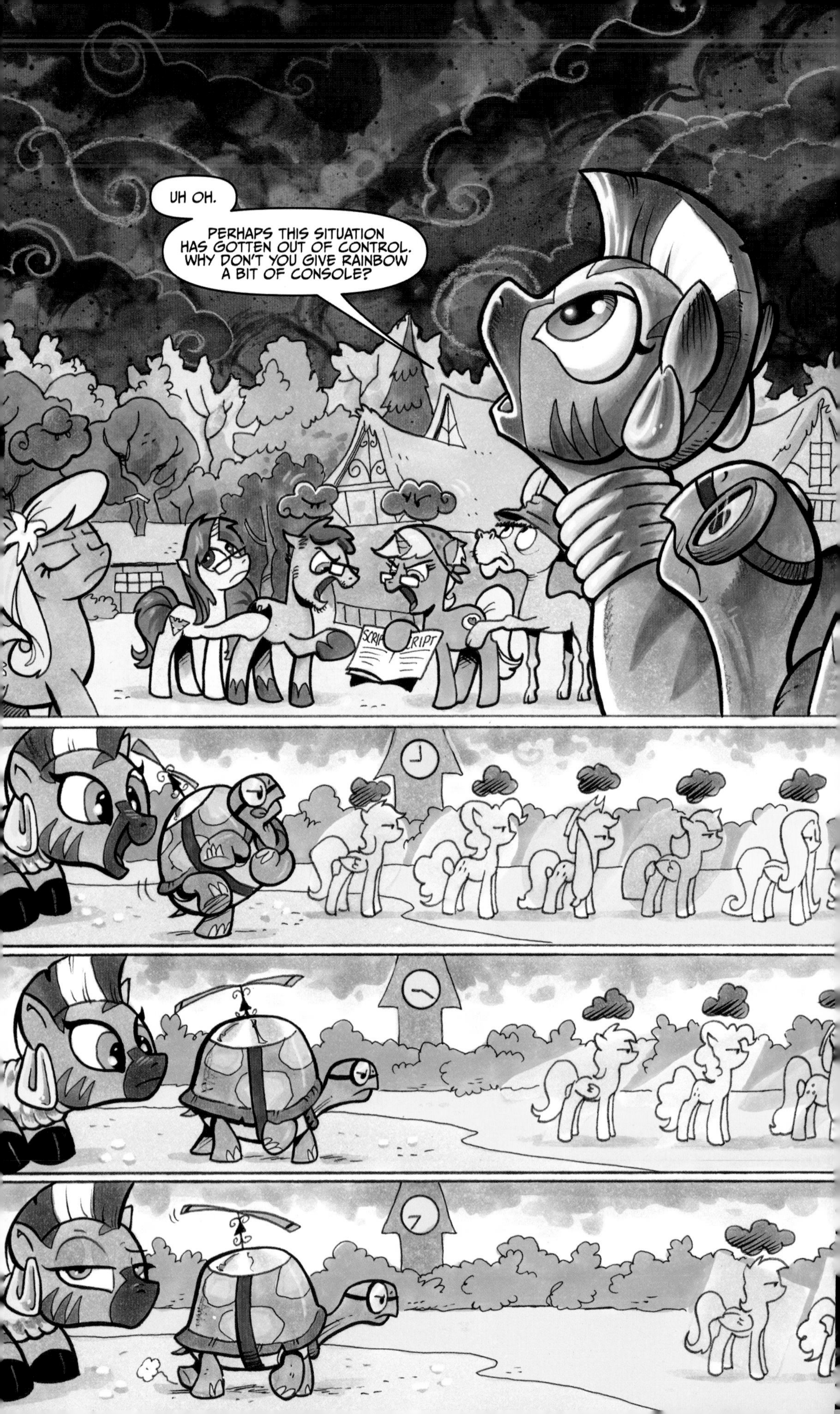
UH OH.
PERHAPS THIS SITUATION HAS GOTTEN OUT OF CONTROL. WHY DON'T YOU GIVE RAINBOW A BIT OF CONSOLE?
SCRIPT
SCRIPT

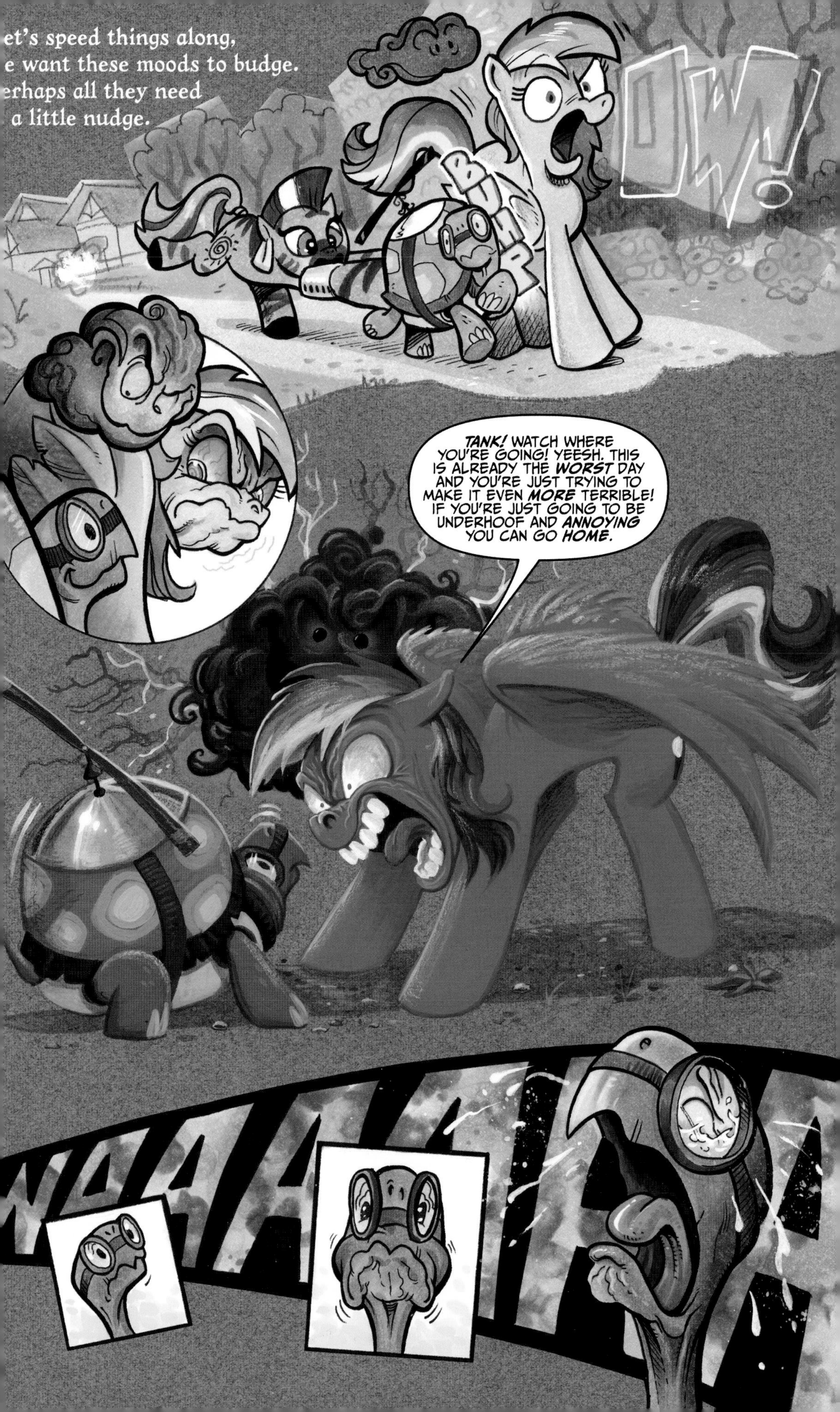
et's speed things along,
e want these moods to budge.
erhaps all they need
a little nudge.
BUMP
OW!
TANK! WATCH WHERE YOU'RE GOING! YEESH. THIS IS ALREADY THE WORST DAY AND YOU'RE JUST TRYING TO MAKE IT EVEN MORE TERRIBLE! IF YOU'RE JUST GOING TO BE UNDERHOOF AND ANNOYING YOU CAN GO HOME.

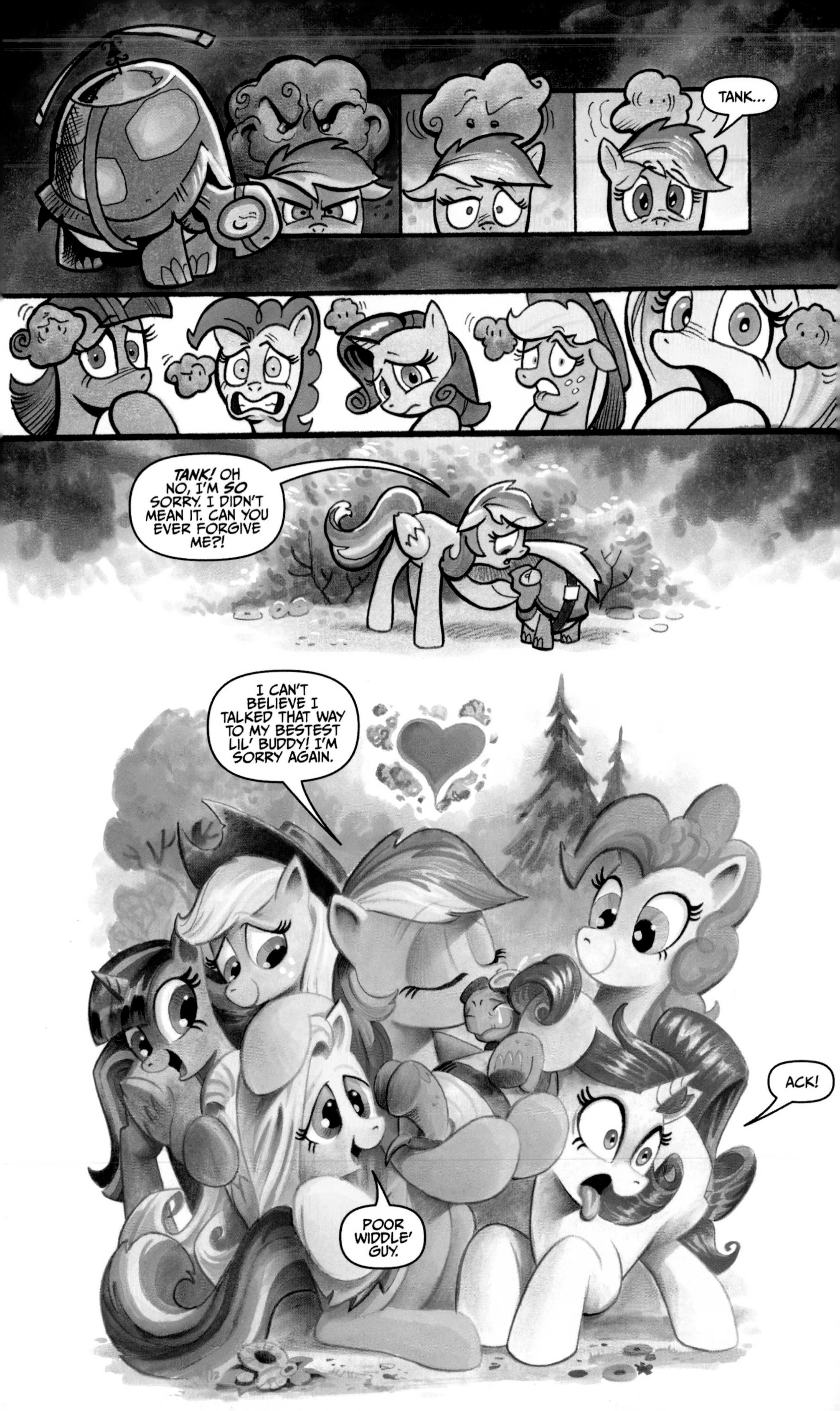
TANK...
TANK! OH NO, I'M SO SORRY. I DIDN'T MEAN IT. CAN YOU EVER FORGIVE ME?!
I CAN'T BELIEVE I TALKED THAT WAY TO MY BESTEST LIL' BUDDY! I'M SORRY AGAIN.
ACK!
POOR WIDDLE' GUY.

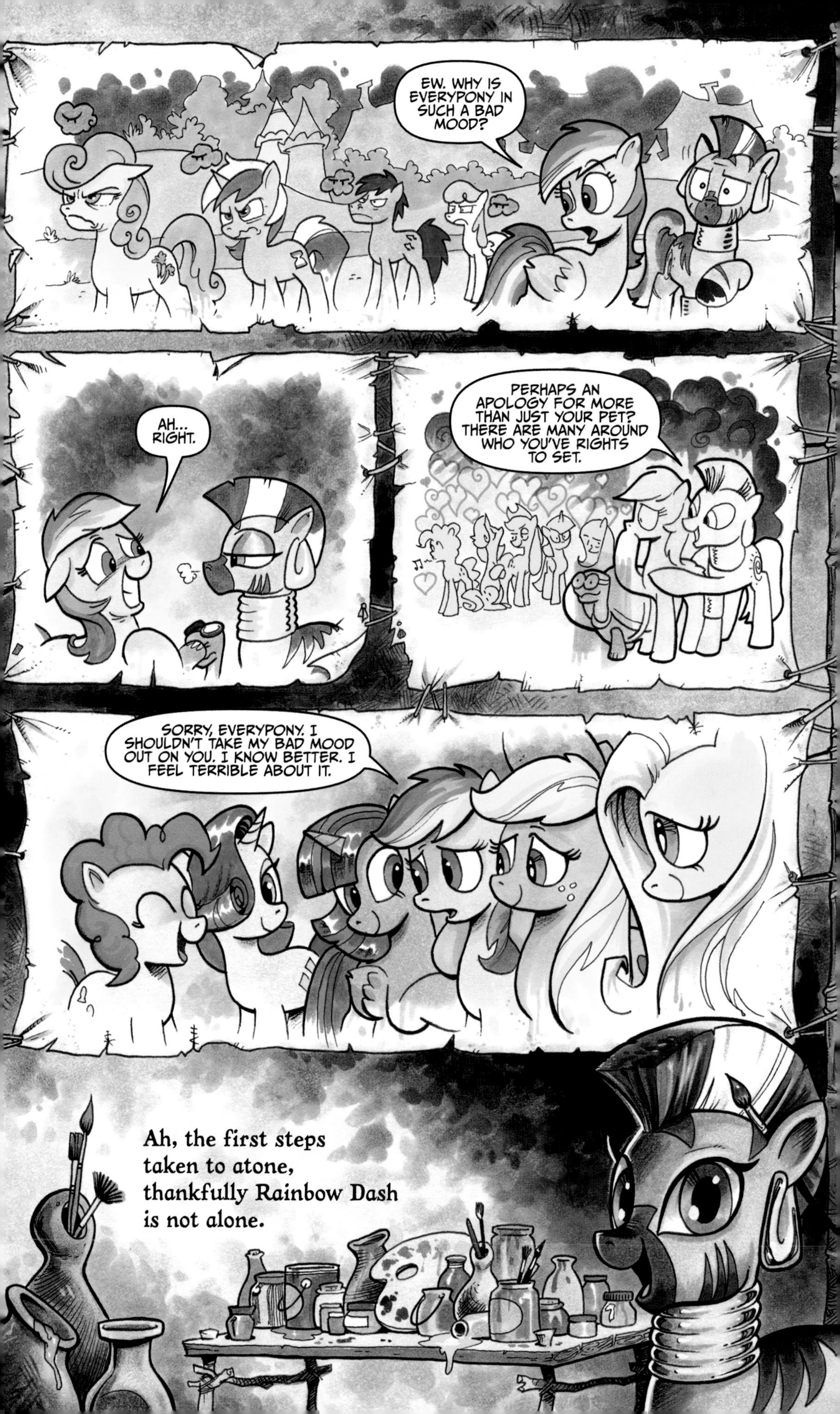
EW. WHY IS EVERYPONY IN SUCH A BAD MOOD?
AH... RIGHT.
PERHAPS AN APOLOGY FOR MORE THAN JUST YOUR PET? THERE ARE MANY AROUND WHO YOU'VE RIGHTS TO SET.
SORRY, EVERYPONY. I SHOULDN'T TAKE MY BAD MOOD OUT ON YOU. I KNOW BETTER. I FEEL TERRIBLE ABOUT IT.
Ah, the first steps taken to atone, thankfully Rainbow Dash is not alone.

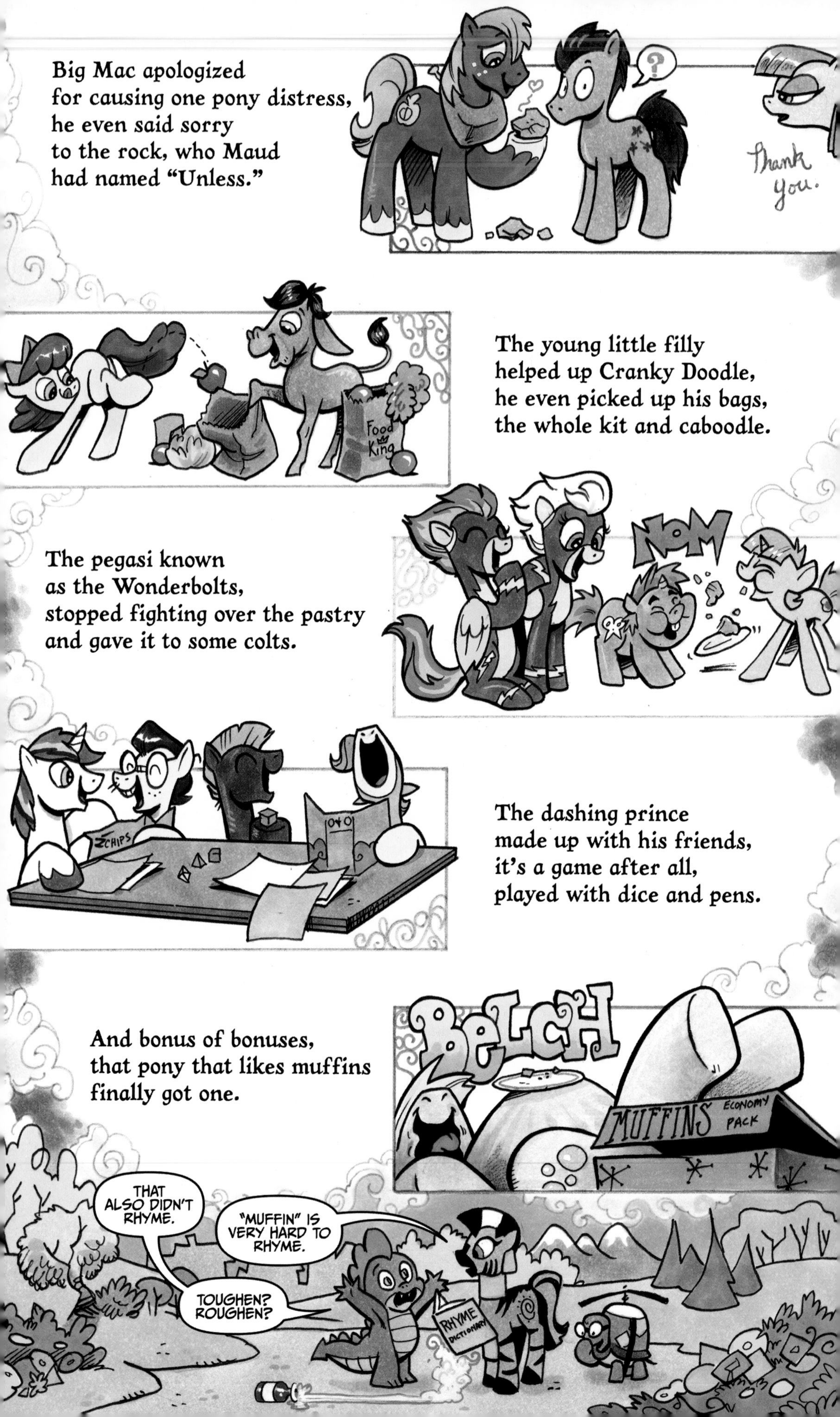
Big Mac apologized
for causing one pony distress,
he even said sorry
to the rock, who Maud
had named "Unless."
?
Thank you.
The young little filly
helped up Cranky Doodle,
he even picked up his bags,
the whole kit and caboodle.
Food King
The pegasi known
as the Wonderbolts,
stopped fighting over the pastry
and gave it to some colts.
NOM
CHIPS
The dashing prince
made up with his friends,
it's a game after all,
played with dice and pens.
And bonus of bonuses,
that pony that likes muffins
finally got one.
BELCH
MUFFINS
ECONOMY PACK
THAT ALSO DIDN'T RHYME.
"MUFFIN" IS VERY HARD TO RHYME.
TOUGHEN? ROUGHEN?
RHYME DICTIONARY

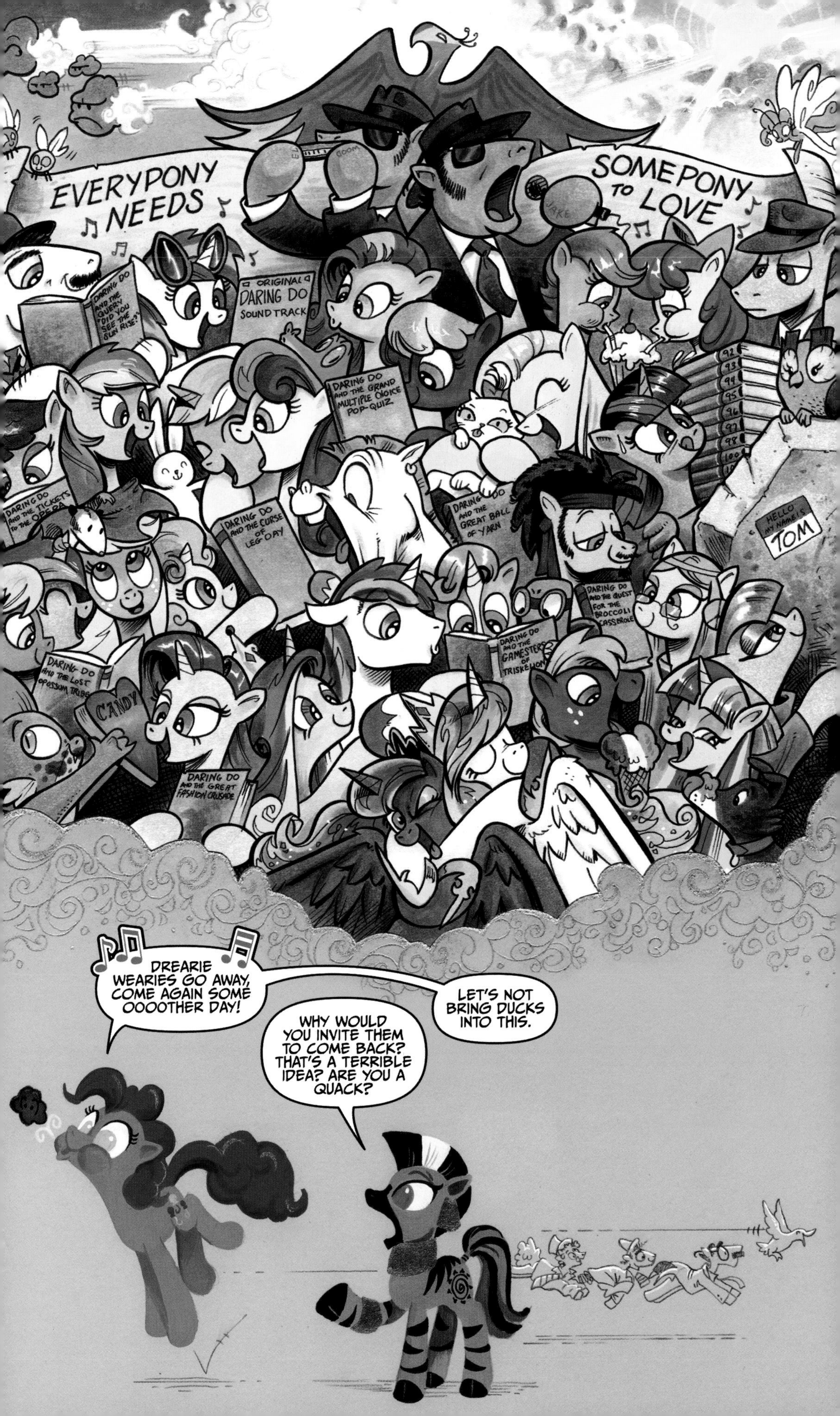
EVERYPONY NEEDS
SOMEPONY TO LOVE
ORIGINAL DARING DO SOUNDTRACK
DARING DO AND THE QUERY "DID YOU SEE THE SUN RISE?"
DARING DO AND THE GRAND MULTIPLE CHOICE POP-QUIZ
DARING DO AND THE TICKETS TO THE OPERA
DARING DO AND THE CURSE OF LEG-DAY
DARING DO AND THE GREAT BALL OF YARN
HELLO MY NAME IS TOM
DARING DO AND THE QUEST FOR THE BROCCOLI CASSEROLE
DARING DO AND THE GAMESTERS OF TRISKELION
DARING DO AND THE LOST OPOSSUM TRIBE
CANDY
DARING DO AND THE GREAT FASHION CRUSADE
DREARIE WEARIES GO AWAY, COME AGAIN SOME OOOOTHER DAY!
LET'S NOT BRING DUCKS INTO THIS.
WHY WOULD YOU INVITE THEM TO COME BACK? THAT'S A TERRIBLE IDEA? ARE YOU A QUACK?

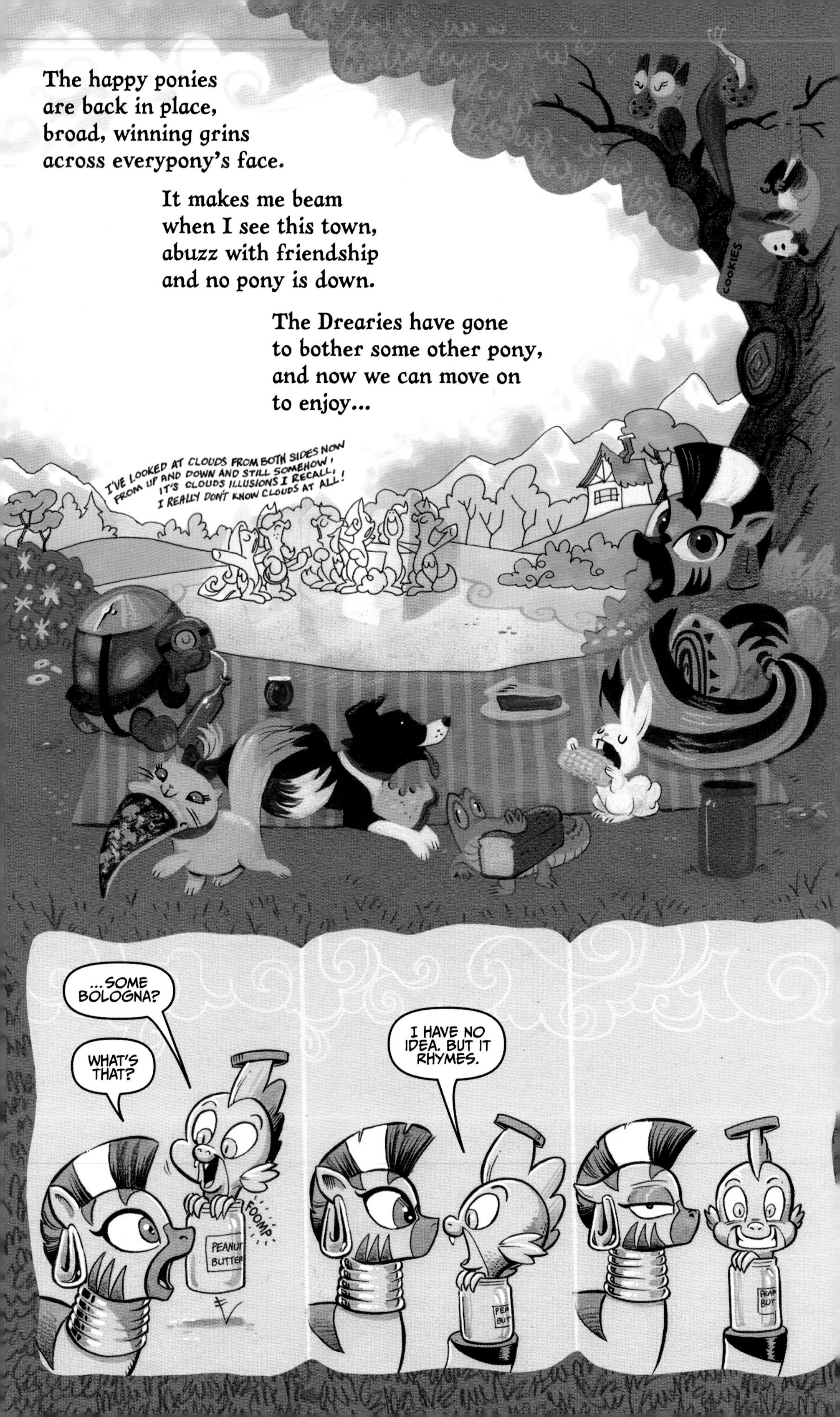
The happy ponies
are back in place,
broad, winning grins
across everypony's face.
It makes me beam
when I see this town,
abuzz with friendship
and no pony is down.
The Drearies have gone
to bother some other pony,
and now we can move on
to enjoy...
I'VE LOOKED AT CLOUDS FROM BOTH SIDES NOW
FROM UP AND DOWN AND STILL SOMEHOW,
IT'S CLOUDS ILLUSIONS I RECALL,
I REALLY DON'T KNOW CLOUDS AT ALL!
COOKIES
...SOME BOLOGNA?
WHAT'S THAT?
FOOMP
PEANUT BUTTER
I HAVE NO IDEA. BUT IT RHYMES.

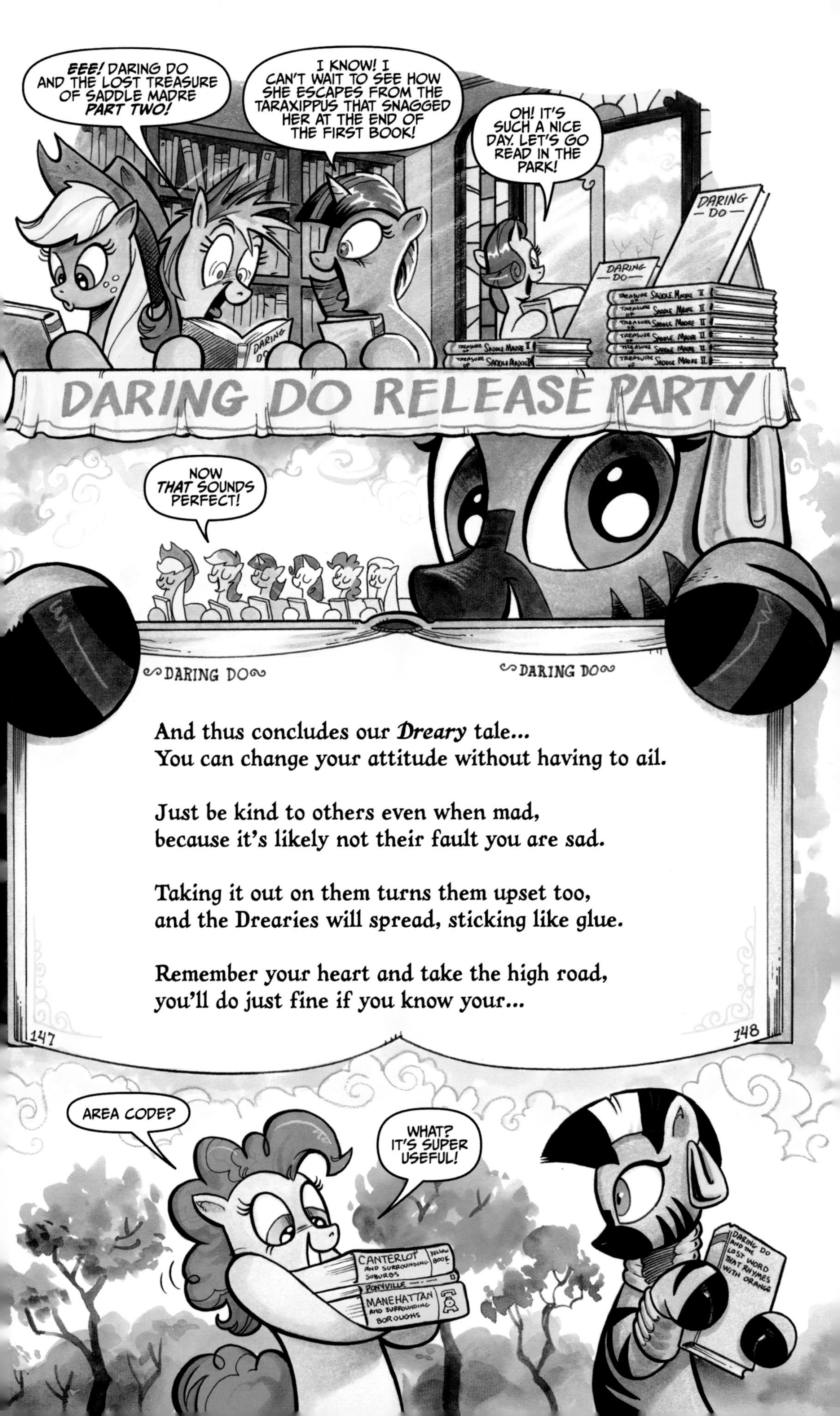
EEE! DARING DO AND THE LOST TREASURE OF SADDLE MADRE PART TWO!
I KNOW! I CAN'T WAIT TO SEE HOW SHE ESCAPES FROM THE TARAXIPPUS THAT SNAGGED HER AT THE END OF THE FIRST BOOK!
OH! IT'S SUCH A NICE DAY. LET'S GO READ IN THE PARK!
DARING DO
DARING DO
DARING DO RELEASE PARTY
NOW THAT SOUNDS PERFECT!
DARING DO
DARING DO
And thus concludes our Dreary tale...
You can change your attitude without having to ail.
Just be kind to others even when mad,
because it's likely not their fault you are sad.
Taking it out on them turns them upset too,
and the Drearies will spread, sticking like glue.
Remember your heart and take the high road,
you'll do just fine if you know your...
147
148
AREA CODE?
WHAT? IT'S SUPER USEFUL!
CANTERLOT AND SURROUNDING SUBURBS
YELLOW BOOK
PONYVILLE
MANEHATTAN AND SURROUNDING BOROUGHS
DARING DO AND THE LOST WORD THAT RHYMES WITH ORANGE

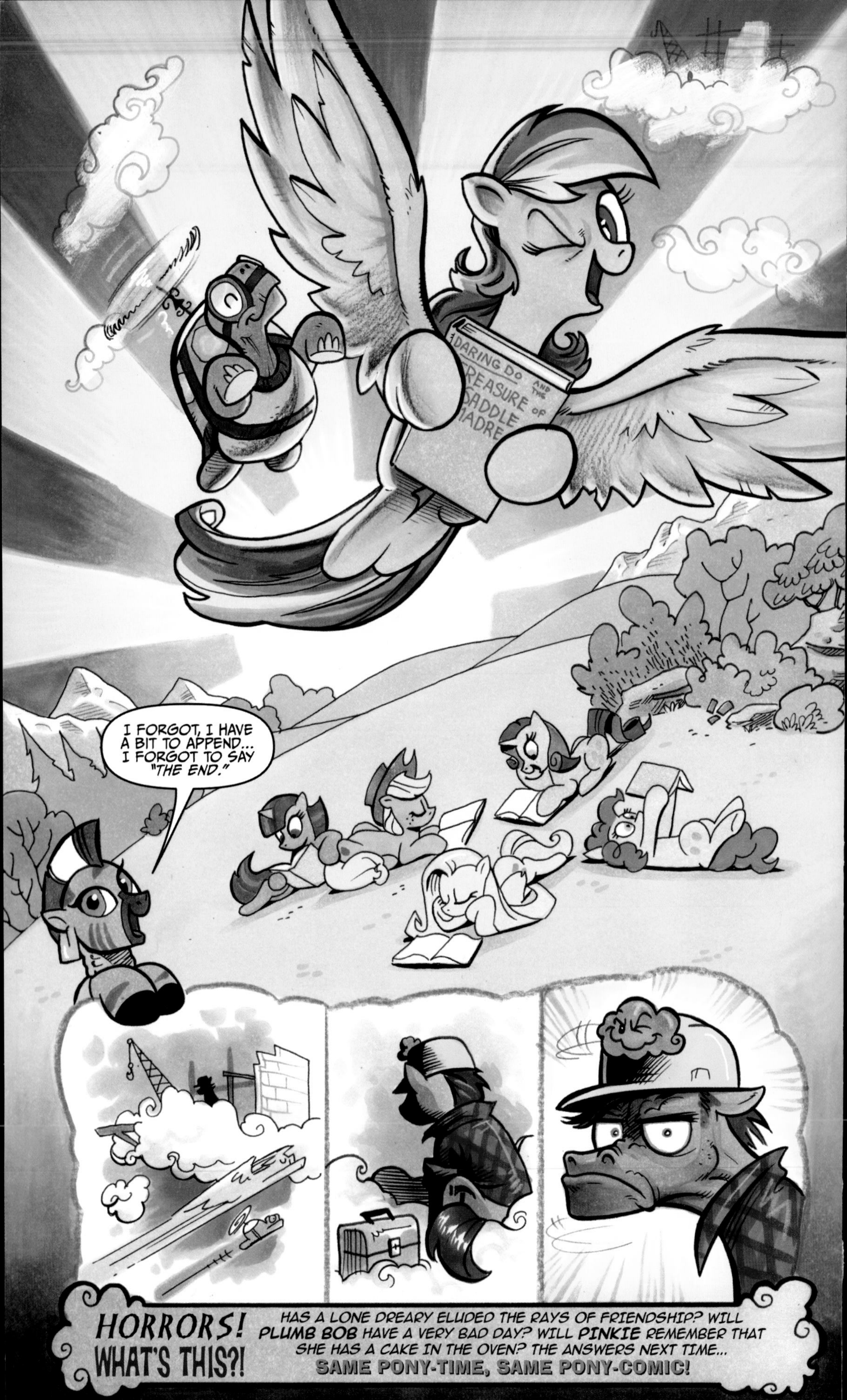
DARING DO AND THE TREASURE OF SADDLE MADRE
I FORGOT, I HAVE A BIT TO APPEND... I FORGOT TO SAY "THE END."
HORRORS! WHAT'S THIS?!
HAS A LONE DREARY ELUDED THE RAYS OF FRIENDSHIP? WILL PLUMB BOB HAVE A VERY BAD DAY? WILL PINKIE REMEMBER THAT SHE HAS A CAKE IN THE OVEN? THE ANSWERS NEXT TIME...
SAME PONY-TIME, SAME PONY-COMIC!

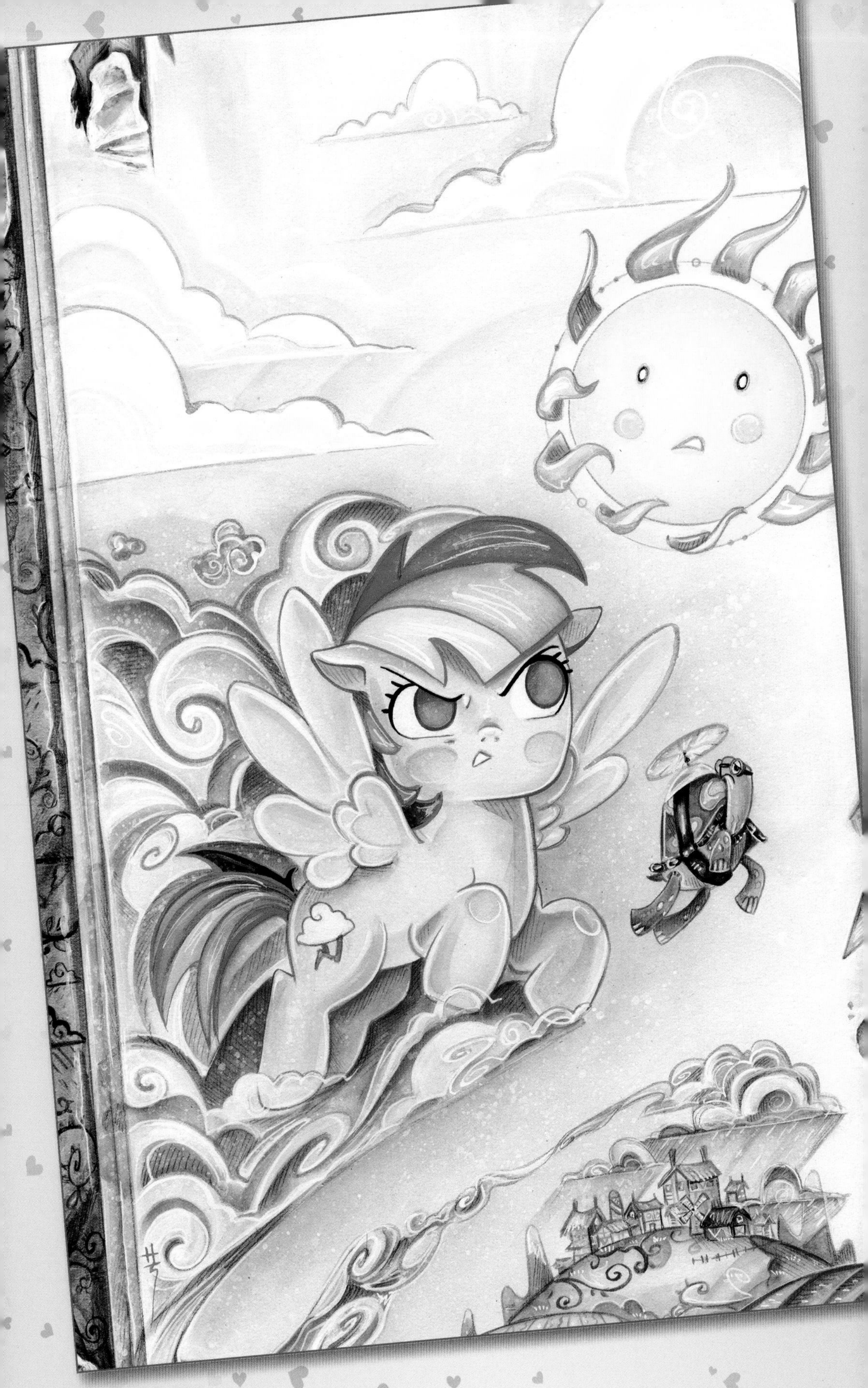

art by Sara Richard

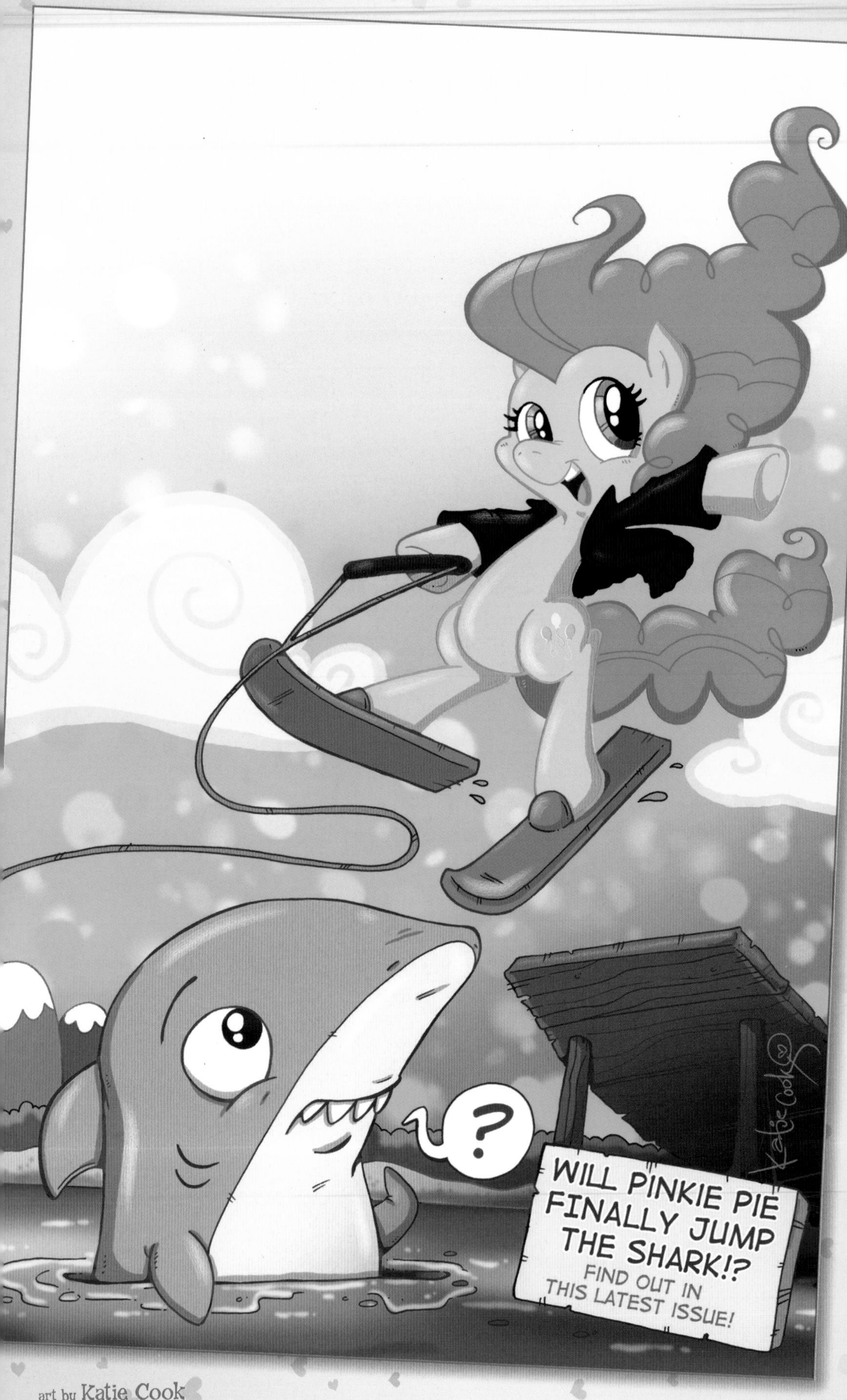
?
WILL PINKIE PIE FINALLY JUMP THE SHARK!?
FIND OUT IN THIS LATEST ISSUE!
Katie Cook

art by Katie Cook

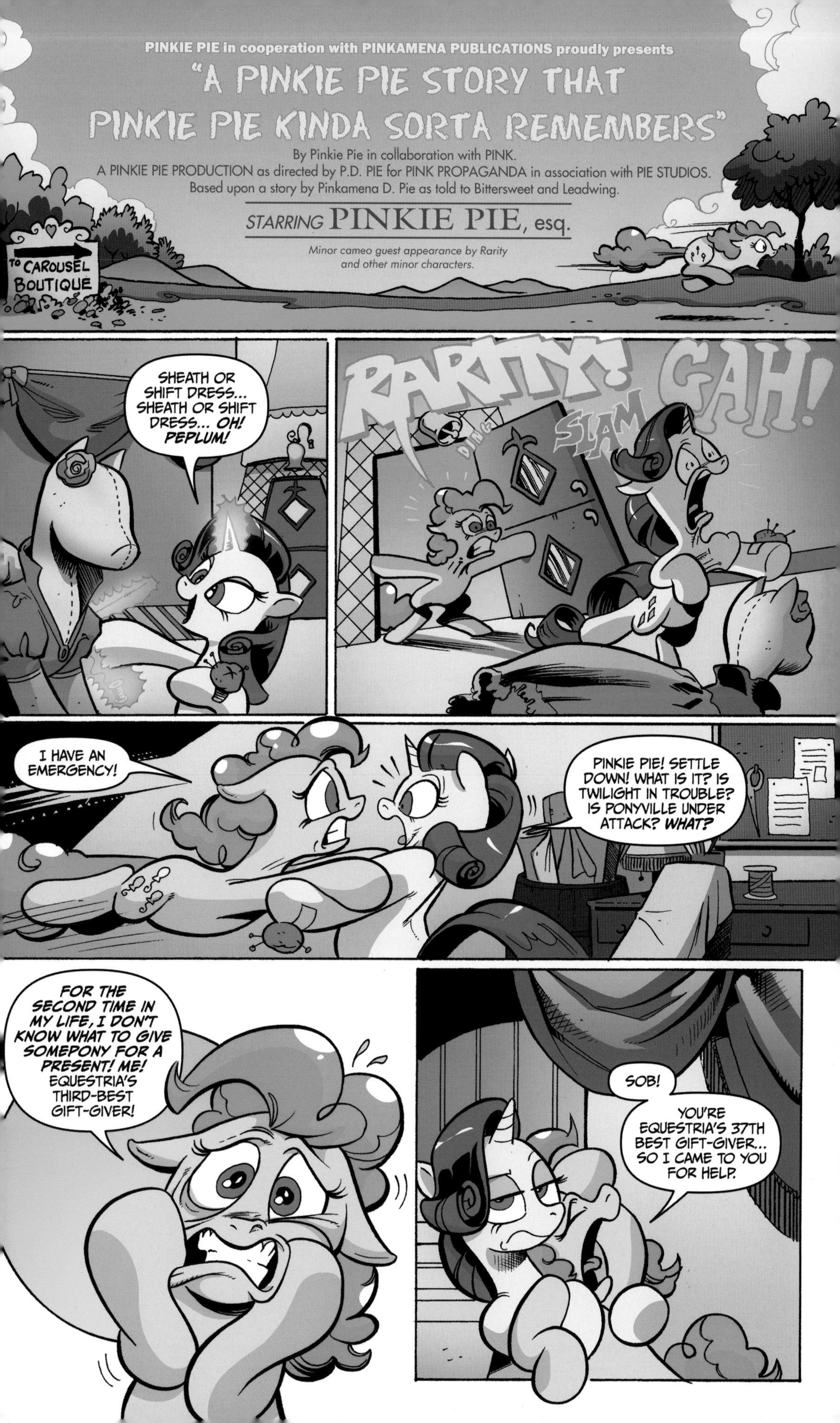
PINKIE PIE in cooperation with PINKAMENA PUBLICATIONS proudly presents
"A PINKIE PIE STORY THAT PINKIE PIE KINDA SORTA REMEMBERS"
By Pinkie Pie in collaboration with PINK.
A PINKIE PIE PRODUCTION as directed by P.D. PIE for PINK PROPAGANDA in association with PIE STUDIOS.
Based upon a story by Pinkamena D. Pie as told to Bittersweet and Leadwing.
STARRING PINKIE PIE, esq.
Minor cameo guest appearance by Rarity and other minor characters.
TO CAROUSEL BOUTIQUE
SHEATH OR SHIFT DRESS... SHEATH OR SHIFT DRESS... OH! PEPLUM!
RARITY!
SLAM
GAH!
I HAVE AN EMERGENCY!
PINKIE PIE! SETTLE DOWN! WHAT IS IT? IS TWILIGHT IN TROUBLE? IS PONYVILLE UNDER ATTACK? WHAT?
FOR THE SECOND TIME IN MY LIFE, I DON'T KNOW WHAT TO GIVE SOMEPONY FOR A PRESENT! ME! EQUESTRIA'S THIRD-BEST GIFT-GIVER!
SOB!
YOU'RE EQUESTRIA'S 37TH BEST GIFT-GIVER... SO I CAME TO YOU FOR HELP.

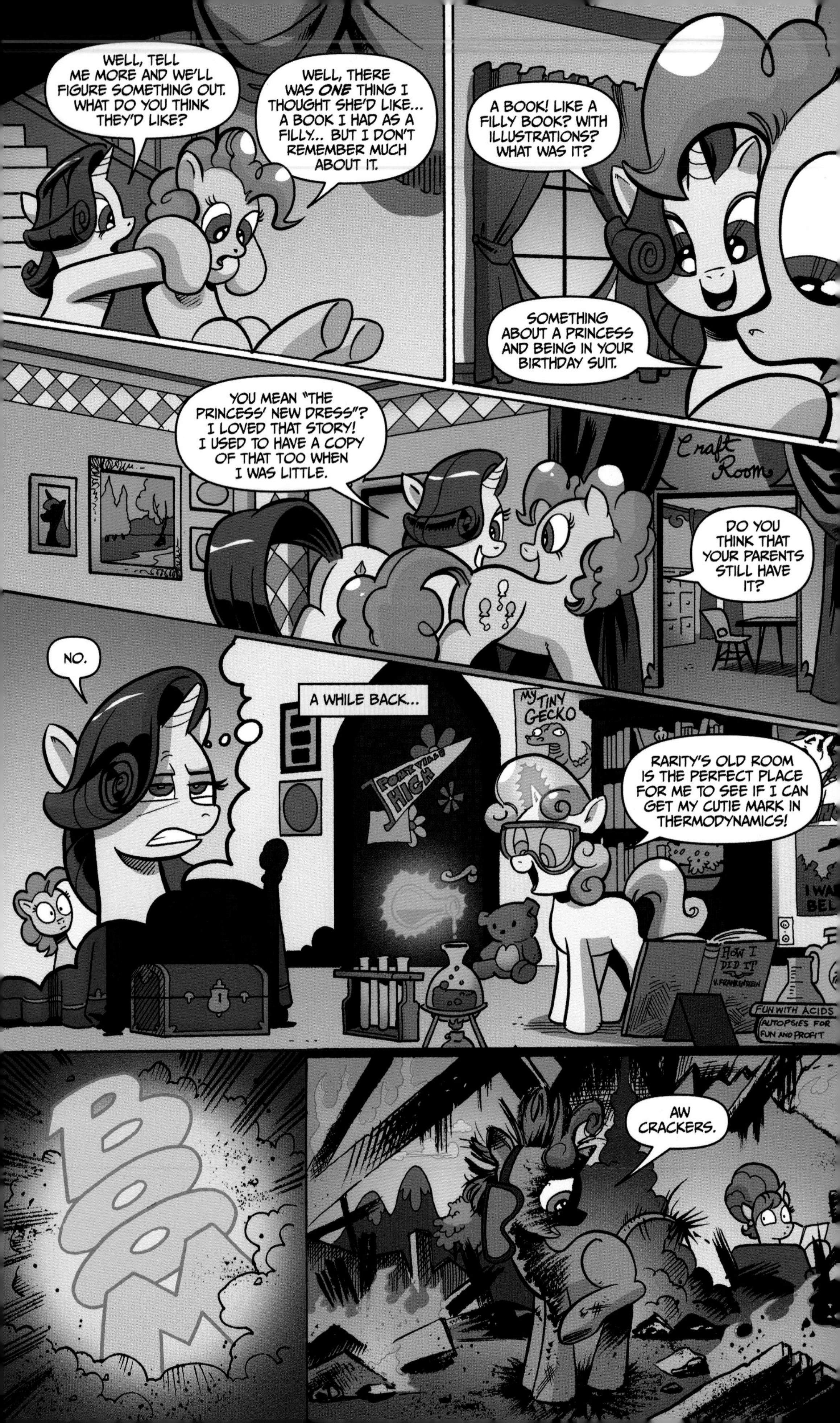
WELL, TELL ME MORE AND WE'LL FIGURE SOMETHING OUT. WHAT DO YOU THINK THEY'D LIKE?
WELL, THERE WAS *ONE* THING I THOUGHT SHE'D LIKE... A BOOK I HAD AS A FILLY... BUT I DON'T REMEMBER MUCH ABOUT IT.
A BOOK! LIKE A FILLY BOOK? WITH ILLUSTRATIONS? WHAT WAS IT?
SOMETHING ABOUT A PRINCESS AND BEING IN YOUR BIRTHDAY SUIT.
YOU MEAN "THE PRINCESS' NEW DRESS"? I LOVED THAT STORY! I USED TO HAVE A COPY OF THAT TOO WHEN I WAS LITTLE.
Craft Room
DO YOU THINK THAT YOUR PARENTS STILL HAVE IT?
NO.
A WHILE BACK...
PONYVILLE HIGH
MY TINY GECKO
RARITY'S OLD ROOM IS THE PERFECT PLACE FOR ME TO SEE IF I CAN GET MY CUTIE MARK IN THERMODYNAMICS!
HOW I DID IT
V. FRANKENSTEIN
FUN WITH ACIDS
AUTOPSIES FOR FUN AND PROFIT
BOOM
AW CRACKERS.

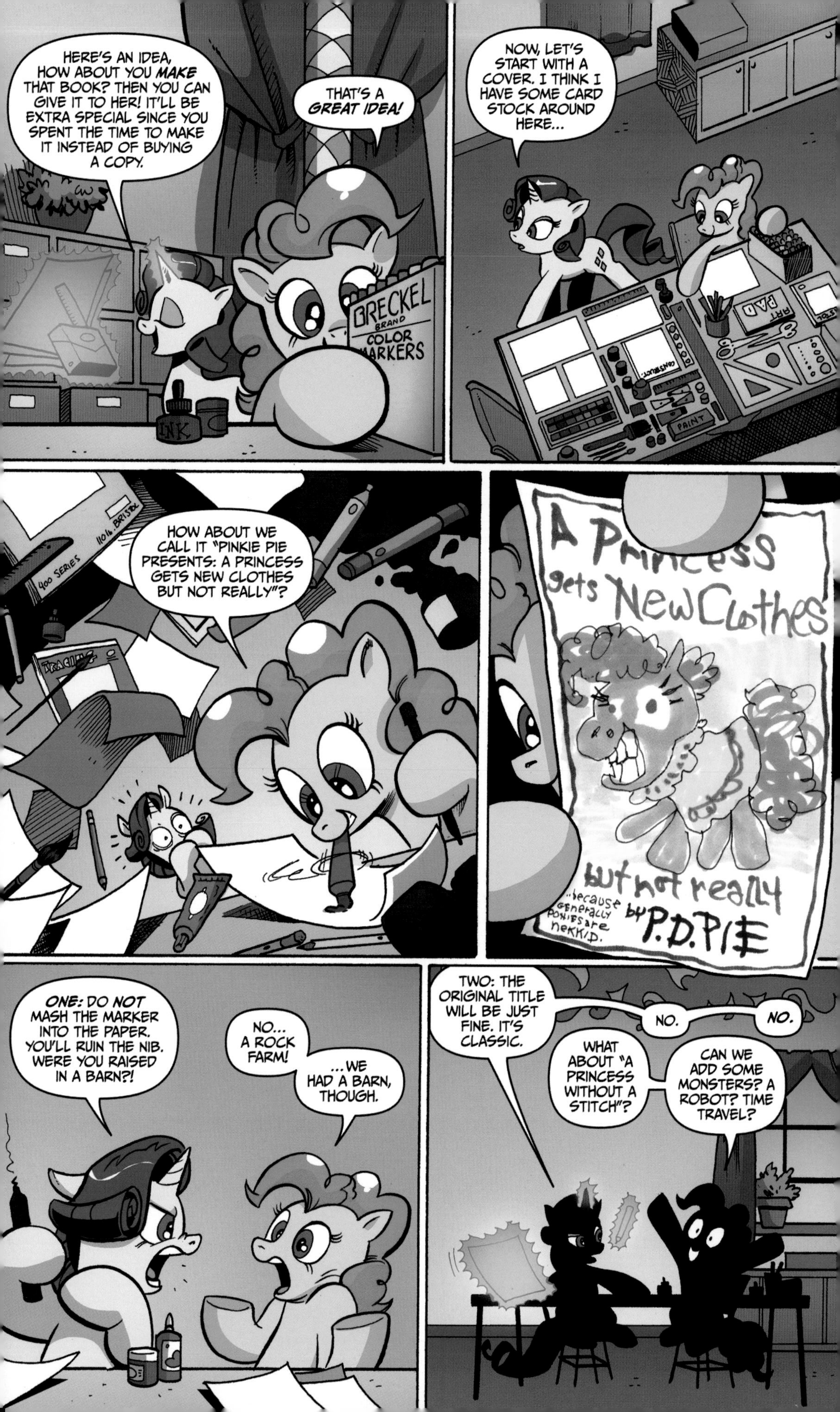
HERE'S AN IDEA, HOW ABOUT YOU MAKE THAT BOOK? THEN YOU CAN GIVE IT TO HER! IT'LL BE EXTRA SPECIAL SINCE YOU SPENT THE TIME TO MAKE IT INSTEAD OF BUYING A COPY.
THAT'S A GREAT IDEA!
BRECKEL BRAND COLOR MARKERS
INK
NOW, LET'S START WITH A COVER. I THINK I HAVE SOME CARD STOCK AROUND HERE...
ART PAD
PAINT
HOW ABOUT WE CALL IT "PINKIE PIE PRESENTS: A PRINCESS GETS NEW CLOTHES BUT NOT REALLY"?
400 SERIES
BRISTOL
A Princess gets New Clothes
but not really
...because generally ponies are nekkid.
by P.D. PIE
ONE: DO NOT MASH THE MARKER INTO THE PAPER. YOU'LL RUIN THE NIB. WERE YOU RAISED IN A BARN?!
NO... A ROCK FARM!
...WE HAD A BARN, THOUGH.
TWO: THE ORIGINAL TITLE WILL BE JUST FINE. IT'S CLASSIC.
NO.
NO.
WHAT ABOUT "A PRINCESS WITHOUT A STITCH"?
CAN WE ADD SOME MONSTERS? A ROBOT? TIME TRAVEL?

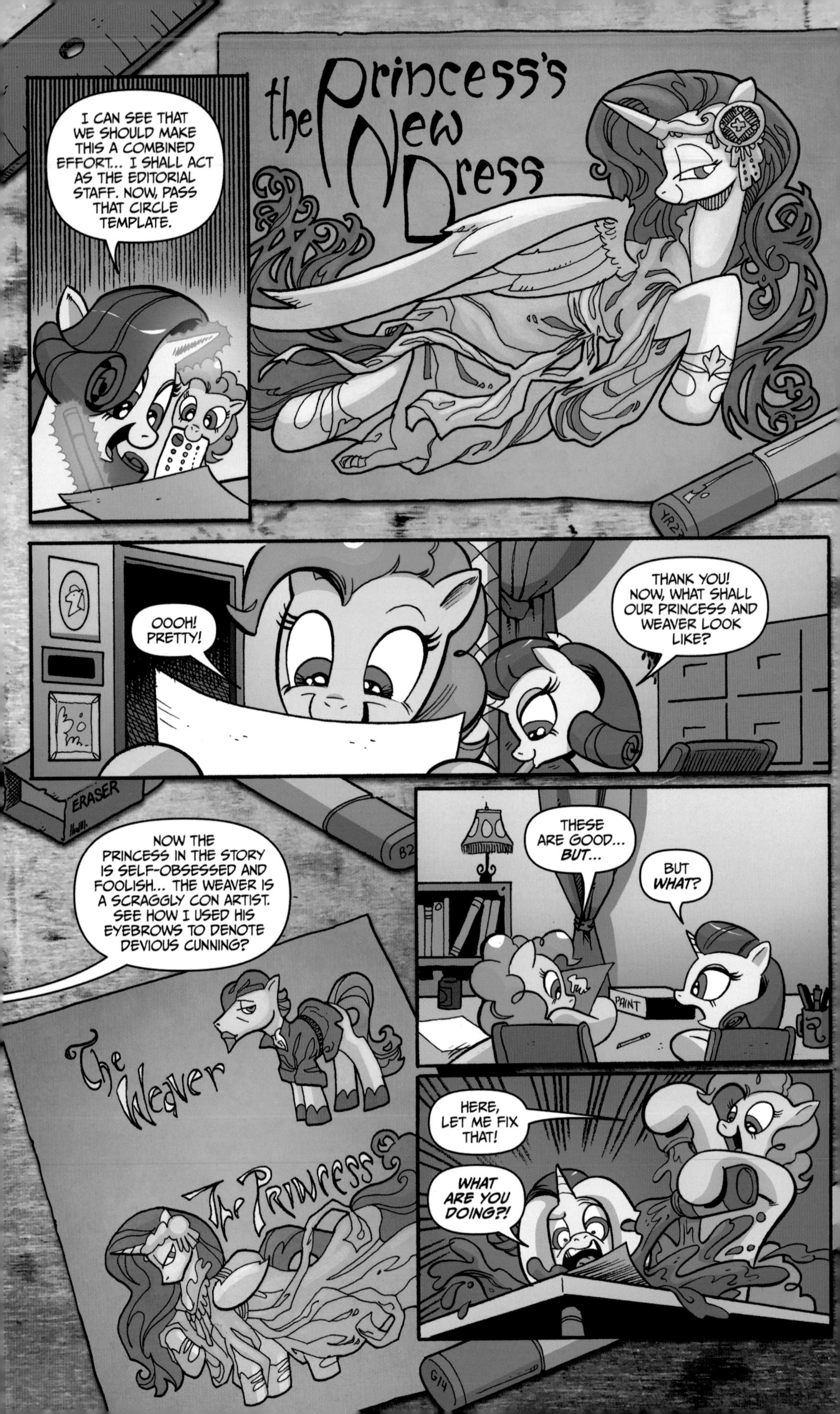
I CAN SEE THAT WE SHOULD MAKE THIS A COMBINED EFFORT... I SHALL ACT AS THE EDITORIAL STAFF. NOW, PASS THAT CIRCLE TEMPLATE.
the Princess's New Dress
OOOH! PRETTY!
THANK YOU! NOW, WHAT SHALL OUR PRINCESS AND WEAVER LOOK LIKE?
ERASER
NOW THE PRINCESS IN THE STORY IS SELF-OBSESSED AND FOOLISH... THE WEAVER IS A SCRAGGLY CON ARTIST. SEE HOW I USED HIS EYEBROWS TO DENOTE DEVIOUS CUNNING?
THESE ARE GOOD... BUT...
BUT WHAT?
PAINT
The Weaver
The Princess
HERE, LET ME FIX THAT!
WHAT ARE YOU DOING?!

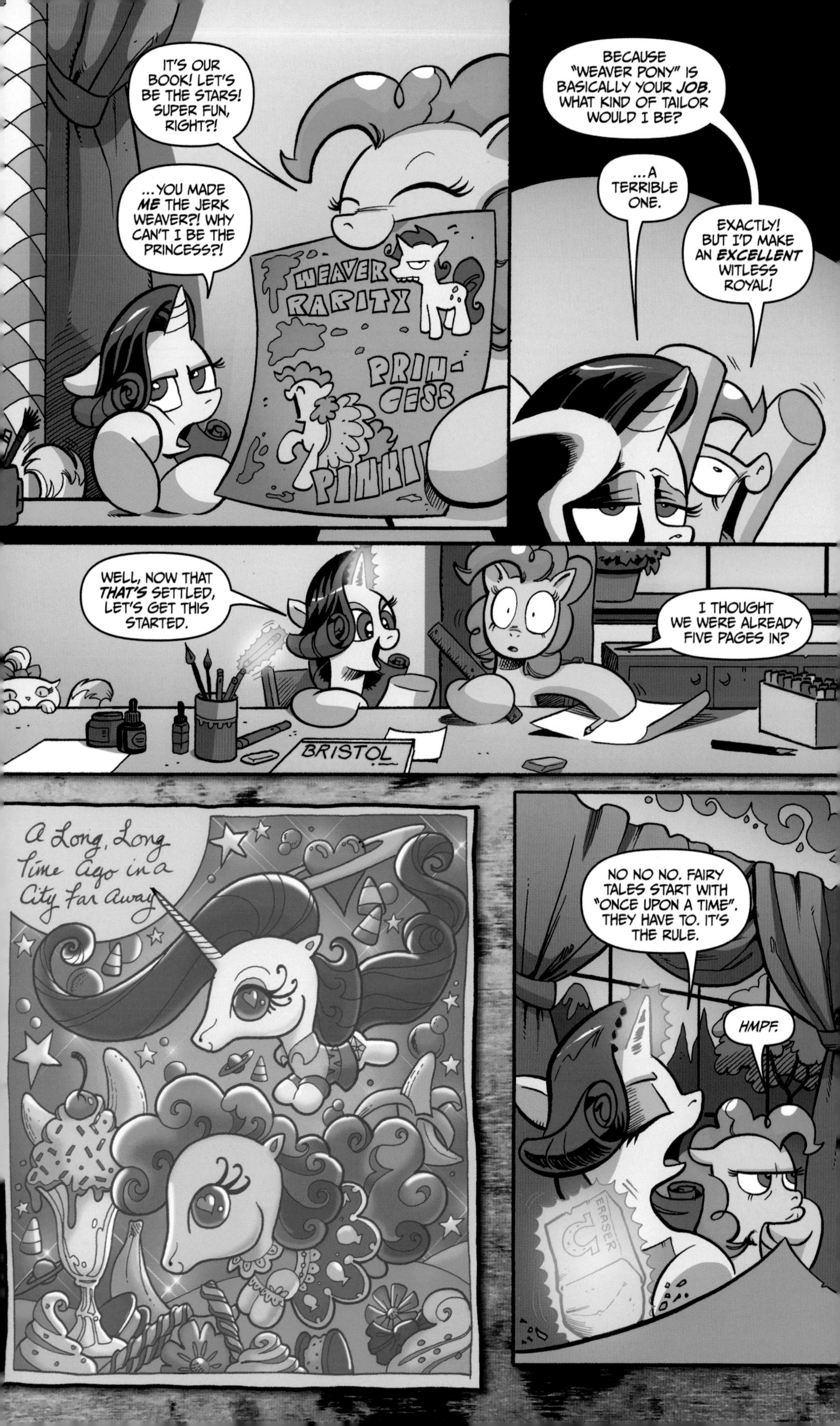
IT'S OUR BOOK! LET'S BE THE STARS! SUPER FUN, RIGHT?!
...YOU MADE ME THE JERK WEAVER?! WHY CAN'T I BE THE PRINCESS?!
WEAVER RARITY
PRIN-CESS
PINKIE
BECAUSE "WEAVER PONY" IS BASICALLY YOUR JOB. WHAT KIND OF TAILOR WOULD I BE?
...A TERRIBLE ONE.
EXACTLY! BUT I'D MAKE AN EXCELLENT WITLESS ROYAL!
WELL, NOW THAT THAT'S SETTLED, LET'S GET THIS STARTED.
I THOUGHT WE WERE ALREADY FIVE PAGES IN?
BRISTOL
A Long, Long Time Ago in a City Far Away
NO NO NO. FAIRY TALES START WITH "ONCE UPON A TIME". THEY HAVE TO. IT'S THE RULE.
HMPF.
ERASER

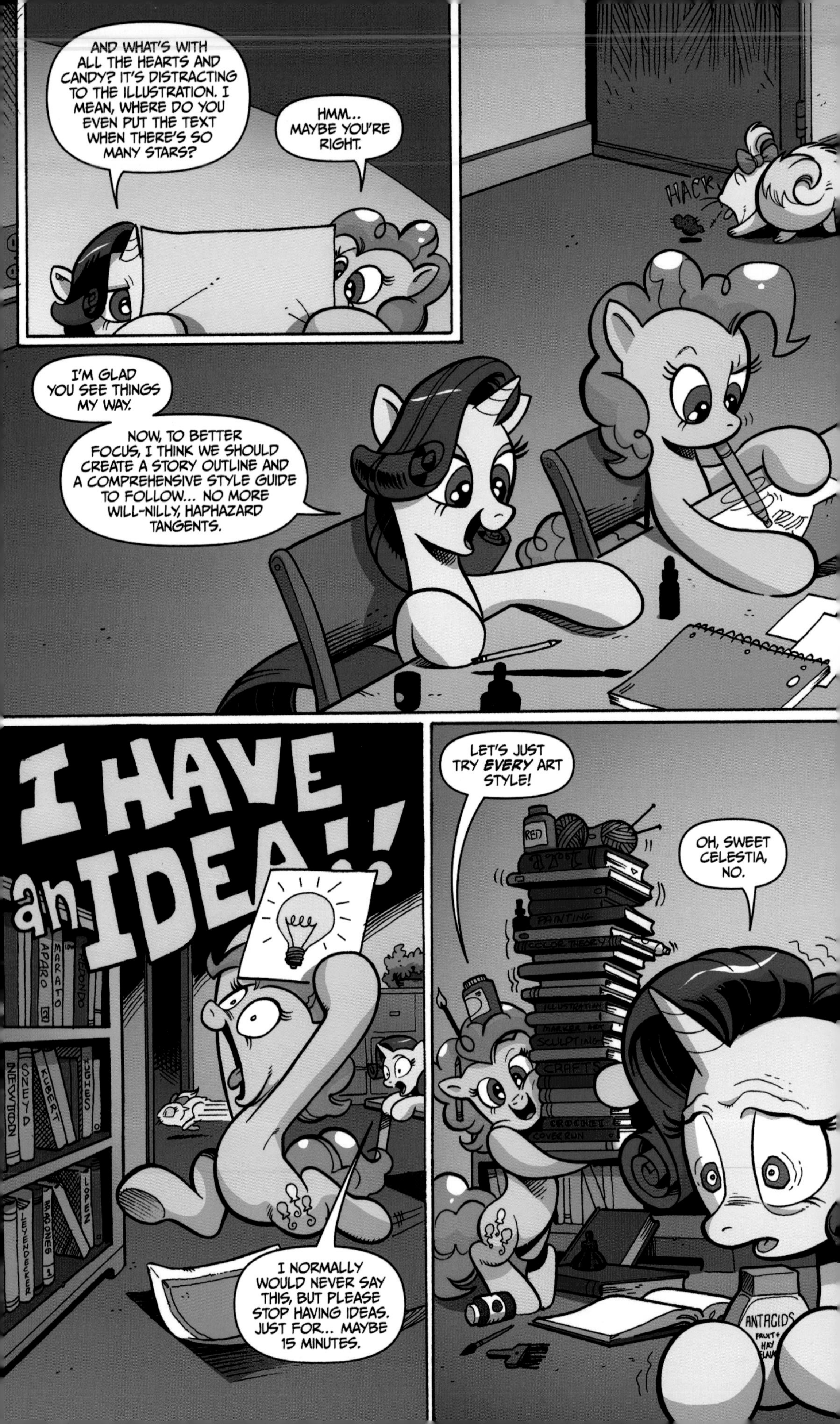
AND WHAT'S WITH ALL THE HEARTS AND CANDY? IT'S DISTRACTING TO THE ILLUSTRATION. I MEAN, WHERE DO YOU EVEN PUT THE TEXT WHEN THERE'S SO MANY STARS?
HMM... MAYBE YOU'RE RIGHT.
HACK
I'M GLAD YOU SEE THINGS MY WAY.
NOW, TO BETTER FOCUS, I THINK WE SHOULD CREATE A STORY OUTLINE AND A COMPREHENSIVE STYLE GUIDE TO FOLLOW... NO MORE WILL-NILLY, HAPHAZARD TANGENTS.
I HAVE an IDEA!!
APARO
KUBERT
HUGHES
LEYENDECKER
LOPEZ
I NORMALLY WOULD NEVER SAY THIS, BUT PLEASE STOP HAVING IDEAS. JUST FOR... MAYBE 15 MINUTES.
LET'S JUST TRY *EVERY* ART STYLE!
RED
PAINTING
COLOR THEORY
ILLUSTRATION
MARKER ART
SCULPTING
CRAFTS
CROCHET
COVER RUN
OH, SWEET CELESTIA, NO.
ANTACIDS

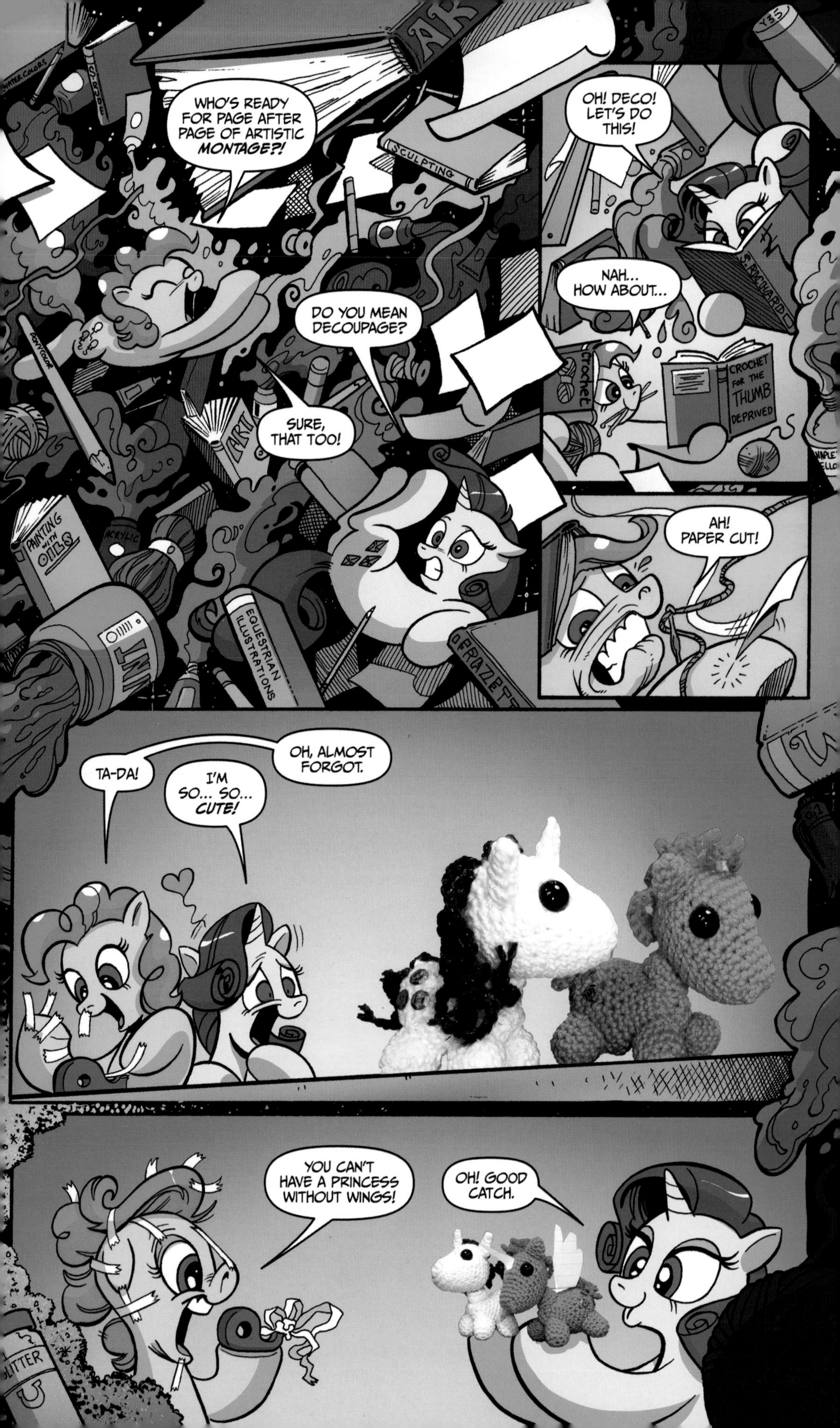
WHO'S READY FOR PAGE AFTER PAGE OF ARTISTIC *MONTAGE?!*
DO YOU MEAN DECOUPAGE?
SURE, THAT TOO!
OH! DECO! LET'S DO THIS!
NAH... HOW ABOUT...
CROCHET FOR THE THUMB DEPRIVED
AH! PAPER CUT!
TA-DA!
OH, ALMOST FORGOT.
I'M SO... SO... *CUTE!*
YOU CAN'T HAVE A PRINCESS WITHOUT WINGS!
OH! GOOD CATCH.

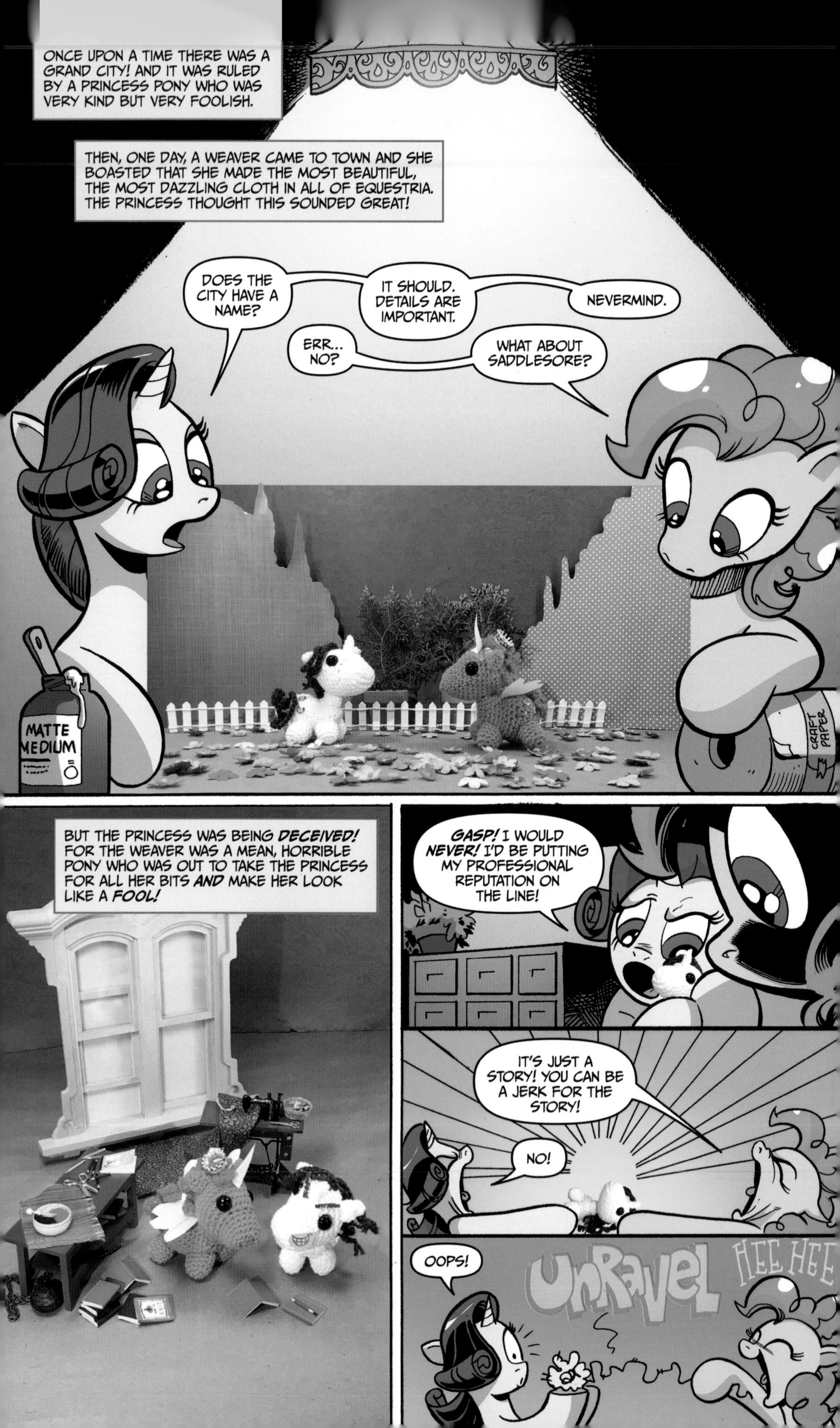

ONCE UPON A TIME THERE WAS A GRAND CITY! AND IT WAS RULED BY A PRINCESS PONY WHO WAS VERY KIND BUT VERY FOOLISH.
THEN, ONE DAY, A WEAVER CAME TO TOWN AND SHE BOASTED THAT SHE MADE THE MOST BEAUTIFUL, THE MOST DAZZLING CLOTH IN ALL OF EQUESTRIA. THE PRINCESS THOUGHT THIS SOUNDED GREAT!
DOES THE CITY HAVE A NAME?
ERR... NO?
IT SHOULD. DETAILS ARE IMPORTANT.
WHAT ABOUT SADDLESORE?
NEVERMIND.
MATTE MEDIUM
CRAFT PAPER
BUT THE PRINCESS WAS BEING DECEIVED! FOR THE WEAVER WAS A MEAN, HORRIBLE PONY WHO WAS OUT TO TAKE THE PRINCESS FOR ALL HER BITS AND MAKE HER LOOK LIKE A FOOL!
GASP! I WOULD NEVER! I'D BE PUTTING MY PROFESSIONAL REPUTATION ON THE LINE!
IT'S JUST A STORY! YOU CAN BE A JERK FOR THE STORY!
NO!
OOPS!
UNRAVEL
HEE HEE

I THINK WE CAN DO THIS BOOK *WITHOUT* THE PROFESSIONAL SLANDER TO MY CAREER THANKYOUVERYMUCH.

LEYENDECKER BRAND OILS

THERE ONCE WAS A BEAUTIFUL, TALENTED WEAVER THAT MAKES HER CLIENTS SHINE LIKE SUNLIGHT WITH HER STUNNING CREATIONS.

THE WEAVER

AFTER LEYENDECKER

BUT, THE WEAVER WAS ALSO VERY *WISE* AND IF SHE THOUGHT THAT THE NOBLE SHE WAS DRESSING WAS A BIT OF A FOOL, SHE'D CUT THEIR FABRIC TO MAKE THEM LOOK A BIT WIDE IN THE SHOULDERS.

AND AFTER THE WEAVER MADE THE DRESS, SHE WAS HIRED TO MAKE *MORE* DRESSES! AND SHE LIVED HAPPILY EVER AFTER!

PERFECT! OR MAYBE IT'S NOT ENOUGH? WE COULD ADD A PRINCE!

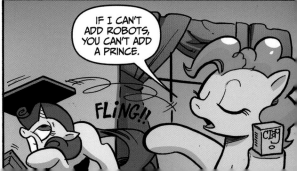

IF I CAN'T ADD ROBOTS, YOU CAN'T ADD A PRINCE.

FLING!!

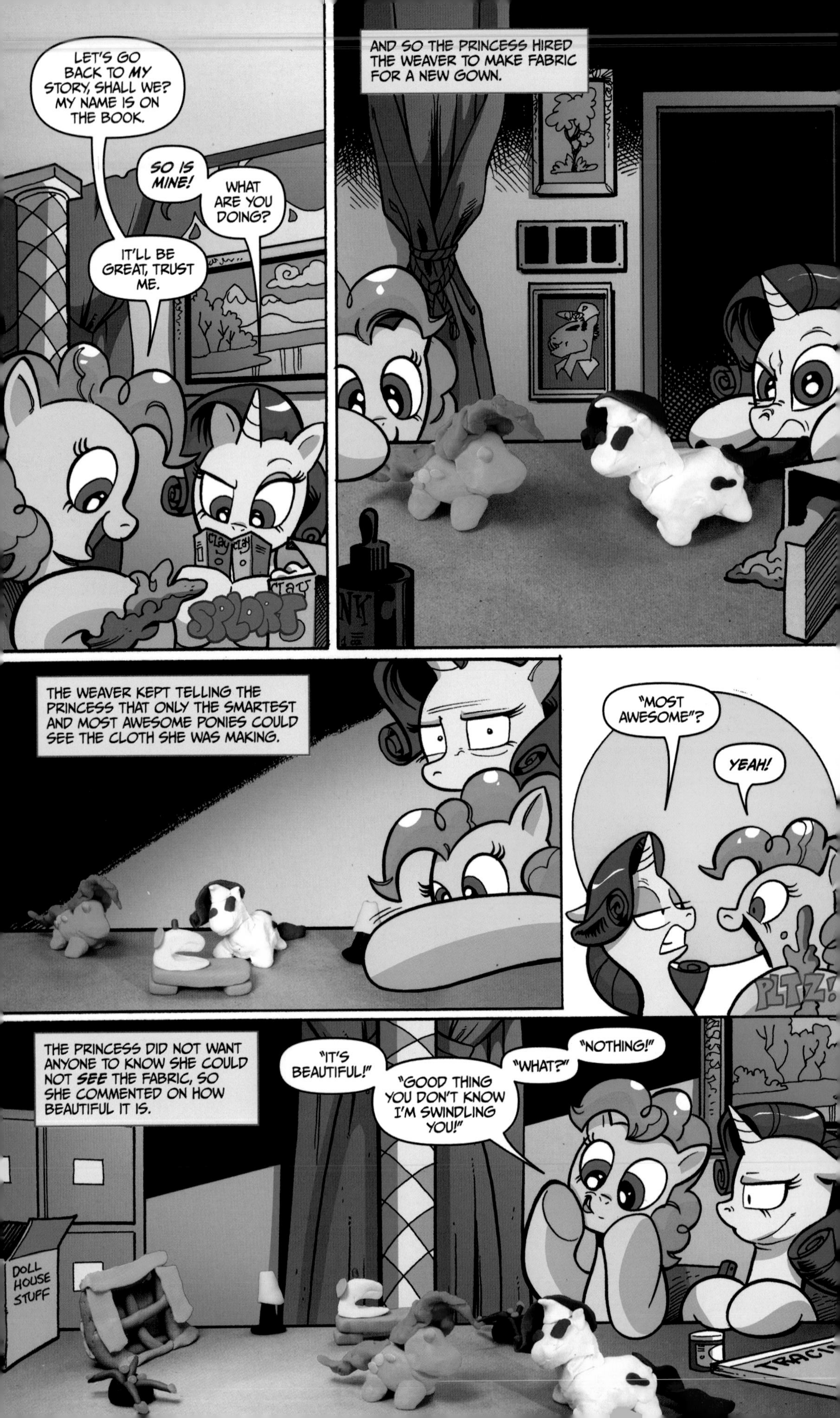
LET'S GO BACK TO MY STORY, SHALL WE? MY NAME IS ON THE BOOK.
SO IS MINE!
WHAT ARE YOU DOING?
IT'LL BE GREAT, TRUST ME.
CLAY
CLAY
CLAY
SPLORT
AND SO THE PRINCESS HIRED THE WEAVER TO MAKE FABRIC FOR A NEW GOWN.
INK
THE WEAVER KEPT TELLING THE PRINCESS THAT ONLY THE SMARTEST AND MOST AWESOME PONIES COULD SEE THE CLOTH SHE WAS MAKING.
"MOST AWESOME"?
YEAH!
PLTZ!
THE PRINCESS DID NOT WANT ANYONE TO KNOW SHE COULD NOT SEE THE FABRIC, SO SHE COMMENTED ON HOW BEAUTIFUL IT IS.
"IT'S BEAUTIFUL!"
"GOOD THING YOU DON'T KNOW I'M SWINDLING YOU!"
"WHAT?"
"NOTHING!"
DOLL HOUSE STUFF

NOPE. NO. I CAN'T GET BEHIND THIS. I LOOK LIKE A POTATO.

AND NOW YOU'RE A MASHED POTATO!

LICHTENSTEIN BRAND CANVAS NOW WITH CARBON PAPER!

PRINT

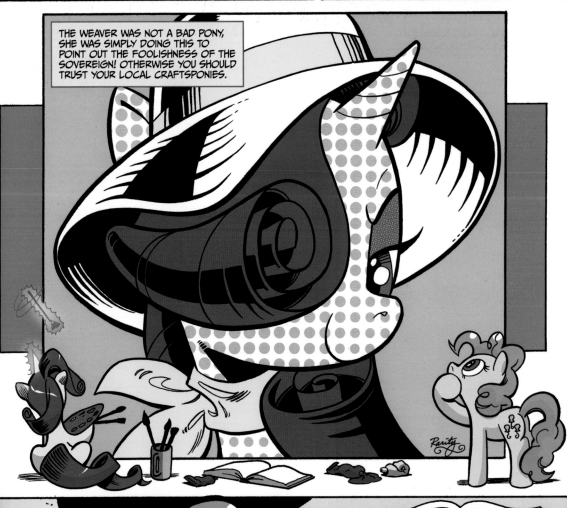

THE WEAVER WAS NOT A BAD PONY, SHE WAS SIMPLY DOING THIS TO POINT OUT THE FOOLISHNESS OF THE SOVEREIGN! OTHERWISE YOU SHOULD TRUST YOUR LOCAL CRAFTSPONIES.

I DON'T KNOW... WHEN I SEE SOMETHING LIKE THIS I ALWAYS THINK I'VE SEEN IT SOMEWHERE BEFORE.

IS IT PLAGARISM OR IS IT ART?

PRICE

KUBERT
ROMITA
ABRUZZO
EISMAN
HEATH

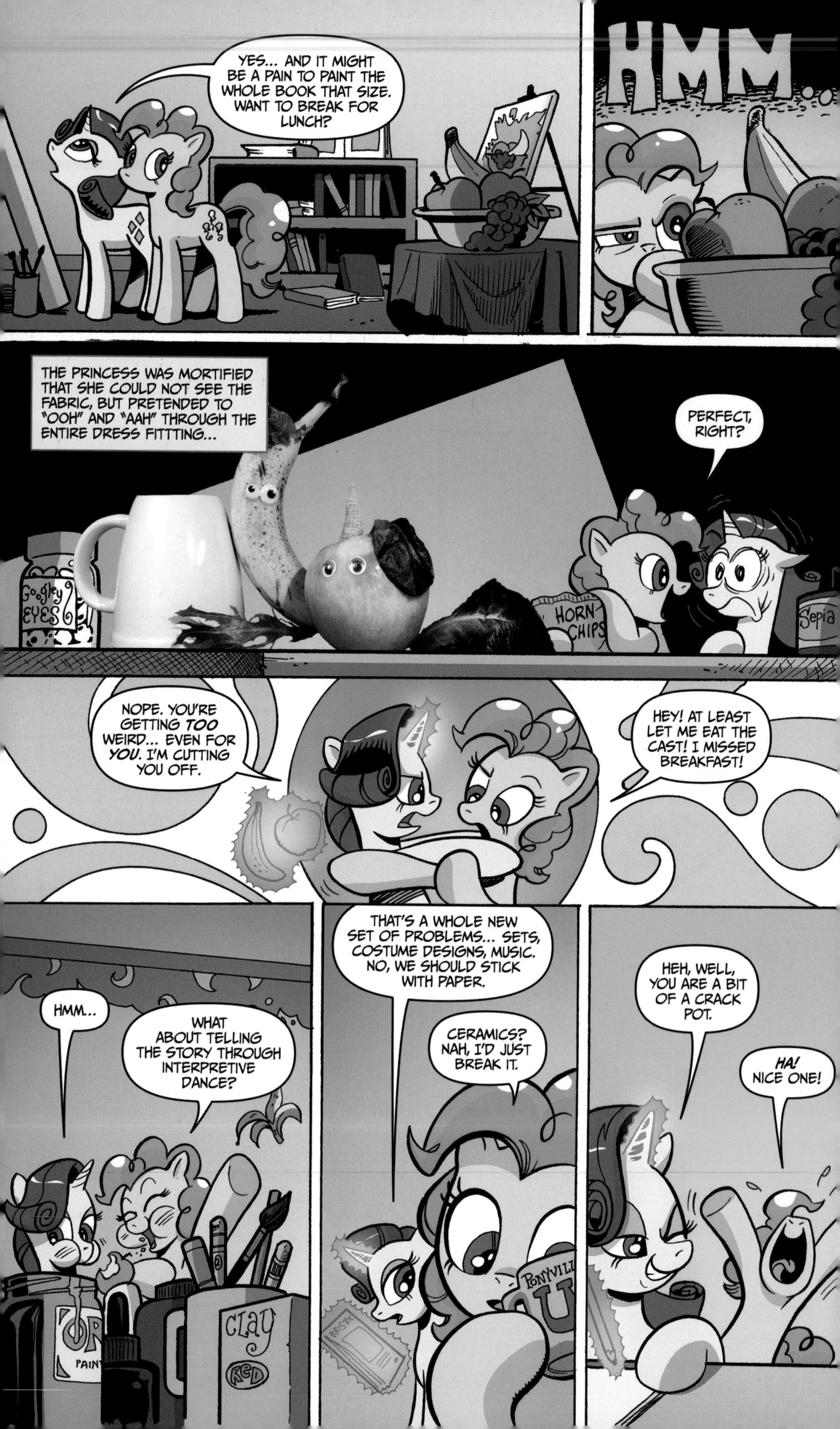
YES... AND IT MIGHT BE A PAIN TO PAINT THE WHOLE BOOK THAT SIZE. WANT TO BREAK FOR LUNCH?
HMM
THE PRINCESS WAS MORTIFIED THAT SHE COULD NOT SEE THE FABRIC, BUT PRETENDED TO "OOH" AND "AAH" THROUGH THE ENTIRE DRESS FITTTING...
PERFECT, RIGHT?
Googley EYES
HORN CHIPS
Sepia
NOPE. YOU'RE GETTING TOO WEIRD... EVEN FOR YOU. I'M CUTTING YOU OFF.
HEY! AT LEAST LET ME EAT THE CAST! I MISSED BREAKFAST!
HMM...
WHAT ABOUT TELLING THE STORY THROUGH INTERPRETIVE DANCE?
PAINT
CLAY
RED
THAT'S A WHOLE NEW SET OF PROBLEMS... SETS, COSTUME DESIGNS, MUSIC. NO, WE SHOULD STICK WITH PAPER.
CERAMICS? NAH, I'D JUST BREAK IT.
PONYVILL
HEH, WELL, YOU ARE A BIT OF A CRACK POT.
HA! NICE ONE!

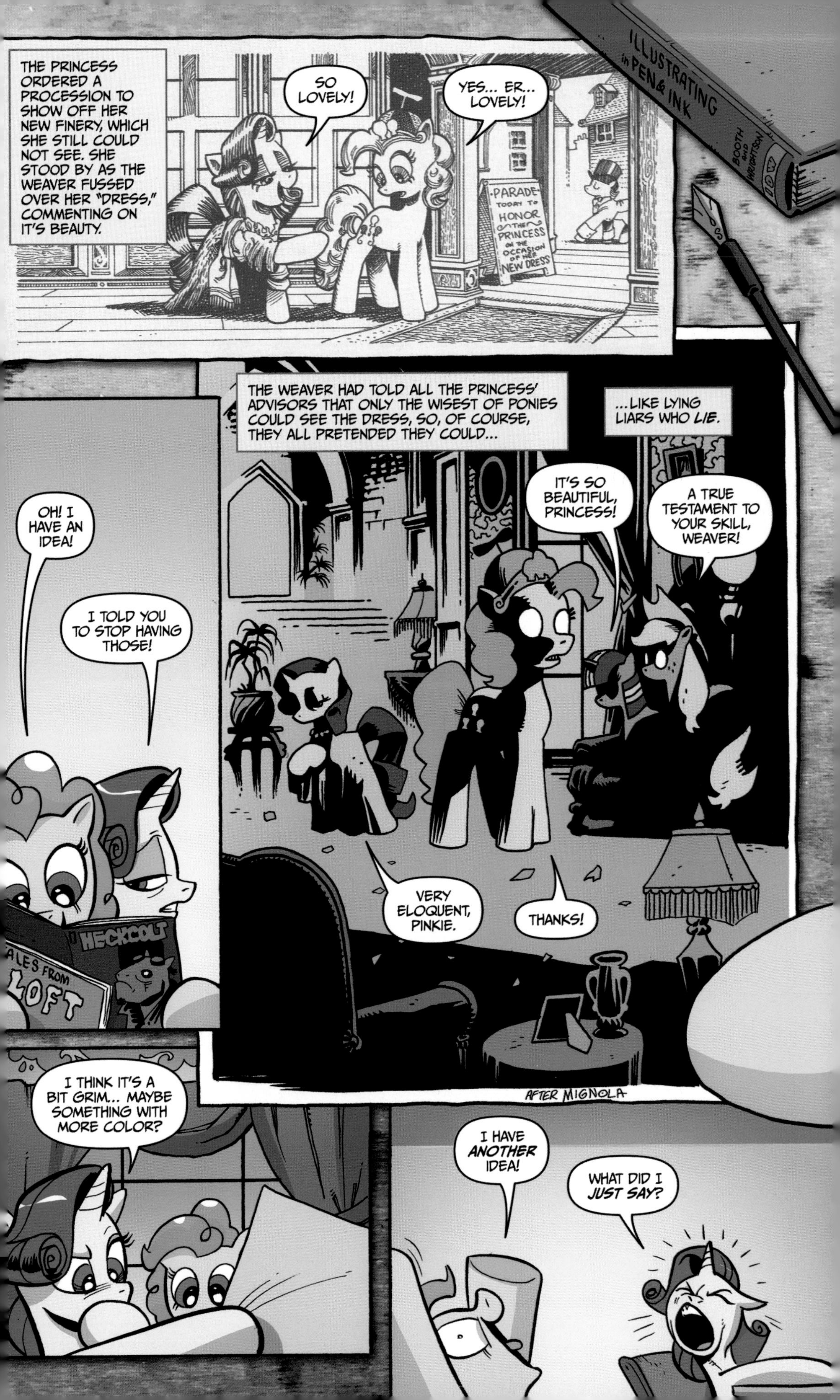
THE PRINCESS ORDERED A PROCESSION TO SHOW OFF HER NEW FINERY, WHICH SHE STILL COULD NOT SEE. SHE STOOD BY AS THE WEAVER FUSSED OVER HER "DRESS," COMMENTING ON IT'S BEAUTY.
SO LOVELY!
YES... ER... LOVELY!
PARADE TODAY TO HONOR THE PRINCESS ON THE OCCASION OF HER NEW DRESS
ILLUSTRATING in PEN & INK
BOOTH AND WRIGHTSON
THE WEAVER HAD TOLD ALL THE PRINCESS' ADVISORS THAT ONLY THE WISEST OF PONIES COULD SEE THE DRESS, SO, OF COURSE, THEY ALL PRETENDED THEY COULD...
...LIKE LYING LIARS WHO *LIE*.
IT'S SO BEAUTIFUL, PRINCESS!
A TRUE TESTAMENT TO YOUR SKILL, WEAVER!
VERY ELOQUENT, PINKIE.
THANKS!
AFTER MIGNOLA
OH! I HAVE AN IDEA!
I TOLD YOU TO STOP HAVING THOSE!
HECKCOLT
TALES FROM LOFT
I THINK IT'S A BIT GRIM... MAYBE SOMETHING WITH MORE COLOR?
I HAVE *ANOTHER* IDEA!
WHAT DID I *JUST SAY?*

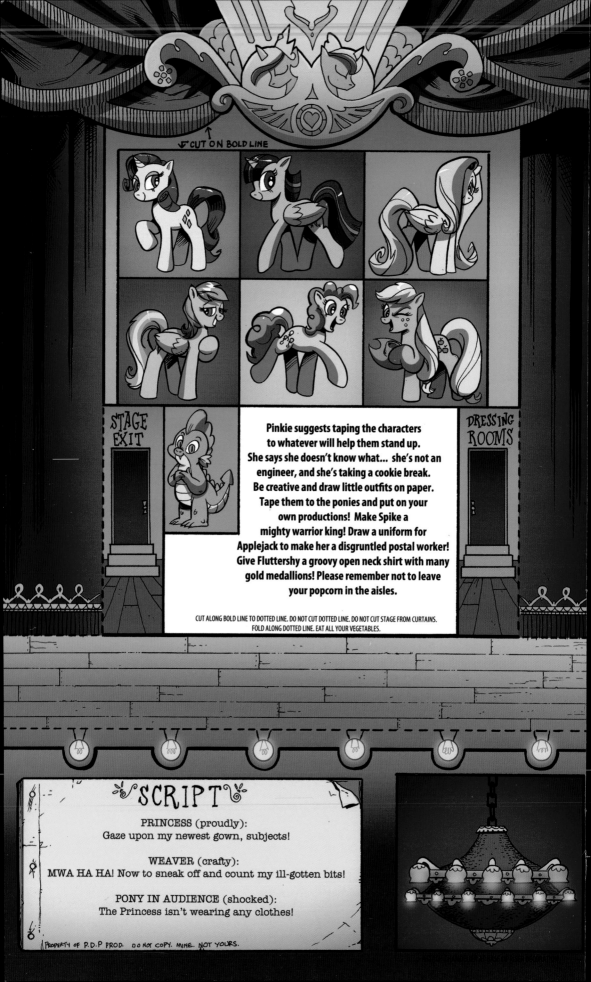

CUT ON BOLD LINE

STAGE EXIT

DRESSING ROOMS

Pinkie suggests taping the characters to whatever will help them stand up. She says she doesn't know what... she's not an engineer, and she's taking a cookie break. Be creative and draw little outfits on paper. Tape them to the ponies and put on your own productions! Make Spike a mighty warrior king! Draw a uniform for Applejack to make her a disgruntled postal worker! Give Fluttershy a groovy open neck shirt with many gold medallions! Please remember not to leave your popcorn in the aisles.

CUT ALONG BOLD LINE TO DOTTED LINE. DO NOT CUT DOTTED LINE. DO NOT CUT STAGE FROM CURTAINS. FOLD ALONG DOTTED LINE. EAT ALL YOUR VEGETABLES.

SCRIPT

PRINCESS (proudly):
Gaze upon my newest gown, subjects!

WEAVER (crafty):
MWA HA HA! Now to sneak off and count my ill-gotten bits!

PONY IN AUDIENCE (shocked):
The Princess isn't wearing any clothes!

PROPERTY OF P.D.P PROD. DO NOT COPY. MINE. NOT YOURS.

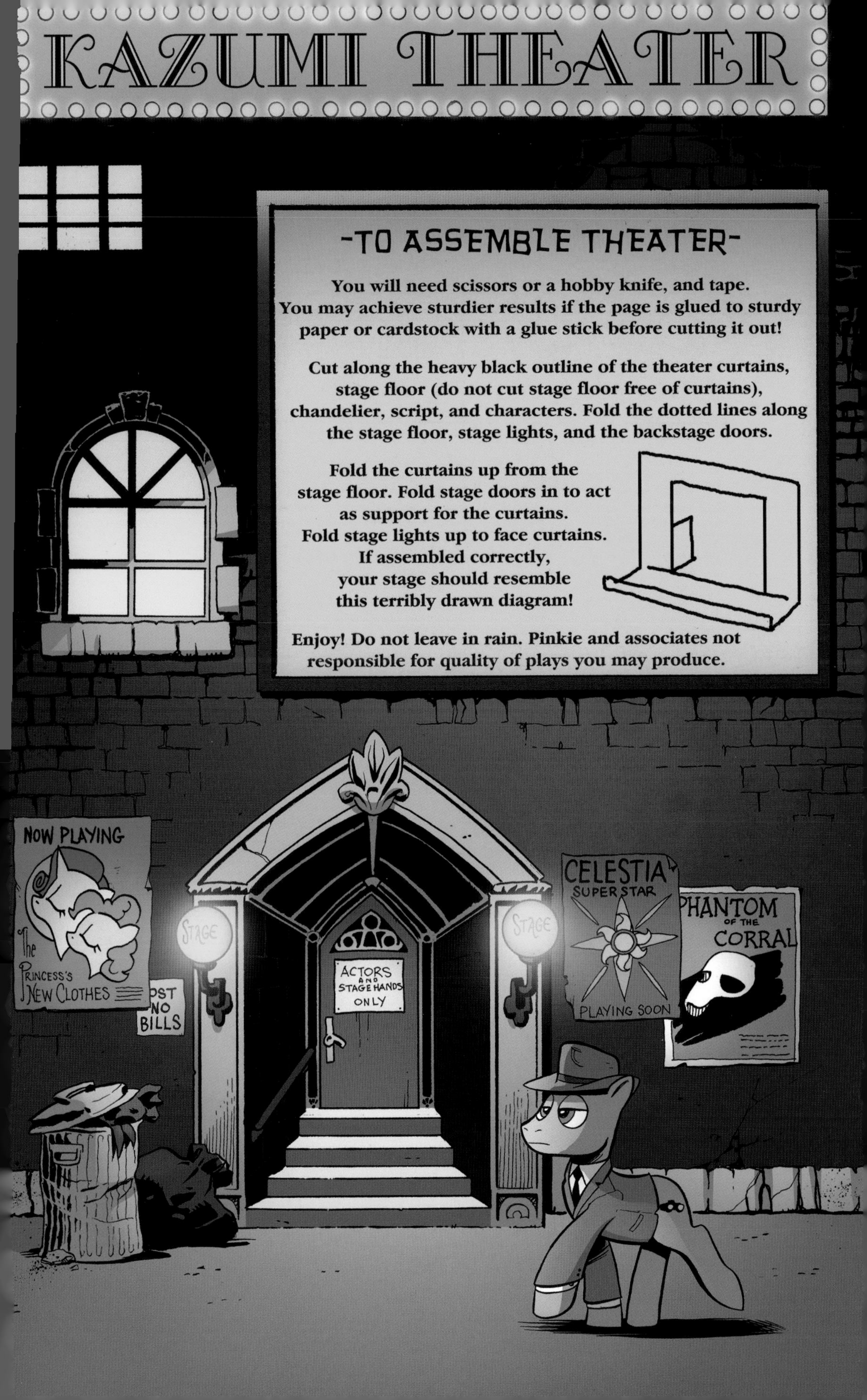
KAZUMI THEATER
-TO ASSEMBLE THEATER-
You will need scissors or a hobby knife, and tape.
You may achieve sturdier results if the page is glued to sturdy paper or cardstock with a glue stick before cutting it out!
Cut along the heavy black outline of the theater curtains, stage floor (do not cut stage floor free of curtains), chandelier, script, and characters. Fold the dotted lines along the stage floor, stage lights, and the backstage doors.
Fold the curtains up from the stage floor. Fold stage doors in to act as support for the curtains. Fold stage lights up to face curtains. If assembled correctly, your stage should resemble this terribly drawn diagram!
Enjoy! Do not leave in rain. Pinkie and associates not responsible for quality of plays you may produce.
NOW PLAYING
The PRINCESS'S NEW CLOTHES
OST NO BILLS
STAGE
STAGE
ACTORS AND STAGE HANDS ONLY
CELESTIA SUPER STAR
PLAYING SOON
PHANTOM OF THE CORRAL

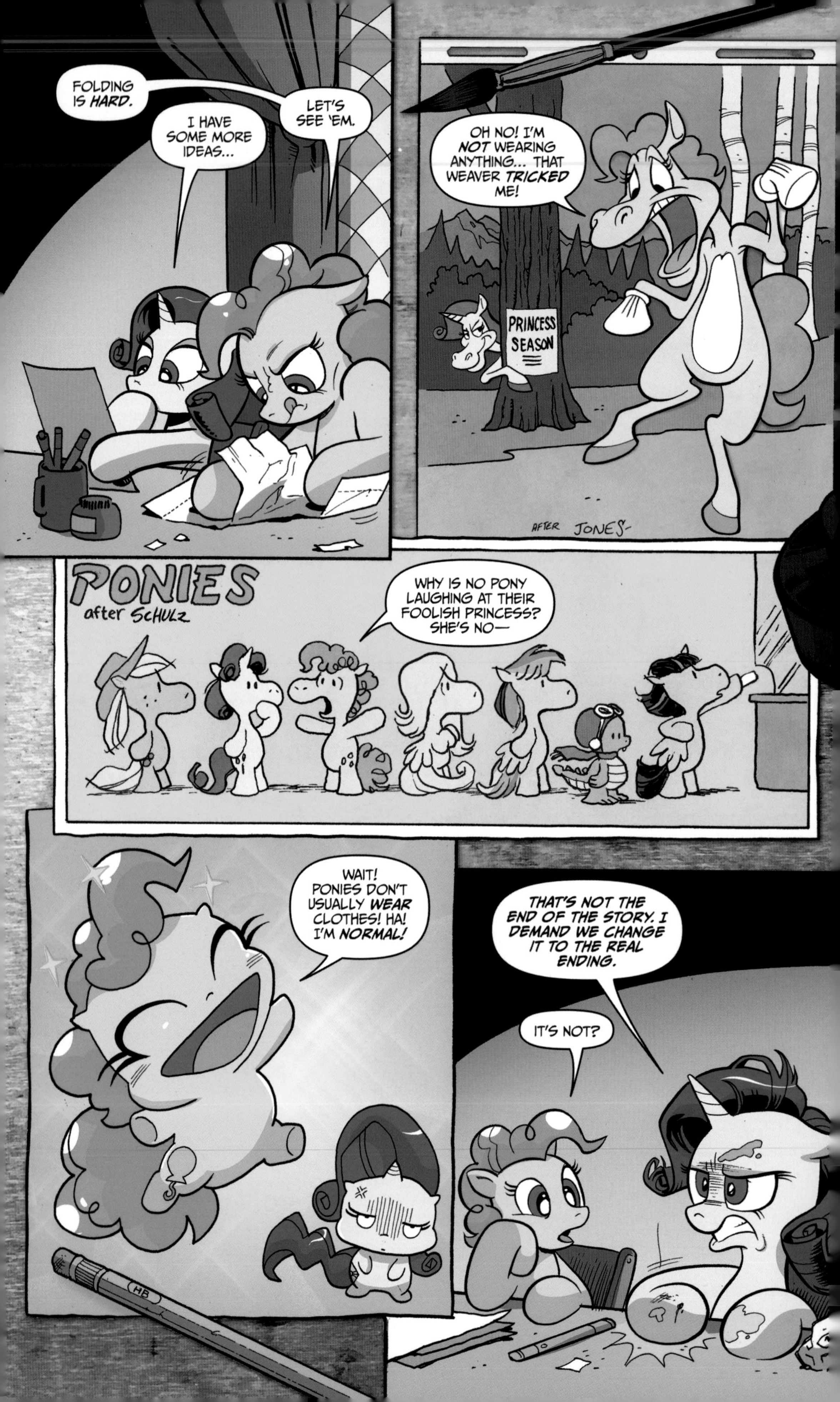
FOLDING IS HARD.
I HAVE SOME MORE IDEAS...
LET'S SEE 'EM.
OH NO! I'M NOT WEARING ANYTHING... THAT WEAVER TRICKED ME!
PRINCESS SEASON
AFTER JONES
PONIES
after SCHULZ
WHY IS NO PONY LAUGHING AT THEIR FOOLISH PRINCESS? SHE'S NO—
WAIT! PONIES DON'T USUALLY WEAR CLOTHES! HA! I'M NORMAL!
THAT'S NOT THE END OF THE STORY. I DEMAND WE CHANGE IT TO THE REAL ENDING.
IT'S NOT?
HB

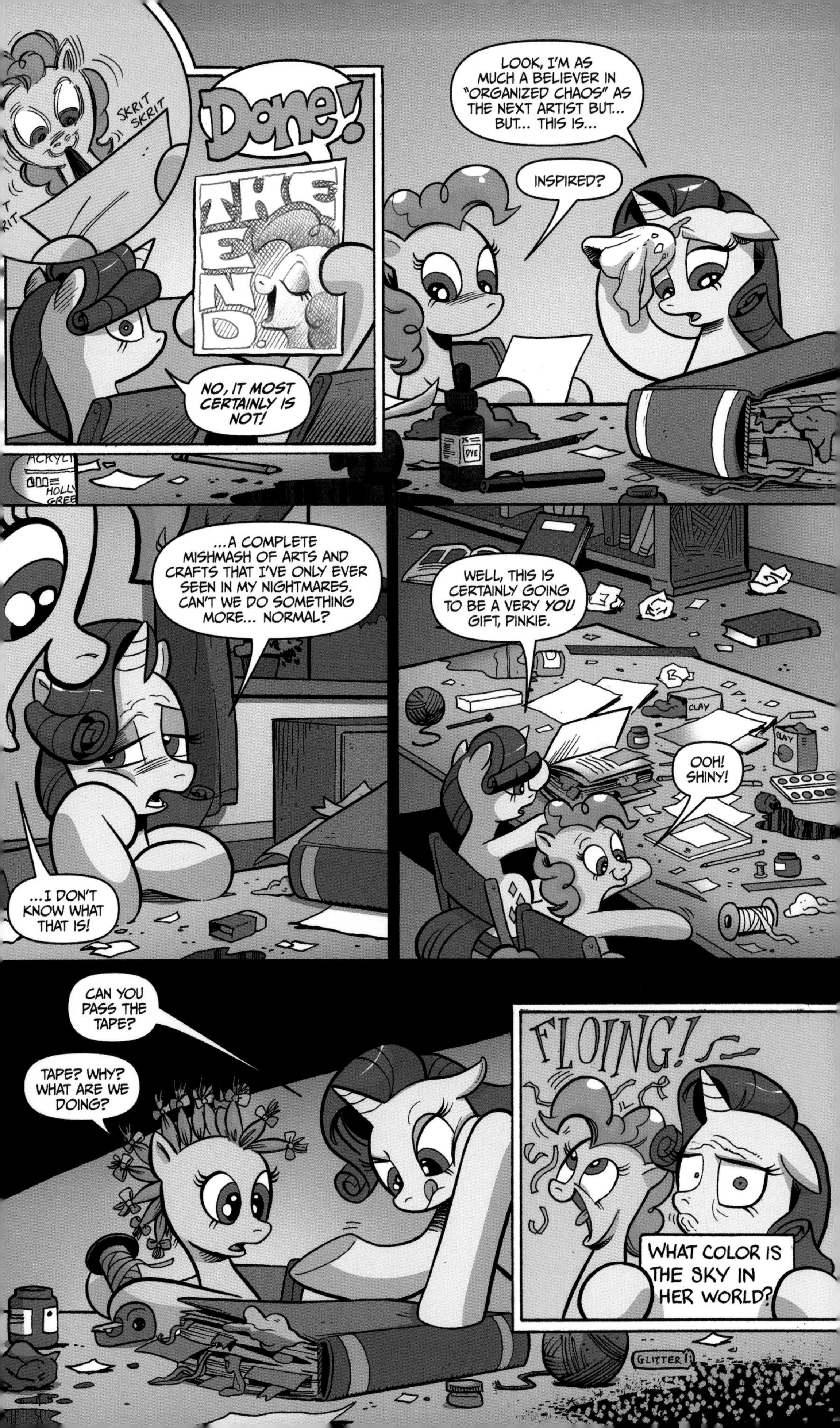
SKRIT SKRIT
Done!
THE END.
NO, IT MOST CERTAINLY IS NOT!
LOOK, I'M AS MUCH A BELIEVER IN "ORGANIZED CHAOS" AS THE NEXT ARTIST BUT... BUT... THIS IS...
INSPIRED?
DYE
ACRYL
HOLLY GREE
...A COMPLETE MISHMASH OF ARTS AND CRAFTS THAT I'VE ONLY EVER SEEN IN MY NIGHTMARES. CAN'T WE DO SOMETHING MORE... NORMAL?
...I DON'T KNOW WHAT THAT IS!
WELL, THIS IS CERTAINLY GOING TO BE A VERY *YOU* GIFT, PINKIE.
CLAY
CLAY
OOH! SHINY!
CAN YOU PASS THE TAPE?
TAPE? WHY? WHAT ARE WE DOING?
FLOING!
WHAT COLOR IS THE SKY IN HER WORLD?
GLITTER!

A GENUINE, ACCEPT NO SUBSTITUTES

PINKIE FOLD-IN!

A > FOLD THIS SECTION OVER LEFT < B FOLD BACK SO "A" MEETS "B"

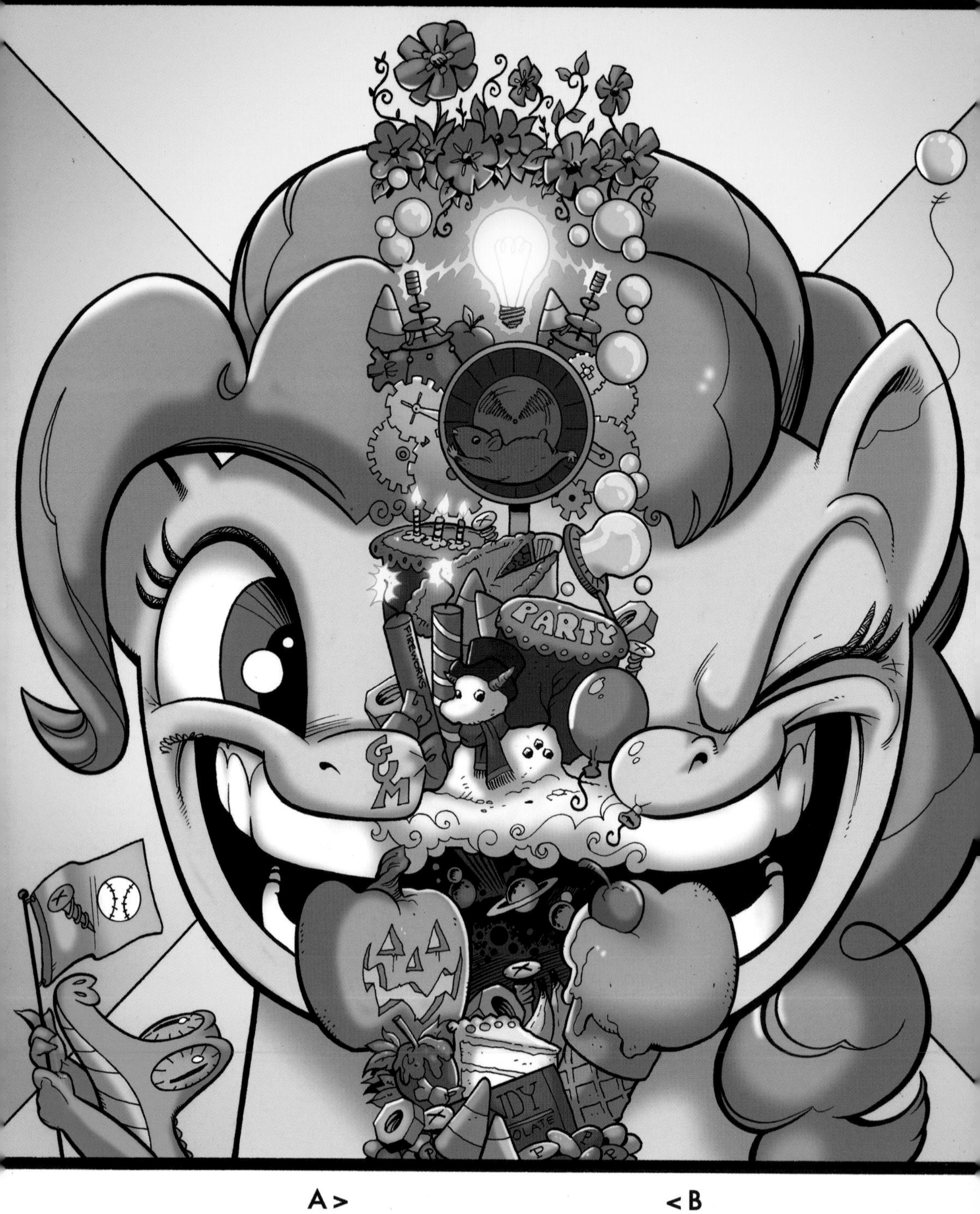

PARTY
FIREWORKS
GUM

A > < B

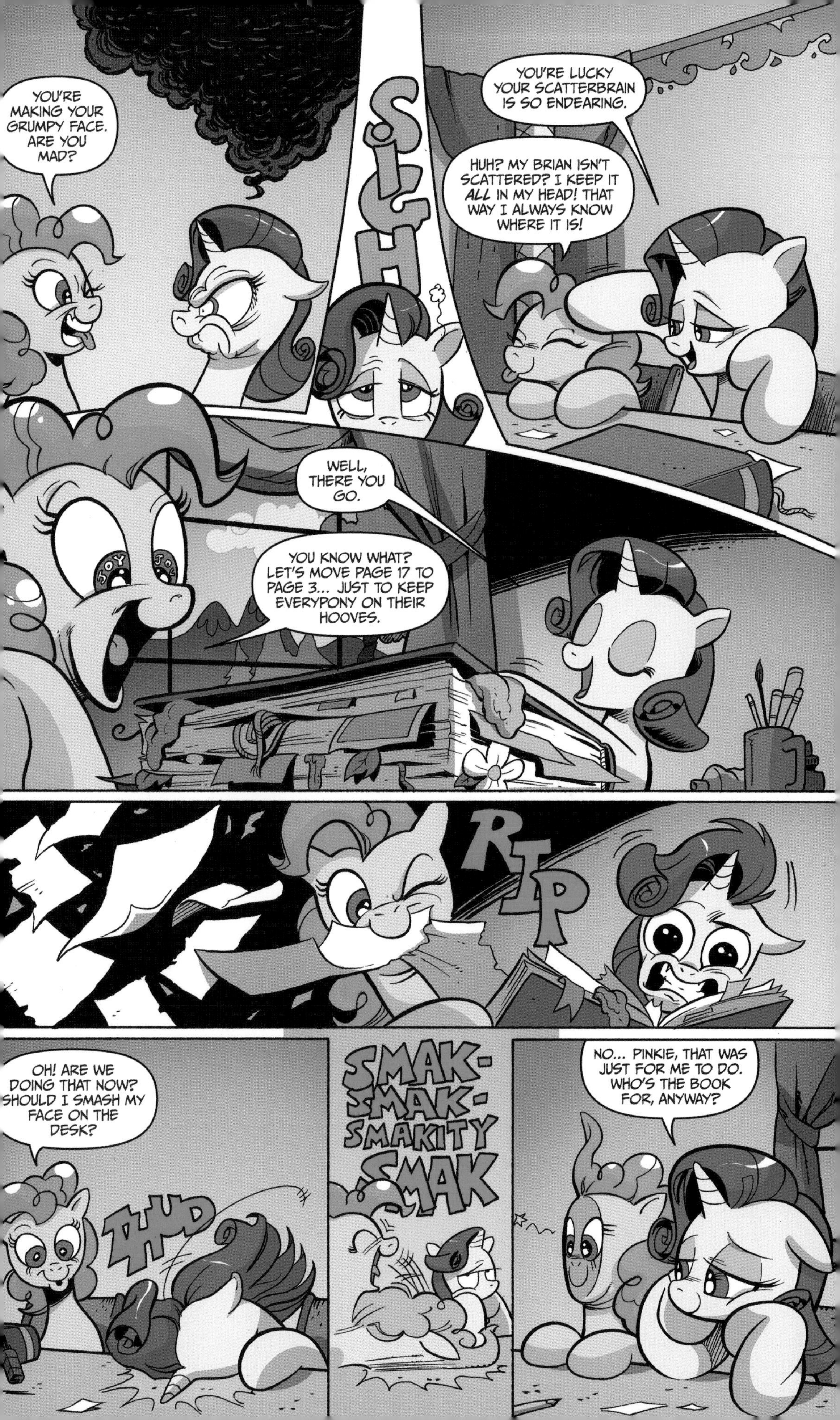
YOU'RE MAKING YOUR GRUMPY FACE. ARE YOU MAD?
SIGH
YOU'RE LUCKY YOUR SCATTERBRAIN IS SO ENDEARING.
HUH? MY BRIAN ISN'T SCATTERED? I KEEP IT ALL IN MY HEAD! THAT WAY I ALWAYS KNOW WHERE IT IS!
WELL, THERE YOU GO.
YOU KNOW WHAT? LET'S MOVE PAGE 17 TO PAGE 3... JUST TO KEEP EVERYPONY ON THEIR HOOVES.
JOY
JOY
RIP
OH! ARE WE DOING THAT NOW? SHOULD I SMASH MY FACE ON THE DESK?
THUD
SMAK-SMAK-SMAKITY SMAK
NO... PINKIE, THAT WAS JUST FOR ME TO DO. WHO'S THE BOOK FOR, ANYWAY?

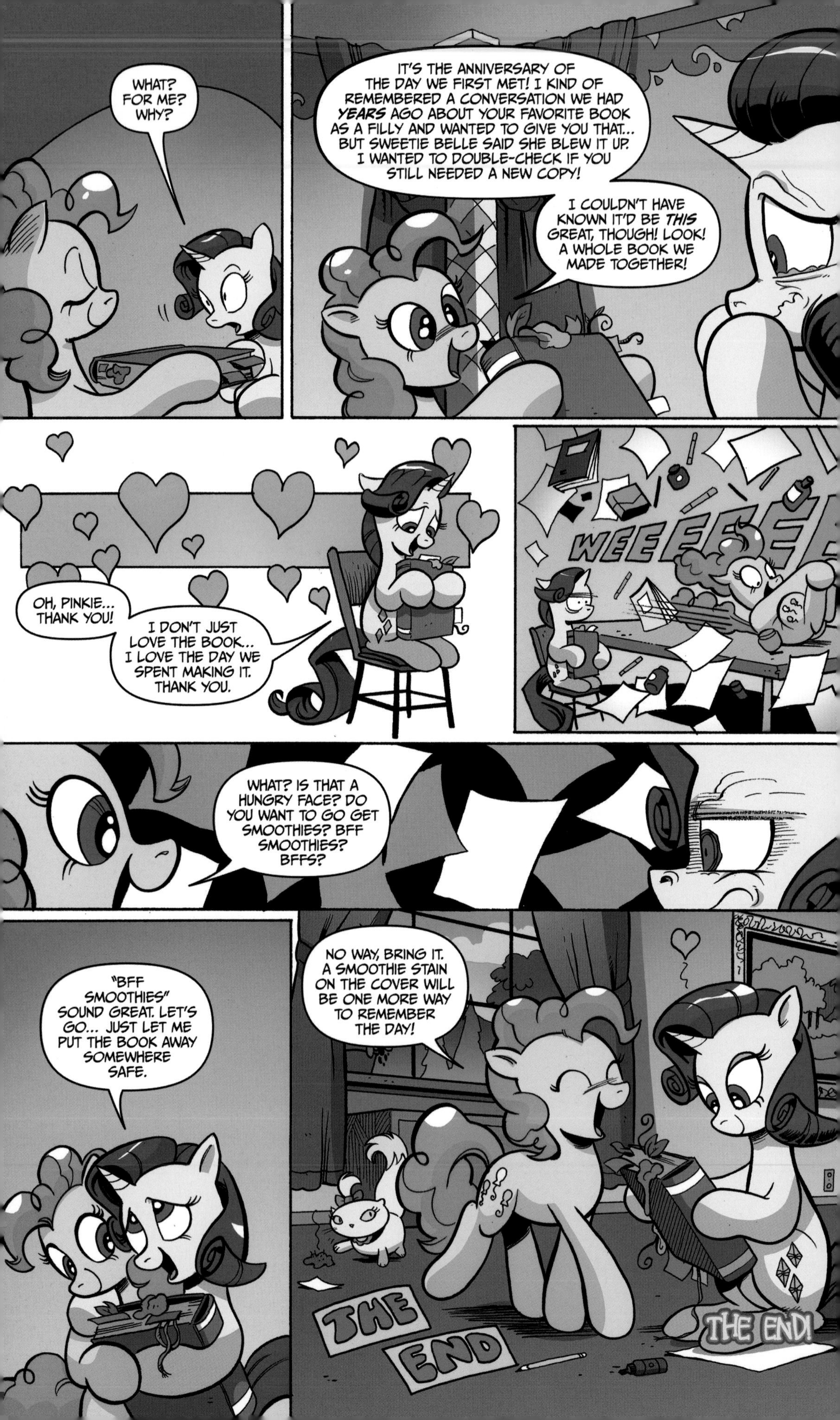
WHAT? FOR ME? WHY?
IT'S THE ANNIVERSARY OF THE DAY WE FIRST MET! I KIND OF REMEMBERED A CONVERSATION WE HAD *YEARS* AGO ABOUT YOUR FAVORITE BOOK AS A FILLY AND WANTED TO GIVE YOU THAT... BUT SWEETIE BELLE SAID SHE BLEW IT UP. I WANTED TO DOUBLE-CHECK IF YOU STILL NEEDED A NEW COPY!
I COULDN'T HAVE KNOWN IT'D BE *THIS* GREAT, THOUGH! LOOK! A WHOLE BOOK WE MADE TOGETHER!
OH, PINKIE... THANK YOU!
I DON'T JUST LOVE THE BOOK... I LOVE THE DAY WE SPENT MAKING IT. THANK YOU.
WEEEEE
WHAT? IS THAT A HUNGRY FACE? DO YOU WANT TO GO GET SMOOTHIES? BFF SMOOTHIES? BFFS?
"BFF SMOOTHIES" SOUND GREAT. LET'S GO... JUST LET ME PUT THE BOOK AWAY SOMEWHERE SAFE.
NO WAY, BRING IT. A SMOOTHIE STAIN ON THE COVER WILL BE ONE MORE WAY TO REMEMBER THE DAY!
THE END
THE END!

PARTY
TIME

art by Sara Richard

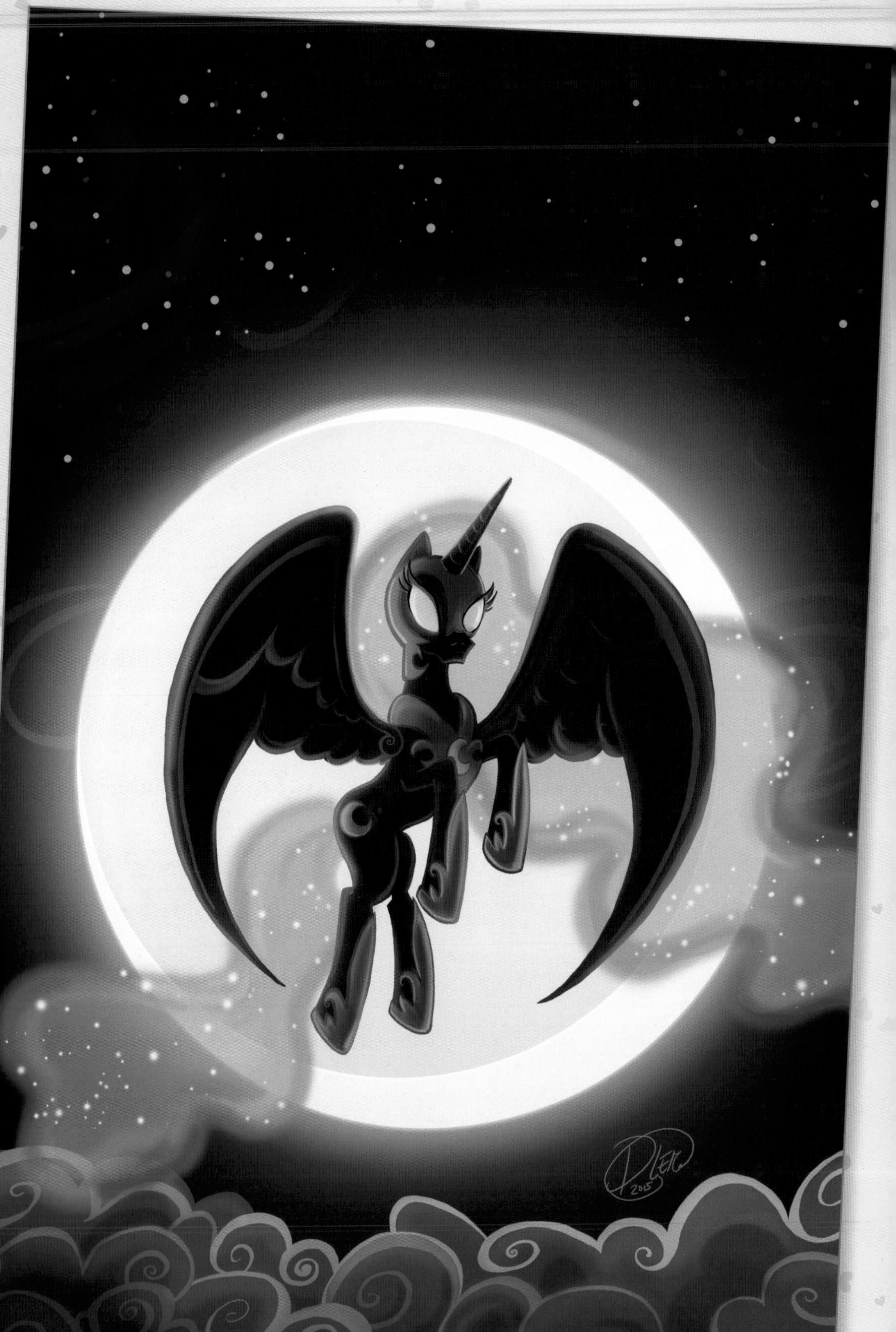

art by Diane Leto

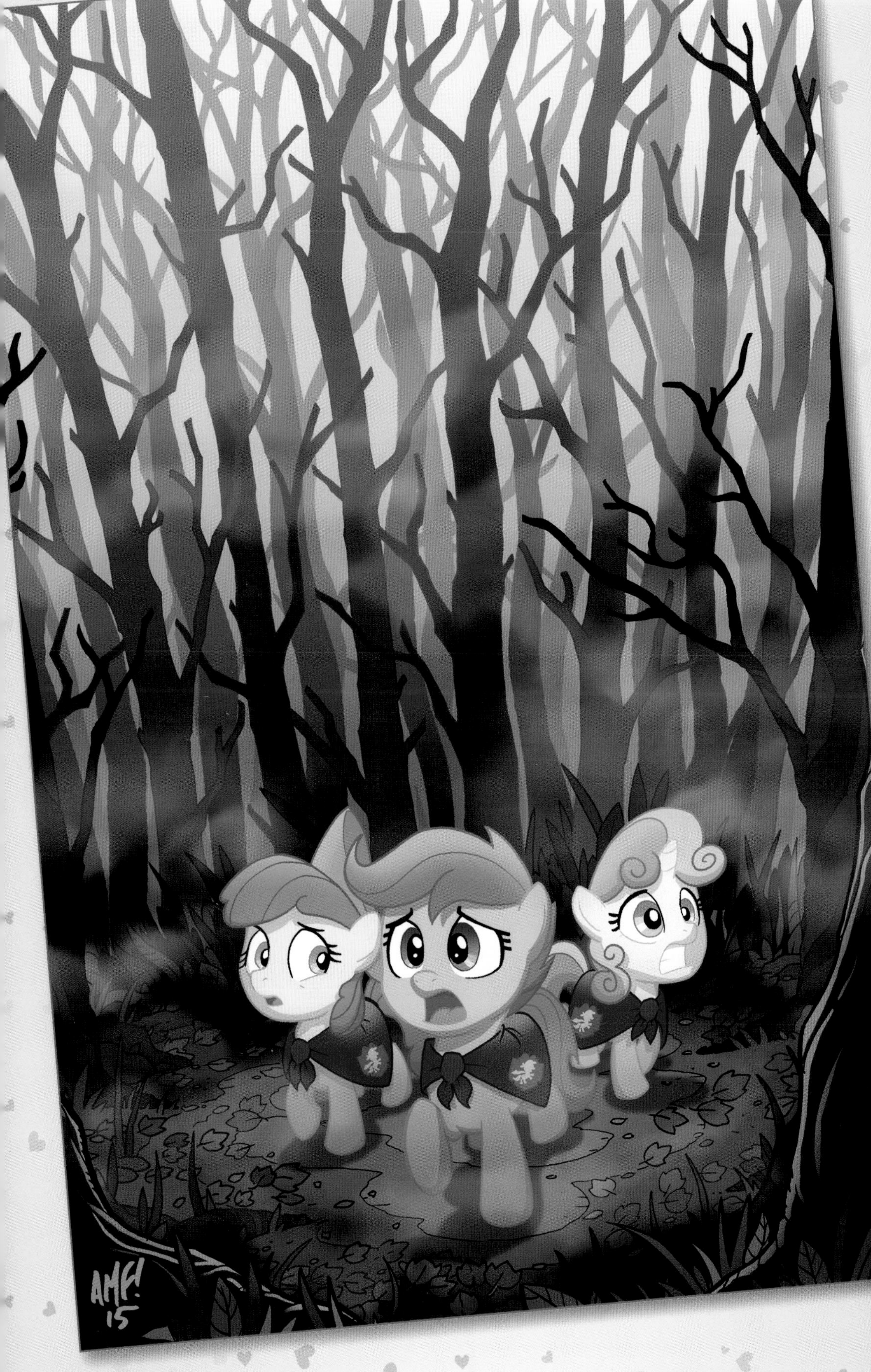
AMF!
15

art by Tony Fleecs

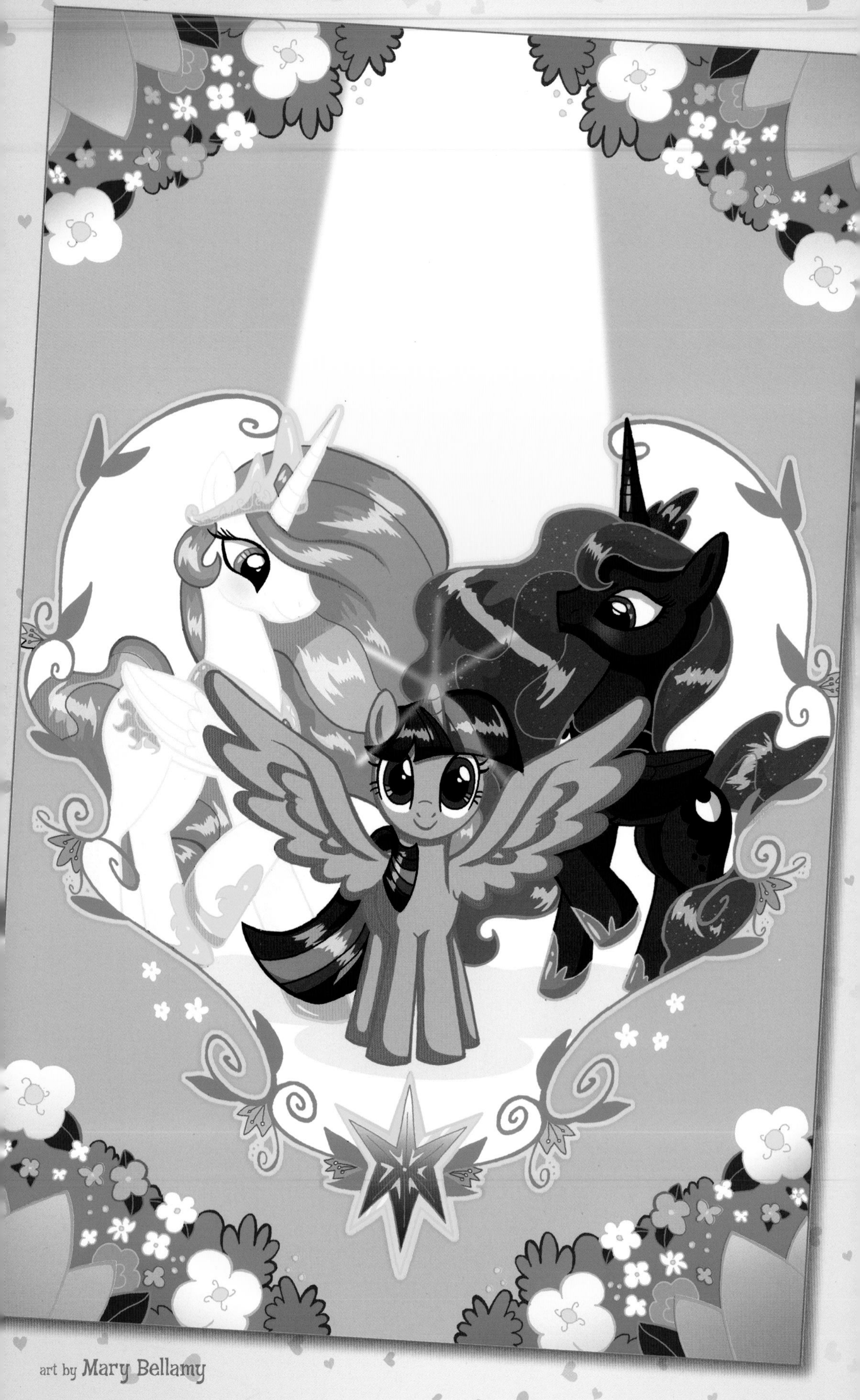

art by Mary Bellamy

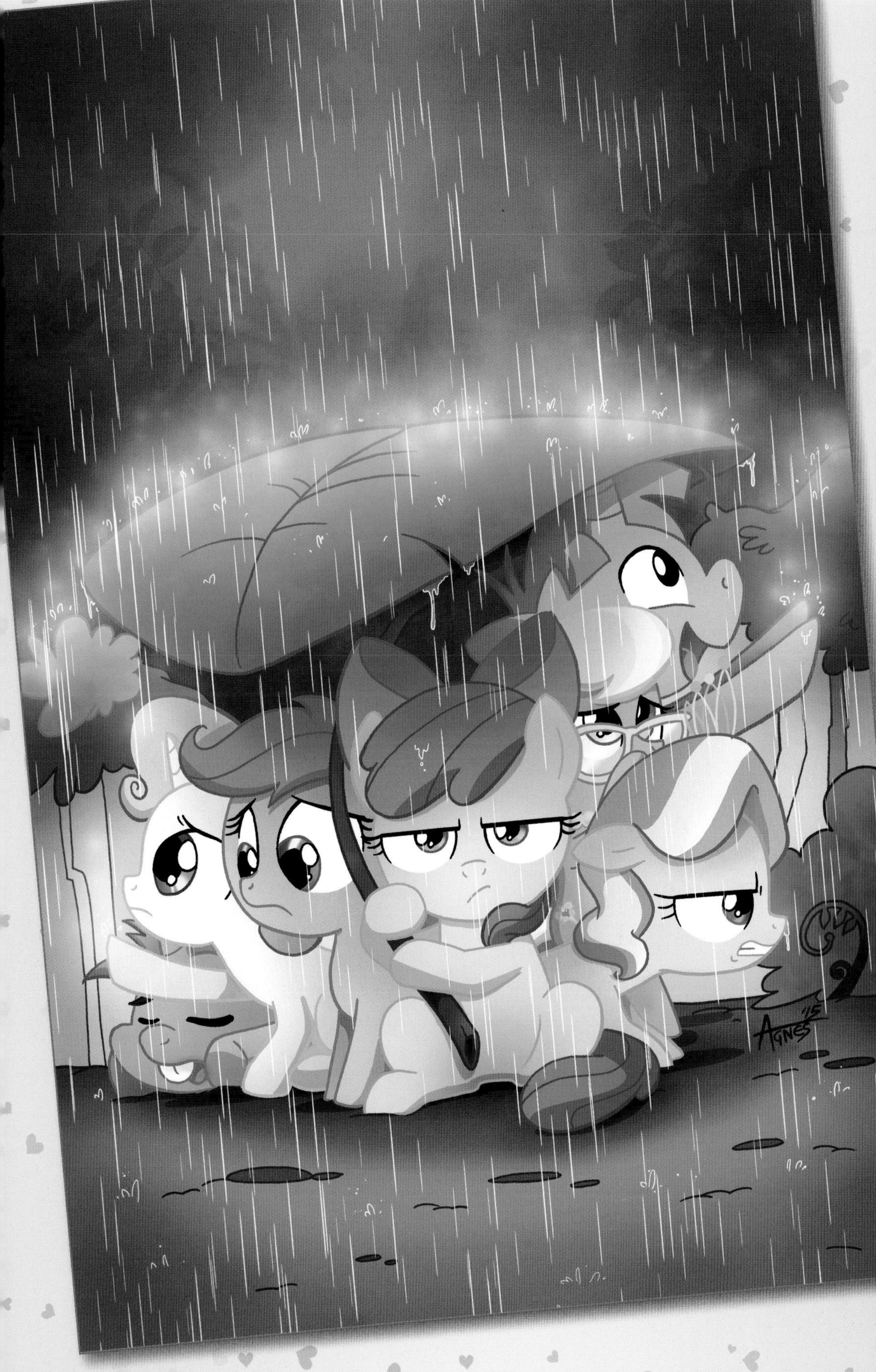
Agnes '15

art by Agnes Garbowska

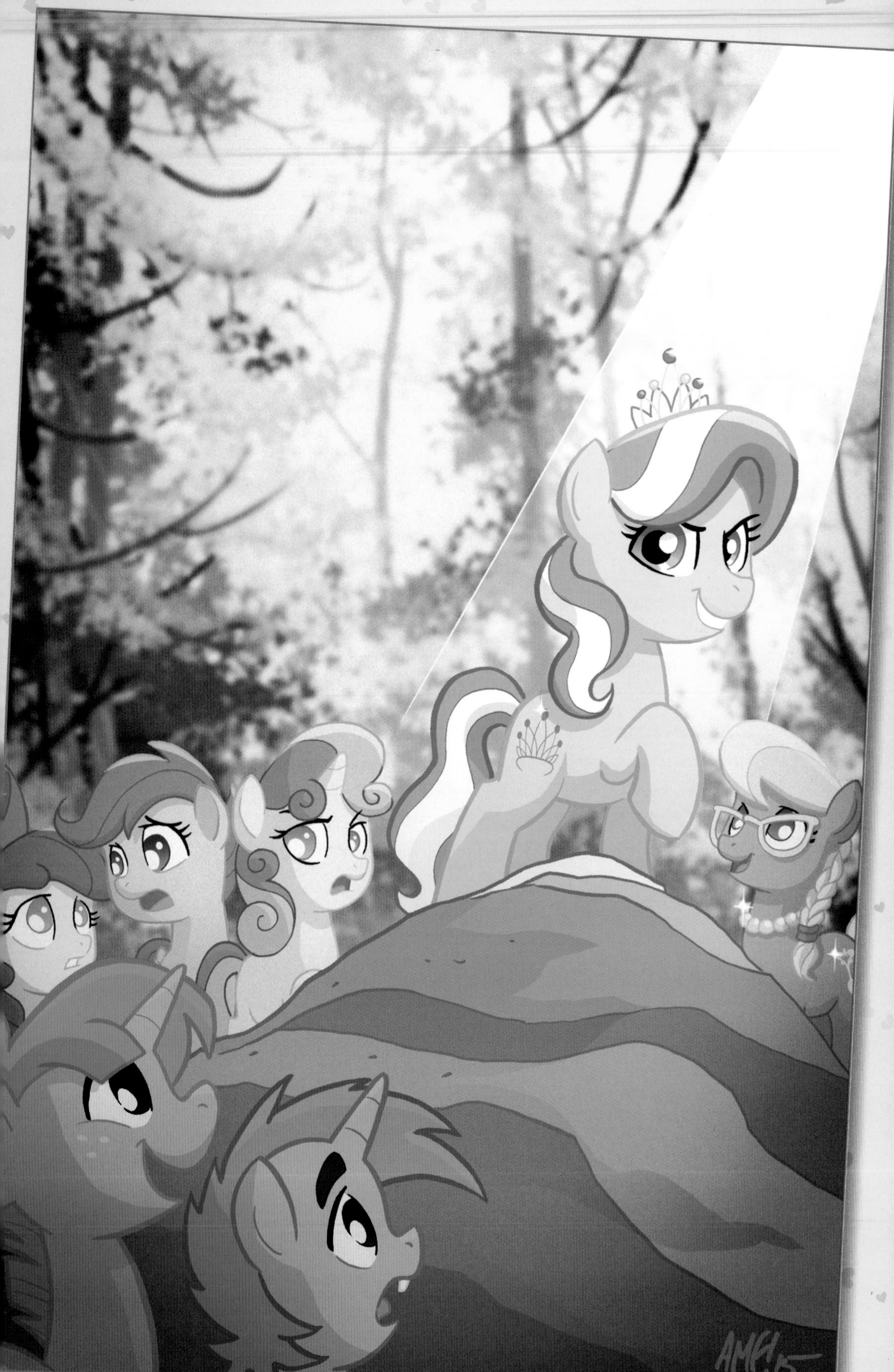
AMF! 15
art by Tony Fleecs

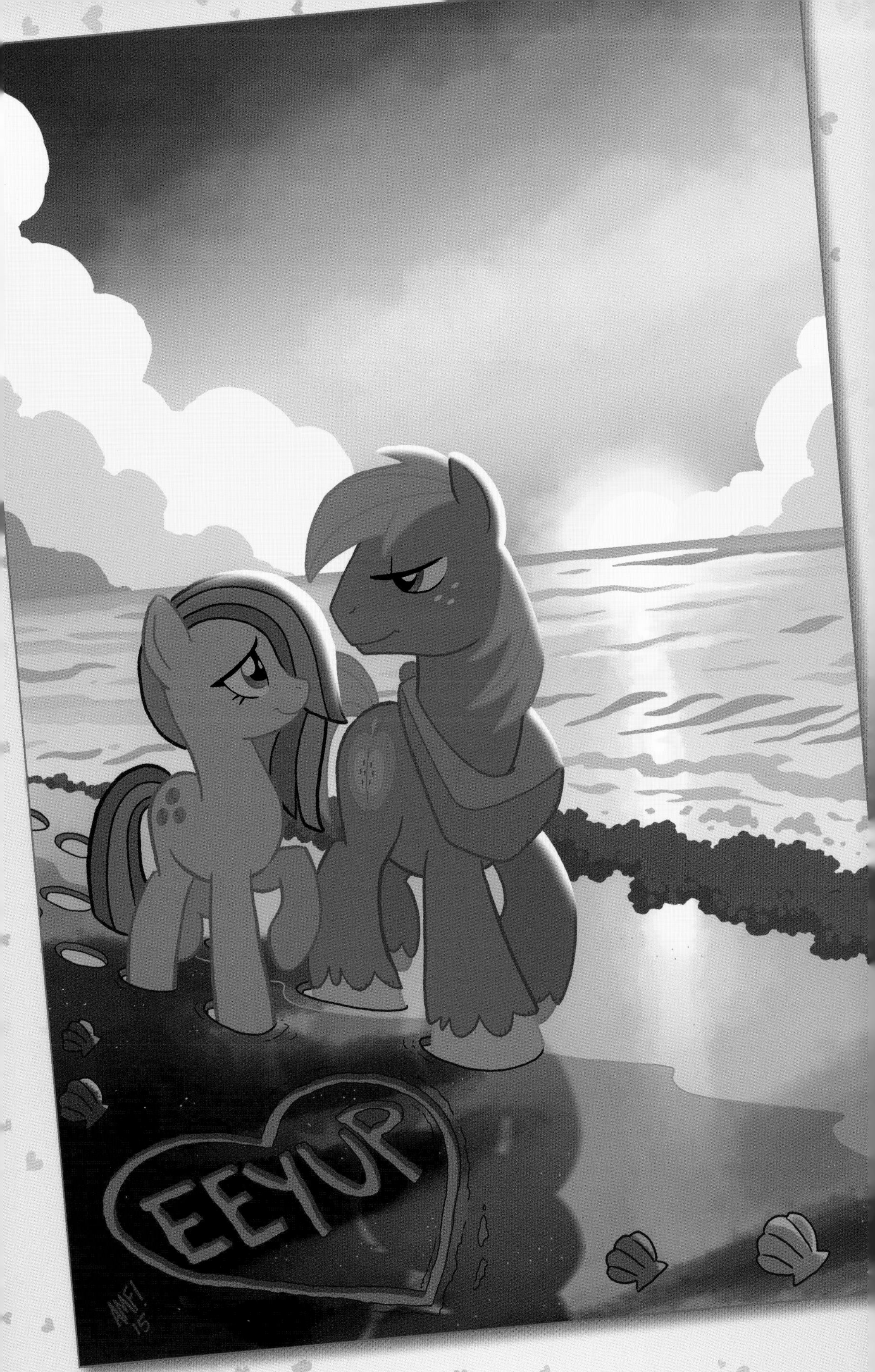

EEYUP
AMF! 15

art by Tony Fleecs

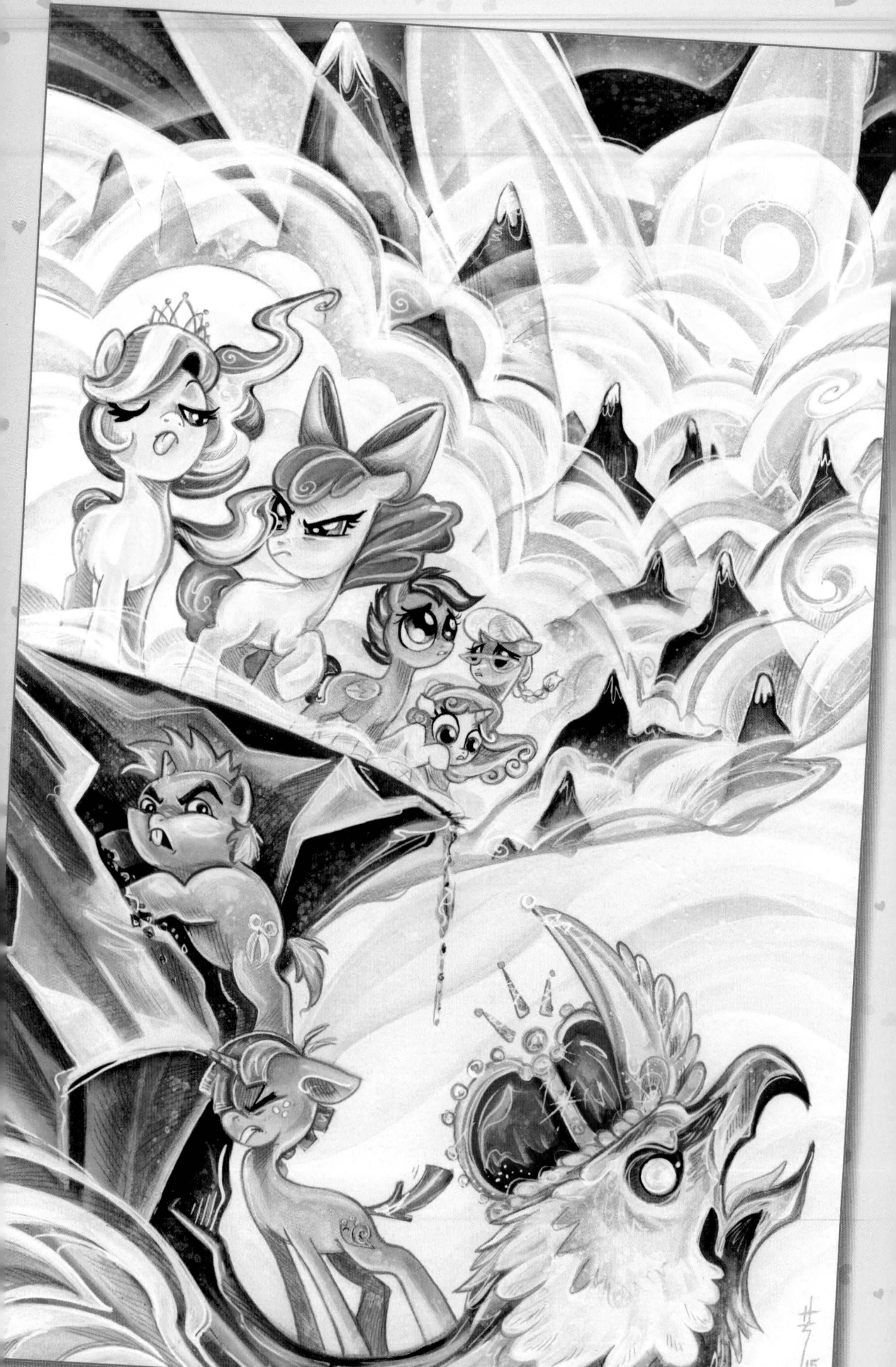

art by Sara Richard

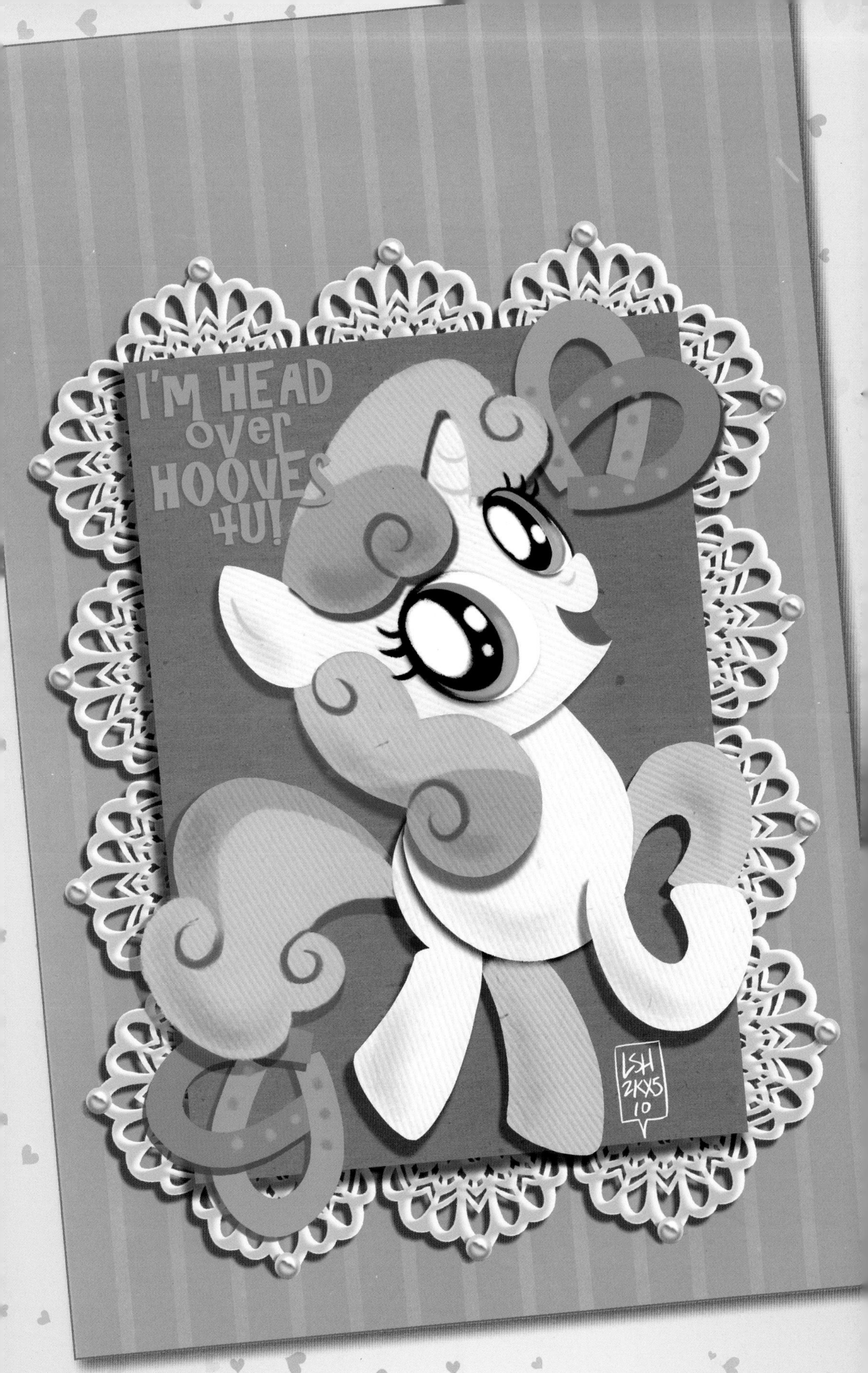
I'M HEAD over HOOVES 4U!
LSH 2KX5 10

art by Lea Hernandez | colors by Summer Cruz

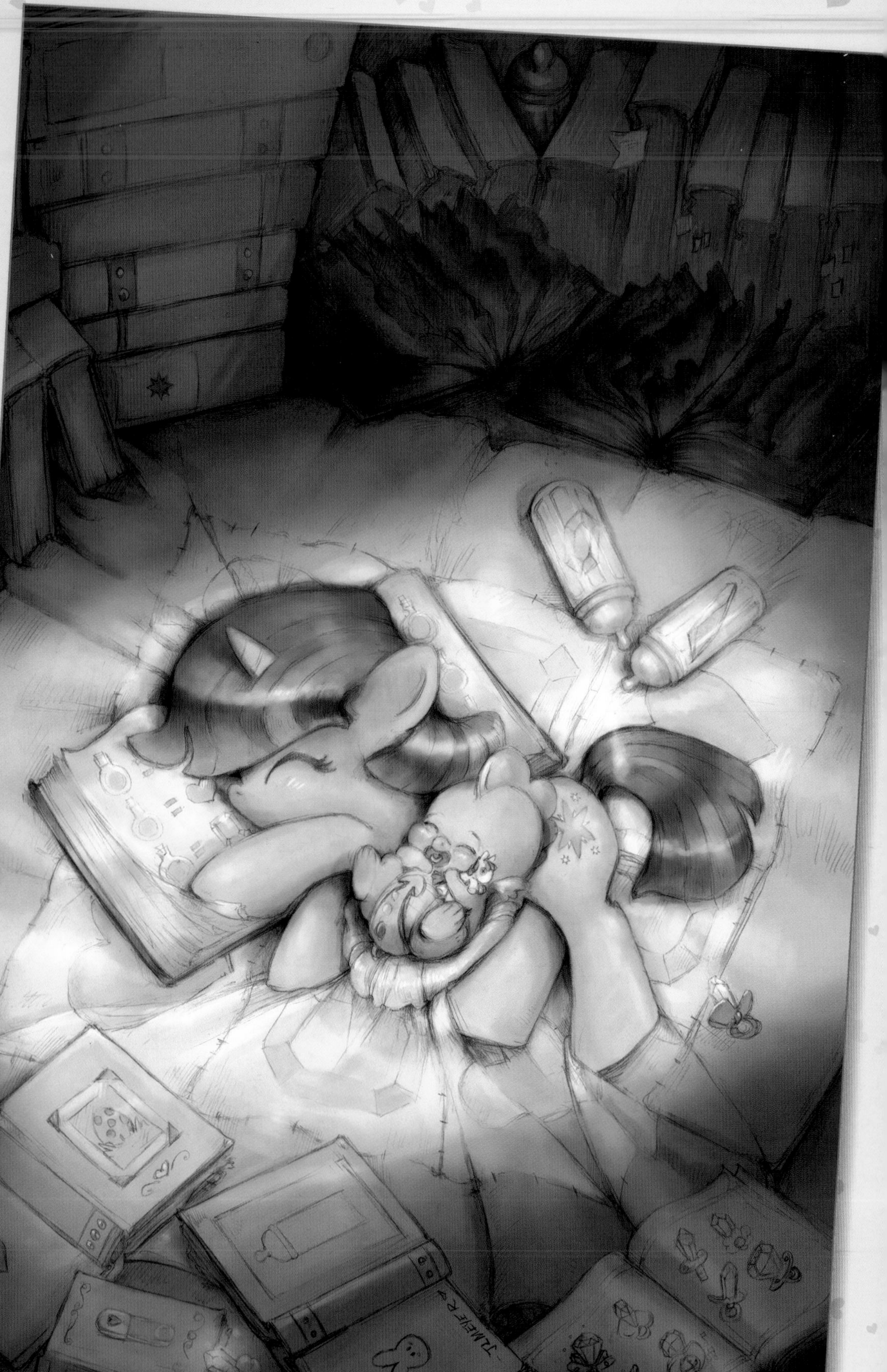

art by Jennifer L. Meyer

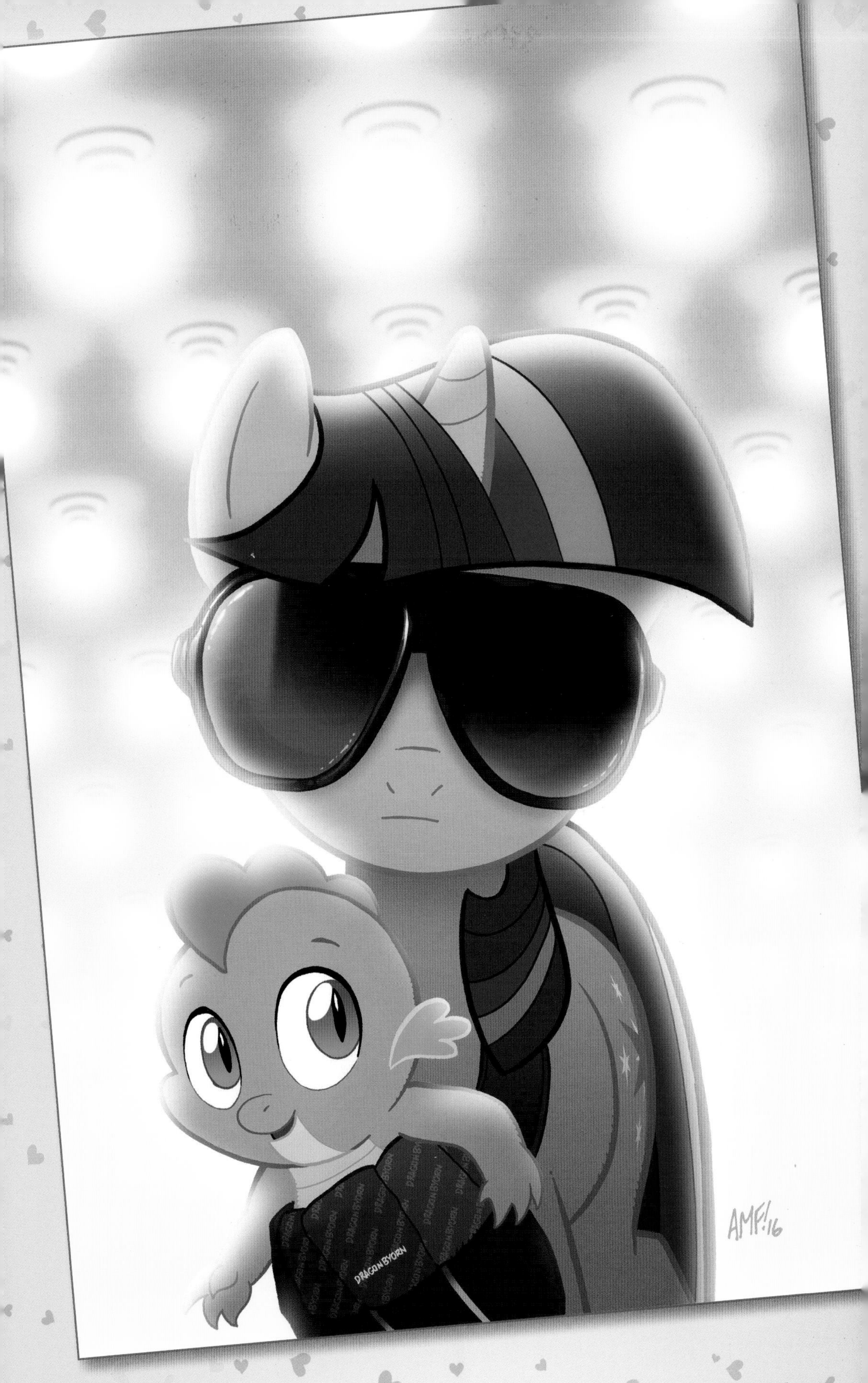
DRAGONBYORN
AMF! '16

art by Tony Fleecs

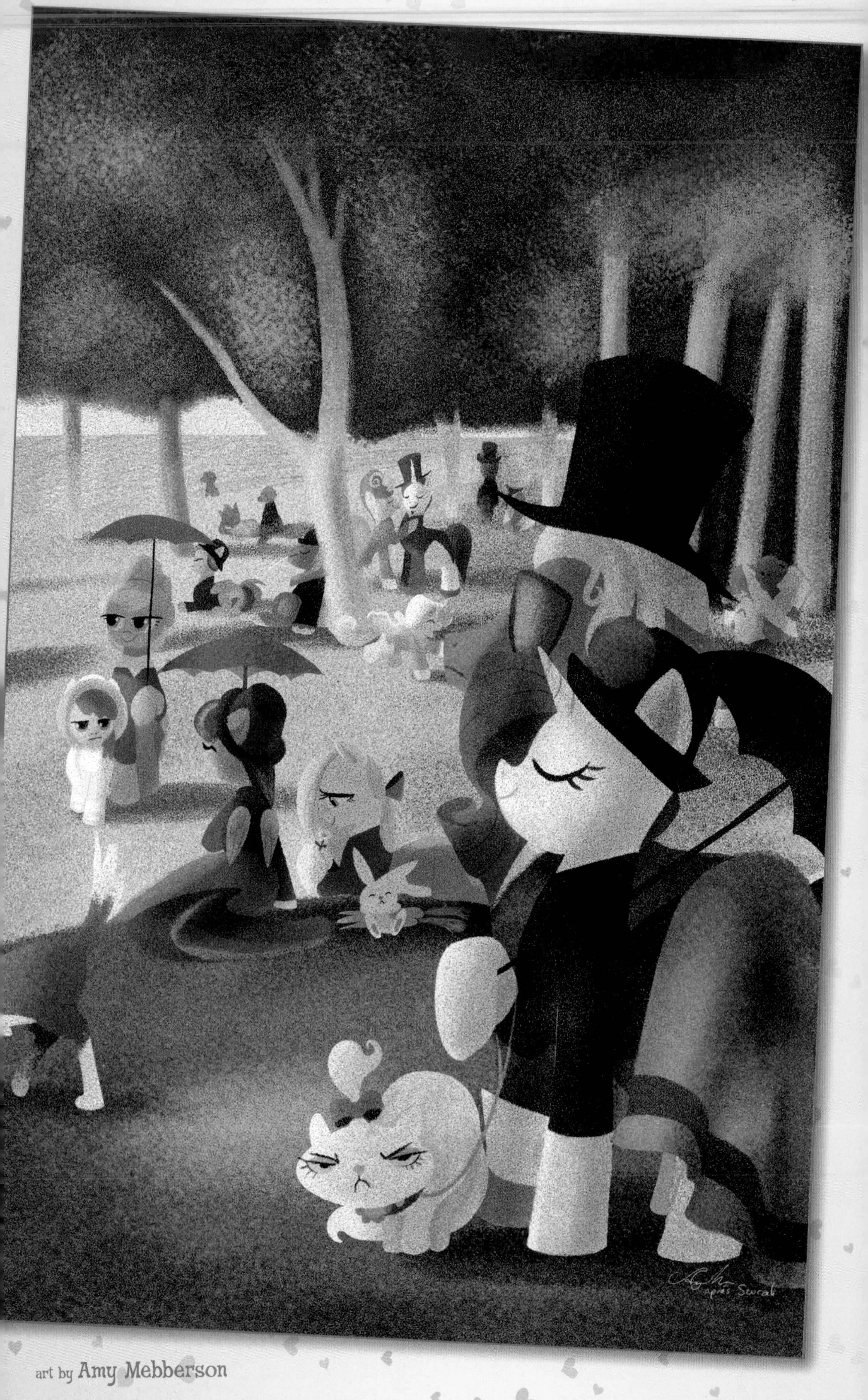

art by Amy Mebberson

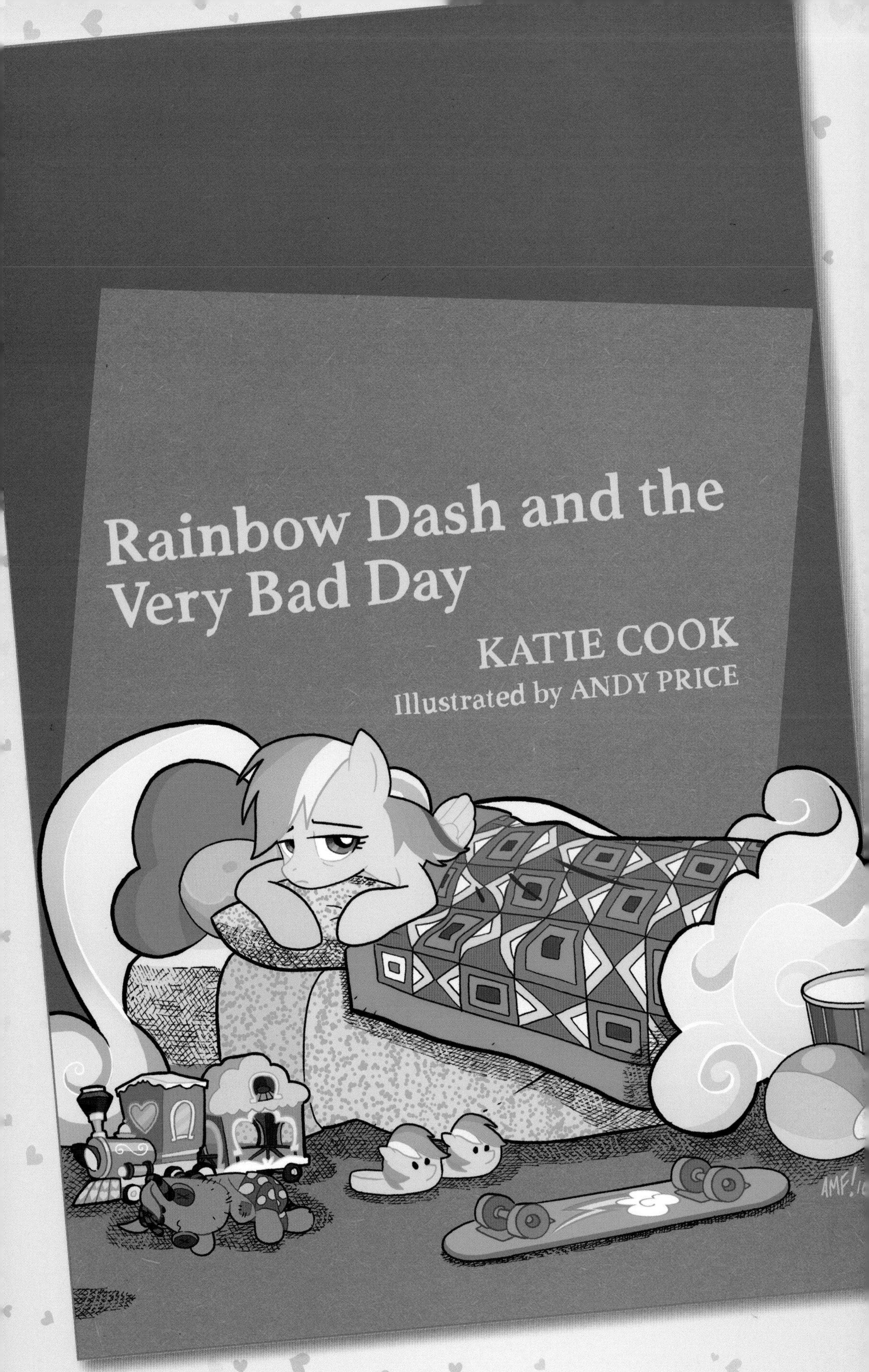
Rainbow Dash and the Very Bad Day
KATIE COOK
Illustrated by ANDY PRICE

art by Tony Fleecs

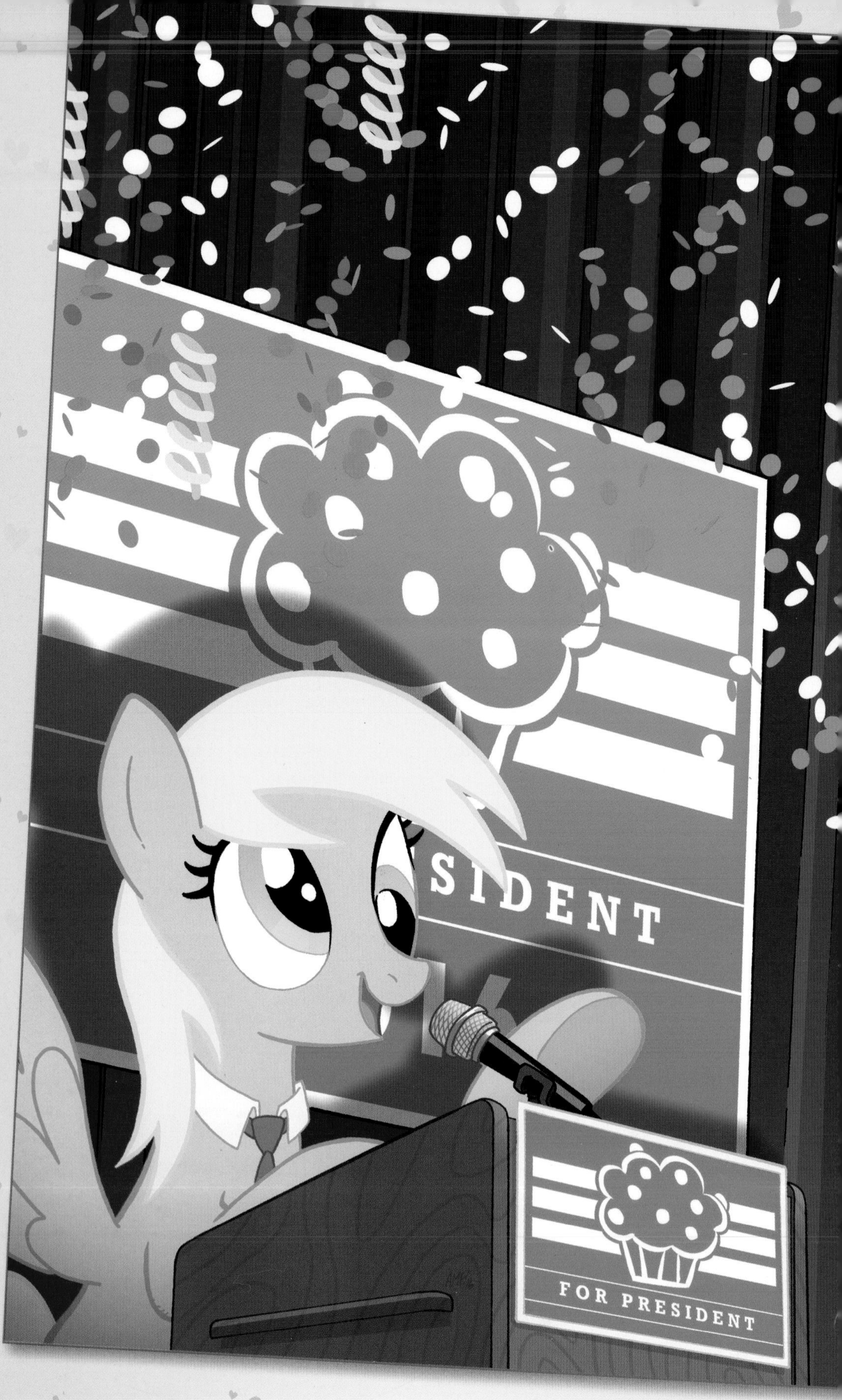
SIDENT
FOR PRESIDENT

art by Tony Fleecs

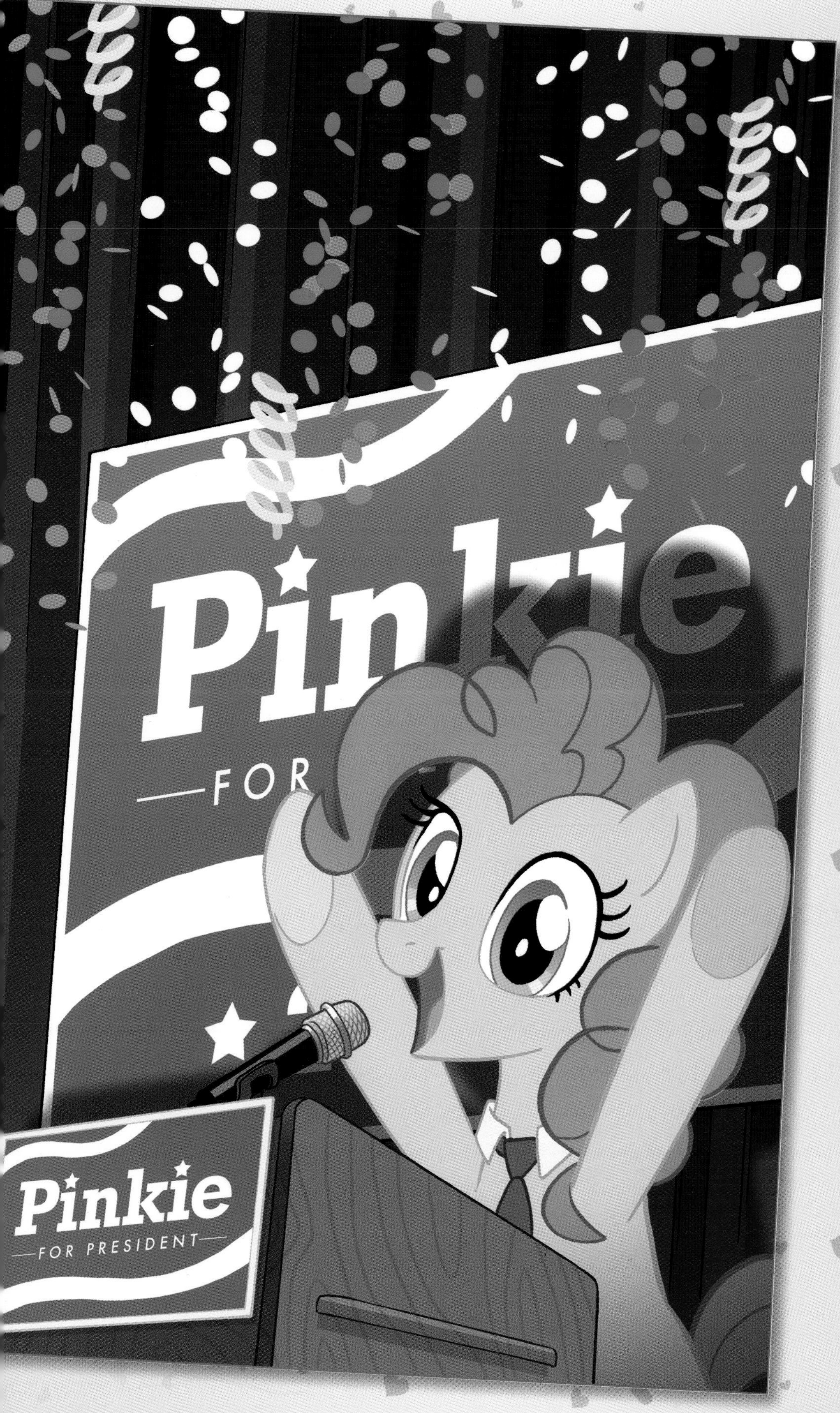
Pinkie
FOR
Pinkie
FOR PRESIDENT

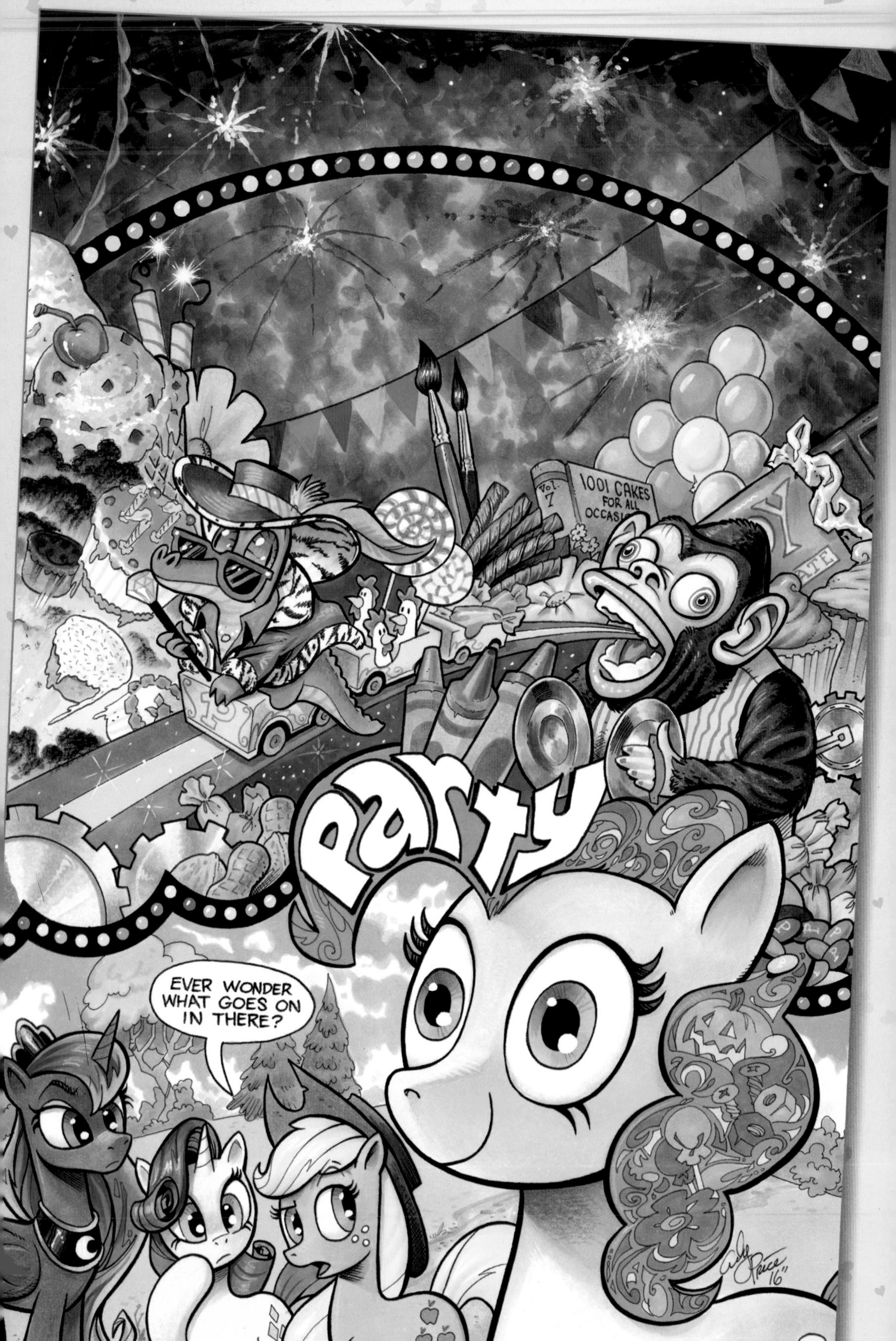
1001 CAKES FOR ALL OCCASI
Vol. 7
Party
EVER WONDER WHAT GOES ON IN THERE?
Andy Price 16'

art by Andy Price

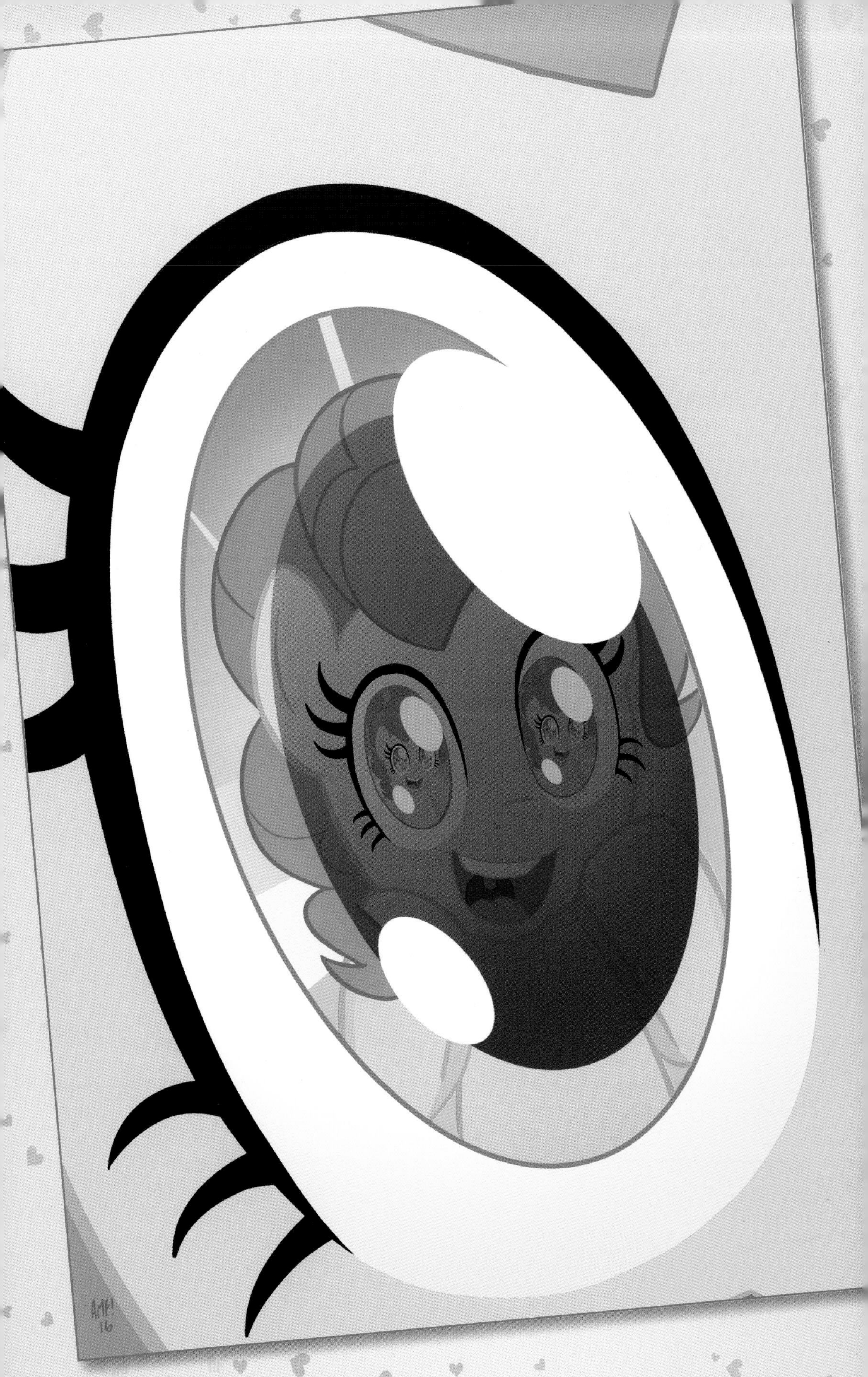
AMF!
16

art by Tony Fleecs

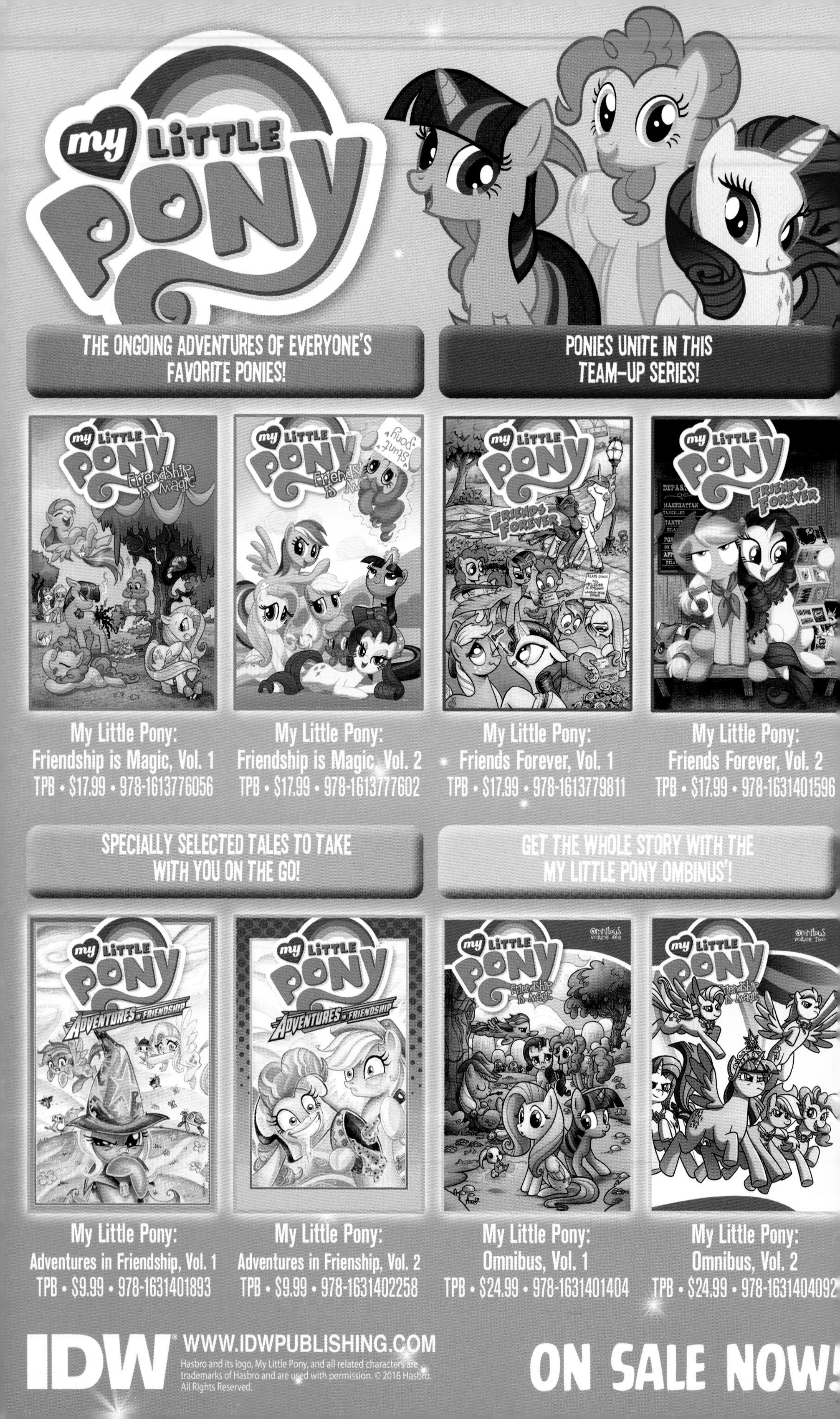
my LITTLE PONY
THE ONGOING ADVENTURES OF EVERYONE'S FAVORITE PONIES!
PONIES UNITE IN THIS TEAM-UP SERIES!
My Little Pony: Friendship is Magic, Vol. 1
TPB • $17.99 • 978-1613776056
My Little Pony: Friendship is Magic, Vol. 2
TPB • $17.99 • 978-1613777602
My Little Pony: Friends Forever, Vol. 1
TPB • $17.99 • 978-1613779811
My Little Pony: Friends Forever, Vol. 2
TPB • $17.99 • 978-1631401596
SPECIALLY SELECTED TALES TO TAKE WITH YOU ON THE GO!
GET THE WHOLE STORY WITH THE MY LITTLE PONY OMBINUS'!
My Little Pony: Adventures in Friendship, Vol. 1
TPB • $9.99 • 978-1631401893
My Little Pony: Adventures in Frienship, Vol. 2
TPB • $9.99 • 978-1631402258
My Little Pony: Omnibus, Vol. 1
TPB • $24.99 • 978-1631401404
My Little Pony: Omnibus, Vol. 2
TPB • $24.99 • 978-1631404092
IDW
WWW.IDWPUBLISHING.COM
Hasbro and its logo, My Little Pony, and all related characters are trademarks of Hasbro and are used with permission. © 2016 Hasbro. All Rights Reserved.
ON SALE NOW!